Hans Christian Andersen 著

任溶溶 譯

# ANDERSEN'S
# BEST FAIRY TALES

## 安徒生童話

商務印書館

本書譯文由上海世紀出版股份有限公司譯文出版社授權繁體字版出版發行。

# 安徒生童話 *Andersen's Best Fairy Tales*

作　　者：Hans Christian Andersen

責任編輯：黃家麗　黃稔茵

封面設計：趙穎珊

出　　版：商務印書館（香港）有限公司

　　　　　香港筲箕灣耀興道 3 號東滙廣場 8 樓

　　　　　http://www.commercialpress.com.hk

發　　行：香港聯合書刊物流有限公司

　　　　　香港新界荃灣德士古道 220-248 號荃灣工業中心 16 樓

印　　刷：永經堂印刷有限公司

　　　　　香港新界荃灣德士古道 188-202 號立泰工業中心第 1 座 3 樓

版　　次：2021 年 7 月第 1 版第 1 次印刷

　　　　　© 2021 商務印書館（香港）有限公司

　　　　　ISBN 978 962 07 0442 0

　　　　　Printed in China

# Publisher's Note 出版說明

　　"世界童話之父"安徒生窮盡一生，發揮無限想像力，創作出許多不朽經典童話故事，作品打破時空地域限制，深受世界各地讀者歡迎。本書選收其作品內許多精彩故事，有觸動人心的〈醜小鴨〉、〈蠟燭〉和〈賣火柴的小女孩〉，有發人深省的〈影子〉、〈她是個廢物〉、〈茶壺〉和〈老約翰妮講的故事〉，也有令人發出會心微笑的〈國王的新衣〉、〈老頭子做的事總是對的〉和〈笨蛋漢斯〉等，風格多樣，趣味盎然。

　　初、中級英語程度讀者使用本書時，先閱讀英文原文，如遇到理解障礙，則參考中譯作為輔助。在英文原文後附註釋，標註古英語、非現代詞彙拼寫形式及語法；在譯文後附加註解，以幫助讀者理解原文背景。讀者如有餘力，可在閱讀原文段落後，查閱相應中譯，揣摩雙語不同的表達。

　　安徒生筆下的童話，題材廣泛，趣味橫生，曾被翻譯成超過125 種文字，體裁雖屬兒童文學，但字裏行間蘊藏豐富的人生哲理，啟發思考，確實值得家長陪伴孩子一起閱讀，細味箇中寓意，是親子共讀的極佳選擇。

商務印書館 (香港) 有限公司

編輯出版部

# Contents 目錄

# Andersen's Best Fairy Tales

# The Tinderbox

A soldier came marching along the high road: 'Left, right—left, right.' He had his knapsack on his back, and a sword at his side; he had been to the wars, and was now returning home.

As he walked on, he met a very frightful-looking old witch in the road. Her underlip hung quite down on her breast, and she stopped and said, 'Good evening, soldier; you have a very fine sword, and a large knapsack, and you are a real soldier; so you shall have as much money as ever you like.'

'Thank you, old witch,' said the soldier.

'Do you see that large tree,' said the witch, pointing to a tree which stood beside them. 'Well, it is quite hollow inside, and you must climb to the top, when you will see a hole, through which you can let yourself down into the tree to a great depth. I will tie a rope round your body, so that I can pull you up again when you call out to me.'

'But what am I to do, down there in the tree?' asked the soldier.

'Get money,' she replied; 'for you must know that when you reach the ground under the tree, you will find yourself in a large hall, lighted up by three hundred lamps; you will then see three doors, which can be easily opened, for the keys are in all the locks. On entering the first of the chambers, to which these doors lead, you will see a large chest, standing in the middle of the floor, and upon it a dog seated, with a pair of eyes as large as teacups. But you need not be at all afraid of him; I will give you my blue checked apron, which you must spread upon the floor, and then boldly seize hold of the dog, and place him upon it. You can then open the chest, and take from it as many pence as you please, they are only copper pence; but if you would rather have silver money, you must go into the second chamber. Here you will find another dog, with eyes as big as mill wheels; but do not let that trouble you. Place him upon my apron, and then take what money you please. If, however, you like gold best, enter the third chamber, where there is another chest full of it. The dog who sits on this chest is very dreadful; his eyes are as big as a tower, but do not mind him. If he also is placed upon my apron, he cannot hurt you, and you may take from the chest what gold you will.'

'This is not a bad story,' said the soldier; 'but what am I to give you, you old witch? For, of course, you do not mean to tell me all this for nothing.'

'No,' said the witch; 'but I do not ask for a single penny. Only promise to bring me an old tinderbox, which my grandmother left behind the last time she went down there.'

'Very well; I promise. Now tie the rope round my body.'

'Here it is,' replied the witch; 'and here is my blue checked apron.'

As soon as the rope was tied, the soldier climbed up the tree, and let himself down through the hollow to the ground beneath; and here he found, as the witch had told him, a large hall, in which many hundred lamps were all burning. Then he opened the first door. 'Ah!' there sat the dog, with the eyes as large as teacups, staring at him.

'You're a pretty fellow,' said the soldier, seizing him, and placing him on the witch's apron, while he filled his pockets from the chest with as many pieces as they would hold. Then he closed the lid, seated the dog upon it again, and walked into another chamber, and, sure enough, there sat the dog with eyes as big as mill wheels.

'You had better not look at me in that way,' said the soldier; 'you will make your eyes water;' and then he seated him also upon the apron, and opened the chest. But when he saw what a quantity of silver money it contained, he very quickly threw away all the coppers he had taken, and filled his pockets and his knapsack with nothing but silver.

Then he went into the third room, and there the dog was really hideous; his eyes were, truly, as big as towers, and they turned round and round in his head like wheels.

'Good morning,' said the soldier, touching his cap, for he had never seen such a dog in his life. But after looking at him more closely, he thought he had been civil enough, so he placed him on the floor, and opened the chest. Good gracious, what a quantity of gold there was! Enough to buy all the sugar sticks of the sweet-stuff women; all the tin soldiers, whips, and rocking-horses in the world, or even the whole town itself. There was, indeed, an immense quantity. So the soldier now threw away all the silver money he had taken, and filled his pockets and his knapsack with gold instead; and not only his pockets and his knapsack, but even his cap and boots, so that he could scarcely walk.

He was really rich now; so he replaced the dog on the chest, closed the door, and called up through the tree, 'Now pull me out, you old witch.'

'Have you got the tinderbox?' asked the witch.

'No; I declare I quite forgot it.' So he went back and fetched the tinderbox, and then the witch drew him up out of the tree, and he stood again in the high road, with his pockets, his knapsack, his cap, and his boots full of gold.

'What are you going to do with the tinderbox?' asked the soldier.

'That is nothing to you,' replied the witch; 'you have the money, now give me the tinderbox.'

'I tell you what,' said the soldier, 'if you don't tell me what you are going to do with it, I will draw my sword and cut off your head.'

'No,' said the witch.

The soldier immediately cut off her head, and there she lay on the ground. Then he tied up all his money in her apron and slung it on his back like a bundle, put the tinderbox in his pocket, and walked off to the nearest town. It was a very nice town, and he put up at the best inn, and ordered a dinner of all his favourite dishes, for now he was rich and had plenty of money.

The servant, who cleaned his boots, thought they certainly

were a shabby pair to be worn by such a rich gentleman, for he had not yet bought any new ones. The next day, however, he procured some good clothes and proper boots, so that our soldier soon became known as a fine gentleman, and the people visited him, and told him all the wonders that were to be seen in the town, and of the king's beautiful daughter, the princess.

'Where can I see her?' asked the soldier.

'She is not to be seen at all,' they said; 'she lives in a large copper castle, surrounded by walls and towers. No one but the king himself can pass in or out, for there has been a prophecy that she will marry a common soldier, and the king cannot bear to think of such a marriage.'

'I should like very much to see her,' thought the soldier; but he could not obtain permission to do so. However, he passed a very pleasant time; went to the theatre, drove in the king's garden, and gave a great deal of money to the poor, which was very good of him; he remembered what it had been in olden times to be without a shilling. Now he was rich, had fine clothes, and many friends, who all declared he was a fine fellow and a real gentleman, and all this gratified him exceedingly. But his money would not last forever; and as he spent and gave away a great deal daily, and received none, he found himself at last with only two shillings left. So he was obliged to leave his elegant rooms, and live in a little garret under the roof, where he had to clean his own boots, and even mend them with a large needle. None of his friends came to see him, there were too many stairs to mount up. One dark evening, he had not even a penny to buy a candle; then all at once he remembered that there was a piece of candle stuck in the tinderbox, which he had brought from the old tree, into which the witch had helped him.

He found the tinderbox, but no sooner had he struck a few sparks from the flint and steel, than the door flew open and the dog with eyes as big as teacups, whom he had seen while down in the tree, stood before him, and said, 'What orders, master?'

'Hallo[1],' said the soldier; 'well this is a pleasant tinderbox, if it brings me all I wish for.'

'Bring me some money,' said he to the dog.

He was gone in a moment, and presently returned, carrying a large bag of coppers in his mouth. The soldier very soon discovered after this the value of the tinderbox. If he struck the flint once, the dog who sat on the chest of copper money made his appearance; if twice, the dog came from the chest of silver; and if three times, the dog with eyes like towers, who watched over the gold. The soldier had now plenty of money; he returned to his elegant rooms, and reappeared in his fine clothes, so that his friends knew him again directly, and made as much of him as before.

After a while he began to think it was very strange that no one could get a look at the princess. 'Everyone says she is very beautiful,' thought he to himself; 'but what is the use of that if she is to be shut up in a copper castle surrounded by so many towers. Can I by any means get to see her. Stop! Where is my tinderbox?' Then he struck a light, and in a moment the dog, with eyes as big as teacups, stood before him.

'It is midnight,' said the soldier, 'yet I should very much like to see the princess, if only for a moment.'

The dog disappeared instantly, and before the soldier could even look round, he returned with the princess. She was lying on the dog's back asleep, and looked so lovely, that everyone who saw her would know she was a real princess. The soldier could not help kissing her, true soldier as he was. Then the dog ran back with the princess; but in the morning, while at breakfast with the king and queen, she told them what a singular dream she had had during the night, of a dog and a soldier, that she had ridden on the dog's back, and been kissed by the soldier.

'That is a very pretty story, indeed,' said the queen. So the next night one of the old ladies of the court was set to watch by the princess's bed, to discover whether it really was a dream, or what else it might be.

The soldier longed very much to see the princess once more, so he sent for the dog again in the night to fetch her, and to run with her as fast as ever he could. But the old lady put on water boots, and ran after him as quickly as he did, and found that he carried the princess into a large house. She thought it would help her to remember the place if she made a large cross on the door with a piece of chalk. Then she went home to bed, and the dog presently returned with the princess. But when he saw that a cross had been made on the door of the house, where the soldier lived, he took another piece of chalk and made crosses on all the doors in the town, so that the lady-in-waiting might not be able to find out the right door.

Early the next morning the king and queen accompanied the lady and all the officers of the household, to see where the princess had been.

'Here it is,' said the king, when they came to the first door with a cross on it.

'No, my dear husband, it must be that one,' said the queen, pointing to a second door having a cross also.

'And here is one, and there is another!' they all exclaimed; for there were crosses on all the doors in every direction.

So they felt it would be useless to search any further. But the queen was a very clever woman; she could do a great deal more than merely ride in a carriage. She took her large gold scissors, cut a piece of silk into squares, and made a neat little bag. This bag she filled with buckwheat flour, and tied it round the princess's neck; and then she cut a small hole in the bag, so that the flour might be scattered on the ground as the princess went along. During the night, the dog came again and carried the princess on his back, and ran with her to the soldier, who loved her very much, and wished that he had been a prince, so that he might have her for a wife. The dog did not observe how the flour ran out of the bag all the way from the castle wall to the soldier's house, and even up to the window, where he had climbed with the princess. Therefore in the morning the king and queen found out where their daughter had been, and the soldier was taken up and put in prison. Oh, how dark and disagreeable it was as he sat there, and the people said to him, 'Tomorrow you will be hanged.' It was not very pleasant news, and besides, he had left the tinderbox at the inn. In the morning he could see through the iron grating of the little window how the people were hastening out of the town to see him hanged; he heard the drums beating, and saw the soldiers marching. Everyone ran out to look at them, and a shoemaker's boy, with a leather apron and slippers on, galloped by so fast, that one of his slippers flew off and struck against the wall where the soldier sat looking through the iron grating. 'Hallo, you shoemaker's boy, you need not be in such a hurry,' cried the soldier to him. 'There will be nothing to see till I come; but if you will run to the house where I have been living, and bring me my tinderbox, you shall have four shillings, but you must put your best foot foremost.'

The shoemaker's boy liked the idea of getting the four shillings, so he ran very fast and fetched the tinderbox, and gave it to the soldier. And now we shall see what happened. Outside the town a large gibbet had been erected, round which stood the soldiers and several thousands of people. The king and the queen sat on splendid thrones opposite to the judges and the whole council. The soldier already stood on the ladder; but as they were about to place the rope around his neck, he said that an innocent request was often granted to a poor criminal before he suffered death. He wished very much to smoke a pipe, as it would be the last pipe he should ever smoke in the world. The king could not refuse this request, so the soldier took his tinderbox, and struck fire, once, twice, thrice[2],—and there in a moment stood all the dogs;—the one with eyes as big as teacups, the one with eyes as large as mill wheels, and the third, whose eyes were like towers. 'Help me now, that I may not be hanged,' cried the soldier.

And the dogs fell upon the judges and all the councillors; seized one by the legs, and another by the nose, and tossed them many feet high in the air, so that they fell down and were dashed to pieces.

'I will not be touched,' said the king. But the largest dog seized him, as well as the queen, and threw them after the others. Then the soldiers and all the people were afraid, and cried, 'Good soldier, you shall be our king, and you shall marry the beautiful princess.'

So they placed the soldier in the king's carriage, and the three dogs ran on in front and cried 'Hurrah!' and the little boys whistled through their fingers, and the soldiers presented arms. The princess came out of the copper castle, and became queen, which was very pleasing to her. The wedding festivities lasted a whole week, and the dogs sat at the table, and stared with all their eyes.

# Great Claus and Little Claus

In a village there once lived two men of the same name. Both of them were called Claus. But because one of them owned four horses while the other had but one, people called the one who had the four horses Big, or Great, Claus and the one who owned but a single horse Little Claus. Now I shall tell you what happened to each of them, for this is a true story.

All the days of the week Little Claus was obliged to plow[3] for Great Claus and to lend him his one horse; then once a week, on Sunday, Great Claus helped Little Claus with his four horses, but always on a holiday.

'Hurrah!' How Little Claus would crack his whip over the five, for they were as good as his own on that one day.

The sun shone brightly, and the church bells rang merrily as the people passed by. The people were dressed in their best, with their prayer books under their arms, for they were going to church to hear the clergyman preach. They looked at Little Claus plowing with five horses, and he was so proud and merry that he cracked his whip and cried, 'Gee up, my fine horses.'

'You mustn't say that,' said Great Claus, 'for only one of them is yours.'

But Little Claus soon forgot what it was that he ought not to say, and when anyone went by he would call out, 'Gee up, my fine horses.'

'I must really beg you not to say that again,' said Great Claus as he passed; 'for if you do, I shall hit your horse on the head so that he will drop down dead on the spot, and then it will be all over with him.'

'I will certainly not say it again, I promise you,' said Little Claus. But as soon as anyone came by, nodding good day to him, he was so pleased, and felt so grand at having five horses plowing his field, that again he cried out, 'Gee up, all my horses.'

'I'll gee up your horses for you,' said Great Claus, and he caught up the tethering mallet and struck Little Claus's one horse on the head, so that it fell down dead.

'Oh, now I haven't[4] any horse at all!' cried Little Claus, and he began to weep. But after a while he flayed the horse and hung up the skin to dry in the wind.

Then he put the dried skin into a bag, and hanging it over his shoulder, went off to the next town to sell it. He had a very long way to go and was obliged to pass through a great, gloomy wood. A dreadful storm came up. He lost his way, and before he found it again, evening was drawing on. It was too late to get to the town, and too late to get home before nightfall.

Near the road stood a large farmhouse. The shutters outside the windows were closed, but lights shone through the crevices and at the top. 'They might let me stay here for the night,' thought Little Claus. So he went up to the door and knocked. The door was opened by the farmer's wife, but when he explained what it was that he wanted, she told him to go away; her husband, she said, was not at home, and she could not let any strangers in.

'Then I shall have to lie out here,' said Little Claus to himself, as the farmer's wife shut the door in his face.

Close to the farmhouse stood a tall haystack, and between it and the house was a small shed with a thatched roof. 'I can lie up there,' said Little Claus, when he saw the roof. 'It will make a capital bed, but I hope the stork won't fly down and bite my legs.' A stork was just then standing near his nest on the house roof.

So Little Claus climbed onto the roof of the shed and proceeded to make himself comfortable. As he turned round to settle himself, he discovered that the wooden shutters did not reach to the tops of the windows. He could look over them straight into the room, in which a large table was laid with wine, roast meat, and a fine, great fish. The farmer's wife and the sexton were sitting at the table all by themselves, and she was pouring out wine for him, while his fork was in the fish, which he seemed to like the best.

'If I could only get some too,' thought Little Claus, and as he stretched his neck toward the window he spied a large, beautiful cake. Goodness! What a glorious feast they had before them.

At that moment someone came riding down the road towards the farm. It was the farmer himself, returning. He was a good man enough, but he had one very singular prejudice—he could not bear the sight of a sexton, and if he came on one he fell into a terrible rage. This was the reason that the sexton had gone to visit the farmer's wife during his absence from home and that the good wife had put before him the best she had.

When they heard the farmer they were frightened, and the woman begged the sexton to creep into a large empty chest which stood in a corner. He did so with all haste, for he well knew how the farmer felt toward a sexton. The woman hid the wine and all the good things in the oven, for if her husband were to see them, he would certainly ask why they had been provided.

'O dear!' sighed Little Claus, on the shed roof, as he saw the good things disappear.

'Is anyone up there?' asked the farmer, looking up where Little Claus was. 'What are you doing up there? You had better come with me into the house.'

Then Little Claus told him how he had lost his way, and asked if he might have shelter for the night.

'Certainly,' replied the farmer; 'but the first thing is to have something to eat.'

The wife received them both in a friendly way, and laid the table, bringing to it a large bowl of porridge. The farmer was hungry and ate with a good appetite. But Little Claus could not help thinking of the capital roast meat, fish, and cake, which he knew were hidden in the oven.

He had put his sack with the hide in it under the table by his feet, for, we must remember, he was on his way to the town to sell it. He did not relish the porridge, so he trod on the sack and made the dried skin squeak quite loudly.

'Hush!' said Little Claus to his bag, at the same time treading upon it again, to make it squeak much louder than before.

'Hollo! What's that you've got in your bag?' asked the farmer.

'Oh, it's a magician,' said Little Claus, 'and he says we needn't eat the porridge, for he has charmed the oven full of roast meat, fish, and cake.'

'What?' cried the farmer, and he opened the oven with all speed and saw all the nice things the woman had hidden, but which he believed the magician had conjured up for their special benefit.

The farmer's wife did not say a word, but set the food before them; and they both made a hearty meal of the fish, the meat, and the cake. Little Claus now trod again upon his sack and made the skin squeak.

'What does he say now?' inquired the farmer.

'He says,' promptly answered Little Claus, 'that he has conjured up three bottles of wine, which are standing in the corner near the stove.' So the woman was obliged to bring the wine which she had hidden, and the farmer and Little Claus became right merry. Would not the farmer like to have such a conjurer as Little Claus carried about in his sack?

'Can he conjure up the Evil One?' inquired the farmer. 'I shouldn't mind seeing him now, when I'm in such a merry mood.'

'Yes,' said Little Claus, 'he will do anything that I please;' and he trod on the bag till it squeaked. 'You hear him answer, "Yes, only the Evil One is so ugly that you had better not see him." '

'Oh, I'm not afraid. What will he look like?'

'Well, he will show himself to you in the image of a sexton.'

'Nay[5], that's bad indeed. You must know that I can't abide a sexton. However, it doesn't matter, for I know he's a demon, and I shan't mind so much. Now my courage is up! Only he mustn't come too close.'

'I'll ask him about it,' said Little Claus, putting his ear down as he trod close to the bag.

'What does he say?'

'He says you can go along and open the chest in the corner, and there you'll see him cowering in the dark. But hold the lid tight, so that he doesn't get out.'

'Will you help me to hold the lid,' asked the farmer, going along to the chest in which his wife had hidden the sexton, who was shivering with fright.

The farmer opened the lid a wee little way and peeped in. 'Ha!' he cried, springing backward. 'I saw him, and he looks exactly like our sexton. It was a shocking sight!'

They must needs[6] drink after this, and there they sat till far into the night.

'You must sell me your conjurer,' said the farmer. 'Ask anything you like for him. Nay, I'll give you a bushel of money for him.'

'No, I can't do that,' said Little Claus. 'You must remember how much benefit I can get from such a conjurer.'

'Oh, but I should so like to have him!' said the farmer, and he went on begging for him.

'Well,' said Little Claus at last, 'since you have been so kind as to give me a night's shelter, I won't say nay. You must give me a bushel of money, only I must have it full to the brim.'

'You shall have it,' said the farmer; 'but you must take that chest away with you. I won't have it in the house an hour longer. You could never know that he might not still be inside.'

So Little Claus gave his sack with the dried hide of the horse in it and received a full bushel of money in return, and the measure was full to the brim. The farmer also gave him a large wheelbarrow, with which to take away the chest and the bushel of money.

'Good-by[7],' said Little Claus, and off he went with his money and the chest with the sexton in it.

On the other side of the forest was a wide, deep river, whose current was so strong that it was almost impossible to swim against it. A large, new bridge had just been built over it, and when they came to the middle of the bridge Little Claus said in a voice loud enough to be heard by the sexton: 'What shall I do with this stupid old chest? It might be full of paving stones, it is so heavy. I am tired of wheeling it. I'll just throw it into the river. If it floats down to my home, well and good; if not, I don't care. It will be no great matter.' And he took hold of the chest and lifted it a little, as if he were going to throw it into the river.

'No, no! Let be!' shouted the sexton. 'Let me get out.'

'Ho!' said Little Claus, pretending to be frightened. 'Why, he is still inside. Then I must heave it into the river to drown him.'

'Oh, no, no, no!' shouted the sexton; 'I'll give you a whole bushelful of money if you'll let me out.'

'Oh, that's another matter,' said Little Claus, opening the chest. He pushed the empty chest into the river and then went home with the sexton to get his bushelful of money. He had already had one from the farmer, you know, so now his wheelbarrow was quite full of money.

'I got a pretty fair price for that horse, I must admit,' said he to himself, when he got home and turned the money out of the wheelbarrow into a heap in the middle of the floor. 'What a rage Great Claus will be in when he discovers how rich I am become through my one horse. But I won't tell him just how it happened.' So he sent a boy to Great Claus to borrow a bushel measure.

'What can he want with it?' thought Great Claus, and he rubbed some tallow on the bottom so that some part of whatever was measured might stick to it. And so it did, for when the measure came back, three new silver threepenny bits were sticking to it.

'What's this!' said Great Claus, and he ran off at once to Little

Claus. 'Where on earth did you get all this money?' he asked.

'Oh, that's for my horse's skin. I sold it yesterday morning.'

'That was well paid for, indeed,' said Great Claus. He ran home, took an ax[8], and hit all his four horses on the head; then he flayed them and carried their skins off to the town.

'Hides! Hides! Who'll buy my hides?' he cried through the streets.

All the shoemakers and tanners in the town came running up and asked him how much he wanted for his hides.

'A bushel of money for each,' said Great Claus.

'Are you mad?' they all said. 'Do you think we have money by the bushel?'

'Skins! Skins! Who'll buy them?' he shouted again, and the shoemakers took up their straps, and the tanners their leather aprons, and began to beat Great Claus.

'Hides! Hides!' they called after him. 'Yes, we'll hide you and tan you. Out of the town with him,' they shouted. And Great Claus made the best haste he could to get out of the town, for he had never yet been thrashed as he was being thrashed now.

'Little Claus shall pay for this,' he said, when he got home. 'I'll kill him for it.'

Little Claus's old grandmother had just died in his house. She had often been harsh and unkind to him, but now that she was dead he felt quite grieved. He took the dead woman and laid her in his warm bed to see if she would not come to life again. He himself intended to sit in a corner all night. He had slept that way before.

As he sat there in the night, the door opened and in came Great Claus with his ax. He knew where Little Claus's bed stood, and he went straight to it and hit the dead grandmother a blow on the forehead, thinking it was Little Claus.

'Just see if you'll make a fool of me again,' said he, and then he went home.

'What a bad, wicked man he is!' said Little Claus. 'He was going to kill me. What a good thing that poor grandmother was dead already! He would have taken her life.'

He now dressed his grandmother in her best Sunday clothes, borrowed a horse of his neighbour, harnessed it to a cart, and set his grandmother on the back seat, so that she could not fall when the cart moved. Then he started off through the woods. When the sun rose, he was just outside a big inn, and he drew up his horse and went in to get something to eat.

The landlord was a very rich man and a very good man, but he was hot-tempered, as if he were made of pepper and snuff. 'Good morning!' said he to Little Claus; 'you have your best clothes on very early this morning.'

'Yes,' said Little Claus, 'I'm going to town with my old grandmother. She's sitting out there in the cart; I can't get her to come in. Won't you take her out a glass of beer? You'll have to shout at her, she's very hard of hearing.'

'Yes, that I'll do,' said the host, and he poured a glass and went out with it to the dead grandmother, who had been placed upright in the cart.

'Here is a glass of beer your son has sent,' said the landlord but she sat quite still and said not a word.

'Don't you hear?' cried he as loud as he could. 'Here is a glass of beer from your son.'

But the dead woman replied not a word, and at last he became quite angry and threw the beer in her face—and at that moment she fell backwards out of the cart, for she was only set upright and not bound fast.

'Now!' shouted Little Claus, as he rushed out of the inn and seized the landlord by the neck, 'you have killed my grandmother! Just look at the big hole in her forehead!'

'Oh! What a misfortune!' cried the man, 'and all because of my quick temper. Good Little Claus, I will pay you a bushel of money, and I will have your poor grandmother buried as if she were my own, if only you will say nothing about it. Otherwise I shall have my head cut off—and that is so dreadful.'

So Little Claus again received a whole bushel of money, and the landlord buried the old grandmother as if she had been his own.

When Little Claus got home again with all his money, he immediately sent his boy to Great Claus to ask to borrow his bushel measure.

'What!' said Great Claus, 'is he not dead? I must go and see about this myself.' So he took the measure over to Little Claus himself.

'I say, where did you get all that money?' asked he, his eyes big and round with amazement at what he saw.

'It was grandmother you killed instead of me,' said Little Claus. 'I have sold her and got a bushel of money for her.'

'That's being well paid, indeed,' said Great Claus, and he hurried home, took an ax and killed his own old grandmother.

He then put her in a carriage and drove off to the town where the apothecary lived, and asked him if he would buy a dead person.

'Who is it and where did you get him?' asked the apothecary.

'It is my grandmother, and I have killed her so as to sell her for a bushel of money.'

'Heaven preserve us!' cried the apothecary. 'You talk like a madman. Pray don't say such things, you may lose your head.' And he told him earnestly what a horribly wicked thing he had done, and that he deserved punishment. Great Claus was so frightened that he rushed out of the shop, jumped into his cart, whipped up his horse, and galloped home through the wood. The apothecary and all the people who saw him thought he was mad, and so they let him drive away.

'You shall be paid for this!' said Great Claus, when he got out on the highroad. 'You shall be paid for this, Little Claus!'

Directly after he got home, Great Claus took the biggest sack he could find and went over to Little Claus.

'You have deceived me again,' he said. 'First I killed my horses, and then my old grandmother. That is all your fault; but you shall never have the chance to trick me again.' And he seized Little Claus around the body and thrust him into the sack; then he threw the sack over his back, calling out to Little Claus, 'Now I'm going to the river to drown you.'

It was a long way that he had to travel before he came to the river, and Little Claus was not light to carry. The road came close to the church, and the people within were singing beautifully. Great Claus put down his sack, with Little Claus in it, at the church door. He thought it would be a very good thing to go in and hear a psalm before he went further, for Little Claus could not get out. So he went in.

'O dear! O dear!' moaned Little Claus in the sack, and he

turned and twisted, but found it impossible to loosen the cord. Then there came by an old drover with snow-white hair and a great staff in his hand. He was driving a whole herd of cows and oxen before him, and they jostled against the sack in which Little Claus was confined, so that it was upset.

'O dear,' again sighed Little Claus, 'I'm so young to be going directly to the kingdom of heaven!'

'And I, poor fellow,' said the drover, 'am so old already, and cannot get there yet.'

'Open the sack,' cried Little Claus, 'and creep into it in my place, and you'll be there directly.'

'With all my heart,' said the drover, and he untied the sack for Little Claus, who crept out at once. 'You must look out for the cattle now,' said the old man, as he crept in. Then Little Claus tied it up and went his way, driving the cows and the oxen.

In a little while Great Claus came out of the church. He took the sack upon his shoulders and thought as he did so that it had certainly grown lighter since he had put it down, for the old cattle-drover was not more than half as heavy as Little Claus.

'How light he is to carry now! That must be because I have heard a psalm in the church.'

He went on to the river, which was both deep and broad, threw the sack containing the old drover into the water, and called after him, thinking it was Little Claus, 'Now lie there! You won't trick me again!'

He turned to go home, but when he came to the place where there was a crossroad he met Little Claus driving his cattle.

'What's this?' cried he. 'Haven't I drowned you?'

'Yes,' said Little Claus, 'you threw me into the river, half an hour ago.'

'But where did you get all those fine cattle?' asked Great Claus.

'These beasts are sea cattle,' said Little Claus, 'and I thank you heartily for drowning me, for now I'm at the top of the tree. I'm a very rich man, I can tell you. But I was frightened when you threw me into the water huddled up in the sack. I sank to the bottom immediately, but I did not hurt myself, for the grass is beautifully soft down there. I fell upon it, and the sack was opened, and the most beautiful maiden in snow-white garments and a green wreath upon her hair took me by the hand, and said to me, "Have you come, Little Claus? Here are cattle for you, and a mile further up the road there is another herd!"

'Then I saw that she meant the river and that it was the highway for the sea folk. Down at the bottom of it they walk directly from the sea, straight into the land where the river ends. Lovely flowers and beautiful fresh grass were there. The fishes which swam there glided about me like birds in the air. How nice the people were, and what fine herds of cattle there were, pasturing on the mounds and about the ditches!'

'But why did you come up so quickly then?' asked Great Claus. 'I shouldn't have done that if it was so fine down there.'

'Why, that was just my cunning. You know, I told you that the mermaid said there was a whole herd of cattle for me a mile further up the stream. Well, you see, I know how the river bends this way and that, and how long a distance it would have been to go that way. If you can come up on the land and take the short cuts, driving across fields and down to the river again, you save almost half a mile and get the cattle much sooner.'

'Oh, you are a fortunate man!' cried Great Claus. 'Do you think

I could get some sea cattle if I were to go down to the bottom of the river?'

'I'm sure you would,' said Little Claus. 'But I cannot carry you. If you will walk to the river and creep into a sack yourself, I will help you into the water with a great deal of pleasure.'

'Thanks!' said Great Claus. 'But if I do not find sea cattle there, I shall beat you soundly, you may be sure.'

'Oh! Do not be so hard on me.'

And so they went together to the river. When the cows and oxen saw the water, they ran to it as fast as they could. 'See how they hurry!' cried Little Claus. 'They want to get back to the bottom again.'

'Yes, but help me first or I'll thrash you,' said Great Claus. He then crept into a big sack, which had been lying across the back of one of the cows. 'Put a big stone in or I'm afraid I shan't sink.'

'Oh, that'll be all right,' said Little Claus, but he put a big stone into the sack and gave it a push. Plump! And there lay Great Claus in the river. He sank at once to the bottom.

'I'm afraid he won't find the cattle,' said Little Claus. Then he drove homeward with his herd.

# 3

# The Real Princess

There was once a prince, and he wanted a princess, but then she must be a real Princess. He travelled right round the world to find one, but there was always something wrong. There were plenty of princesses, but whether they were real princesses he had great difficulty in discovering; there was always something which was not quite right about them. So at last he had to come home again, and he was very sad because he wanted a real princess so badly.

One evening there was a terrible storm; it thundered and lightened and the rain poured down in torrents; indeed it was a fearful night.

In the middle of the storm somebody knocked at the town gate, and the old King himself went to open it.

It was a princess who stood outside, but she was in a terrible state from the rain and the storm. The water streamed out of her hair and her clothes; it ran in at the top of her shoes and out at the heel, but she said that she was a real princess.

'Well we shall soon see if that is true,' thought the old Queen, but she said nothing. She went into the bedroom, took all the bedclothes off and laid a pea on the bedstead; then she took twenty mattresses and piled them on the top of the pea, and then twenty feather beds on the top of the mattresses. This was where the princess was to sleep that night. In the morning they asked her how she had slept.

'Oh terribly badly!' said the princess. 'I have hardly closed my eyes the whole night! Heaven knows what was in the bed. I seemed to be lying upon some hard thing, and my whole body is black and blue this morning. It is terrible!'

They saw at once that she must be a real princess when she had felt the pea through twenty mattresses and twenty feather beds. Nobody but a real princess could have such a delicate skin.

So the prince took her to be his wife, for now he was sure that he had found a real princess, and the pea was put into the Museum, where it may still be seen if no one has stolen it.

Now this is a true story.

# 4

# Little Ida's Flowers

'My poor flowers are quite faded!' said little Ida. 'Only yesterday evening they were so pretty, and now all the leaves are drooping. Why do they do that?' she asked of the student, who sat on the sofa. He was a great favourite with her, because he used to tell her the prettiest of stories and cut out the most amusing things in paper—hearts with little ladies dancing in them, and high castles with doors which one could open and shut. He was a merry student. 'Why do the flowers look so wretched today?' asked she again, showing him a bouquet of faded flowers.

'Do you not know?' replied the student. 'The flowers went to a ball last night, and are tired. That's why they hang their heads.'

'What an idea,' exclaimed little Ida. 'Flowers cannot dance!'

'Of course they can dance! When it is dark, and we are all gone to bed, they jump about as merrily as possible. They have a ball almost every night.'

'And can their children go to the ball?' asked Ida.

'Oh, yes,' said the student; 'daisies and lilies of the valley, that are quite little.'

'And when is it that the prettiest flowers dance?'

'Have you not been to the large garden outside the town gate, in front of the castle where the king lives in summer—the garden that is so full of lovely flowers? You surely remember the swans which come swimming up when you give them crumbs of bread? Believe me, they have capital balls there.'

'I was out there only yesterday with my mother,' said Ida, 'but there were no leaves on the trees, and I did not see a single flower. What has become of them? There were so many in the summer.'

'They are inside the palace now,' replied the student. 'As soon as the king and all his court go back to the town, the flowers hasten out of the garden and into the palace, where they have famous times. Oh, if you could but see them! The two most beautiful roses seat themselves on the throne and act king and queen. All the tall red cockscombs stand before them on either side and bow; they are the chamberlains. Then all the pretty flowers come, and there is a great ball. The blue violets represent the naval cadets; they dance with hyacinths and crocuses, who take the part of young ladies. The tulips and the tall tiger lilies are old ladies,—dowagers,—who see to it that the dancing is well done and that all things go on properly.'

'But,' asked little Ida, 'is there no one there to harm the flowers for daring to dance in the king's castle?'

'No one knows anything about it,' replied the student. 'Once during the night, perhaps, the old steward of the castle does, to be sure, come in with his great bunch of keys to see that all is right; but the moment the flowers hear the clanking of the keys they stand stock-still or hide themselves behind the long silk window curtains. Then the old steward will say, "Do I not smell flowers here?" but he can't see them.'

'That is very funny,' exclaimed little Ida, clapping her hands with glee; 'but should not I be able to see the flowers?'

'To be sure you can see them,' replied the student. 'You have only to remember to peep in at the windows the next time you go to the palace. I did so this very day, and saw a long yellow lily lying on the sofa. She was a court lady.'

'Do the flowers in the Botanical Garden go to the ball? Can they go all that long distance?'

'Certainly,' said the student; 'for the flowers can fly if they please. Have you not seen the beautiful red and yellow butterflies that look so much like flowers? They are in fact nothing else. They have flown off their stalks high into the air and flapped their little petals just as if they were wings, and thus they came to fly about. As a reward for always behaving well they have leave to fly about in the daytime, too, instead of sitting quietly on their stalks at home, till at last the flower petals have become real wings. That you have seen yourself.

'It may be, though, that the flowers in the Botanical Garden have never been in the king's castle. They may not have heard what frolics take place there every night. But I'll tell you; if, the next time you go to the garden, you whisper to one of the flowers that a great ball is to be given yonder[9] in the castle, the news will spread from flower to flower and they will all fly away. Then should the professor come to his garden there won't be a flower there, and he will not be able to imagine what has become of them.'

'But how can one flower tell it to another? For I am sure the flowers cannot speak.'

'No; you are right there,' returned the student. 'They cannot speak, but they can make signs. Have you ever noticed that when the wind blows a little the flowers nod to each other and move all their green leaves? They can make each other understand in this way just as well as we do by talking.'

'And does the professor understand their pantomime?' asked Ida.

'Oh, certainly; at least part of it. He came into his garden one morning and saw that a great stinging nettle was making signs with its leaves to a beautiful red carnation. It was saying, "You are so beautiful, and I love you with all my heart!" But the professor doesn't like that sort of thing, and he rapped the nettle on her leaves, which are her fingers; but she stung him, and since then he has never dared to touch a nettle.'

'Ha! Ha!' laughed little Ida, 'that is very funny.'

'How can one put such stuff into a child's head?' said a tiresome councillor, who had come to pay a visit. He did not like the student and always used to scold when he saw him cutting out the droll pasteboard figures, such as a man hanging on a gibbet and holding a heart in his hand to show that he was a stealer of hearts, or an old witch riding on a broomstick and carrying her husband on the end of her nose. The councillor could not bear such jokes, and he would always say, as now: 'How can anyone put such notions into a child's head? They are only foolish fancies.'

But to little Ida all that the student had told her was very entertaining, and she kept thinking it over. She was sure now that her pretty yesterday's flowers hung their heads because they were tired, and that they were tired because they had been to the ball. So she took them to the table where stood her toys. Her doll lay sleeping, but Ida said to her, 'You must get up, and be content to sleep tonight in the table drawer, for the poor flowers are ill and must have your bed to sleep in; then perhaps they will be well again by tomorrow.'

And she at once took the doll out, though the doll looked vexed at giving up her cradle to the flowers.

Ida laid the flowers in the doll's bed and drew the coverlet quite over them, telling them to lie still while she made some tea for them to drink, in order that they might be well next day. And she drew the curtains about the bed, that the sun might not shine into their eyes.

All the evening she thought of nothing but what the student had told her; and when she went to bed herself, she ran to the window where her mother's tulips and hyacinths stood. She whispered to them, 'I know very well that you are going to a ball tonight.' The flowers pretended not to understand and did not stir so much as a leaf, but that did not prevent Ida from knowing what she knew.

When she was in bed she lay for a long time thinking how delightful it must be to see the flower dance in the king's castle, and said to herself, 'I wonder if my flowers have really been there.' Then she fell asleep.

In the night she woke. She had been dreaming of the student and the flowers and the councillor, who told her they were making game of her. All was still in the room, the night lamp was burning on the table, and her father and mother were both asleep.

'I wonder if my flowers are still lying in Sophie's bed,' she thought to herself. 'How I should like to know!' She raised herself a little and looked towards the door, which stood half open; within lay the flowers and all her playthings. She listened, and it seemed to her that she heard someone playing upon the piano, but quite softly, and more sweetly than she had ever heard before.

'Now all the flowers are certainly dancing,' thought she. 'Oh, how I should like to see them!' but she dared not get up for fear of waking her father and mother. 'If they would only come in here!' But the flowers did not come, and the music went on so prettily that she could restrain herself no longer, and she crept out of her little bed, stole softly to the door, and peeped into the room. Oh, what a pretty sight it was!

There was no night lamp in the room, still it was quite bright; the moon shone through the window down upon the floor, and it was almost like daylight. The hyacinths and tulips stood there in two rows. Not one was left on the window, where stood the empty flower pots. On the floor all the flowers danced gracefully, making all the turns, and holding each other by their long green leaves as they twirled around. At the piano sat a large yellow lily, which little Ida remembered to have seen in the summer, for she recollected that the student had said, 'How like she is to Miss Laura,' and how everyone had laughed at the remark. But now she really thought that the lily was very like the young lady. It had exactly her manner of playing—bending its long yellow face, now to one side and now to the other, and nodding its head to mark the time of the beautiful music.

A tall blue crocus now stepped forward, sprang upon the table on which lay Ida's playthings, went straight to the doll's cradle, and drew back the curtains. There lay the sick flowers; but they rose at once, greeted the other flowers, and made a sign that they would like to join in the dance. They did not look at all ill now.

Suddenly a heavy noise was heard, as of something falling from the table. Ida glanced that way and saw that it was the rod she had found on her bed on Shrove Tuesday, and that it seemed to wish to belong to the flowers. It was a pretty rod, for a wax figure that looked exactly like the councillor sat upon the head of it.

The rod began to dance, and the wax figure that was riding on it became long and great, like the councillor himself, and began to exclaim, 'How can one put such stuff into a child's head?' It was very funny to see, and little Ida could not help laughing, for the rod kept on dancing, and the councillor had to dance too,—there was no help for it,—whether he remained tall and big or became a little wax figure again. But the other flowers said a good word for him, especially those that had lain in the doll's bed, so that at last the rod left it in peace.

At the same time there was a loud knocking inside the drawer where Sophie, Ida's doll, lay with many other toys. She put out her head and asked in great astonishment: 'Is there a ball here? Why has no one told me of it?' She sat down upon the table, expecting some of the flowers to ask her to dance with them; but as they did not, she let herself fall upon the floor so as to make a great noise; and then the flowers all came crowding about to ask if she were hurt, and they were very polite—especially those that had lain in her bed.

She was not at all hurt, and the flowers thanked her for the use of her pretty bed and took her into the middle of the room, where the moon shone, and danced with her, while the other flowers formed a circle around them. So now Sophie was pleased and said they might keep her bed, for she did not mind sleeping in the drawer the least in the world.

But the flowers replied: 'We thank you most heartily for your kindness, but we shall not live long enough to need it; we shall be quite dead by tomorrow. But tell little Ida she is to bury us out in the garden near the canary bird's grave; and then we shall wake again next summer and be even more beautiful than we have been this year.'

'Oh, no, you must not die,' said Sophie, kissing them as she spoke; and then a great company of flowers came dancing in. Ida could not imagine where they could have come from, unless from the king's garden. Two beautiful roses led the way, wearing golden crowns; then followed wallflowers and pinks, who bowed to all present. They brought a band of music with them. Wild hyacinths and little white snowdrops jingled merry bells. It was a most remarkable orchestra. Following these were an immense number of flowers, all dancing—violets, daisies, lilies of the valley, and others which it was a delight to see.

At last all the happy flowers wished one another good night. Little Ida, too, crept back to bed, to dream of all that she had seen.

When she rose next morning she went at once to her little table to see if her flowers were there. She drew aside the curtains of her little bed; yes, there lay the flowers, but they were much more faded today than yesterday. Sophie too was in the drawer, but she looked very sleepy.

'Do you remember what you were to say to me?' asked Ida of her.

But Sophie looked quite stupid and had not a word to say.

'You are not kind at all,' said Ida; 'and yet all the flowers let you dance with them.'

Then she chose from her playthings a little pasteboard box with birds painted on it, and in it she laid the dead flowers.

'That shall be your pretty casket,' said she; 'and when my cousins come to visit me, by and by, they shall help me to bury you in the garden, in order that next summer you may grow again and be still more beautiful.'

The two cousins were two merry boys, Gustave and Adolphe. Their father had given them each a new crossbow, which they brought with them to show to Ida. She told them of the poor flowers that were dead and were to be buried in the garden. So the two boys walked in front, with their bows slung across their shoulders, and little Ida followed, carrying the dead flowers in their pretty coffin. A little grave was dug for them in the garden. Ida first kissed the flowers and then laid them in the earth, and Adolphe and Gustave shot with their crossbows over the grave, for they had neither guns nor cannons.

# 5

# Thumbelina

There was once a woman who wished very much to have a little child. She went to a fairy and said: 'I should so very much like to have a little child. Can you tell me where I can find one?'

'Oh, that can be easily managed,' said the fairy. 'Here is a barleycorn; it is not exactly of the same sort as those which grow in the farmers' fields, and which the chickens eat. Put it into a flowerpot and see what will happen.'

'Thank you,' said the woman; and she gave the fairy twelve shillings, which was the price of the barleycorn. Then she went home and planted it, and there grew up a large, handsome flower, somewhat like a tulip in appearance, but with its leaves tightly closed, as if it were still a bud.

'It is a beautiful flower,' said the woman, and she kissed the red and golden-coloured petals; and as she did so the flower opened, and she could see that it was a real tulip. But within the flower, upon the green velvet stamens, sat a very delicate and graceful little maiden. She was scarcely half as long as a thumb, and they gave her the name of Little Thumb, or Thumbelina, because she was so small.

A walnut shell, elegantly polished, served her for a cradle; her bed was formed of blue violet leaves, with a rose leaf for a counterpane. Here she slept at night, but during the day she amused herself on a table, where the peasant wife had placed a plate full of water.

Round this plate were wreaths of flowers with their stems in the water, and upon it floated a large tulip leaf, which served the little one for a boat. Here she sat and rowed herself from side to side, with two oars made of white horsehair. It was a very pretty sight. Thumbelina could also sing so softly and sweetly that nothing like her singing had ever before been heard.

One night, while she lay in her pretty bed, a large, ugly, wet toad crept through a broken pane of glass in the window and leaped right upon the table where she lay sleeping under her rose-leaf quilt.

'What a pretty little wife this would make for my son,' said the toad, and she took up the walnut shell in which Thumbelina lay asleep, and jumped through the window with it, into the garden.

In the swampy margin of a broad stream in the garden lived the toad with her son. He was uglier even than his mother; and when he saw the pretty little maiden in her elegant bed, he could only cry 'Croak, croak, croak.'

'Don't speak so loud, or she will wake,' said the toad, 'and then she might run away, for she is as light as swan's-down. We will place her on one of the water lily leaves out in the stream; it will be like an island to her, she is so light and small, and then she cannot escape; and while she is there we will make haste and prepare the stateroom under the marsh, in which you are to live when you are married.'

Far out in the stream grew a number of water lilies with broad green leaves which seemed to float on the top of the water.

The largest of these leaves appeared further off than the rest, and the old toad swam out to it with the walnut shell, in which Thumbelina still lay asleep.

The tiny creature woke very early in the morning and began to cry bitterly when she found where she was, for she could see nothing but water on every side of the large green leaf, and no way of reaching the land.

Meanwhile the old toad was very busy under the marsh, decking her room with rushes and yellow wildflowers, to make it look pretty for her new daughter-in-law. Then she swam out with her ugly son to the leaf on which she had placed poor Thumbelina. She wanted to bring the pretty bed, that she might put it in the bridal chamber to be ready for her. The old toad bowed low to her in the water and said, 'Here is my son; he will be your husband, and you will live happily together in the marsh by the stream.'

'Croak, croak, croak,' was all her son could say for himself. So the toad took up the elegant little bed and swam away with it, leaving Thumbelina all alone on the green leaf, where she sat and wept. She could not bear to think of living with the old toad and having her ugly son for a husband. The little fishes who swam about in the water beneath had seen the toad and heard what she said, so now they lifted their heads above the water to look at the little maiden.

As soon as they caught sight of her they saw she was very pretty, and it vexed them to think that she must go and live with the ugly toads.

'No, it must never be!' So they gathered together in the water, round the green stalk which held the leaf on which the little maiden stood, and gnawed it away at the root with their teeth.

Then the leaf floated down the stream, carrying Thumbelina far away out of reach of land.

Thumbelina sailed past many towns, and the little birds in the bushes saw her and sang, 'What a lovely little creature.' So the leaf swam away with her further and further, till it brought her to other lands. A graceful little white butterfly constantly fluttered round her and at last alighted on the leaf. The little maiden pleased him, and she was glad of it, for now the toad could not possibly reach her, and the country through which she sailed was beautiful, and the sun shone upon the water till it glittered like liquid gold. She took off her girdle and tied one end of it round the butterfly, fastening the other end of the ribbon to the leaf, which now glided on much faster than before, taking Thumbelina with it as she stood.

Presently a large cockchafer flew by. The moment he caught sight of her he seized her round her delicate waist with his claws and flew with her into a tree. The green leaf floated away on the brook, and the butterfly flew with it, for he was fastened to it and could not get away.

Oh, how frightened Thumbelina felt when the cockchafer flew with her to the tree! But especially was she sorry for the beautiful white butterfly which she had fastened to the leaf, for if he could not free himself he would die of hunger. But the cockchafer did not trouble himself at all about the matter. He seated himself by her side, on a large green leaf, gave her some honey from the flowers to eat, and told her she was very pretty, though not in the least like a cockchafer.

After a time all the cockchafers who lived in the tree came to pay Thumbelina a visit. They stared at her, and then the young lady cockchafers turned up their feelers and said, 'She has only two legs! How ugly that looks.' 'She has no feelers,' said another. 'Her waist is quite slim. Pooh! She is like a human being.'

'Oh, she is ugly,' said all the lady cockchafers. The cockchafer who had run away with her believed all the others when they said she was ugly. He would have nothing more to say to her, and told her she might go where she liked. Then he flew down with her from the tree and placed her on a daisy, and she wept at the thought that she was so ugly that even the cockchafers would have nothing to say to her. And all the while she was really the loveliest creature that one could imagine, and as tender and delicate as a beautiful rose leaf.

During the whole summer poor little Thumbelina lived quite alone in the wide forest. She wove herself a bed with blades of grass and hung it up under a broad leaf, to protect herself from the rain. She sucked the honey from the flowers for food and drank the dew from their leaves every morning.

So passed away the summer and the autumn, and then came the winter—the long, cold winter. All the birds who had sung to her so sweetly had flown away, and the trees and the flowers had withered. The large shamrock under the shelter of which she had lived was now rolled together and shrivelled up; nothing remained but a yellow, withered stalk. She felt dreadfully cold, for her clothes were torn, and she was herself so frail and delicate that she was nearly frozen to death. It began to snow, too; and the snowflakes, as they fell upon her, were like a whole shovelful falling upon one of us, for we are tall, but she was only an inch high. She wrapped herself in a dry leaf, but it cracked in the middle and could not keep her warm, and she shivered with cold.

Near the wood in which she had been living was a large cornfield, but the corn had been cut a long time; nothing remained but the bare, dry stubble, standing up out of the frozen ground. It was to her like struggling through a large wood.

Oh! How she shivered with the cold. She came at last to the door of a field mouse, who had a little den under the corn stubble. There dwelt the field mouse in warmth and comfort, with a whole roomful of corn, a kitchen, and a beautiful dining room. Poor Thumbelina stood before the door, just like a little beggar girl, and asked for a small piece of barleycorn, for she had been without a morsel to eat for two days.

'You poor little creature,' said the field mouse, for she was really a good old mouse, 'come into my warm room and dine with me.'

She was pleased with Thumbelina, so she said, 'You are quite welcome to stay with me all the winter, if you like; but you must keep my rooms clean and neat, and tell me stories, for I shall like to hear them very much.' And Thumbelina did all that the field mouse asked her, and found herself very comfortable.

'We shall have a visitor soon,' said the field mouse one day; 'my neighbour pays me a visit once a week. He is better off than I am; he has large rooms, and wears a beautiful black velvet coat. If you could only have him for a husband, you would be well provided for indeed. But he is blind, so you must tell him some of your prettiest stories.'

Thumbelina did not feel at all interested about this neighbour, for he was a mole. However, he came and paid his visit, dressed in his black velvet coat.

'He is very rich and learned, and his house is twenty times larger than mine,' said the field mouse.

He was rich and learned, no doubt, but he always spoke slightingly of the sun and the pretty flowers, because he had never seen them. Thumbelina was obliged to sing to him, 'Ladybird, ladybird, fly away home,' and many other pretty songs. And the mole fell in love with her because she had so sweet a voice; but he said nothing yet, for he was very prudent and cautious. A short time before, the mole had dug a long passage under the earth, which led from the dwelling of the field mouse to his own, and here she had permission to walk with Thumbelina whenever she liked. But he warned them not to be alarmed at the sight of a dead bird which lay in the passage. It was a perfect bird, with a beak and feathers, and could not have been dead long. It was lying just where the mole had made his passage. The mole took in his mouth a piece of phosphorescent wood, which glittered like fire in the dark. Then he went before them to light them through the long, dark passage. When they came to the spot where the dead bird lay, the mole pushed his broad nose through the ceiling, so that the earth gave way and the daylight shone into the passage.

In the middle of the floor lay a swallow, his beautiful wings pulled close to his sides, his feet and head drawn up under his feathers—the poor bird had evidently died of the cold. It made little Thumbelina very sad to see it, she did so love the little birds; all the summer they had sung and twittered for her so beautifully. But the mole pushed it aside with his crooked legs and said: 'He will sing no more now. How miserable it must be to be born a little bird! I am thankful that none of my children will ever be birds, for they can do nothing but cry "Tweet, tweet," and must always die of hunger in the winter.'

'Yes, you may well say that, as a clever man!' exclaimed the field mouse. 'What is the use of his twittering if, when winter comes, he must either starve or be frozen to death? Still, birds are very high bred.'

Thumbelina said nothing, but when the two others had turned their backs upon the bird, she stooped down and stroked aside the soft feathers which covered his head, and kissed the closed eyelids. 'Perhaps this was the one who sang to me so sweetly in the summer,' she said; 'and how much pleasure it gave me, you dear, pretty bird.'

The mole now stopped up the hole through which the daylight shone, and then accompanied the ladies home. But during the night Thumbelina could not sleep; so she got out of bed and wove a large, beautiful carpet of hay. She carried it to the dead bird and spread it over him, with some down from the flowers which she had found in the field mouse's room. It was as soft as wool, and she spread some of it on each side of the bird, so that he might lie warmly in the cold earth.

'Farewell, pretty little bird,' said she, 'farewell. Thank you for your delightful singing during the summer, when all the trees were green and the warm sun shone upon us.' Then she laid her head on the bird's breast, but she was alarmed, for it seemed as if something inside the bird went 'thump, thump.' It was the bird's heart; he was not really dead, only benumbed with the cold, and the warmth had restored him to life. In autumn all the swallows fly away into warm countries; but if one happens to linger, the cold seizes it, and it becomes chilled and falls down as if dead. It remains where it fell, and the cold snow covers it.

Thumbelina trembled very much; she was quite frightened, for the bird was large, a great deal larger than herself (she was only an inch high). But she took courage, laid the wool more thickly over the poor swallow, and then took a leaf which she had used for her own counterpane and laid it over his head.

The next night she again stole out to see him. He was alive, but very weak; he could only open his eyes for a moment to look at Thumbelina, who stood by, holding a piece of decayed wood in her hand, for she had no other lantern. 'Thank you, pretty little maiden,' said the sick swallow; 'I have been so nicely warmed that I shall soon regain my strength and be able to fly about again in the warm sunshine.'

'Oh,' said she, 'it is cold out of doors now; it snows and freezes. Stay in your warm bed; I will take care of you.'

She brought the swallow some water in a flower leaf, and after he had drunk, he told her that he had wounded one of his wings in a thornbush and could not fly as fast as the others, who were soon far away on their journey to warm countries. At last he had fallen to the earth, and could remember nothing more, nor how he came to be where she had found him.

All winter the swallow remained underground, and Thumbelina nursed him with care and love. She did not tell either the mole or the field mouse anything about it, for they did not like swallows. Very soon the springtime came, and the sun warmed the earth. Then the swallow bade farewell to Thumbelina, and she opened the hole in the ceiling which the mole had made. The sun shone in upon them so beautifully that the swallow asked her if she would go with him. She could sit on his back, he said, and he would fly away with her into the green woods. But she knew it would grieve the field mouse if she left her in that manner, so she said, 'No, I cannot.'

'Farewell, then, farewell, you good, pretty little maiden,' said the swallow, and he flew out into the sunshine.

Thumbelina looked after him, and the tears rose in her eyes. She was very fond of the poor swallow.

'Tweet, tweet,' sang the bird, as he flew out into the green woods, and Thumbelina felt very sad. She was not allowed to go out into the warm sunshine. The corn which had been sowed in the field over the house of the field mouse had grown up high into the air and formed a thick wood to Thumbelina, who was only an inch in height.

'You are going to be married, little one,' said the field mouse. 'My neighbour has asked for you. What good fortune for a poor child like you! Now we will prepare your wedding clothes. They must be woollen and linen. Nothing must be wanting when you are the wife of the mole.'

Thumbelina had to turn the spindle, and the field mouse hired four spiders, who were to weave day and night. Every evening the mole visited her and was continually speaking of the time when the summer would be over. Then he would keep his wedding day with Thumbelina; but now the heat of the sun was so great that it burned the earth and made it hard, like stone. As soon as the summer was over the wedding should take place. But Thumbelina was not at all pleased, for she did not like the tiresome mole.

Every morning when the sun rose and every evening when it went down she would creep out at the door, and as the wind blew aside the ears of corn so that she could see the blue sky, she thought how beautiful and bright it seemed out there and wished so much to see her dear friend, the swallow, again. But he never returned, for by this time he had flown far away into the lovely green forest.

When autumn arrived Thumbelina had her outfit quite ready, and the field mouse said to her, 'In four weeks the wedding must take place.'

Then she wept and said she would not marry the disagreeable mole.

'Nonsense,' replied the field mouse. 'Now don't be obstinate, or I shall bite you with my white teeth. He is a very handsome mole; the queen herself does not wear more beautiful velvets and furs. His kitchens and cellars are quite full. You ought to be very thankful for such good fortune.'

So the wedding day was fixed, on which the mole was to take her away to live with him, deep under the earth, and never again to see the warm sun, because he did not like it. The poor child was very unhappy at the thought of saying farewell to the beautiful sun, and as the field mouse had given her permission to stand at the door, she went to look at it once more.

'Farewell, bright sun,' she cried, stretching out her arm towards it; and then she walked a short distance from the house, for the corn had been cut, and only the dry stubble remained in the fields. 'Farewell, farewell,' she repeated, twining her arm around a little red flower that grew just by her side. 'Greet the little swallow from me, if you should see him again.'

'Tweet, tweet,' sounded over her head suddenly. She looked up, and there was the swallow himself flying close by. As soon as he spied Thumbelina he was delighted. She told him how unwilling she was to marry the ugly mole, and to live always beneath the earth, nevermore to see the bright sun. And as she told him, she wept.

'Cold winter is coming,' said the swallow, 'and I am going to fly away into warmer countries. Will you go with me? You can sit on my back and fasten yourself on with your sash. Then we can fly away from the ugly mole and his gloomy rooms—far away, over the mountains, into warmer countries, where the sun shines more brightly than here; where it is always summer, and the flowers bloom in greater beauty. Fly now with me, dear little one; you saved my life when I lay frozen in that dark, dreary passage.'

'Yes, I will go with you,' said Thumbelina; and she seated herself on the bird's back, with her feet on his outstretched wings, and tied her girdle to one of his strongest feathers.

The swallow rose in the air and flew over forest and over sea—high above the highest mountains, covered with eternal snow. Thumbelina would have been frozen in the cold air, but she crept under the bird's warm feathers, keeping her little head uncovered, so that she might admire the beautiful lands over which they passed. At length they reached the warm countries, where the sun shines brightly and the sky seems so much higher above the earth. Here on the hedges and by the wayside grew purple, green, and white grapes, lemons and oranges hung from trees in the fields, and the air was fragrant with myrtles and orange blossoms. Beautiful children ran along the country lanes, playing with large gay butterflies; and as the swallow flew further and further, every place appeared still more lovely[10].

At last they came to a blue lake, and by the side of it, shaded by trees of the deepest green, stood a palace of dazzling white marble, built in the olden times. Vines clustered round its lofty pillars, and at the top were many swallows' nests, and one of these was the home of the swallow who carried Thumbelina.

'This is my house,' said the swallow; 'but it would not do for you to live there—you would not be comfortable. You must choose for yourself one of those lovely flowers, and I will put you down upon it, and then you shall have everything that you can wish to make you happy.'

'That will be delightful,' she said, and clapped her little hands for joy.

A large marble pillar lay on the ground, which, in falling, had been broken into three pieces. Between these pieces grew the most beautiful large white flowers, so the swallow flew down with Thumbelina and placed her on one of the broad leaves. But how surprised she was to see in the middle of the flower a tiny little man, as white and transparent as if he had been made of crystal! He had a gold crown on his head, and delicate wings at his shoulders, and was not much larger than was she herself. He was the angel of the flower, for a tiny man and a tiny woman dwell in every flower, and this was the king of them all.

'Oh, how beautiful he is!' whispered Thumbelina to the swallow.

The little prince was at first quite frightened at the bird, who was like a giant compared to such a delicate little creature as himself; but when he saw Thumbelina he was delighted and thought her the prettiest little maiden he had ever seen. He took the gold crown from his head and placed it on hers, and asked her name and if she would be his wife and queen over all the flowers.

This certainly was a very different sort of husband from the son of the toad, or the mole with his black velvet and fur, so she said "Yes" to the handsome prince. Then all the flowers opened, and out of each came a little lady or a tiny lord, all so pretty it was quite a pleasure to look at them. Each of them brought Thumbelina a present; but the best gift was a pair of beautiful wings, which had belonged to a large white fly, and they fastened them to Thumbelina's shoulders, so that she might fly from flower to flower.

Then there was much rejoicing, and the little swallow, who sat above them in his nest, was asked to sing a wedding song, which he did as well as he could; but in his heart he felt sad, for he was very fond of Thumbelina and would have liked never to part from her again.

'You must not be called Thumbelina any more,' said the spirit of the flowers to her. 'It is an ugly name, and you are so very lovely. We will call you Maia.'

'Farewell, farewell,' said the swallow, with a heavy heart, as he left the warm countries, to fly back into Denmark. There he had a nest over the window of a house in which dwelt the writer of fairy tales. The swallow sang 'Tweet, tweet,' and from his song came the whole story.

# 6

# The Naughty Boy

Once upon a time an old poet—a really nice and kind old poet—was sitting cozily by his potbelly stove toasting apples. Outside a storm was raging and the rain was coming down by the bucket. 'Anyone caught out tonight won't have a dry stitch on,' remarked the poet, and sighed.

'Open the door! I am wet and freezing!' cried a little child, and banged on the poet's door, while the wind made all the windows rattle.

'Poor little fellow!' exclaimed the poet, and hurried to open the door. There stood a little boy; he was stark naked and the water was streaming down his golden hair. He was so cold that he was trembling all over; and had he not been let in, he certainly would have died that night out in the awful storm.

'You poor little boy.' The poet took him by the hand. 'Come in and sit down by the stove and get dry. I'll give you wine and toasted apples. You are a beautiful child!'

And that he was. His eyes shone like two stars, and even though his golden hair was wet, it curled most becomingly. He looked like an angel as he stood there pale and shivering. In his hands he had a bow and some arrows, which were much the worse for having been out in the rain, for all the colours on the pretty arrows had run into each other.

The old poet sat down next to the stove with the child in his lap. He dried his hair and warmed his hands in his own; then he gave him a toasted apple and a glass of mulled wine. The boy soon recovered. The colour returned to his cheeks. He jumped down from the poet's knees and began to dance around his chair.

'You are a lively child,' said the old poet, and smiled. 'What is your name?'

'I am called Cupid,' answered the boy. 'Don't you know me? There are my bow and arrows. I am good at shooting. Look, the moon has come out; the weather is fine now.'

'But I am afraid your bow and arrows are spoiled,' the poet said.

'That is too bad!' The boy picked up the bow and glanced at it. 'Now that it's dry it looks all right,' he argued. 'Look, the string is taut. No harm has come to it.' Cupid slipped an arrow into the bow and bent it. He took aim and the arrow pierced the old man's heart! 'There, you can see for yourself, my bow is fine,' the naughty, ungrateful boy said laughingly to the poor old poet who had taken him into his warm living room and given him mulled wine and the very best of his toasted apples.

The old poet lay on the floor, weeping. He had really been hit, right in the heart. 'Oh... oh...' he moaned. 'The mischievous child! I am going to tell all the other boys and girls to beware of Cupid and never to play with him, so he cannot do them any harm.'

All the boys and girls who were warned by the old poet did their best to be on the alert against Cupid; but he fooled them anyway, because he is very cunning. When a student is returning from a lecture at the university, Cupid runs along beside him, wearing a black robe and with a book under his arm. The student

cannot recognise him; he mistakes him for another student and takes his arm; then Cupid shoots an arrow into his heart. The girls are not safe from him, even in church when they are being confirmed. In the theatre, he sits astride the chandelier and nobody notices him up there among the burning candles, but they feel it when he shoots his arrows at them. He runs about in the royal parks and on the embankment where your parents love to go for a walk. He has hit their hearts with his arrows once, too. Ask them, and see what they say. Cupid is a rascal! Don't ever have anything to do with him! Imagine, he once shot your poor old grandmother, right through the heart; it's so long ago that it no longer hurts, but she hasn't forgotten it. Pooh! That mischievous Cupid! Now you know what he is like and what a naughty boy he is.

# 7

# The Little Mermaid

Far out in the ocean, where the water is as blue as the prettiest cornflower and as clear as crystal, it is very, very deep; so deep, indeed, that no cable could sound it, and many church steeples, piled one upon another, would not reach from the ground beneath to the surface of the water above. There dwell the Sea King and his subjects.

We must not imagine that there is nothing at the bottom of the sea but bare yellow sand. No, indeed, for on this sand grow the strangest flowers and plants, the leaves and stems of which are so pliant that the slightest agitation of the water causes them to stir as if they had life. Fishes, both large and small, glide between the branches as birds fly among the trees here upon land.

In the deepest spot of all stands the castle of the Sea King. Its walls are built of coral, and the long Gothic windows are of the clearest amber. The roof is formed of shells that open and close as the water flows over them. Their appearance is very beautiful, for in each lies a glittering pearl which would be fit for the diadem of a queen.

The Sea King had been a widower for many years, and his aged mother kept house for him. She was a very sensible woman, but exceedingly proud of her high birth, and on that account wore twelve oysters on her tail, while others of high rank were only allowed to wear six.

She was, however, deserving of very great praise, especially for her care of the little sea princesses, her six granddaughters. They were beautiful children, but the youngest was the prettiest of them all. Her skin was as clear and delicate as a rose leaf, and her eyes as blue as the deepest sea; but, like all the others, she had no feet and her body ended in a fish's tail. All day long they played in the great halls of the castle or among the living flowers that grew out of the walls. The large amber windows were open, and the fish swam in, just as the swallows fly into our houses when we open the windows; only the fishes swam up to the princesses, ate out of their hands, and allowed themselves to be stroked.

Outside the castle there was a beautiful garden, in which grew bright-red and dark-blue flowers, and blossoms like flames of fire; the fruit glittered like gold, and the leaves and stems waved to and fro continually. The earth itself was the finest sand, but blue as the flame of burning sulphur. Over everything lay a peculiar blue radiance, as if the blue sky were everywhere, above and below, instead of the dark depths of the sea. In calm weather the sun could be seen, looking like a reddish-purple flower with light streaming from the calyx.

Each of the young princesses had a little plot of ground in the garden, where she might dig and plant as she pleased. One arranged her flower bed in the form of a whale; another preferred to make hers like the figure of a little mermaid; while the youngest child made hers round, like the sun, and in it grew flowers as red as his rays at sunset.

She was a strange child, quiet and thoughtful. While her sisters showed delight at the wonderful things which they obtained from the wrecks of vessels, she cared only for her pretty flowers, red like the sun, and a beautiful marble statue. It was the representation of a handsome boy, carved out of pure white stone, which had fallen to the bottom of the sea from a wreck.

She planted by the statue a rose-coloured weeping willow. It grew rapidly and soon hung its fresh branches over the statue, almost down to the blue sands. The shadows had the colour of violet and waved to and fro like the branches, so that it seemed as if the crown of the tree and the root were at play, trying to kiss each other.

Nothing gave her so much pleasure as to hear about the world above the sea. She made her old grandmother tell her all she knew of the ships and of the towns, the people and the animals. To her it seemed most wonderful and beautiful to hear that the flowers of the land had fragrance, while those below the sea had none; that the trees of the forest were green; and that the fishes among the trees could sing so sweetly that it was a pleasure to listen to them. Her grandmother called the birds fishes, or the little mermaid would not have understood what was meant, for she had never seen birds.

'When you have reached your fifteenth year,' said the grandmother, 'you will have permission to rise up out of the sea and sit on the rocks in the moonlight, while the great ships go sailing by. Then you will see both forests and towns.'

In the following year, one of the sisters would be fifteen, but as each was a year younger than the other, the youngest would have to wait five years before her turn came to rise up from the bottom of the ocean to see the earth as we do. However, each promised to tell the others what she saw on her first visit and what she thought was most beautiful. Their grandmother could not tell them enough—there were so many things about which they wanted to know.

None of them longed so much for her turn to come as the youngest—she who had the longest time to wait and who was so quiet and thoughtful. Many nights she stood by the open window, looking up through the dark blue water and watching the fish as they splashed about with their fins and tails. She could see the moon and stars shining faintly, but through the water they looked larger than they do to our eyes. When something like a black cloud passed between her and them, she knew that it was either a whale swimming over her head, or a ship full of human beings who never imagined that a pretty little mermaid was standing beneath them, holding out her white hands towards the keel of their ship.

At length the eldest was fifteen and was allowed to rise to the surface of the ocean.

When she returned she had hundreds of things to talk about. But the finest thing, she said, was to lie on a sand bank in the quiet moonlit sea, near the shore, gazing at the lights of the near-by town, that twinkled like hundreds of stars, and listening to the sounds of music, the noise of carriages, the voices of human beings, and the merry pealing of the bells in the church steeples. Because she could not go near all these wonderful things, she longed for them all the more.

Oh, how eagerly did the youngest sister listen to all these descriptions! And afterwards, when she stood at the open window looking up through the dark-blue water, she thought of the great city, with all its bustle and noise, and even fancied she could hear the sound of the church bells down in the depths of the sea.

In another year the second sister received permission to rise to the surface of the water and to swim about where she pleased. She rose just as the sun was setting, and this, she said, was the most beautiful sight of all. The whole sky looked like gold, and violet and rose-coloured clouds, which she could not describe, drifted across it. And more swiftly than the clouds, flew a large flock of wild swans toward the setting sun, like a long white veil across the sea. She also swam towards the sun, but it sank into the waves, and the rosy tints faded from the clouds and from the sea.

The third sister's turn followed, and she was the boldest of them all, for she swam up a broad river that emptied into the sea. On the banks she saw green hills covered with beautiful vines, and palaces and castles peeping out from amid the proud trees of the forest. She heard birds singing and felt the rays of the sun so strongly that she was obliged often to dive under the water to cool her burning face. In a narrow creek she found a large group of little human children, almost naked, sporting about in the water. She wanted to play with them, but they fled in a great fright; and then a little black animal—it was a dog, but she did not know it, for she had never seen one before—came to the water and barked at her so furiously that she became frightened and rushed back to the open sea. But she said she should never forget the beautiful forest, the green hills, and the pretty children who could swim in the water although they had no tails.

The fourth sister was more timid. She remained in the midst of the sea, but said it was quite as beautiful there as nearer the land. She could see many miles around her, and the sky above looked like a bell of glass. She had seen the ships, but at such a great distance that they looked like sea gulls. The dolphins sported in the waves, and the great whales spouted water from their nostrils till it seemed as if a hundred fountains were playing in every direction.

The fifth sister's birthday occurred in the winter, so when her turn came she saw what the others had not seen the first time they went up. The sea looked quite green, and large icebergs were floating about, each like a pearl, she said, but larger and loftier than the churches built by men. They were of the most singular shapes and glittered like diamonds. She had seated herself on one of the largest and let the wind play with her long hair. She noticed that all the ships sailed past very rapidly, steering as far away as they could, as if they were afraid of the iceberg. Towards evening, as the sun went down, dark clouds covered the sky, the thunder rolled, and the flashes of lightning glowed red on the icebergs as they were tossed about by the heaving sea. On all the ships the sails were reefed with fear and trembling, while she sat on the floating iceberg, calmly watching the lightning as it darted its forked flashes into the sea.

Each of the sisters, when first she had permission to rise to the surface, was delighted with the new and beautiful sights. Now that they were grown-up girls and could go when they pleased, they had become quite indifferent about it. They soon wished themselves back again, and after a month had passed they said it was much more beautiful down below and pleasanter[11] to be at home.

Yet often, in the evening hours, the five sisters would twine their arms about each other and rise to the surface together. Their voices were more charming than that of any human beings, and before the approach of a storm, when they feared that a ship might be lost, they swam before the vessel, singing enchanting songs of the delights to be found in the depths of the sea and begging the voyagers not to fear if they sank to the bottom. But the sailors could not understand the song and thought it was the sighing of the storm. These things were never beautiful to them, for if the ship sank, the men were drowned and their dead bodies alone reached the palace of the Sea King.

When the sisters rose, arm in arm, through the water, their youngest sister would stand quite alone, looking after them, ready to cry—only, since mermaids have no tears, she suffered more acutely.

'Oh, were I but fifteen years old!' said she. 'I know that I shall love the world up there, and all the people who live in it.'

At last she reached her fifteenth year.

'Well, now you are grown up,' said the old dowager, her grandmother. 'Come, and let me adorn you like your sisters.' And she placed in her hair a wreath of white lilies, of which every flower leaf was half a pearl. Then the old lady ordered eight great oysters to attach themselves to the tail of the princess to show her high rank.

'But they hurt me so,' said the little mermaid.

'Yes, I know; pride must suffer pain,' replied the old lady.

Oh, how gladly she would have shaken off all this grandeur and laid aside the heavy wreath! The red flowers in her own garden would have suited her much better. But she could not change herself, so she said farewell and rose as lightly as a bubble to the surface of the water.

The sun had just set when she raised her head above the waves. The clouds were tinted with crimson and gold, and through the glimmering twilight beamed the evening star in all its beauty. The sea was calm, and the air mild and fresh. A large ship with three masts lay becalmed on the water; only one sail was set, for not a breeze stirred, and the sailors sat idle on deck or amidst the rigging. There was music and song on board, and as darkness came on, a hundred coloured lanterns were lighted, as if the flags of all nations waved in the air.

The little mermaid swam close to the cabin windows, and now and then, as the waves lifted her up, she could look in through glass window-panes and see a number of gayly dressed people.

Among them, and the most beautiful of all, was a young prince with large, black eyes. He was sixteen years of age, and his birthday was being celebrated with great display. The sailors were dancing on deck, and when the prince came out of the cabin, more than a hundred rockets rose in the air, making it as bright as day. The little mermaid was so startled that she dived under water, and when she again stretched out her head, it looked as if all the stars of heaven were falling around her.

She had never seen such fireworks before. Great suns spurted fire about, splendid fireflies flew into the blue air, and everything was reflected in the clear, calm sea beneath. The ship itself was so brightly illuminated that all the people, and even the smallest rope, could be distinctly seen. How handsome the young prince looked, as he pressed the hands of all his guests and smiled at them, while the music resounded through the clear night air!

It was very late, yet the little mermaid could not take her eyes from the ship or from the beautiful prince. The coloured lanterns had been extinguished, no more rockets rose in the air, and the cannon had ceased firing; but the sea became restless, and a moaning, grumbling sound could be heard beneath the waves. Still the little mermaid remained by the cabin window, rocking up and down on the water, so that she could look within. After a while the sails were quickly set, and the ship went on her way. But soon the waves rose higher, heavy clouds darkened the sky, and lightning appeared in the distance. A dreadful storm was approaching. Once more the sails were furled, and the great ship pursued her flying course over the raging sea. The waves rose mountain high, as if they would overtop the mast, but the ship dived like a swan between them, then rose again on their lofty, foaming crests. To the little mermaid this was pleasant sport; but not so to the sailors. At length the ship groaned and creaked; the thick planks gave way under the lashing of the sea, as the waves broke over the deck; the mainmast snapped asunder like a reed, and as the ship lay over on her side, the water rushed in.

The little mermaid now perceived that the crew were in danger; even she was obliged to be careful, to avoid the beams and planks of the wreck which lay scattered on the water. At one moment it was pitch dark so that she could not see a single object, but when a flash of lightning came it revealed the whole scene; she could see everyone who had been on board except the prince. When the ship parted, she had seen him sink into the deep waves, and she was glad, for she thought he would now be with her. Then she remembered that human beings could not live in the water, so that when he got down to her father's palace he would certainly be quite dead.

No, he must not die! So she swam about among the beams and planks which strewed the surface of the sea, forgetting that they could crush her to pieces. Diving deep under the dark waters, rising and falling with the waves, she at length managed to reach the young prince, who was fast losing the power to swim in that stormy sea. His limbs were failing him, his beautiful eyes were closed, and he would have died had not the little mermaid come to his assistance. She held his head above the water and let the waves carry them where they would.

In the morning the storm had ceased, but of the ship not a single fragment could be seen. The sun came up red and shining out of the water, and its beams brought back the hue of health to the prince's cheeks, but his eyes remained closed. The mermaid kissed his high, smooth forehead and stroked back his wet hair. He seemed to her like the marble statue in her little garden, so she kissed him again and wished that he might live.

Presently they came in sight of land, and she saw lofty blue mountains on which the white snow rested as if a flock of swans were lying upon them. Beautiful green forests were near the shore, and close by stood a large building, whether a church or a convent she could not tell. Orange and citron trees grew in the garden, and before the door stood lofty palms. The sea here formed a little bay, in which the water lay quiet and still, but very deep. She swam with the handsome prince to the beach, which was covered with fine white sand, and there she laid him in the warm sunshine, taking care to raise his head higher than his body. Then bells sounded in the large white building, and some young girls came into the garden. The little mermaid swam out further from the shore and hid herself among some high rocks that rose out of the water. Covering her head and neck with the foam of the sea, she watched there to see what would become of the poor prince.

It was not long before she saw a young girl approach the spot where the prince lay. She seemed frightened at first, but only for a moment; then she brought a number of people, and the mermaid saw that the prince came to life again and smiled upon those who stood about him. But to her he sent no smile; he knew not that she had saved him. This made her very sorrowful, and when he was led away into the great building, she dived down into the water and returned to her father's castle.

She had always been silent and thoughtful, and now she was more so than ever. Her sisters asked her what she had seen during her first visit to the surface of the water, but she could tell them nothing. Many an evening and morning did she rise to the place where she had left the prince. She saw the fruits in the garden ripen and watched them gathered; she watched the snow on the mountain tops melt away; but never did she see the prince, and therefore she always returned home more sorrowful than before.

It was her only comfort to sit in her own little garden and fling her arm around the beautiful marble statue, which was like the prince. She gave up tending her flowers, and they grew in wild confusion over the paths, twining their long leaves and stems round the branches of the trees so that the whole place became dark and gloomy.

At length she could bear it no longer and told one of her sisters all about it. Then the others heard the secret, and very soon it became known to several mermaids, one of whom had an intimate friend who happened to know about the prince. She had also seen the festival on board ship, and she told them where the prince came from and where his palace stood.

'Come, little sister,' said the other princesses. Then they entwined their arms and rose together to the surface of the water, near the spot where they knew the prince's palace stood. It was built of bright-yellow, shining stone and had long flights of marble steps, one of which reached quite down to the sea. Splendid gilded cupolas rose over the roof, and between the pillars that surrounded the whole building stood lifelike statues of marble. Through the clear crystal of the lofty windows could be seen noble rooms, with costly silk curtains and hangings of tapestry and walls covered with beautiful paintings. In the centre of the largest salon a fountain threw its sparkling jets high up into the glass cupola of the ceiling, through which the sun shone in upon the water and upon the beautiful plants that grew in the basin of the fountain.

Now that the little mermaid knew where the prince lived, she spent many an evening and many a night on the water near the palace. She would swim much nearer the shore than any of the others had ventured, and once she went up the narrow channel under the marble balcony, which threw a broad shadow on the water. Here she sat and watched the young prince, who thought himself alone in the bright moonlight.

She often saw him evenings, sailing in a beautiful boat on which music sounded and flags waved. She peeped out from among the green rushes, and if the wind caught her long silvery-white veil, those who saw it believed it to be a swan, spreading out its wings.

Many a night, too, when the fishermen set their nets by the light of their torches, she heard them relate many good things about the young prince. And this made her glad that she had saved his life when he was tossed about half dead on the waves. She remembered how his head had rested on her bosom and how heartily she had kissed him, but he knew nothing of all this and could not even dream of her.

She grew more and more to like human beings and wished more and more to be able to wander about with those whose world seemed to be so much larger than her own. They could fly over the sea in ships and mount the high hills which were far above the clouds; and the lands they possessed, their woods and their fields, stretched far away beyond the reach of her sight. There was so much that she wished to know! But her sisters were unable to answer all her questions. She then went to her old grandmother, who knew all about the upper world, which she rightly called 'the lands above the sea.'

'If human beings are not drowned,' asked the little mermaid, 'can they live forever? Do they never die, as we do here in the sea?'

'Yes,' replied the old lady, 'they must also die, and their term of life is even shorter than ours. We sometimes live for three hundred years, but when we cease to exist here, we become only foam on the surface of the water and have not even a grave among those we love. We have not immortal souls, we shall never live again;

like the green seaweed when once it has been cut off, we can never flourish more. Human beings, on the contrary, have souls which live forever, even after the body has been turned to dust. They rise up through the clear, pure air, beyond the glittering stars. As we rise out of the water and behold all the land of the earth, so do they rise to unknown and glorious regions which we shall never see.'

'Why have not we immortal souls?' asked the little mermaid, mournfully. 'I would gladly give all the hundreds of years that I have to live, to be a human being only for one day and to have the hope of knowing the happiness of that glorious world above the stars.'

'You must not think that,' said the old woman. 'We believe that we are much happier and much better off than human beings.'

'So I shall die,' said the little mermaid, 'and as the foam of the sea I shall be driven about, never again to hear the music of the waves or to see the pretty flowers or the red sun? Is there anything I can do to win an immortal soul?'

'No,' said the old woman; 'unless a man should love you so much that you were more to him than his father or his mother, and if all his thoughts and all his love were fixed upon you, and the priest placed his right hand in yours, and he promised to be true to you here and hereafter—then his soul would glide into your body, and you would obtain a share in the future happiness of mankind. He would give to you a soul and retain his own as well; but this can never happen. Your fish's tail, which among us is considered so beautiful, on earth is thought to be quite ugly. They do not know any better, and they think it necessary, in order to be handsome, to have two stout props, which they call legs.'

Then the little mermaid sighed and looked sorrowfully at her fish's tail. 'Let us be happy,' said the old lady, 'and dart and spring about during the three hundred years that we have to live, which is really quite long enough. After that we can rest ourselves all the better. This evening we are going to have a court ball.'

It was one of those splendid sights which we can never see on earth. The walls and the ceiling of the large ballroom were of thick but transparent crystal. Many hundreds of colossal shells,—some of a deep red, others of a grass green,—with blue fire in them, stood in rows on each side. These lighted up the whole salon, and shone through the walls so that the sea was also illuminated. Innumerable fishes, great and small, swam past the crystal walls; on some of them the scales glowed with a purple brilliance, and on others shone like silver and gold. Through the halls flowed a broad stream, and in it danced the mermen and the mermaids to the music of their own sweet singing.

No one on earth has such lovely voices as they, but the little mermaid sang more sweetly than all. The whole court applauded her with hands and tails, and for a moment her heart felt quite gay, for she knew she had the sweetest voice either on earth or in the sea. But soon she thought again of the world above her; she could not forget the charming prince, nor her sorrow that she had not an immortal soul like his. She crept away silently out of her father's palace, and while everything within was gladness and song, she sat in her own little garden, sorrowful and alone. Then she heard the bugle sounding through the water and thought: 'He is certainly sailing above, he in whom my wishes centre and in whose hands I should like to place the happiness of my life. I will venture all for him and to win an immortal soul. While my sisters are dancing in my father's palace I will go to the sea witch, of whom I have always been so much afraid; she can give me counsel and help.'

Then the little mermaid went out from her garden and took the road to the foaming whirlpools, behind which the sorceress lived. She had never been that way before. Neither flowers nor grass grew there; nothing but bare, grey, sandy ground stretched out to the whirlpool, where the water, like foaming mill wheels, seized everything that came within its reach and cast it into the fathomless deep. Through the midst of these crushing whirlpools the little mermaid was obliged to pass before she could reach the dominions of the sea witch. Then, for a long distance, the road lay across a stretch of warm, bubbling mire, called by the witch her turf moor.

Beyond this was the witch's house, which stood in the centre of a strange forest, where all the trees and flowers were polypi, half animals and half plants. They looked like serpents with a hundred heads, growing out of the ground. The branches were long, slimy arms, with fingers like flexible worms, moving limb after limb from the root to the top. All that could be reached in the sea they seized upon and held fast, so that it never escaped from their clutches.

The little mermaid was so alarmed at what she saw that she stood still and her heart beat with fear. She came very near turning back, but she thought of the prince and of the human soul for which she longed, and her courage returned. She fastened her long, flowing hair round her head, so that the polypi should not lay hold of it. She crossed her hands on her bosom, and then darted forward as a fish shoots through the water, between the supple arms and fingers of the ugly polypi, which were stretched out on each side of her. She saw that they all held in their grasp something they had seized with their numerous little arms, which were as strong as iron bands. Tightly grasped in their clinging arms were white skeletons of human beings who had perished at sea and had sunk down into the deep waters; skeletons of land animals; and oars, rudders, and chests, of ships. There was even a little mermaid whom they had caught and strangled, and this seemed the most shocking of all to the little princess.

She now came to a space of marshy ground in the wood, where large, fat water snakes were rolling in the mire and showing their ugly, drab-coloured bodies. In the midst of this spot stood a house, built of the bones of shipwrecked human beings. There sat the sea witch, allowing a toad to eat from her mouth just as people sometimes feed a canary with pieces of sugar. She called the ugly water snakes her little chickens and allowed them to crawl all over her bosom.

'I know what you want,' said the sea witch. 'It is very stupid of you, but you shall have your way, though it will bring you to sorrow, my pretty princess. You want to get rid of your fish's tail and to have two supports instead, like human beings on earth, so that the young prince may fall in love with you and so that you may have an immortal soul.' And then the witch laughed so loud and so disgustingly that the toad and the snakes fell to the ground and lay there wriggling.

'You are but just in time,' said the witch, 'for after sunrise tomorrow I should not be able to help you till the end of another year. I will prepare a draft for you, with which you must swim to land tomorrow before sunrise; seat yourself there and drink it. Your tail will then disappear, and shrink up into what men call legs.

'You will feel great pain, as if a sword were passing through you. But all who see you will say that you are the prettiest little human being they ever saw. You will still have the same floating gracefulness of movement, and no dancer will ever tread so lightly. Every step you take, however, will be as if you were treading upon sharp knives and as if the blood must flow. If you will bear all this, I will help you.'

'Yes, I will,' said the little princess in a trembling voice, as she thought of the prince and the immortal soul.

'But think again,' said the witch, 'for when once your shape has become like a human being, you can no more be a mermaid. You will never return through the water to your sisters or to your father's palace again. And if you do not win the love of the prince, so that he is willing to forget his father and mother for your sake and to love you with his whole soul and allow the priest to join your hands that you may be man and wife, then you will never have an immortal soul. The first morning after he marries another, your heart will break and you will become foam on the crest of the waves.'

'I will do it,' said the little mermaid, and she became pale as death.

'But I must be paid, also,' said the witch, 'and it is not a trifle that I ask. You have the sweetest voice of any who dwell here in the depths of the sea, and you believe that you will be able to charm the prince with it. But this voice you must give to me. The best thing you possess will I have as the price of my costly draft, which must be mixed with my own blood so that it may be as sharp as a two-edged sword.'

'But if you take away my voice,' said the little mermaid, 'what is left for me?'

'Your beautiful form, your graceful walk, and your expressive eyes. Surely with these you can enchain a man's heart. Well, have you lost your courage? Put out your little tongue, that I may cut it off as my payment; then you shall have the powerful draft.'

'It shall be,' said the little mermaid.

Then the witch placed her caldron on the fire, to prepare the magic draft.

'Cleanliness is a good thing,' said she, scouring the vessel with snakes which she had tied together in a large knot. Then she pricked herself in the breast and let the black blood drop into the caldron. The steam that rose twisted itself into such horrible shapes that no one could look at them without fear. Every moment the witch threw a new ingredient into the vessel, and when it began to boil, the sound was like the weeping of a crocodile. When at last the magic draft was ready, it looked like the clearest water.

'There it is for you,' said the witch. Then she cut off the mermaid's tongue, so that she would never again speak or sing. 'If the polypi should seize you as you return through the wood,' said the witch, 'throw over them a few drops of the potion, and their fingers will be torn into a thousand pieces.' But the little mermaid had no occasion to do this, for the polypi sprang back in terror when they caught sight of the glittering draft, which shone in her hand like a twinkling star.

So she passed quickly through the wood and the marsh and between the rushing whirlpools. She saw that in her father's palace the torches in the ballroom were extinguished and that all within were asleep. But she did not venture to go in to them, for now that she was dumb and going to leave them forever she felt as if her heart would break. She stole into the garden, took a flower from the flower bed of each of her sisters, kissed her hand towards the palace a thousand times, and then rose up through the dark-blue waters.

The sun had not risen when she came in sight of the prince's palace and approached the beautiful marble steps, but the moon shone clear and bright. Then the little mermaid drank the magic draft, and it seemed as if a two-edged sword went through her delicate body. She fell into a swoon and lay like one dead. When the sun rose and shone over the sea, she recovered and felt a sharp pain, but before her stood the handsome young prince.

He fixed his coal-black eyes upon her so earnestly that she cast down her own and then became aware that her fish's tail was gone and that she had as pretty a pair of white legs and tiny feet as any little maiden could have. But she had no clothes, so she wrapped herself in her long, thick hair. The prince asked her who she was and whence[12] she came. She looked at him mildly and sorrowfully with her deep blue eyes, but could not speak. He took her by the hand and led her to the palace.

Every step she took was as the witch had said it would be; she felt as if she were treading upon the points of needles or sharp knives. She bore it willingly, however, and moved at the prince's side as lightly as a bubble, so that he and all who saw her wondered at her graceful, swaying movements. She was very soon arrayed in costly robes of silk and muslin and was the most beautiful creature in the palace; but she was dumb and could neither speak nor sing.

Beautiful female slaves, dressed in silk and gold, stepped

forward and sang before the prince and his royal parents. One sang better than all the others, and the prince clapped his hands and smiled at her. This was a great sorrow to the little mermaid, for she knew how much more sweetly she herself once could sing, and she thought, 'Oh, if he could only know that I have given away my voice forever, to be with him!'

The slaves next performed some pretty fairy-like dances, to the sound of beautiful music. Then the little mermaid raised her lovely white arms, stood on the tips of her toes, glided over the floor, and danced as no one yet had been able to dance. At each moment her beauty was more revealed, and her expressive eyes appealed more directly to the heart than the songs of the slaves. Everyone was enchanted, especially the prince, who called her his little foundling. She danced again quite readily, to please him, though each time her foot touched the floor it seemed as if she trod on sharp knives.

The prince said she should remain with him always, and she was given permission to sleep at his door, on a velvet cushion. He had a page's dress made for her, that she might accompany him on horseback. They rode together through the sweet-scented woods, where the green boughs touched their shoulders, and the little birds sang among the fresh leaves. She climbed with him to the tops of high mountains, and although her tender feet bled so that even her steps were marked, she only smiled, and followed him till they could see the clouds beneath them like a flock of birds flying to distant lands. While at the prince's palace, and when all the household were asleep, she would go and sit on the broad marble steps, for it eased her burning feet to bathe them in the cold sea water. It was then that she thought of all those below in the deep.

Once during the night her sisters came up arm in arm, singing sorrowfully as they floated on the water. She beckoned to them, and they recognised her and told her how she had grieved them; after that, they came to the same place every night. Once she saw in the distance her old grandmother, who had not been to the surface of the sea for many years, and the old Sea King, her father, with his crown on his head. They stretched out their hands towards her, but did not venture so near the land as her sisters had.

As the days passed she loved the prince more dearly, and he loved her as one would love a little child. The thought never came to him to make her his wife. Yet unless he married her, she could not receive an immortal soul, and on the morning after his marriage with another, she would dissolve into the foam of the sea.

'Do you not love me the best of them all?' the eyes of the little mermaid seemed to say when he took her in his arms and kissed her fair forehead.

'Yes, you are dear to me,' said the prince, 'for you have the best heart and you are the most devoted to me. You are like a young maiden whom I once saw, but whom I shall never meet again. I was in a ship that was wrecked, and the waves cast me ashore near a holy temple where several young maidens performed the service. The youngest of them found me on the shore and saved my life. I saw her but twice, and she is the only one in the world whom I could love. But you are like her, and you have almost driven her image from my mind. She belongs to the holy temple, and good fortune has sent you to me in her stead. We will never part.'

'Ah, he knows not that it was I who saved his life,' thought the little mermaid. 'I carried him over the sea to the wood where the temple stands; I sat beneath the foam and watched till the human beings came to help him. I saw the pretty maiden that he loves better than he loves me.' The mermaid sighed deeply, but she could not weep. 'He says the maiden belongs to the holy temple, therefore she will never return to the world—they will meet no more. I am by his side and see him every day. I will take care of him, and love him, and give up my life for his sake.'

Very soon it was said that the prince was to marry and that the beautiful daughter of a neighbouring king would be his wife, for a fine ship was being fitted out. Although the prince gave out that he intended merely to pay a visit to the king, it was generally supposed that he went to court the princess. A great company were to go with him. The little mermaid smiled and shook her head. She knew the prince's thoughts better than any of the others.

'I must travel,' he had said to her; 'I must see this beautiful princess. My parents desire it, but they will not oblige me to bring her home as my bride. I cannot love her, because she is not like the beautiful maiden in the temple, whom you resemble. If I were forced to choose a bride, I would choose you, my dumb foundling, with those expressive eyes.' Then he kissed her rosy mouth, played with her long, waving hair, and laid his head on her heart, while she dreamed of human happiness and an immortal soul.

'You are not afraid of the sea, my dumb child, are you?' he said, as they stood on the deck of the noble ship which was to carry them to the country of the neighbouring king. Then he told her of storm and of calm, of strange fishes in the deep beneath them, and of what the divers had seen there. She smiled at his descriptions, for she knew better than anyone what wonders were at the bottom of the sea.

In the moonlight night, when all on board were asleep except the man at the helm, she sat on deck, gazing down through the clear water. She thought she could distinguish her father's castle, and upon it her aged grandmother, with the silver crown on her head, looking through the rushing tide at the keel of the vessel. Then her sisters came up on the waves and gazed at her mournfully, wringing their white hands. She beckoned to them, and smiled, and wanted to tell them how happy and well off she was. But the cabin boy approached, and when her sisters dived down, he thought what he saw was only the foam of the sea.

The next morning the ship sailed into the harbour of a beautiful town belonging to the king whom the prince was going to visit. The church bells were ringing, and from the high towers sounded a flourish of trumpets. Soldiers, with flying colours and glittering bayonets, lined the roads through which they passed. Every day was a festival, balls and entertainments following one another. But the princess had not yet appeared. People said that she had been brought up and educated in a religious house, where she was learning every royal virtue.

At last she came. Then the little mermaid, who was anxious to see whether she was really beautiful, was obliged to admit that she had never seen a more perfect vision of beauty. Her skin was delicately fair, and beneath her long, dark eyelashes her laughing blue eyes shone with truth and purity.

'It was you,' said the prince, 'who saved my life when I lay as if dead on the beach,' and he folded his blushing bride in his arms.

'Oh, I am too happy!' said he to the little mermaid; 'my fondest hopes are now fulfilled. You will rejoice at my happiness, for your devotion to me is great and sincere.'

The little mermaid kissed his hand and felt as if her heart were already broken. His wedding morning would bring death to her, and she would change into the foam of the sea.

All the church bells rang, and the heralds rode through the town proclaiming the betrothal. Perfumed oil was burned in costly silver lamps on every altar. The priests waved the censers, while the bride and the bridegroom joined their hands and received the blessing of the bishop. The little mermaid, dressed in silk and gold, held up the bride's train; but her ears heard nothing of the festive music, and her eyes saw not the holy ceremony. She thought of the night of death which was coming to her, and of all she had lost in the world.

On the same evening the bride and bridegroom went on board the ship. Cannons were roaring, flags waving, and in the centre of the ship a costly tent of purple and gold had been erected. It contained elegant sleeping couches for the bridal pair during the night. The ship, under a favourable wind, with swelling sails, glided away smoothly and lightly over the calm sea.

When it grew dark, a number of coloured lamps were lighted and the sailors danced merrily on the deck. The little mermaid could not help thinking of her first rising out of the sea, when she had seen similar joyful festivities, so she too joined in the dance, poised herself in the air as a swallow when he pursues his prey, and all present cheered her wonderingly. She had never danced so gracefully before. Her tender feet felt as if cut with sharp knives, but she cared not for the pain; a sharper pang had pierced her heart.

She knew this was the last evening she should ever see the prince for whom she had forsaken her kindred and her home.

She had given up her beautiful voice and suffered unheard-of pain daily for him, while he knew nothing of it. This was the last evening that she should breathe the same air with him or gaze on the starry sky and the deep sea. An eternal night, without a thought or a dream, awaited her. She had no soul, and now could never win one.

All was joy and gaiety on the ship until long after midnight. She smiled and danced with the rest, while the thought of death was in her heart. The prince kissed his beautiful bride and she played with his raven hair till they went arm in arm to rest in the sumptuous tent. Then all became still on board the ship, and only the pilot, who stood at the helm, was awake. The little mermaid leaned her white arms on the edge of the vessel and looked towards the east for the first blush of morning—for that first ray of the dawn which was to be her death. She saw her sisters rising out of the flood. They were as pale as she, but their beautiful hair no longer waved in the wind; it had been cut off.

'We have given our hair to the witch,' said they, 'to obtain help for you, that you may not die tonight. She has given us a knife; see, it is very sharp. Before the sun rises you must plunge it into the heart of the prince. When the warm blood falls upon your feet they will grow together again into a fish's tail, and you will once more be a mermaid and can return to us to live out your three hundred years before you are changed into the salt sea foam. Haste, then; either he or you must die before sunrise. Our old grandmother mourns so for you that her white hair is falling, as ours fell under the witch's scissors. Kill the prince, and come back. Hasten! Do you not see the first red streaks in the sky? In a few minutes the sun will rise, and you must die.'

Then they sighed deeply and mournfully, and sank beneath the waves.

The little mermaid drew back the crimson curtain of the tent and beheld the fair bride, whose head was resting on the prince's breast. She bent down and kissed his noble brow, then looked at the sky, on which the rosy dawn grew brighter and brighter. She glanced at the sharp knife and again fixed her eyes on the prince, who whispered the name of his bride in his dreams.

She was in his thoughts, and the knife trembled in the hand of the little mermaid—but she flung it far from her into the waves. The water turned red where it fell, and the drops that spurted up looked like blood. She cast one more lingering, half-fainting glance at the prince, then threw herself from the ship into the sea and felt her body dissolving into foam.

The sun rose above the waves, and his warm rays fell on the cold foam of the little mermaid, who did not feel as if she were dying. She saw the bright sun, and hundreds of transparent, beautiful creatures floating around her—she could see through them the white sails of the ships and the red clouds in the sky. Their speech was melodious, but could not be heard by mortal ears—just as their bodies could not be seen by mortal eyes. The little mermaid perceived that she had a body like theirs and that she continued to rise higher and higher out of the foam. 'Where am I?' asked she, and her voice sounded ethereal, like the voices of those who were with her. No earthly music could imitate it.

'Among the daughters of the air,' answered one of them. 'A mermaid has not an immortal soul, nor can she obtain one unless she wins the love of a human being. On the will of another hangs her eternal destiny. But the daughters of the air, although they do not possess an immortal soul, can, by their good deeds, procure one for themselves. We fly to warm countries and cool the sultry air that destroys mankind with the pestilence. We carry the perfume of the flowers to spread health and restoration.

'After we have striven for three hundred years to do all the good in our power, we receive an immortal soul and take part in the happiness of mankind. You, poor little mermaid, have tried with your whole heart to do as we are doing. You have suffered and endured, and raised yourself to the spirit world by your good deeds, and now, by striving for three hundred years in the same way, you may obtain an immortal soul.'

The little mermaid lifted her glorified eyes toward the sun and, for the first time, felt them filling with tears.

On the ship in which she had left the prince there were life and noise, and she saw him and his beautiful bride searching for her. Sorrowfully they gazed at the pearly foam, as if they knew she had thrown herself into the waves. Unseen she kissed the forehead of the bride and fanned the prince, and then mounted with the other children of the air to a rosy cloud that floated above.

'After three hundred years, thus shall we float into the kingdom of heaven,' said she. 'And we may even get there sooner,' whispered one of her companions. 'Unseen we can enter the houses of men where there are children, and for every day on which we find a good child that is the joy of his parents and deserves their love, our time of probation is shortened. The child does not know, when we fly through the room, that we smile with joy at his good conduct—for we can count one year less of our three hundred years. But when we see a naughty or a wicked child we shed tears of sorrow, and for every tear a day is added to our time of trial.'

# 8

# The Emperor's New Clothes

Many years ago there was an emperor who was so fond of new clothes that he spent all his money on them. He did not give himself any concern about his army; he cared nothing about the theatre or for driving about in the woods, except for the sake of showing himself off in new clothes. He had a costume for every hour in the day, and just as they say of a king or emperor, 'He is in his council chamber,' they said of him, 'The emperor is in his dressing room.'

Life was merry and gay in the town where the emperor lived, and numbers of strangers came to it every day. Among them there came one day two rascals, who gave themselves out as weavers and said that they knew how to weave the most exquisite stuff imaginable. Not only were the colours and patterns uncommonly beautiful, but the clothes that were made of the stuff had the peculiar property of becoming invisible to every person who was unfit for the office he held or who was exceptionally stupid.

'Those must be valuable clothes,' thought the emperor. 'By wearing them I should be able to discover which of the men in my empire are not fit for their posts. I should distinguish wise men from fools. Yes, I must order some of the stuff to be woven for me directly.' And he paid the swindlers a handsome sum of money in advance, as they required.

As for them, they put up two looms and pretended to be weaving, though there was nothing whatever on their shuttles. They called for a quantity of the finest silks and of the purest gold thread, all of which went into their own bags, while they worked at their empty looms till late into the night.

'I should like to know how those weavers are getting on with the stuff,' thought the emperor. But he felt a little queer when he reflected that those who were stupid or unfit for their office would not be able to see the material. He believed, indeed, that he had nothing to fear for himself, but still he thought it better to send someone else first, to see how the work was coming on. All the people in the town had heard of the peculiar property of the stuff, and everyone was curious to see how stupid his neighbour might be.

'I will send my faithful old prime minister to the weavers,' thought the emperor. 'He will be best capable of judging of this stuff, for he is a man of sense and nobody is more fit[13] for his office than he.'

So the worthy old minister went into the room where the two swindlers sat working the empty looms. 'Heaven save us!' thought the old man, opening his eyes wide. 'Why, I can't see anything at all!' But he took care not to say so aloud.

Both the rogues begged him to step a little nearer and asked him if he did not think the patterns very pretty and the colouring fine. They pointed to the empty loom as they did so, and the poor old minister kept staring as hard as he could—but without being able to see anything on it, for of course there was nothing there to see.

'Heaven save us!' thought the old man. 'Is it possible that I am a fool? I have never thought[14] it, and nobody must know it. Is it true that I am not fit for my office? It will never do for me to say that I cannot see the stuffs.'

'Well, sir, do you say nothing about the cloth?' asked the one who was pretending to go on with his work.

'Oh, it is most elegant, most beautiful!' said the dazed old man, as he peered again through his spectacles. 'What a fine pattern, and what fine colours! I will certainly tell the emperor how pleased I am with the stuff.'

'We are glad of that,' said both the weavers; and then they named the colours and pointed out the special features of the pattern. To all of this the minister paid great attention, so that he might be able to repeat it to the emperor when he went back to him.

And now the cheats called for more money, more silk, and more gold thread, to be able to proceed with the weaving, but they put it all into their own pockets, and not a thread went into the stuff, though they went on as before, weaving at the empty looms.

After a little time the emperor sent another honest statesman to see how the weaving was progressing, and if the stuff would soon be ready. The same thing happened with him as with the minister. He gazed and gazed, but as there was nothing but empty looms, he could see nothing else.

'Is not this an exquisite piece of stuff?' asked the weavers, pointing to one of the looms and explaining the beautiful pattern and the colours which were not there to be seen.

'I am not stupid, I know I am not!' thought the man, 'so it must be that I am not fit for my good office. It is very strange, but I must not let it be noticed.' So he praised the cloth he did not see and assured the weavers of his delight in the lovely colours and the exquisite pattern. 'It is perfectly charming,' he reported to the emperor.

Everybody in the town was talking of the splendid cloth. The emperor thought he should like to see it himself while it was still on the loom. With a company of carefully selected men, among whom were the two worthy officials who had been there before, he went to visit the crafty impostors, who were working as hard as ever at the empty looms.

'Is it not magnificent?' said both the honest statesmen. 'See, your Majesty, what splendid colours, and what a pattern!' And they pointed to the looms, for they believed that others, no doubt, could see what they did not.

'What!' thought the emperor. 'I see nothing at all. This is terrible! Am I a fool? Am I not fit to be mperor? Why nothing more dreadful could happen to me!'

'Oh, it is very pretty! It has my highest approval,' the emperor said aloud. He nodded with satisfaction as he gazed at the empty looms, for he would not betray that he could see nothing.

His whole suite gazed and gazed, each seeing no more than the others; but, like the emperor, they all exclaimed, 'Oh, it is beautiful!' They even suggested to the emperor that he wear the splendid new clothes for the first time on the occasion of a great procession which was soon to take place.

'Splendid! Gorgeous! Magnificent!' went from mouth to mouth. All were equally delighted with the weavers' workmanship. The emperor gave each of the impostors an order of knighthood to be worn in their buttonholes, and the title Gentleman Weaver of the Imperial Court.

Before the day on which the procession was to take place, the weavers sat up the whole night, burning sixteen candles, so that people might see how anxious they were to get the emperor's new clothes ready. They pretended to take the stuff from the loom, they cut it out in the air with huge scissors, and they stitched away with needles which had no thread in them. At last they said, 'Now the clothes are finished.'

The emperor came to them himself with his grandest courtiers, and each of the rogues lifted his arm as if he held something, saying, 'See! Here are the trousers! Here is the coat! Here is the cloak,' and so on. 'It is as light as a spider's web. One would almost feel as if one had nothing on, but that is the beauty of it!'

'Yes,' said all the courtiers, but they saw nothing, for there was nothing to see.

'Will your Majesty be graciously pleased to take off your clothes so that we may put on the new clothes here, before the great mirror?'

The emperor took off his clothes, and the rogues pretended to put on first one garment and then another of the new ones they had pretended to make. They pretended to fasten something round his waist and to tie on something. This they said was the train, and the emperor turned round and round before the mirror.

'How well his Majesty looks in the new clothes! How becoming they are!' cried all the courtiers in turn. 'That is a splendid costume!'

'The canopy that is to be carried over your Majesty in the procession is waiting outside,' said the master of ceremonies.

'Well, I am ready,' replied the emperor. 'Don't the clothes look well?' and he turned round and round again before the mirror, to appear as if he were admiring his new costume.

The chamberlains, who were to carry the train, stooped and put their hands near the floor as if they were lifting it; then they pretended to be holding something in the air. They would not let it be noticed that they could see and feel nothing.

So the emperor went along in the procession, under the splendid canopy, and everyone in the streets said: 'How beautiful the emperor's new clothes are! What a splendid train! And how well they fit!'

No one wanted to let it appear that he could see nothing, for that would prove him not fit for his post. None of the emperor's clothes had been so great a success before.

'But he has nothing on!' said a little child.

'Just listen to the innocent,' said its[15] father; and one person whispered to another what the child had said. 'He has nothing on;

a child says he has nothing on!'

'But he has nothing on,' cried all the people. The emperor was startled by this, for he had a suspicion that they were right. But he thought, 'I must face this out to the end and go on with the procession.' So he held himself more stiffly than ever, and the chamberlains held up the train that was not there at all.

# 9

# The Steadfast Tin Soldier

There were once five and twenty tin soldiers. They were brothers, for they had all been made out of the same old tin spoon. They all shouldered their bayonets, held themselves upright, and looked straight before them. Their uniforms were very smart-looking—red and blue—and very splendid. The first thing they heard in the world, when the lid was taken off the box in which they lay, was the words 'Tin soldiers!' These words were spoken by a little boy, who clapped his hands for joy. The soldiers had been given[16] him because it was his birthday, and now he was putting them out upon the table.

Each was exactly like the rest to a hair, except one who had but one leg. He had been cast last of all, and there had not been quite enough tin to finish him; but he stood as firmly upon his one leg as the others upon their two, and it was he whose fortunes became so remarkable.

On the table where the tin soldiers had been set up were several other toys, but the one that attracted most attention was a pretty little paper castle. Through its tiny windows one could see straight into the hall. In front of the castle stood little trees, clustering round a small mirror which was meant to represent a transparent lake. Swans of wax swam upon its surface, and it reflected back their images.

All this was very pretty, but prettiest of all was a little lady who stood at the castle's open door. She too was cut out of paper, but she wore a frock of the clearest gauze and a narrow blue ribbon over her shoulders, like a scarf, and in the middle of the ribbon was placed a shining tinsel rose. The little lady stretched out both her arms, for she was a dancer, and then she lifted one leg so high that the Soldier quite lost sight of it. He thought that, like himself, she had but one leg.

'That would be just the wife for me,' thought he, 'if she were not too grand. But she lives in a castle, while I have only a box, and there are five and twenty of us in that. It would be no place for a lady. Still, I must try to make her acquaintance.' A snuffbox happened to be upon the table and he lay down at full length behind it, and here he could easily watch the dainty little lady, who still remained standing on one leg without losing her balance.

When the evening came all the other tin soldiers were put away in their box, and the people in the house went to bed. Now the playthings began to play in their turn. They visited, fought battles, and gave balls. The tin soldiers rattled in the box, for they wished to join the rest, but they could not lift the lid. The nutcrackers turned somersaults, and the pencil jumped about in a most amusing way. There was such a din that the canary woke and began to speak—and in verse, too. The only ones who did not move from their places were the Tin Soldier and the Lady Dancer. She stood on tiptoe with outstretched arms, and he was just as persevering on his one leg; he never once turned away his eyes from her.

Twelve o'clock struck—crash! Up sprang the lid of the snuffbox. There was no snuff in it, but a little black goblin. You see it was not a real snuffbox, but a jack-in-the-box.

'Tin Soldier,' said the Goblin, 'keep thine[17] eyes to thyself[18]. Gaze not at what does not concern thee[19]!'

But the Tin Soldier pretended not to hear.

'Only wait, then, till tomorrow,' remarked the Goblin.

Next morning, when the children got up, the Tin Soldier was placed on the window sill, and, whether it was the Goblin or the wind that did it, all at once the window flew open and the Tin Soldier fell head foremost from the third story to the street below. It was a tremendous fall! Over and over he turned in the air, till at last he rested, his cap and bayonet sticking fast between the paving stones, while his one leg stood upright in the air.

The maidservant and the little boy came down at once to look for him, but, though they nearly trod upon him, they could not manage to find him. If the Soldier had but once called 'Here am I!' they might easily enough have heard him, but he did not think it becoming to cry out for help, being in uniform.

It now began to rain; faster and faster fell the drops, until there was a heavy shower; and when it was over, two street boys came by.

'Look you,' said one, 'there lies a tin soldier. He must come out and sail in a boat.'

So they made a boat out of an old newspaper and put the Tin Soldier in the middle of it, and away he sailed down the gutter, while the boys ran along by his side, clapping their hands.

Goodness! How the waves rocked that paper boat, and how fast the stream ran! The Tin Soldier became quite giddy, the boat veered round so quickly; still he moved not a muscle, but looked straight before him and held his bayonet tightly.

All at once the boat passed into a drain, and it became as dark as his own old home in the box. 'Where am I going now?' thought he. 'Yes, to be sure, it is all that Goblin's doing. Ah! If the little lady were but sailing with me in the boat, I would not care if it were twice as dark.'

Just then a great water rat, that lived under the drain, darted suddenly out.

'Have you[20] a passport?' asked the rat. 'Where is your passport?'

But the Tin Soldier kept silence and only held his bayonet with a firmer grasp.

The boat sailed on, but the rat followed. Whew! How he gnashed his teeth and cried to the sticks and straws: 'Stop him! Stop him! He hasn't paid toll! He hasn't shown his passport!'

But the stream grew stronger and stronger. Already the Tin Soldier could see daylight at the point where the tunnel ended; but at the same time he heard a rushing, roaring noise, at which a bolder man might have trembled. Think! Just where the tunnel ended, the drain widened into a great sheet that fell into the mouth of a sewer. It was as perilous a situation for the Soldier as sailing down a mighty waterfall would be for us.

He was now so near it that he could not stop. The boat dashed on, and the Tin Soldier held himself so well that no one might say of him that he so much as winked an eye. Three or four times the boat whirled round and round; it was full of water to the brim and must certainly sink.

The Tin Soldier stood up to his neck in water; deeper and deeper sank the boat, softer and softer grew the paper; and now the water closed over the Soldier's head. He thought of the pretty little dancer whom he should never see again, and in his ears rang the words of the song:

Wild adventure, mortal danger,

Be thy[21] portion, valiant stranger.

The paper boat parted in the middle, and the Soldier was about to sink, when he was swallowed by a great fish.

Oh, how dark it was! Darker even than in the drain, and so narrow; but the Tin Soldier retained his courage; there he lay at full length, shouldering his bayonet as before.

To and fro swam the fish, turning and twisting and making the strangest movements, till at last he became perfectly still.

Something like a flash of daylight passed through him, and a voice said, 'Tin Soldier!' The fish had been caught, taken to market, sold and bought, and taken to the kitchen, where the cook had cut him with a large knife. She seized the Tin Soldier between her finger and thumb and took him to the room where the family sat, and where all were eager to see the celebrated man who had travelled in the maw of a fish; but the Tin Soldier remained unmoved. He was not at all proud.

They set him upon the table there. But how could so curious a thing happen? The Soldier was in the very same room in which he had been before. He saw the same children, the same toys stood upon the table, and among them the pretty dancing maiden, who still stood upon one leg. She too was steadfast. That touched the Tin Soldier's heart. He could have wept tin tears, but that would not have been proper. He looked at her and she looked at him, but neither spoke a word.

And now one of the little boys took the Tin Soldier and threw him into the stove. He gave no reason for doing so, but no doubt the Goblin in the snuffbox had something to do with it.

The Tin Soldier stood now in a blaze of red light. The heat he felt was terrible, but whether it proceeded from the fire or from the love in his heart, he did not know. He saw that the colours were quite gone from his uniform, but whether that had happened on the journey or had been caused by grief, no one could say. He looked at the little lady, she looked at him, and he felt himself melting; still he stood firm as ever, with his bayonet on his shoulder. Then suddenly the door flew open; the wind caught the Dancer, and she flew straight into the stove to the Tin Soldier, flashed up in a flame, and was gone! The Tin Soldier melted into a lump; and in the ashes the maid found him next day, in the shape of a little tin heart, while of the Dancer nothing remained save the tinsel rose, and that was burned as black as a coal.

# The Wild Swans

Far away, in the land to which the swallows fly when it is winter, dwelt a king who had eleven sons, and one daughter, named Eliza.

The eleven brothers were princes, and each went to school with a star on his breast and a sword by his side. They wrote with diamond pencils on golden slates and learned their lessons so quickly and read so easily that everyone knew they were princes. Their sister Eliza sat on a little stool of plate-glass and had a book full of pictures, which had cost as much as half a kingdom.

Happy, indeed, were these children; but they were not long to remain so, for their father, the king, married a queen who did not love the children, and who proved to be a wicked sorceress.

The queen began to show her unkindness the very first day. While the great festivities were taking place in the palace, the children played at receiving company; but the queen, instead of sending them the cakes and apples that were left from the feast, as was customary, gave them some sand in a teacup and told them to pretend it was something good. The next week she sent the little Eliza into the country to a peasant and his wife. Then she told the king so many untrue things about the young princes that he gave himself no more trouble about them.

'Go out into the world and look after yourselves,' said the

queen. 'Fly like great birds without a voice.' But she could not make it so bad for them as she would have liked, for they were turned into eleven beautiful wild swans.

With a strange cry, they flew through the windows of the palace, over the park, to the forest beyond. It was yet early morning when they passed the peasant's cottage where their sister lay asleep in her room. They hovered over the roof, twisting their long necks and flapping their wings, but no one heard them or saw them, so they at last flew away, high up in the clouds, and over the wide world they sped till they came to a thick, dark wood, which stretched far away to the seashore.

Poor little Eliza was alone in the peasant's room playing with a green leaf, for she had no other playthings. She pierced a hole in the leaf, and when she looked through it at the sun she seemed to see her brothers' clear eyes, and when the warm sun shone on her cheeks she thought of all the kisses they had given her.

One day passed just like another. Sometimes the winds rustled through the leaves of the rosebush and whispered to the roses, 'Who can be more beautiful than you?' And the roses would shake their heads and say, 'Eliza is.' And when the old woman sat at the cottage door on Sunday and read her hymn book, the wind would flutter the leaves and say to the book, 'Who can be more pious than you?' And then the hymn book would answer, 'Eliza.' And the roses and the hymn book told the truth.

When she was fifteen she returned home, but because she was so beautiful the witch-queen became full of spite and hatred toward her. Willingly would she have turned her into a swan like her brothers, but she did not dare to do so for fear of the king.

Early one morning the queen went into the bathroom; it was

built of marble and had soft cushions trimmed with the most beautiful tapestry. She took three toads with her, and kissed them, saying to the first, 'When Eliza comes to bathe seat yourself upon her head, that she may become as stupid as you are.' To the second toad she said, 'Place yourself on her forehead, that she may become as ugly as you are, and that her friends may not know her.' 'Rest on her heart,' she whispered to the third; 'then she will have evil inclinations and suffer because of them.' So she put the toads into the clear water, which at once turned green. She next called Eliza and helped her undress and get into the bath.

As Eliza dipped her head under the water one of the toads sat on her hair, a second on her forehead, and a third on her breast. But she did not seem to notice them, and when she rose from the water there were three red poppies floating upon it. Had not the creatures been venomous or had they not been kissed by the witch, they would have become red roses. At all events they became flowers, because they had rested on Eliza's head and on her heart. She was too good and too innocent for sorcery to have any power over her.

When the wicked queen saw this, she rubbed Eliza's face with walnut juice, so that she was quite brown; then she tangled her beautiful hair and smeared it with disgusting ointment until it was quite impossible to recognise her.

The king was shocked, and declared she was not his daughter. No one but the watchdog and the swallows knew her, and they were only poor animals and could say nothing. Then poor Eliza wept and thought of her eleven brothers who were far away. Sorrowfully she stole from the palace and walked the whole day over fields and moors, till she came to the great forest. She knew not in what direction to go, but she was so unhappy and longed so for her brothers, who, like herself, had been driven out into the world, that she had determined to seek them.

She had been in the wood only a short time when night came on and she quite lost the path; so she laid herself down on the soft moss, offered up her evening prayer, and leaned her head against the stump of a tree. All nature was silent, and the soft, mild air fanned her forehead. The light of hundreds of glowworms shone amidst the grass and the moss like green fire, and if she touched a twig with her hand, ever so lightly, the brilliant insects fell down around her like shooting stars.

All night long she dreamed of her brothers. She thought they were all children again, playing together. She saw them writing with their diamond pencils on golden slates, while she looked at the beautiful picture book which had cost half a kingdom. They were not writing lines and letters, as they used to do, but descriptions of the noble deeds they had performed and of all that they had discovered and seen. In the picture book, too, everything was living. The birds sang, and the people came out of the book and spoke to Eliza and her brothers; but as the leaves were turned over they darted back again to their places, that all might be in order.

When she awoke, the sun was high in the heavens. She could not see it, for the lofty trees spread their branches thickly overhead, but its gleams here and there shone through the leaves like a gauzy golden mist. There was a sweet fragrance from the fresh verdure, and the birds came near and almost perched on her shoulders. She heard water rippling from a number of springs, all flowing into a lake with golden sands. Bushes grew thickly round the lake, and at one spot, where an opening had been made by a deer, Eliza went down to the water.

The lake was so clear that had not the wind rustled the branches of the trees and the bushes so that they moved, they would have seemed painted in the depths of the lake; for every leaf, whether in the shade or in the sunshine, was reflected in the water.

When Eliza saw her own face she was quite terrified at finding it so brown and ugly, but after she had wet her little hand and rubbed her eyes and forehead, the white skin gleamed forth once more; and when she had undressed and dipped herself in the fresh water, a more beautiful king's daughter could not have been found anywhere in the wide world.

As soon as she had dressed herself again and braided her long hair, she went to the bubbling spring and drank some water out of the hollow of her hand. Then she wandered far into the forest, not knowing whither[22] she went. She thought of her brothers and of her father and mother and felt sure that God would not forsake her. It is God who makes the wild apples grow in the wood to satisfy the hungry, and He now showed her one of these trees, which was so loaded with fruit that the boughs bent beneath the weight. Here she ate her noonday meal, and then placing props under the boughs, she went into the gloomiest depths of the forest.

It was so still that she could hear the sound of her own footsteps, as well as the rustling of every withered leaf which she crushed under her feet. Not a bird was to be seen, not a sunbeam could penetrate the large, dark boughs of the trees. The lofty trunks stood so close together that when she looked before her it seemed as if she were enclosed within trelliswork. Here was such solitude as she had never known before!

The night was very dark. Not a glowworm was glittering in the moss. Sorrowfully Eliza laid herself down to sleep. After a while it seemed to her as if the branches of the trees parted over her head and the mild eyes of angels looked down upon her from heaven.

In the morning, when she awoke, she knew not whether this had really been so or whether she had dreamed it. She continued her wandering, but she had not gone far when she met an old woman who had berries in her basket and who gave her a few to eat. Eliza asked her if she had not seen eleven princes riding through the forest.

'No,' replied the old woman, 'but I saw yesterday eleven swans with gold crowns on their heads, swimming in the river close by.' Then she led Eliza a little distance to a sloping bank, at the foot of which ran a little river. The trees on its banks stretched their long leafy branches across the water toward each other, and where they did not meet naturally the roots had torn themselves away from the ground, so that the branches might mingle their foliage as they hung over the water.

Eliza bade the old woman farewell and walked by the flowing river till she reached the shore of the open sea. And there, before her eyes, lay the glorious ocean, but not a sail appeared on its surface; not even a boat could be seen. How was she to go further? She noticed how the countless pebbles on the shore had been smoothed and rounded by the action of the water. Glass, iron, stones, everything that lay there mingled together, had been shaped by the same power until they were as smooth as her own delicate hand.

'The water rolls on without weariness,' she said, 'till all that is hard becomes smooth; so will I be unwearied in my task. Thanks for your lesson, bright rolling waves; my heart tells me you will one day lead me to my dear brothers.'

On the foam-covered seaweeds lay eleven white swan feathers, which she gathered and carried with her. Drops of water lay upon them; whether they were dewdrops or tears no one could say. It was lonely on the seashore, but she did not know it, for the ever-moving sea showed more changes in a few hours than the most varying lake could produce in a whole year. When a black, heavy cloud arose, it was as if the sea said, 'I can look dark and angry too'; and then the wind blew, and the waves turned to white foam as they rolled. When the wind slept and the clouds glowed with the red sunset, the sea looked like a rose leaf. Sometimes it became green and sometimes white. But, however quietly it lay, the waves were always restless on the shore and rose and fell like the breast of a sleeping child.

When the sun was about to set, Eliza saw eleven white swans, with golden crowns on their heads, flying toward the land, one behind the other, like a long white ribbon. She went down the slope from the shore and hid herself behind the bushes. The swans alighted quite close to her, flapping their great white wings. As soon as the sun had disappeared under the water, the feathers of the swans fell off and eleven beautiful princes, Eliza's brothers, stood near her.

She uttered a loud cry, for, although they were very much changed, she knew them immediately. She sprang into their arms and called them each by name. Very happy the princes were to see their little sister again; they knew her, although she had grown so tall and beautiful. They laughed and wept and told each other how cruelly they had been treated by their stepmother.

'We brothers,' said the eldest, 'fly about as wild swans while the sun is in the sky, but as soon as it sinks behind the hills we recover our human shape. Therefore we must always be near a resting place before sunset; for if we were flying toward the clouds when we recovered our human form, we should sink deep into the sea.

'We do not dwell here, but in a land just as fair that lies far across the ocean; the way is long, and there is no island upon which we can pass the night—nothing but a little rock rising out of the sea, upon which, even crowded together, we can scarcely stand with safety. If the sea is rough, the foam dashes over us; yet we thank God for this rock. We have passed whole nights upon it, or we should never have reached our beloved fatherland, for our flights across the sea occupies two of the longest days in the year.

'We have permission to visit our home once every year and to remain eleven days. Then we fly across the forest to look once more at the palace where our father dwells and where we were born, and at the church beneath whose shade our mother lies buried. The very trees and bushes here seem related to us. The wild horses leap over the plains as we have seen them in our childhood. The charcoal burners sing the old songs to which we have danced as children. This is our fatherland, to which we are drawn by loving ties; and here we have found you, our dear little sister. Two days longer we can remain here, and then we must fly away to a beautiful land which is not our home. How can we take you with us? We have neither ship nor boat.'

'How can I break this spell?' asked the sister. And they talked about it nearly the whole night, slumbering only a few hours.

Eliza was awakened by the rustling of the wings of swans

soaring above her. Her brothers were again changed to swans. They flew in circles, wider and wider, till they were far away; but one of them, the youngest, remained behind and laid his head in his sister's lap, while she stroked his wings. They remained together the whole day.

Towards evening the rest came back, and as the sun went down they resumed their natural forms. 'Tomorrow,' said one, 'we shall fly away, not to return again till a whole year has passed. But we cannot leave you here. Have you courage to go with us? My arm is strong enough to carry you through the wood, and will not all our wings be strong enough to bear you over the sea?'

'Yes, take me with you,' said Eliza. They spent the whole night in weaving a large, strong net of the pliant willow and rushes. On this Eliza laid herself down to sleep, and when the sun rose and her brothers again became wild swans, they took up the net with their beaks, and flew up to the clouds with their dear sister, who still slept. When the sunbeams fell on her face, one of the swans soared over her head so that his broad wings might shade her.

They were far from the land when Eliza awoke. She thought she must still be dreaming, it seemed so strange to feel herself being carried high in the air over the sea. By her side lay a branch full of beautiful ripe berries and a bundle of sweet-tasting roots; the youngest of her brothers had gathered them and placed them there. She smiled her thanks to him; she knew it was the same one that was hovering over her to shade her with his wings. They were now so high that a large ship beneath them looked like a white sea gull skimming the waves. A great cloud floating behind them appeared like a vast mountain, and upon it Eliza saw her own shadow and those of the eleven swans, like gigantic flying things. Altogether it formed a more beautiful picture than she had ever before seen; but as the sun rose higher and the clouds were left behind, the picture vanished.

Onward the whole day they flew through the air like winged arrows, yet more slowly than usual, for they had their sister to carry. The weather grew threatening, and Eliza watched the sinking sun with great anxiety, for the little rock in the ocean was not yet in sight. It seemed to her as if the swans were exerting themselves to the utmost. Alas! She was the cause of their not advancing more quickly. When the sun set they would change to men, fall into the sea, and be drowned.

Then she offered a prayer from her inmost heart, but still no rock appeared. Dark clouds came nearer, the gusts of wind told of the coming storm, while from a thick, heavy mass of clouds the lightning burst forth, flash after flash. The sun had reached the edge of the sea, when the swans darted down so swiftly that Eliza's heart trembled; she believed they were falling, but they again soared onward.

Presently, and by this time the sun was half hidden by the waves, she caught sight of the rock just below them. It did not look larger than a seal's head thrust out of the water. The sun sank so rapidly that at the moment their feet touched the rock it shone only like a star, and at last disappeared like the dying spark in a piece of burnt paper. Her brothers stood close around her with arms linked together, for there was not the smallest space to spare. The sea dashed against the rock and covered them with spray. The heavens were lighted up with continual flashes, and thunder rolled from the clouds. But the sister and brothers stood holding each other's hands, and singing hymns.

In the early dawn the air became calm and still, and at sunrise the swans flew away from the rock, bearing their sister with them. The sea was still rough, and from their great height the white foam on the dark-green waves looked like millions of swans swimming on the water. As the sun rose higher, Eliza saw before her, floating in the air, a range of mountains with shining masses of ice on their summits. In the centre rose a castle that seemed a mile long, with rows of columns rising one above another, while around it palm trees waved and flowers as large as mill wheels bloomed. She asked if this was the land to which they were hastening. The swans shook their heads, for what she beheld were the beautiful, ever-changing cloud-palaces of the Fata Morgana, into which no mortal can enter.

Eliza was still gazing at the scene, when mountains, forests, and castles melted away, and twenty stately churches rose in their stead, with high towers and pointed Gothic windows. She even fancied she could hear the tones of the organ, but it was the music of the murmuring sea. As they drew nearer to the churches, these too were changed and became a fleet of ships, which seemed to be sailing beneath her; but when she looked again she saw only a sea mist gliding over the ocean.

One scene melted into another, until at last she saw the real land to which they were bound, with its blue mountains, its cedar forests, and its cities and palaces. Long before the sun went down she was sitting on a rock in front of a large cave, the floor of which was overgrown with delicate green creeping plants, like an embroidered carpet.

'Now we shall expect to hear what you dream of tonight,' said the youngest brother, as he showed his sister her bedroom.

'Heaven grant that I may dream how to release you!' she replied. And this thought took such hold upon her mind that she prayed earnestly to God for help, and even in her sleep she continued to pray. Then it seemed to her that she was flying high in the air toward the cloudy palace of the Fata Morgana, and that a fairy came out to meet her, radiant and beautiful, yet much like the old woman who had given her berries in the wood, and who had told her of the swans with golden crowns on their heads.

'Your brothers can be released,' said she, 'if you only have courage and perseverance. Water is softer than your own delicate hands, and yet it polishes and shapes stones. But it feels no pain such as your fingers will feel; it has no soul and cannot suffer such agony and torment as you will have to endure. Do you see the stinging nettle which I hold in my hand? Quantities of the same sort grow round the cave in which you sleep, but only these, and those that grow on the graves of a churchyard, will be of any use to you. These you must gather, even while they burn blisters on your hands. Break them to pieces with your hands and feet, and they will become flax, from which you must spin and weave eleven coats with long sleeves; if these are then thrown over the eleven swans, the spell will be broken. But remember well, that from the moment you commence your task until it is finished, even though it occupy years of your life, you must not speak. The first word you utter will pierce the hearts of your brothers like a deadly dagger. Their lives hang upon your tongue. Remember all that I have told you.'

And as she finished speaking, she touched Eliza's hand lightly with the nettle, and a pain as of burning fire awoke her.

It was broad daylight, and near her lay a nettle like the one she had seen in her dream. She fell on her knees and offered thanks to God. Then she went forth from the cave to begin work with her delicate hands. She groped in amongst the ugly nettles, which burned great blisters on her hands and arms, but she was determined to bear the pain gladly if she could only release her dear brothers. So she bruised the nettles with her bare feet and spun the flax.

At sunset her brothers returned, and were much frightened when she did not speak. They believed her to be under the spell of some new sorcery, but when they saw her hands they understood what she was doing in their behalf. The youngest brother wept, and where his tears touched her the pain ceased and the burning blisters vanished. Eliza kept to her work all night, for she could not rest till she had released her brothers. During the whole of the following day, while her brothers were absent, she sat in solitude, but never before had the time flown so quickly.

One coat was already finished and she had begun the second, when she heard a huntsman's horn and was struck with fear. As the sound came nearer and nearer, she also heard dogs barking, and fled with terror into the cave. She hastily bound together the nettles she had gathered, and sat upon them. In a moment there came bounding toward her out of the ravine a great dog, and then another and another; they ran back and forth barking furiously, until in a few minutes all the huntsmen stood before the cave. The handsomest of them was the king of the country, who, when he saw the beautiful maiden, advanced toward her, saying, 'How did you come here, my sweet child?'

Eliza shook her head. She dared not speak, for it would cost her brothers their deliverance and their lives. And she hid her hands under her apron, so that the king might not see how she was suffering.

'Come with me,' he said; 'here you cannot remain. If you are as good as you are beautiful, I will dress you in silk and velvet, I will place a golden crown on your head, and you shall rule and make your home in my richest castle.' Then he lifted her onto his horse. She wept and wrung her hands, but the king said: 'I wish only your happiness. A time will come when you will thank me for this.'

He galloped away over the mountains, holding her before him on his horse, and the hunters followed behind them. As the sun went down they approached a fair, royal city, with churches and cupolas. On arriving at the castle, the king led her into marble halls, where large fountains played and where the walls and the ceilings were covered with rich paintings. But she had no eyes for all these glorious sights; she could only mourn and weep. Patiently she allowed the women to array her in royal robes, to weave pearls in her hair, and to draw soft gloves over her blistered fingers. As she stood arrayed in her rich dress, she looked so dazzlingly beautiful that the court bowed low in her presence.

Then the king declared his intention of making her his bride, but the archbishop shook his head and whispered that the fair young maiden was only a witch, who had blinded the king's eyes and ensnared his heart. The king would not listen to him, however, and ordered the music to sound, the daintiest dishes to be served, and the loveliest maidens to dance before them.

Afterwards he led her through fragrant gardens and lofty halls, but not a smile appeared on her lips or sparkled in her eyes. She looked the very picture of grief. Then the king opened the door of a little chamber in which she was to sleep. It was adorned with rich green tapestry and resembled the cave in which he had found her. On the floor lay the bundle of flax which she had spun from the nettles, and under the ceiling hung the coat she had made. These things had been brought away from the cave as curiosities, by one of the huntsmen.

'Here you can dream yourself back again in the old home in the cave,' said the king; 'here is the work with which you employed yourself. It will amuse you now, in the midst of all this splendour, to think of that time.'

When Eliza saw all these things which lay so near her heart, a smile played around her mouth, and the crimson blood rushed to her cheeks. The thought of her brothers and their release made her so joyful that she kissed the king's hand. Then he pressed her to his heart.

Very soon the joyous church bells announced the marriage

feast, and that the beautiful dumb girl out of the wood was to be made the queen of the country. Then the archbishop whispered wicked words in the king's ear, but they did not sink into his heart. The marriage was still to take place, and the archbishop himself had to place the crown on the bride's head; in his wicked spite, he pressed the narrow circlet so tightly on her forehead that it caused her pain. But a heavier weight encircled her heart—sorrow for her brothers. She felt not bodily pain. Her mouth was closed; a single word would cost the lives of her brothers. But she loved the king, handsome king, who did everything to make her happy more and more each day; she loved him with all her heart, and her eyes beamed with the love she dared not speak. Oh! If she had only been able to confide in him and tell him of her grief. But dumb she must remain till her task was finished.

Therefore at night she crept away into her little chamber which had been decked out to look like the cave and quickly wove one coat after another. But when she began the seventh, she found she had no more flax. She knew that the nettles she wanted to use grew in the churchyard and that she must pluck them herself. How should she get out there? 'Oh, what is the pain in my fingers to the torment which my heart endures?' thought she. 'I must venture; I shall not be denied help from heaven.'

Then with a trembling heart, as if she were about to perform a wicked deed, she crept into the garden in the broad moonlight, and passed through the narrow walks and the deserted streets, till she reached the churchyard. Then she saw on one of the broad tombstones a group of ghouls. These hideous creatures took off their rags, as if they intended to bathe, and then clawing open the fresh graves with their long, skinny fingers, pulled out the dead bodies and ate the flesh! Eliza had to pass close by them, and they fixed their wicked glances upon her, but she prayed silently, gathered the burning nettles, and carried them home with her to the castle.

One person only had seen her, and that was the archbishop—he was awake while others slept. Now he felt sure that his suspicions were correct; all was not right with the queen; she was a witch and had bewitched the king and all the people. Secretly he told the king what he had seen and what he feared, and as the hard words came from his tongue, the carved images of the saints shook their heads as if they would say, 'It is not so; Eliza is innocent.'

But the archbishop interpreted it in another way; he believed that they witnessed against her and were shaking their heads at her wickedness. Two tears rolled down the king's cheeks. He went home with doubt in his heart, and at night pretended to sleep. But no real sleep came to his eyes, for every night he saw Eliza get up and disappear from her chamber. Day by day his brow became darker, and Eliza saw it, and although she did not understand the reason, it alarmed her and made her heart tremble for her brothers. Her hot tears glittered like pearls on the regal velvet and diamonds, while all who saw her were wishing they could be queen.

In the meantime she had almost finished her task; only one of her brothers' coats was wanting, but she had no flax left and not a single nettle. Once more only, and for the last time, must she venture to the churchyard and pluck a few handfuls. She thought with terror of the solitary walk, and of the horrible ghouls, but her will was firm, as well as her trust in Providence. Eliza went, and the king and the archbishop followed her. They saw her vanish through the wicket gate into the churchyard, and when they came nearer they saw the ghouls sitting on the tombstone, as Eliza had seen them, and the king turned away his head, for he thought she was with them—she whose head had rested on his breast that very evening. 'The people must condemn her,' said he, and she was very quickly condemned by everyone to suffer death by fire.

Away from the gorgeous regal halls she was led to a dark, dreary cell, where the wind whistled through the iron bars. Instead of the velvet and silk dresses, they gave her the ten coats which she had woven, to cover her, and the bundle of nettles for a pillow. But they could have given her nothing that would have pleased her more. She continued her task with joy and prayed for help, while the street boys sang jeering songs about her and not a soul comforted her with a kind word.

Toward evening she heard at the grating the flutter of a swan's wing; it was her youngest brother. He had found his sister, and she sobbed for joy, although she knew that probably this was the last night she had to live. Still, she had hope, for her task was almost finished and her brothers were coming.

Then the archbishop arrived, to be with her during her last hours as he had promised the king. She shook her head and begged him, by looks and gestures, not to stay; for in this night she knew she must finish her task, otherwise all her pain and tears and sleepless nights would have been suffered in vain. The archbishop withdrew, uttering bitter words against her, but she knew that she was innocent and diligently continued her work.

Little mice ran about the floor, dragging the nettles to her feet, to help as much as they could; and a thrush, sitting outside the grating of the window, sang to her the whole night long as sweetly as possible, to keep up her spirits.

It was still twilight, and at least an hour before sunrise, when the eleven brothers stood at the castle gate and demanded to be brought before the king. They were told it could not be; it was yet night; the king slept and could not be disturbed. They threatened, they entreated, until the guard appeared, and even the king himself, inquiring what all the noise meant. At this moment the sun rose, and the eleven brothers were seen no more, but eleven wild swans flew away over the castle.

Now all the people came streaming forth from the gates of the city to see the witch burned. An old horse drew the cart on which she sat. They had dressed her in a garment of coarse sackcloth. Her lovely hair hung loose on her shoulders, her cheeks were deadly pale, her lips moved silently while her fingers still worked at the green flax. Even on the way to death she would not give up her task. The ten finished coats lay at her feet; she was working hard at the eleventh, while the mob jeered her and said: 'See the witch; how she mutters! She has no hymn book in her hand; she sits there with her ugly sorcery. Let us tear it into a thousand pieces.'

They pressed toward her, and doubtless would have destroyed the coats had not, at that moment, eleven wild swans flown over her and alighted on the cart. They flapped their large wings, and the crowd drew back in alarm.

'It is a sign from Heaven that she is innocent,' whispered many of them; but they did not venture to say it aloud.

As the executioner seized her by the hand to lift her out of the cart, she hastily threw the eleven coats over the eleven swans, and they immediately became eleven handsome princes; but the youngest had a swan's wing instead of an arm, for she had not been able to finish the last sleeve of the coat.

'Now I may speak,' she exclaimed. 'I am innocent.'

Then the people, who saw what had happened, bowed to her as before a saint; but she sank unconscious in her brothers' arms, overcome with suspense, anguish, and pain.

'Yes, she is innocent,' said the eldest brother, and related all that had taken place. While he spoke, there rose in the air a fragrance as from millions of roses. Every piece of fagot in the pile made to burn her had taken root, and threw out branches until the whole appeared like a thick hedge, large and high, covered with roses; while above all bloomed a white, shining flower that glittered like a star. This flower the king plucked, and when he placed it in Eliza's bosom she awoke from her swoon with peace and happiness in her heart. Then all the church bells rang of themselves, and the birds came in great flocks. And a marriage procession, such as no king had ever before seen, returned to the castle.

# 11

# The Angel

'Whenever a good child dies, an angel of God comes down from heaven, takes the dead child in his arms, spreads out his great white wings, and flies with him over all the places which the child had loved during his life. Then he gathers a large handful of flowers, which he carries up to the Almighty, that they may bloom more brightly in heaven than they do on earth. And the Almighty presses the flowers to His heart, but He kisses the flower that pleases Him best, and it receives a voice, and is able to join the song of the chorus of bliss.'

These words were spoken by an angel of God, as he carried a dead child up to heaven, and the child listened as if in a dream. Then they passed over well-known spots, where the little one had often played, and through beautiful gardens full of lovely flowers.

'Which of these shall we take with us to heaven to be transplanted there?' asked the angel.

Close by grew a slender, beautiful rosebush, but some wicked hand had broken the stem, and the half-opened rosebuds hung faded and withered on the trailing branches.

'Poor rosebush!' said the child, 'let us take it with us to heaven, that it may bloom above in God's garden.'

The angel took up the rosebush; then he kissed the child, and the little one half opened his eyes. The angel gathered also some beautiful flowers, as well as a few humble buttercups and heart's-ease.

'Now we have flowers enough[23],' said the child; but the angel only nodded, he did not fly upward to heaven.

It was night, and quite still in the great town. Here they remained, and the angel hovered over a small, narrow street, in which lay a large heap of straw, ashes, and sweepings from the houses of people who had removed. There lay fragments of plates, pieces of plaster, rags, old hats, and other rubbish not pleasant to see. Amidst all this confusion, the angel pointed to the pieces of a broken flowerpot, and to a lump of earth which had fallen out of it. The earth had been kept from falling to pieces by the roots of a withered field flower, which had been thrown amongst the rubbish.

'We will take this with us,' said the angel, 'I will tell you why as we fly along.'

And as they flew the angel related the history.

'Down in that narrow lane, in a low cellar, lived a poor sick boy; he had been afflicted from his childhood, and even in his best days he could just manage to walk up and down the room on crutches once or twice, but no more. During some days in summer, the sunbeams would lie on the floor of the cellar for about half an hour. In this spot the poor sick boy would sit warming himself in the sunshine, and watching the red blood through his delicate fingers as he held them before his face.

Then he would say he had been out, yet he knew nothing of the green forest in its spring verdure, till a neighbour's son brought him a green bough from a beech tree. This he would place over his head, and fancy that he was in the beechwood while the sun shone, and the birds carolled gayly. One spring day the neighbour's boy brought him some field flowers, and among them was one to which the root still adhered. This he carefully planted in a flowerpot, and placed in a window seat near his bed. And the flower had been planted by a fortunate hand, for it grew, put forth fresh shoots, and blossomed every year. It became a splendid flower garden to the sick boy, and his little treasure upon earth. He watered it, and cherished it, and took care it should have the benefit of every sunbeam that found its way into the cellar, from the earliest morning ray to the evening sunset. The flower entwined itself even in his dreams—for him it bloomed, for him spread its perfume. And it gladdened his eyes, and to the flower he turned, even in death, when the Lord called him. He has been one year with God. During that time the flower has stood in the window, withered and forgotten, till at length cast out among the sweepings into the street, on the day of the lodgers' removal. And this poor flower, withered and faded as it is, we have added to our nosegay, because it gave more real joy than the most beautiful flower in the garden of a queen.'

'But how do you know all this?' asked the child whom the angel was carrying to heaven.

'I know it,' said the angel, 'because I myself was the poor sick boy who walked upon crutches, and I know my own flower well.'

Then the child opened his eyes and looked into the glorious happy face of the angel, and at the same moment they found themselves in that heavenly home where all is happiness and joy. And God pressed the dead child to His heart, and wings were given him so that he could fly with the angel, hand in hand. Then the Almighty pressed all the flowers to His heart; but He kissed

the withered field flower, and it received a voice. Then it joined in the song of the angels, who surrounded the throne, some near, and others in a distant circle, but all equally happy. They all joined in the chorus of praise, both great and small,—the good, happy child, and the poor field flower, that once lay withered and cast away on a heap of rubbish in a narrow, dark street.

12

# The Nightingale

In China, as you know, the Emperor is a Chinaman, and all the people around him are Chinamen too. It is many years since the story I am going to tell you happened, but that is all the more reason for telling it, lest it should be forgotten. The emperor's palace was the most beautiful thing in the world; it was made entirely of the finest porcelain, very costly, but at the same time so fragile that it could only be touched with the very greatest care. There were the most extraordinary flowers to be seen in the garden; the most beautiful ones had little silver bells tied to them, which tinkled perpetually, so that one should not pass the flowers without looking at them. Every little detail in the garden had been most carefully thought out, and it was so big, that even the gardener himself did not know where it ended. If one went on walking, one came to beautiful woods with lofty trees and deep lakes. The wood extended to the sea, which was deep and blue, deep enough for large ships to sail up right under the branches of the trees. Among these trees lived a nightingale, which sang so deliciously, that even the poor fisherman, who had plenty of other things to do, lay still to listen to it, when he was out at night drawing in his nets. 'Heavens, how beautiful it is!' he said, but then he had to attend to his business and forgot it. The next night when he heard it again he would again exclaim, 'Heavens, how beautiful it is!'

Travellers came to the emperor's capital, from every country in the world; they admired everything very much, especially the palace and the gardens, but when they heard the nightingale they all said, 'This is better than anything!'

When they got home they described it, and the learned ones wrote many books about the town, the palace and the garden; but nobody forgot the nightingale, it was always put above everything else. Those among them who were poets wrote the most beautiful poems, all about the nightingale in the woods by the deep blue sea. These books went all over the world, and in course of time some of them reached the emperor. He sat in his golden chair reading and reading, and nodding his head, well pleased to hear such beautiful descriptions of the town, the palace and the garden. 'But the nightingale is the best of all,' he read.

'What is this?' said the emperor. 'The nightingale? Why, I know nothing about it. Is there such a bird in my kingdom, and in my own garden into the bargain, and I have never heard of it? Imagine my having to discover this from a book?'

Then he called his gentleman-in-waiting, who was so grand that when anyone of a lower rank dared to speak to him, or to ask him a question, he would only answer 'P,' which means nothing at all.

'There is said to be a very wonderful bird called a nightingale here,' said the emperor. 'They say that it is better than anything else in all my great kingdom! Why have I never been told anything about it?'

'I have never heard it mentioned,' said the gentleman-in-waiting. 'It has never been presented at court.'

'I wish it to appear here this evening to sing to me,' said the emperor. 'The whole world knows what I am possessed of, and I know nothing about it!'

'I have never heard it mentioned before,' said the gentleman-in-waiting. 'I will seek it, and I will find it!' But where was it to be found? The gentleman-in-waiting ran upstairs and downstairs and in and out of all the rooms and corridors. No one of all those he met had ever heard anything about the nightingale; so the gentleman-in-waiting ran back to the emperor, and said that it must be a myth, invented by the writers of the books. 'Your imperial majesty must not believe everything that is written; books are often mere inventions, even if they do not belong to what we call the black art!'

'But the book in which I read it is sent to me by the powerful Emperor of Japan, so it can't be untrue. I will hear this nightingale; I insist upon its being here tonight. I extend my most gracious protection to it, and if it is not forthcoming, I will have the whole court trampled upon after supper!'

'Tsing-pe!' said the gentleman-in-waiting, and away he ran again, up and down all the stairs, in and out of all the rooms and corridors; half the court ran with him, for they none of them wished to be trampled on. There was much questioning about this nightingale, which was known to all the outside world, but to no one at court. At last they found a poor little maid in the kitchen. She said, 'Oh heavens, the nightingale? I know it very well. Yes, indeed it can sing. Every evening I am allowed to take broken meat to my poor sick mother: she lives down by the shore. On my way back, when I am tired, I rest awhile in the wood, and then I hear the nightingale. Its song brings the tears into my eyes; I feel as if my mother were kissing me!'

'Little kitchenmaid,' said the gentleman-in-waiting, 'I will procure you a permanent position in the kitchen, and permission to see the emperor dining, if you will take us to the nightingale. It is commanded to appear at court tonight.'

Then they all went out into the wood where the nightingale usually sang. Half the court was there. As they were going along at their best pace a cow began to bellow.

'Oh!' said a young courtier, 'there we have it. What wonderful power for such a little creature; I have certainly heard it before.'

'No, those are the cows bellowing; we are a long way yet from the place.' Then the frogs began to croak in the marsh.

'Beautiful!' said the Chinese chaplain, 'it is just like the tinkling of church bells.'

'No, those are the frogs!' said the little kitchenmaid. 'But I think we shall soon hear it now!'

Then the nightingale began to sing.

'There it is!' said the little girl. 'Listen, listen, there it sits!' and she pointed to a little grey bird up among the branches.

'Is it possible?' said the gentleman-in-waiting. 'I should never have thought it was like that. How common it looks! Seeing so many grand people must have frightened all its colours away.'

'Little nightingale!' called the kitchenmaid quite loud, 'our gracious emperor wishes you to sing to him!'

'With the greatest of pleasure!' said the nightingale, warbling away in the most delightful fashion.

'It is just like crystal bells,' said the gentleman-in-waiting. 'Look at its little throat, how active it is. It is extraordinary that we have never heard it before! I am sure it will be a great success at court!'

'Shall I sing again to the emperor?' said the nightingale, who thought he was present.

'My precious little nightingale,' said the gentleman-in-waiting, 'I have the honour to command your attendance at a court festival tonight, where you will charm his gracious majesty the emperor with your fascinating singing.'

'It sounds best among the trees,' said the nightingale, but it went with them willingly when it heard that the emperor wished it.

The palace had been brightened up for the occasion. The walls and the floors, which were all of china, shone by the light of many thousand golden lamps. The most beautiful flowers, all of the tinkling kind, were arranged in the corridors; there was hurrying to and fro, and a great draught, but this was just what made the bells ring; one's ears were full of the tinkling. In the middle of the large reception room where the emperor sat a golden rod had been fixed, on which the nightingale was to perch. The whole court was assembled, and the little kitchenmaid had been permitted to stand behind the door, as she now had the actual title of cook. They were all dressed in their best; everybody's eyes were turned towards the little grey bird at which the emperor was nodding. The nightingale sang delightfully, and the tears came into the emperor's eyes, nay, they rolled down his cheeks; and then the nightingale sang more beautifully than ever, its notes touched all hearts. The emperor was charmed, and said the nightingale should have his gold slipper to wear round its neck. But the nightingale declined with thanks; it had already been sufficiently rewarded.

'I have seen tears in the eyes of the emperor; that is my richest reward. The tears of an emperor have a wonderful power! God knows I am sufficiently recompensed!' and then it again burst into its sweet heavenly song.

'That is the most delightful coquetting I have ever seen!' said the ladies, and they took some water into their mouths to try and make the same gurgling when anyone spoke to them, thinking so to equal the nightingale. Even the lackeys and the chambermaids announced that they were satisfied, and that is saying a great deal; they are always the most difficult people to please. Yes, indeed, the nightingale had made a sensation. It was to stay at court now, and to have its own cage, as well as liberty to walk out twice a day, and once in the night. It always had twelve footmen, with each one holding a ribbon which was tied round its leg. There was not much pleasure in an outing of that sort.

The whole town talked about the marvellous bird, and if two people met, one said to the other 'Night,' and the other answered 'Gale,' and then they sighed, perfectly understanding each other. Eleven cheesemongers' children were called after it, but they had not got a voice among them.

One day a large parcel came for the emperor; outside was written the word 'Nightingale.'

'Here we have another new book about this celebrated bird,'

said the emperor. But it was no book; it was a little work of art in a box, an artificial nightingale, exactly like the living one, but it was studded all over with diamonds, rubies and sapphires.

When the bird was wound up it could sing one of the songs the real one sang, and it wagged its tail, which glittered with silver and gold. A ribbon was tied round its neck on which was written, 'The Emperor of Japan's nightingale is very poor compared to the Emperor of China's.'

Everybody said, 'Oh, how beautiful!' And the person who brought the artificial bird immediately received the title of Imperial Nightingale Carrier in Chief.

'Now, they must sing together; what a duet that will be.'

Then they had to sing together, but they did not get on very well, for the real nightingale sang in its own way, and the artificial one could only sing waltzes.

'There is no fault in that,' said the music master; 'it is perfectly in time and correct in every way!'

Then the artificial bird had to sing alone. It was just as great a success as the real one, and then it was so much prettier to look at; it glittered like bracelets and breastpins.

It sang the same tune three and thirty times over, and yet it was not tired; people would willingly have heard it from the beginning again, but the emperor said that the real one must have a turn now—but where was it? No one had noticed that it had flown out of the open window, back to its own green woods.

'But what is the meaning of this?' said the emperor.

All the courtiers railed at it, and said it was a most ungrateful bird.

'We have got the best bird though,' said they, and then the

artificial bird had to sing again, and this was the thirty-fourth time that they heard the same tune, but they did not know it thoroughly even yet, because it was so difficult.

The music master praised the bird tremendously, and insisted that it was much better than the real nightingale, not only as regarded the outside with all the diamonds, but the inside too.

'Because you see, my ladies and gentlemen, and the emperor before all, in the real nightingale you never know what you will hear, but in the artificial one everything is decided beforehand! So it is, and so it must remain, it can't be otherwise. You can account for things, you can open it and show the human ingenuity in arranging the waltzes, how they go, and how one note follows upon another!'

'Those are exactly my opinions,' they all said, and the music master got leave to show the bird to the public next Sunday. They were also to hear it sing, said the emperor. So they heard it, and all became as enthusiastic over it as if they had drunk themselves merry on tea, because that is a thoroughly Chinese habit.

Then they all said 'Oh,' and stuck their forefingers in the air and nodded their heads; but the poor fishermen who had heard the real nightingale said, 'It sounds very nice, and it is very like the real one, but there is something wanting, we don't know what.'

The real nightingale was banished from the kingdom.

The artificial bird had its place on a silken cushion, close to the emperor's bed; all the presents it had received of gold and precious jewels were scattered round it. Its title had risen to be 'Chief Imperial Singer of the Bedchamber,' in rank number one, on the left side; for the emperor reckoned that side the important one, where the heart was seated. And even an emperor's heart is on the left side. The music master wrote five-and-twenty volumes about the artificial bird; the treatise was very long and written in all the most difficult Chinese characters. Everybody said they had read and understood it, for otherwise they would have been reckoned stupid, and then their bodies would have been trampled upon. Things went on in this way for a whole year. The emperor, the court, and all the other Chinamen knew every little gurgle in the song of the artificial bird by heart; but they liked it all the better for this, and they could all join in the song themselves. Even the street boys sang 'zizizi' and 'cluck, cluck, cluck,' and the emperor sang it too.

But one evening when the bird was singing its best, and the emperor was lying in bed listening to it, something gave way inside the bird with a 'whizz.' Then a spring burst, 'whirr' went all the wheels, and the music stopped. The emperor jumped out of bed and sent for his private physicians, but what good could they do? Then they sent for the watchmaker, and after a good deal of talk and examination he got the works to go again somehow; but he said it would have to be saved as much as possible, because it was so worn out, and he could not renew the works so as to be sure of the tune. This was a great blow! They only dared to let the artificial bird sing once a year, and hardly that; but then the music master made a little speech, using all the most difficult words. He said it was just as good as ever, and his saying it made it so.

Five years now passed, and then a great grief came upon the nation, for they were all very fond of their emperor, and he was ill and could not live, it was said. A new emperor was already chosen, and people stood about in the street, and asked the gentleman-in-waiting how their emperor was going on.

'P,' answered he, shaking his head.

The emperor lay pale and cold in his gorgeous bed, the courtiers thought he was dead, and they all went off to pay their respects to their new emperor. The lackeys ran off to talk matters over, and the chambermaids gave a great coffee party. Cloth had been laid down in all the rooms and corridors so as to deaden the sound of footsteps, so it was very, very quiet. But the emperor was not dead yet. He lay stiff and pale in the gorgeous bed with its velvet hangings and heavy golden tassels. There was an open window high above him, and the moon streamed in upon the emperor, and the artificial bird beside him.

The poor emperor could hardly breathe, he seemed to have a weight on his chest, he opened his eyes, and then he saw that it was Death sitting upon his chest, wearing his golden crown. In one hand he held the emperor's golden sword, and in the other his imperial banner. Round about, from among the folds of the velvet hangings peered many curious faces; some were hideous, others gentle and pleasant. They were all the emperor's good and bad deeds, which now looked him in the face when Death was weighing him down.

'Do you remember that?' whispered one after the other; 'do you remember this?' and they told him so many things that the perspiration poured down his face.

'I never knew that,' said the emperor. 'Music, music, sound the great Chinese drums!' he cried, 'that I may not hear what they are saying.' But they went on and on, and Death sat nodding his head, just like a Chinaman, at everything that was said.

'Music, music!' shrieked the emperor. 'You precious little golden bird, sing, sing! I have loaded you with precious stones, and even hung my own golden slipper round your neck; sing, I tell you, sing!'

But the bird stood silent; there was nobody to wind it up, so of course it could not go. Death continued to fix the great empty sockets of his eyes upon him, and all was silent, so terribly silent.

Suddenly, close to the window, there was a burst of lovely song; it was the living nightingale, perched on a branch outside. It had heard of the emperor's need, and had come to bring comfort and hope to him. As it sang the faces round became fainter and fainter, and the blood coursed with fresh vigour in the emperor's veins and through his feeble limbs. Even Death himself listened to the song and said, 'Go on, little nightingale, go on!'

'Yes, if you give me the gorgeous golden sword; yes, if you give me the imperial banner; yes, if you give me the emperor's crown.'

And Death gave back each of these treasures for a song, and the nightingale went on singing. It sang about the quiet churchyard, when the roses bloom, where the elder flower scents the air, and where the fresh grass is ever moistened anew by the tears of the mourner. This song brought to Death a longing for his own garden, and, like a cold grey mist, he passed out of the window.

'Thanks, thanks!' said the emperor; 'you heavenly little bird, I know you! I banished you from my kingdom, and yet you have charmed the evil visions away from my bed by your song, and even Death away from my heart! How can I ever repay you?'

'You have rewarded me,' said the nightingale. 'I brought the tears to your eyes, the very first time I ever sang to you, and I shall never forget it! Those are the jewels which gladden the heart of a singer;—but sleep now, and wake up fresh and strong! I will sing to you!'

Then it sang again, and the emperor fell into a sweet refreshing sleep. The sun shone in at his window, when he woke refreshed and well; none of his attendants had yet come back to him, for they thought he was dead, but the nightingale still sat there singing.

'You must always stay with me!' said the emperor. 'You shall only sing when you like, and I will break the artificial bird into a thousand pieces!'

'Don't do that!' said the nightingale, 'it did all the good it could! Keep it as you have always done! I can't build my nest and live in this palace, but let me come whenever I like, then I will sit on the branch in the evening, and sing to you. I will sing to cheer you and to make you thoughtful too; I will sing to you of the happy ones, and of those that suffer too. I will sing about the good and the evil, which are kept hidden from you. The little singing bird flies far and wide, to the poor fisherman, and the peasant's home, to numbers who are far from you and your court. I love your heart more than your crown, and yet there is an odour of sanctity round the crown too!—I will come, and I will sing to you!—But you must promise me one thing!—

'Everything!' said the emperor, who stood there in his imperial robes which he had just put on, and he held the sword heavy with gold upon his heart.

'One thing I ask you! Tell no one that you have a little bird who tells you everything; it will be better so!'

Then the nightingale flew away. The attendants came in to see after their dead emperor, and there he stood, bidding them 'Good morning!'

# 13

# The Ugly Duckling

It was so beautiful in the country. It was the summer time. The wheat fields were golden, the oats were green, and the hay stood in great stacks in the green meadows. The stork paraded about among them on his long red legs, chattering away in Egyptian, the language he had learned from his lady mother.

All around the meadows and cornfields grew thick woods, and in the midst of the forest was a deep lake. Yes, it was beautiful, it was delightful in the country.

In a sunny spot stood a pleasant old farmhouse circled all about with deep canals; and from the walls down to the water's edge grew great burdocks, so high that under the tallest of them a little child might stand upright. The spot was as wild as if it had been in the very centre of the thick wood.

In this snug retreat sat a duck upon her nest, watching for her young brood to hatch; but the pleasure she had felt at first was almost gone; she had begun to think it a wearisome task, for the little ones were so long coming out of their shells, and she seldom had visitors. The other ducks liked much better to swim about in the canals than to climb the slippery banks and sit under the burdock leaves to have a gossip with her. It was a long time to stay so much by herself.

At length, however, one shell cracked, and soon another, and from each came a living creature that lifted its head and cried 'Peep, peep.'

'Quack, quack!' said the mother; and then they all tried to say it, too, as well as they could, while they looked all about them on every side at the tall green leaves. Their mother allowed them to look about as much as they liked, because green is good for the eyes.

'What a great world it is, to be sure,' said the little ones, when they found how much more room they had than when they were in the eggshell.

'Is this all the world, do you imagine?' said the mother. 'Wait till you have seen the garden. Far beyond that it stretches down to the pastor's field, though I have never ventured to such a distance. Are you all out?' she continued, rising to look. 'No, not all; the largest egg lies there yet, I declare. I wonder how long this business is to last. I'm really beginning to be tired of it;' but for all that she sat down again.

'Well, and how are you today?' quacked an old duck who came to pay her a visit.

'There's one egg that takes a deal of hatching. The shell is hard and will not break,' said the fond mother, who sat still upon her nest. 'But just look at the others. Have I not[24] a pretty family? Are they not the prettiest little ducklings you ever saw? They are the image of their father—the good for naught[25]! He never comes to see me.'

'Let me see the egg that will not break,' said the old duck. 'I've no doubt it's a Guinea fowl's egg. The same thing happened to me once, and a deal of trouble it gave me, for the young ones are afraid of the water. I quacked and clucked, but all to no purpose.

Let me take a look at it. Yes, I am right; it's a Guinea fowl, upon my word; so take my advice and leave it where it is. Come to the water and teach the other children to swim.'

'I think I will sit a little while longer,' said the mother. 'I have sat so long, a day or two more won't matter.'

'Very well, please yourself,' said the old duck, rising; and she went away.

At last the great egg broke, and the latest bird cried 'Peep, peep,' as he crept forth from the shell. How big and ugly he was! The mother duck stared at him and did not know what to think. 'Really,' she said, 'this is an enormous duckling, and it is not at all like any of the others. I wonder if he will turn out to be a Guinea fowl. Well, we shall see when we get to the water—for into the water he must go, even if I have to push him in myself.'

On the next day the weather was delightful. The sun shone brightly on the green burdock leaves, and the mother duck took her whole family down to the water and jumped in with a splash. 'Quack, quack!' cried she, and one after another the little ducklings jumped in. The water closed over their heads, but they came up again in an instant and swam about quite prettily, with their legs paddling under them as easily as possible; their legs went of their own accord; and the ugly grey-coat was also in the water, swimming with them.

'Oh,' said the mother, 'that is not a Guinea fowl. See how well he uses his legs, and how erect he holds himself! He is my own child, and he is not so very ugly after all, if you look at him properly. Quack, quack! Come with me now. I will take you into grand society and introduce you to the farmyard, but you must keep close to me or you may be trodden upon; and, above all, beware of the cat.'

When they reached the farmyard, there was a wretched riot going on; two families were fighting for an eel's head, which, after all, was carried off by the cat. 'See, children, that is the way of the world,' said the mother duck, whetting her beak, for she would have liked the eel's head herself. 'Come, now, use your legs, and let me see how well you can behave. You must bow your heads prettily to that old duck yonder; she is the highest born of them all and has Spanish blood; therefore she is well off. Don't you see she has a red rag tied to her leg, which is something very grand and a great honour for a duck; it shows that everyone is anxious not to lose her, and that she is to be noticed by both man and beast. Come, now, don't turn in your toes; a well-bred duckling spreads his feet wide apart, just like his father and mother, in this way; now bend your necks and say "Quack!" '

The ducklings did as they were bade, but the other ducks stared, and said, 'Look, here comes another brood—as if there were not enough of us already! And bless me, what a queer-looking object one of them is; we don't want him here'; and then one flew out and bit him in the neck.

'Let him alone,' said the mother; 'he is not doing any harm.'

'Yes, but he is so big and ugly. He's a perfect fright,' said the spiteful duck, 'and therefore he must be turned out. A little biting will do him good.'

'The others are very pretty children,' said the old duck with the rag on her leg, 'all but that one. I wish his mother could smooth him up a bit; he is really ill-favoured.'

'That is impossible, your grace,' replied the mother. 'He is not pretty, but he has a very good disposition and swims as well as the others or even better. I think he will grow up pretty, and perhaps be smaller. He has remained too long in the egg, and therefore his figure is not properly formed;' and then she stroked his neck and smoothed the feathers, saying: 'It is a drake, and therefore not of so much consequence. I think he will grow up strong and able to take care of himself.'

'The other ducklings are graceful enough,' said the old duck. 'Now make yourself at home, and if you find an eel's head you can bring it to me.'

And so they made themselves comfortable; but the poor duckling who had crept out of his shell last of all and looked so ugly was bitten and pushed and made fun of, not only by the ducks but by all the poultry.

'He is too big,' they all said; and the turkey cock, who had been born into the world with spurs and fancied himself really an emperor, puffed himself out like a vessel in full sail and flew at the duckling. He became quite red in the head with passion, so that the poor little thing did not know where to go, and was quite miserable because he was so ugly as to be laughed at by the whole farmyard.

So it went on from day to day; it got worse and worse. The poor duckling was driven about by everyone; even his brothers and sisters were unkind to him and would say, 'Ah, you ugly creature, I wish the cat would get you' and his mother had been heard to say she wished he had never been born. The ducks pecked him, the chickens beat him, and the girl who fed the poultry pushed him with her feet. So at last he ran away, frightening the little birds in the hedge as he flew over the palings. 'They are afraid because I am so ugly,' he said. So he flew still further, until he came out on a large moor inhabited by wild ducks. Here he remained the whole night, feeling very sorrowful.

In the morning, when the wild ducks rose in the air, they stared at their new comrade. 'What sort of a duck are you?' they all said, coming round him.

He bowed to them and was as polite as he could be, but he did not reply to their question. 'You are exceedingly ugly,' said the wild ducks; 'but that will not matter if you do not want to marry one of our family.'

Poor thing! He had no thoughts of marriage; all he wanted was permission to lie among the rushes and drink some of the water on the moor. After he had been on the moor two days, there came two wild geese, or rather goslings, for they had not been out of the egg long, which accounts for their impertinence. 'Listen, friend,' said one of them to the duckling; 'you are so ugly that we like you very well. Will you go with us and become a bird of passage? Not far from here is another moor, in which there are some wild geese, all of them unmarried. It is a chance for you to get a wife. You may make your fortune, ugly as you are.'

'Bang, bang,' sounded in the air, and the two wild geese fell dead among the rushes, and the water was tinged with blood. 'Bang, bang,' echoed far and wide in the distance, and whole flocks of wild geese rose up from the rushes.

The sound continued from every direction, for the sportsmen surrounded the moor, and some were even seated on branches of trees, overlooking the rushes. The blue smoke from the guns rose like clouds over the dark trees, and as it floated away across the water, a number of sporting dogs bounded in among the rushes, which bent beneath them wherever they went. How they terrified the poor duckling! He turned away his head to hide it under his wing, and at the same moment a large, terrible dog passed quite near him. His jaws were open, his tongue hung from his mouth, and his eyes glared fearfully. He thrust his nose close to the duckling, showing his sharp teeth, and then 'splash, splash,' he went into the water, without touching him.

'Oh,' sighed the duckling, 'how thankful I am for being so ugly; even a dog will not bite me.'

And so he lay quite still, while the shot rattled through the rushes, and gun after gun was fired over him. It was late in the day before all became quiet, but even then the poor young thing did not dare to move. He waited quietly for several hours and then, after looking carefully around him, hastened away from the moor as fast as he could. He ran over field and meadow till a storm arose, and he could hardly struggle against it.

Towards evening he reached a poor little cottage that seemed ready to fall, and only seemed to remain standing because it could not decide on which side to fall first. The storm continued so violent that the duckling could go no further. He sat down by the cottage, and then he noticed that the door was not quite closed, in consequence of one of the hinges having given way. There was, therefore, a narrow opening near the bottom large enough for him to slip through, which he did very quietly, and got a shelter for the night. Here, in this cottage, lived a woman, a cat, and a hen. The cat, whom his mistress called 'My little son,' was a great favourite; he could raise his back, and purr, and could even throw out sparks from his fur if it were stroked the wrong way. The hen had very short legs, so she was called 'Chickie Short-legs.' She laid good eggs, and her mistress loved her as if she had been her own child. In the morning the strange visitor was discovered; the cat began to purr and the hen to cluck.

'What is that noise about?' said the old woman, looking around the room. But her sight was not very good; therefore when she saw the duckling she thought it must be a fat duck that had strayed from home. 'Oh, what a prize!' she exclaimed. 'I hope it is not a drake, for then I shall have some ducks' eggs. I must wait and see.' So the duckling was allowed to remain on trial for three weeks; but there were no eggs.

Now the cat was the master of the house, and the hen was the mistress; and they always said, 'We and the world,' for they believed themselves to be half the world, and by far the better half, too. The duckling thought that others might hold a different opinion on the subject, but the hen would not listen to such doubts.

'Can you lay eggs?' she asked. 'No.' 'Then have the goodness to cease talking.' 'Can you raise your back, or purr, or throw out sparks?' said the cat. 'No.' 'Then you have no right to express an opinion when sensible people are speaking.' So the duckling sat in a corner, feeling very low-spirited; but when the sunshine and the fresh air came into the room through the open door, he began to feel such a great longing for a swim that he could not help speaking of it.

'What an absurd idea!' said the hen. 'You have nothing else to do; therefore you have foolish fancies. If you could purr or lay eggs, they would pass away.'

'But it is so delightful to swim about on the water,' said the duckling, 'and so refreshing to feel it close over your head while you dive down to the bottom.'

'Delightful, indeed! It must be a queer sort of pleasure,' said the hen. 'Why, you must be crazy! Ask the cat—he is the cleverest animal I know; ask him how he would like to swim about on the water, or to dive under it, for I will not speak of my own opinion. Ask our mistress, the old woman; there is no one in the world more clever[26] than she is. Do you think she would relish swimming and letting the water close over her head?'

'I see you don't understand me,' said the duckling.

'We don't understand you? Who can understand you, I wonder? Do you consider yourself more clever than the cat or the old woman?—I will say nothing of myself. Don't imagine such nonsense, child, and thank your good fortune that you have been so well received here. Are you not in a warm room and in society from which you may learn something? But you are a chatterer, and your company is not very agreeable. Believe me, I speak only for your good. I may tell you unpleasant truths, but that is a proof of my friendship. I advise you, therefore, to lay eggs and learn to purr as quickly as possible.'

'I believe I must go out into the world again,' said the duckling.

'Yes, do,' said the hen. So the duckling left the cottage and soon found water on which it could swim and dive, but he was avoided by all other animals because of his ugly appearance.

Autumn came, and the leaves in the forest turned to orange and gold; then, as winter approached, the wind caught them as they fell and whirled them into the cold air. The clouds, heavy with hail and snowflakes, hung low in the sky, and the raven stood among the reeds, crying, 'Croak, croak.' It made one shiver with cold to look at him. All this was very sad for the poor little duckling.

One evening, just as the sun was setting amid radiant clouds, there came a large flock of beautiful birds out of the bushes. The duckling had never seen any like them before. They were swans; and they curved their graceful necks, while their soft plumage shone with dazzling whiteness. They uttered a singular cry as they spread their glorious wings and flew away from those cold regions to warmer countries across the sea. They mounted higher and higher in the air, and the ugly little duckling had a strange sensation as he watched them. He whirled himself in the water like a wheel, stretched out his neck towards them, and uttered a cry so strange that it frightened even himself. Could he ever forget those beautiful, happy birds! And when at last they were out of his sight, he dived under the water and rose again almost beside himself with excitement. He knew not the names of these birds nor where they had flown, but he felt towards them as he had never felt towards any other bird in the world.

He was not envious of these beautiful creatures; it never

occurred to him to wish to be as lovely as they. Poor ugly creature, how gladly he would have lived even with the ducks, had they only treated him kindly and given him encouragement.

The winter grew colder and colder; he was obliged to swim about on the water to keep it from freezing, but every night the space on which he swam became smaller and smaller. At length it froze so hard that the ice in the water crackled as he moved, and the duckling had to paddle with his legs as well as he could, to keep the space from closing up. He became exhausted at last and lay still and helpless, frozen fast in the ice.

Early in the morning a peasant who was passing by saw what had happened. He broke the ice in pieces with his wooden shoe and carried the duckling home to his wife. The warmth revived the poor little creature; but when the children wanted to play with him, the duckling thought they would do him some harm, so he started up in terror, fluttered into the milk pan, and splashed the milk about the room. Then the woman clapped her hands, which frightened him still more. He flew first into the butter cask, then into the meal tub and out again. What a condition he was in! The woman screamed and struck at him with the tongs; the children laughed and screamed and tumbled over each other in their efforts to catch him, but luckily he escaped. The door stood open; the poor creature could just manage to slip out among the bushes and lie down quite exhausted in the newly fallen snow.

It would be very sad were I to relate all the misery and privations which the poor little duckling endured during the hard winter; but when it had passed he found himself lying one morning in a moor, amongst the rushes. He felt the warm sun shining and heard the lark singing and saw that all around was beautiful spring.

Then the young bird felt that his wings were strong, as he flapped them against his sides and rose high into the air. They bore him onwards until, before he well knew how it had happened, he found himself in a large garden. The apple trees were in full blossom, and the fragrant elders bent their long green branches down to the stream, which wound round a smooth lawn. Everything looked beautiful in the freshness of early spring. From a thicket close by came three beautiful white swans, rustling their feathers and swimming lightly over the smooth water. The duckling saw these lovely birds and felt more strangely unhappy than ever.

'I will fly to these royal birds,' he exclaimed, 'and they will kill me because, ugly as I am, I dare to approach them. But it does not matter; better be killed by them than pecked by the ducks, beaten by the hens, pushed about by the maiden who feeds the poultry, or starved with hunger in the winter.'

Then he flew to the water and swam towards the beautiful swans. The moment they espied the stranger they rushed to meet him with outstretched wings.

'Kill me,' said the poor bird and he bent his head down to the surface of the water and awaited death.

But what did he see in the clear stream below? His own image—no longer a dark-grey bird, ugly and disagreeable to look at, but a graceful and beautiful swan.

To be born in a duck's nest in a farmyard is of no consequence to a bird if it is hatched from a swan's egg. He now felt glad at having suffered sorrow and trouble, because it enabled him to enjoy so much better all the pleasure and happiness around him; for the great swans swam round the newcomer and stroked his neck with their beaks, as a welcome.

Into the garden presently came some little children and threw bread and cake into the water.

'See,' cried the youngest, 'there is a new one;' and the rest were delighted, and ran to their father and mother, dancing and clapping their hands and shouting joyously, 'There is another swan come; a new one has arrived.'

Then they threw more bread and cake into the water and said, 'The new one is the most beautiful of all, he is so young and pretty.' And the old swans bowed their heads before him.

Then he felt quite ashamed and hid his head under his wing, for he did not know what to do, he was so happy—yet he was not at all proud. He had been persecuted and despised for his ugliness, and now he heard them say he was the most beautiful of all the birds. Even the elder tree bent down its boughs into the water before him, and the sun shone warm and bright. Then he rustled his feathers, curved his slender neck, and cried joyfully, from the depths of his heart, 'I never dreamed of such happiness as this while I was the despised ugly duckling.'

# 14

# Grandmother

Grandmother is very old, her face is wrinkled, and her hair is quite white; but her eyes are like two stars, and they have a mild, gentle expression in them when they look at you, which does you good. She wears a dress of heavy, rich silk, with large flowers worked on it; and it rustles when she moves. And then she can tell the most wonderful stories. Grandmother knows a great deal, for she was alive before father and mother—that's quite certain. She has a hymn book with large silver clasps, in which she often reads; and in the book, between the leaves, lies a rose, quite flat and dry; it is not so pretty as the roses which are standing in the glass, and yet she smiles at it most pleasantly, and tears even come into her eyes. 'I wonder why grandmother looks at the withered flower in the old book that way? Do you know?' Why, when grandmother's tears fall upon the rose, and she is looking at it, the rose revives, and fills the room with its fragrance; the walls vanish as in a mist, and all around her is the glorious green wood, where in summer the sunlight streams through thick foliage; and grandmother, why she is young again, a charming maiden, fresh as a rose, with round, rosy cheeks, fair, bright ringlets, and a figure pretty and graceful; but the eyes, those mild, saintly eyes, are the same,— they have been left to grandmother. At her side sits a young man, tall and strong; he gives her a rose and she smiles. Grandmother cannot smile like that now. Yes, she is smiling at the memory of that day, and many thoughts and recollections of the past; but the handsome young man is gone, and the rose has withered in the old book, and grandmother is sitting there, again an old woman, looking down upon the withered rose in the book.

Grandmother is dead now. She had been sitting in her armchair, telling us a long, beautiful tale; and when it was finished, she said she was tired, and leaned her head back to sleep awhile. We could hear her gentle breathing as she slept; gradually it became quieter and calmer, and on her countenance beamed happiness and peace. It was as if lighted up with a ray of sunshine. She smiled once more, and then people said she was dead. She was laid in a black coffin, looking mild and beautiful in the white folds of the shrouded linen, though her eyes were closed; but every wrinkle had vanished, her hair looked white and silvery, and around her mouth lingered a sweet smile. We did not feel at all afraid to look at the corpse of her who had been such a dear, good grandmother. The hymn book, in which the rose still lay, was placed under her head, for so she had wished it; and then they buried grandmother.

On the grave, close by the churchyard wall, they planted a rose tree; it was soon full of roses, and the nightingale sat among the flowers, and sang over the grave. From the organ in the church sounded the music and the words of the beautiful psalms, which were written in the old book under the head of the dead one.

The moon shone down upon the grave, but the dead was not there; every child could go safely, even at night, and pluck a rose from the tree by the churchyard wall. The dead know more than we do who are living. They know what a terror would come upon

us if such a strange thing were to happen, as the appearance of a dead person among us. They are better off than we are; the dead return no more. The earth has been heaped on the coffin, and it is earth only that lies within it. The leaves of the hymn book are dust; and the rose, with all its recollections, has crumbled to dust also. But over the grave fresh roses bloom, the nightingale sings, and the organ sounds and there still lives a remembrance of old grandmother, with the loving, gentle eyes that always looked young. *Eyes can never die.* Ours will once again behold dear grandmother, young and beautiful as when, for the first time, she kissed the fresh, red rose, that is now dust in the grave.

# 15

# The Shepherdess and the Chimney-Sweep

Have you ever seen an old wooden cupboard quite black with age, and ornamented with carved foliage and curious figures? Well, just such a cupboard stood in a parlour, and had been left to the family as a legacy by the great-grandmother. It was covered from top to bottom with carved roses and tulips; the most curious scrolls were drawn upon it, and out of them peeped little stags' heads, with antlers. In the middle of the cupboard door was the carved figure of a man most ridiculous to look at. He grinned at you, for no one could call it laughing. He had goat's legs, little horns on his head, and a long beard; the children in the room always called him 'Major general-field-sergeant-commander Billy-goat's-legs.' It was certainly a very difficult name to pronounce, and there are very few who ever receive such a title, but then it seemed wonderful how he came to be carved at all; yet there he was, always looking at the table under the looking glass, where stood a very pretty little shepherdess made of china. Her shoes were gilt, and her dress had a red rose or an ornament. She wore a hat, and carried a crook, that were both gilded, and looked very bright and pretty. Close by her side stood a little chimney-sweep, as black as coal, and also made of china. He was, however, quite as clean and neat as any other china figure; he only represented a black chimney-sweep, and the china workers might just as well have made him a prince, had they felt inclined to do so. He stood holding his ladder quite handily, and his face was as fair and rosy as a girl's; indeed, that was rather a mistake, it should have had some black marks on it. He and the shepherdess had been placed close together, side by side; and, being so placed, they became engaged to each other, for they were very well suited, being both made of the same sort of china, and being equally fragile. Close to them stood another figure, three times as large as they were, and also made of china. He was an old Chinaman, who could nod his head, and used to pretend that he was the grandfather of the shepherdess, although he could not prove it. He however assumed authority over her, and therefore when 'Major-general-field-sergeant-commander Billy-goat's-legs' asked for the little shepherdess to be his wife, he nodded his head to show that he consented. 'You will have a husband,' said the old Chinaman to her, 'who I really believe is made of mahogany. He will make you a lady of Major-general-field-sergeant-commander Billy-goat's-legs. He has the whole cupboard full of silver plate, which he keeps locked up in secret drawers.'

'I won't go into the dark cupboard,' said the little shepherdess. 'I have heard that he has eleven china wives there already.'

'Then you shall be the twelfth,' said the old Chinaman. 'Tonight as soon as you hear a rattling in the old cupboard, you shall be married, as true as I am a Chinaman;' and then he nodded his head and fell asleep.

Then the little shepherdess cried, and looked at her sweetheart, the china chimney-sweep. 'I must entreat you,' said she, 'to go out with me into the wide world, for we cannot stay here.'

'I will do whatever you wish,' said the little chimney-sweep; 'let us go immediately: I think I shall be able to maintain you with my profession.'

'If we were but safely down from the table!' said she; 'I shall not be happy till we are really out in the world.'

Then he comforted her, and showed her how to place her little foot on the carved edge and gilt leaf ornaments of the table. He brought his little ladder to help her, and so they contrived to reach the floor. But when they looked at the old cupboard, they saw it was all in an uproar. The carved stags pushed out their heads, raised their antlers, and twisted their necks. The major-general sprung up in the air; and cried out to the old Chinaman, 'They are running away! They are running away!' The two were rather frightened at this, so they jumped into the drawer of the window seat. Here were three or four packs of cards not quite complete, and a doll's theatre, which had been built up very neatly. A comedy was being performed in it, and all the queens of diamonds, clubs, and hearts, and spades, sat in the first row fanning themselves with tulips, and behind them stood all the knaves, showing that they had heads above and below as playing cards generally have. The play was about two lovers, who were not allowed to marry, and the shepherdess wept because it was so like her own story. 'I cannot bear it,' said she, 'I must get out of the drawer;' but when they reached the floor, and cast their eyes on the table, there was the old Chinaman awake and shaking his whole body, till all at once down he came on the floor, 'plump.' 'The old Chinaman is coming,' cried the little shepherdess in a fright, and down she fell on one knee.

'I have thought of something,' said the chimney-sweep; 'let us get into the great potpourri jar which stands in the corner; there we can lie on rose leaves and lavender, and throw salt in his eyes if he comes near us.'

'No, that will never do,' said she, 'because I know that the Chinaman and the potpourri jar were lovers once, and there always remains behind a feeling of goodwill between those who have been so intimate as that. No, there is nothing left for us but to go out into the wide world.'

'Have you really courage enough to go out into the wide world with me?' said the chimney-sweep; 'have you thought how large it is, and that we can never come back here again?'

'Yes, I have,' she replied.

When the chimney-sweep saw that she was quite firm, he said, 'My way is through the stove and up the chimney. Have you courage to creep with me through the firebox, and the iron pipe? When we get to the chimney I shall know how to manage very well. We shall soon climb too high for anyone to reach us, and we shall come through a hole in the top out into the wide world.' So he led her to the door of the stove.

'It looks very dark,' said she; still she went in with him through the stove and through the pipe, where it was as dark as pitch.

'Now we are in the chimney,' said he; 'and look, there is a beautiful star shining above it.' It was a real star shining down upon them as if it would show them the way. So they clambered, and crept on, and a frightful steep place it was; but the chimney-sweep helped her and supported her, till they got higher and higher. He showed her the best places on which to set her little china foot, so at last they reached the top of the chimney, and sat themselves down, for they were very tired, as may be supposed.

The sky, with all its stars, was over their heads, and below were the roofs of the town. They could see for a very long distance out into the wide world, and the poor little shepherdess leaned her head on her chimney-sweep's shoulder, and wept till she washed the gilt off her sash; the world was so different to what she expected. 'This is too much,' she said; 'I cannot bear it, the world is too large. Oh, I wish I were safe back on the table. Again, under the looking glass; I shall never be happy till I am safe back again. Now I have followed you out into the wide world, you will take me back, if you love me.'

Then the chimney-sweep tried to reason with her, and spoke of the old Chinaman, and of the Major-general-field-sergeant-commander Billy-goat's legs; but she sobbed so bitterly, and kissed her little chimney-sweep till he was obliged to do all she asked, foolish as it was. And so, with a great deal of trouble, they climbed down the chimney, and then crept through the pipe and stove, which were certainly not very pleasant places. Then they stood in the dark firebox, and listened behind the door, to hear what was going on in the room. As it was all quiet, they peeped out. Alas! There lay the old Chinaman on the floor; he had fallen down from the table as he attempted to run after them, and was broken into three pieces; his back had separated entirely, and his head had rolled into a corner of the room. The major-general stood in his old place, and appeared lost in thought.

'This is terrible,' said the little shepherdess. 'My poor old grandfather is broken to pieces, and it is our fault. I shall never live after this;' and she wrung her little hands.

'He can be riveted,' said the chimney-sweep; 'he can be riveted. Do not be so hasty. If they cement his back, and put a good rivet in it, he will be as good as new, and be able to say as many disagreeable things to us as ever.'

'Do you think so?' said she; and then they climbed up to the table, and stood in their old places.

'As we have done no good,' said the chimney-sweep, 'we might as well have remained here, instead of taking so much trouble.'

'I wish grandfather was riveted,' said the shepherdess. 'Will it cost much, I wonder?'

And she had her wish. The family had the Chinaman's back mended, and a strong rivet put through his neck; he looked as good as new, but he could no longer nod his head.

'You have become proud since your fall broke you to pieces,' said Major-general-field-sergeant-commander Billy-goat's-legs. 'You have no reason to give yourself such airs. Am I to have her or not?'

The chimney-sweep and the little shepherdess looked piteously at the old Chinaman, for they were afraid he might nod; but he was not able: besides, it was so tiresome to be always telling strangers he had a rivet in the back of his neck.

And so the little china people remained together, and were glad of the grandfather's rivet, and continued to love each other till they were broken to pieces.

# 16

# The Little Match Girl

It was dreadfully cold; it was snowing fast, and was almost dark, as evening came on—the last evening of the year. In the cold and the darkness, there went along the street a poor little girl, bareheaded and with naked feet. When she left home she had slippers on, it is true; but they were much too large for her feet— slippers that her mother had used till then, and the poor little girl lost them in running across the street when two carriages were passing terribly fast. When she looked for them, one was not to be found, and a boy seized the other and ran away with it, saying he would use it for a cradle some day, when he had children of his own.

So on the little girl went with her bare feet, that were red and blue with cold. In an old apron that she wore were bundles of matches, and she carried a bundle also in her hand. No one had bought so much as a bunch all the long day, and no one had given her even a penny.

Poor little girl! Shivering with cold and hunger she crept along, a perfect picture of misery.

The snowflakes fell on her long flaxen hair, which hung in pretty curls about her throat; but she thought not of her beauty nor of the cold. Lights gleamed in every window, and there came to her the savory smell of roast goose, for it was New Year's Eve.

And it was this of which she thought.

In a corner formed by two houses, one of which projected beyond the other, she sat cowering down. She had drawn under her little feet, but still she grew colder and colder; yet she dared not go home, for she had sold no matches and could not bring a penny of money. Her father would certainly beat her; and, besides, it was cold enough at home, for they had only the house roof above them, and though the largest holes had been stopped with straw and rags, there were left many through which the cold wind could whistle.

And now her little hands were nearly frozen with cold. Alas! A single match might do her good if she might only draw it from the bundle, rub it against the wall, and warm her fingers by it. So at last she drew one out. Whisht[27]! How it blazed and burned! It gave out a warm, bright flame like a little candle, as she held her hands over it. A wonderful little light it was. It really seemed to the little girl as if she sat before a great iron stove with polished brass feet and brass shovel and tongs. So blessedly it burned that the little maiden stretched out her feet to warm them also. How comfortable she was! But lo[28]! The flame went out, the stove vanished, and nothing remained but the little burned match in her hand.

She rubbed another match against the wall. It burned brightly, and where the light fell upon the wall it became transparent like a veil, so that she could see through it into the room. A snow-white cloth was spread upon the table, on which was a beautiful china dinner service, while a roast goose, stuffed with apples and prunes, steamed famously and sent forth a most savory smell. And what was more delightful still, and wonderful, the goose jumped from the dish, with knife and fork still in its breast, and waddled along the floor straight to the little girl.

But the match went out then, and nothing was left to her but the thick, damp wall.

She lighted another match. And now she was under a most beautiful Christmas tree, larger and far more prettily trimmed than the one she had seen through the glass doors at the rich merchant's. Hundreds of wax tapers were burning on the green branches, and gay figures, such as she had seen in shop windows, looked down upon her. The child stretched out her hands to them; then the match went out.

Still the lights of the Christmas tree rose higher and higher. She saw them now as stars in heaven, and one of them fell, forming a long trail of fire.

'Now someone is dying,' murmured the child softly; for her grandmother, the only person who had loved her, and who was now dead, had told her that whenever a star falls a soul mounts up to God.

She struck yet another match against the wall, and again it was light; and in the brightness there appeared before her the dear old grandmother, bright and radiant, yet sweet and mild, and happy as she had never looked on earth.

'Oh, grandmother,' cried the child, 'take me with you. I know you will go away when the match burns out. You, too, will vanish, like the warm stove, the splendid New Year's feast, the beautiful Christmas tree.' And lest her grandmother should disappear, she rubbed the whole bundle of matches against the wall.

And the matches burned with such a brilliant light that it became brighter than noonday. Her grandmother had never looked so grand and beautiful. She took the little girl in her arms, and both flew together, joyously and gloriously, mounting higher and higher, far above the earth; and for them there was neither hunger, nor cold, nor care—they were with God.

But in the corner, at the dawn of day, sat the poor girl, leaning against the wall, with red cheeks and smiling mouth—frozen to death on the last evening of the old year. Stiff and cold she sat, with the matches, one bundle of which was burned.

'She wanted to warm herself, poor little thing,' people said. No one imagined what sweet visions she had had, or how gloriously she had gone with her grandmother to enter upon the joys of a new year.

# 17

# The Old Street Lamp

D id you ever hear the story of the old street lamp? It is not remarkably interesting, but for once in a way you may as well listen to it. It was a most respectable old lamp, which had seen many, many years of service, and now was to retire with a pension. It was this evening at its post for the last time, giving light to the street. His feelings were something like those of an old dancer at the theatre, who is dancing for the last time, and knows that on the morrow she will be in her garret, alone and forgotten. The lamp had very great anxiety about the next day, for he knew that he had to appear for the first time at the town hall, to be inspected by the mayor and the council, who were to decide if he were fit for further service or not;—whether the lamp was good enough to be used to light the inhabitants of one of the suburbs, or in the country, at some factory; and if not, it would be sent at once to an iron foundry, to be melted down. In this latter case it might be turned into anything, and he wondered very much whether he would then be able to remember that he had once been a street lamp, and it troubled him exceedingly. Whatever might happen, one thing seemed certain, that he would be separated from the watchman and his wife, whose family he looked upon as his own. The lamp had first been hung up on that very evening that the watchman, then a robust young man, had entered upon the duties of his office. Ah, well, it was a very long time since one became a lamp and the other a watchman. His wife had a little pride in those days; she seldom condescended to glance at the lamp, excepting when she passed by in the evening, never in the daytime. But in later years, when all these,—the watchman, the wife, and the lamp—had grown old, she had attended to it, cleaned it, and supplied it with oil. The old people were thoroughly honest, they had never cheated the lamp of a single drop of the oil provided for it.

This was the lamp's last night in the street, and tomorrow he must go to the town hall,—two very dark things to think of. No wonder he did not burn brightly. Many other thoughts also passed through his mind. How many persons he had lighted on their way, and how much he had seen; as much, very likely, as the mayor and corporation themselves! None of these thoughts were uttered aloud, however; for he was a good, honourable old lamp, who would not willingly do harm to anyone, especially to those in authority. As many things were recalled to his mind, the light would flash up with sudden brightness; he had, at such moments, a conviction that he would be remembered. 'There was a handsome young man once,' thought he; 'it is certainly a long while ago, but I remember he had a little note, written on pink paper with a gold edge; the writing was elegant, evidently a lady's hand: twice he read it through, and kissed it, and then looked up at me, with eyes that said quite plainly, "I am the happiest of men!" Only he and I know what was written on this his first letter from his ladylove. Ah, yes, and there was another pair of eyes that I remember,—it is really wonderful how the thoughts jump from one thing to another! A funeral passed through the street; a young and beautiful woman lay on a bier, decked with garlands of flowers, and attended by torches, which quite overpowered my light. All along the street stood the people from the houses, in crowds, ready to join the procession. But when the torches had passed from before me, and I could look round, I saw one person alone, standing, leaning against my post, and weeping. Never shall I forget the sorrowful eyes that looked up at me.' These and similar reflections occupied the old street lamp, on this the last time that his light would shine. The sentry, when he is relieved from his post, knows at least who will succeed him, and may whisper a few words to him, but the lamp did not know his successor, or he could have given him a few hints respecting rain, or mist, and could have informed him how far the moon's rays would rest on the pavement, and from which side the wind generally blew, and so on.

On the bridge over the canal stood three persons, who wished to recommend themselves to the lamp, for they thought he could give the office to whomsoever[29] he chose. The first was a herring's head, which could emit light in the darkness. He remarked that it would be a great saving of oil if they placed him on the lamppost. Number two was a piece of rotten wood, which also shines in the dark. He considered himself descended from an old stem, once the pride of the forest. The third was a glow-worm, and how he found his way there the lamp could not imagine, yet there he was, and could really give light as well as the others. But the rotten wood and the herring's head declared most solemnly, by all they held sacred, that the glow-worm only gave light at certain times, and must not be allowed to compete with themselves. The old lamp assured them that not one of them could give sufficient light to fill the position of a street lamp; but they would believe nothing he said. And when they discovered that he had not the power of naming his successor, they said they were very glad to hear it, for the lamp was too old and worn-out to make a proper choice.

At this moment the wind came rushing round the corner of the street, and through the air holes of the old lamp. 'What is this I hear?' said he; 'that you are going away tomorrow? Is this evening the last time we shall meet? Then I must present you with a farewell gift. I will blow into your brain, so that in future you shall not only be able to remember all that you have seen or heard in the past, but your light within shall be so bright, that you shall be able to understand all that is said or done in your presence.'

'Oh, that is really a very, very great gift,' said the old lamp; 'I thank you most heartily. I only hope I shall not be melted down.'

'That is not likely to happen yet,' said the wind; 'and I will also blow a memory into you, so that should you receive other similar presents your old age will pass very pleasantly.'

'That is if I am not melted down,' said the lamp. 'But should I in that case still retain my memory?'

'Do be reasonable, old lamp,' said the wind, puffing away.

At this moment the moon burst forth from the clouds. 'What will you give the old lamp?' asked the wind.

'I can give nothing,' she replied; 'I am on the wane, and no lamps have ever given me light while I have frequently shone upon them.' And with these words the moon hid herself again behind the clouds, that she might be saved from further importunities. Just then a drop fell upon the lamp, from the roof of the house, but the drop explained that he was a gift from those grey clouds, and perhaps the best of all gifts. 'I shall penetrate you so thoroughly,' he said, 'that you will have the power of becoming rusty, and, if you wish it, to crumble into dust in one night.'

But this seemed to the lamp a very shabby present, and the wind thought so too. 'Does no one give any more? Will no one give any more?' shouted the breath of the wind, as loud as it could. Then a bright falling star came down, leaving a broad, luminous streak behind it.

'What was that?' cried the herring's head. 'Did not a star fall? I really believe it went into the lamp. Certainly, when such highborn personages try for the office, we may as well say "Good-night," and go home.'

And so they did, all three, while the old lamp threw a wonderfully strong light all around him.

'This is a glorious gift,' said he; 'the bright stars have always been a joy to me, and have always shone more brilliantly than I ever could shine, though I have tried with my whole might; and now they have noticed me, a poor old lamp, and have sent me a gift that will enable me to see clearly everything that I remember, as if it still stood before me, and to be seen by all those who love me. And herein lies the truest pleasure, for joy which we cannot share with others is only half enjoyed.'

'That sentiment does you honour,' said the wind; 'but for this purpose wax lights will be necessary. If these are not lighted in you, your particular faculties will not benefit others in the least. The stars have not thought of this; they suppose that you and every other light must be a wax taper: but I must go down now.' So he laid himself to rest.

'Wax tapers, indeed!' said the lamp, 'I have never yet had these, nor is it likely I ever shall. If I could only be sure of not being melted down!'

The next day. Well, perhaps we had better pass over the next day. The evening had come, and the lamp was resting in a grandfather's chair, and guess where! Why, at the old watchman's house. He had begged, as a favour, that the mayor and corporation would allow him to keep the street lamp, in consideration of his long and faithful service, as he had himself hung it up and lit it on the day he first commenced his duties, four and twenty years ago. He looked upon it almost as his own child; he had no children, so the lamp was given to him. There it lay in the great armchair near to the warm stove. It seemed almost as if it had grown larger, for it appeared quite to fill the chair. The old people sat at their supper, casting friendly glances at the old lamp, whom they would willingly have admitted to a place at the table. It is quite true that they dwelt in a cellar, two yards deep in the earth, and they had to cross a stone passage to get to their room, but within it was warm and comfortable and strips of list had been nailed round the door. The bed and the little window had curtains, and everything looked clean and neat. On the window seat stood two curious flower pots which a sailor, named Christian, had brought over from the East or West Indies. They were of clay, and in the form of two elephants, with open backs; they were hollow and filled with earth, and through the open space flowers bloomed. In one grew some very fine chives or leeks; this was the kitchen garden. The other elephant, which contained a beautiful geranium, they called their flower garden. On the wall hung a large coloured print, representing the congress of Vienna, and all the kings and emperors at once. A clock, with heavy weights, hung on the wall and went 'tick, tick,' steadily enough; yet it was always rather too fast, which, however, the old people said was better than being too slow. They were now eating their supper, while the old street lamp, as we have heard, lay in the grandfather's armchair near the stove. It seemed to the lamp as if the whole world had turned round; but after a while the old watchman looked at the lamp, and spoke of what they had both gone through together,—in rain and in fog; during the short bright nights of summer, or in the long winter nights, through the drifting snowstorms, when he longed to be at home in the cellar. Then the lamp felt it was all right again. He saw everything that had happened quite clearly, as if it were passing before him. Surely the wind had given him an excellent gift. The old people were very active and industrious, they were never idle for even a single hour. On Sunday afternoons they would bring out some books, generally a book of travels which they were very fond of. The old man would read aloud about Africa, with its great forests and the wild elephants, while his wife would listen attentively, stealing a glance now and then at the clay elephants, which served as flower pots.

'I can almost imagine I am seeing it all,' she said; and then how the lamp wished for a wax taper to be lighted in him, for then the old woman would have seen the smallest detail as clearly as he did himself. The lofty trees, with their thickly entwined branches, the naked negroes on horseback, and whole herds of elephants treading down bamboo thickets with their broad, heavy feet.

'What is the use of all my capabilities,' sighed the old lamp, 'when I cannot obtain any wax lights; they have only oil and tallow here, and these will not do.' One day a great heap of wax candle ends found their way into the cellar. The larger pieces were burnt, and the smaller ones the old woman kept for waxing her thread. So there were now candles enough, but it never occurred to anyone to put a little piece in the lamp.

'Here I am now with my rare powers,' thought the lamp, 'I have faculties within me, but I cannot share them; they do not know that I could cover these white walls with beautiful tapestry, or change them into noble forests, or, indeed, to anything else they might wish for.' The lamp, however, was always kept clean and shining in a corner where it attracted all eyes. Strangers looked upon it as lumber, but the old people did not care for that; they loved the lamp. One day—it was the watchman's birthday—the old woman approached the lamp, smiling to herself, and said, 'I will have an illumination today in honour of my old man.' And the lamp rattled in his metal frame, for he thought, 'Now at last I shall have a light within me,' but after all no wax light was placed in the lamp, but oil as usual. The lamp burned through the whole evening, and began to perceive too clearly that the gift of the stars would remain a hidden treasure all his life. Then he had a dream; for, to one with his faculties, dreaming was no difficulty. It appeared to him that the old people were dead, and that he had been taken to the iron foundry to be melted down. It caused him quite as much anxiety as on the day when he had been called upon to appear before the mayor and the council at the town hall. But though he had been endowed with the power of falling into decay from rust when he pleased, he did not make use of it. He was therefore put into the melting furnace and changed into as elegant an iron candlestick as you could wish to see, one intended to hold a wax taper. The candlestick was in the form of an angel holding a nosegay, in the centre of which the wax taper was to be placed. It was to stand on a green writing table, in a very pleasant room; many books were scattered about, and splendid paintings hung on the walls. The owner of the room was a poet, and a man of intellect; everything he thought or wrote was pictured around him. Nature showed herself to him sometimes in the dark forests, at others in cheerful meadows where the storks were strutting about, or on the deck of a ship sailing across the foaming sea with the clear, blue sky above, or at night the glittering stars. 'What powers I possess!' said the lamp, awaking from his dream; 'I could almost wish to be melted down; but no, that must not be while the old people live. They love me for myself alone, they keep me bright, and supply me with oil. I am as well off as the picture of the congress, in which they take so much pleasure.' And from that time he felt at rest in himself, and not more so than such an honourable old lamp really deserved to be.

# 18

# The Shadow

It is in the hot lands that the sun burns, sure enough! There
the people become quite a mahogany brown, ay[30], and in the
HOTTEST lands they are burnt to Negroes. But now it was only to
the HOT lands that a learned man had come from the cold; there
he thought that he could run about just as when at home, but he
soon found out his mistake.

He, and all sensible folks, were obliged to stay within doors—
the window shutters and doors were closed the whole day; it
looked as if the whole house slept, or there was no one at home.

The narrow street with the high houses, was built so that the
sunshine must fall there from morning till evening—it was really
not to be borne.

The learned man from the cold lands—he was a young man,
and seemed to be a clever man—sat in a glowing oven; it took
effect on him, he became quite meagre—even his shadow shrunk
in, for the sun had also an effect on it. It was first towards evening
when the sun was down, that they began to freshen up again.

In the warm lands every window has a balcony, and the people
came out on all the balconies in the street—for one must have air,
even if one be accustomed to be mahogany! It was lively both up
and down the street. Tailors, and shoemakers, and all the folks,
moved out into the street—chairs and tables were brought forth—

and candles burnt—yes, above a thousand lights were burning—
and the one talked and the other sung; and people walked and
church bells rang, and asses went along with a dingle-dingle-dong!
For they too had bells on. The street boys were screaming and
hooting, and shouting and shooting, with devils and detonating
balls—and there came corpse bearers and hood wearers—for there
were funerals with psalm and hymn—and then the din of carriages
driving and company arriving: yes, it was, in truth, lively enough
down in the street. Only in that single house, which stood opposite
that in which the learned foreigner lived, it was quite still; and yet
someone lived there, for there stood flowers in the balcony—they
grew so well in the sun's heat! And that they could not do unless
they were watered—and someone must water them—there must
be somebody there. The door opposite was also opened late in the
evening, but it was dark within, at least in the front room; further
in there was heard the sound of music. The learned foreigner
thought it quite marvellous, but now—it might be that he only
imagined it—for he found everything marvellous out there, in the
warm lands, if there had only been no sun. The stranger's landlord
said that he didn't know who had taken the house opposite, one
saw no person about, and as to the music, it appeared to him to

be extremely tiresome. 'It is as if someone sat there, and practised a piece that he could not master—always the same piece. "I shall master it!" says he; but yet he cannot master it, however long he plays.'

One night the stranger awoke—he slept with the doors of the balcony open—the curtain before it was raised by the wind, and he thought that a strange lustre came from the opposite neighbour's house; all the flowers shone like flames, in the most beautiful colours, and in the midst of the flowers stood a slender, graceful maiden—it was as if she also shone; the light really hurt his eyes. He now opened them quite wide—yes, he was quite awake; with one spring he was on the floor; he crept gently behind the curtain, but the maiden was gone; the flowers shone no longer, but there they stood, fresh and blooming as ever; the door was ajar, and, far within, the music sounded so soft and delightful, one could really melt away in sweet thoughts from it. Yet it was like a piece of enchantment. And who lived there? Where was the actual entrance? The whole of the ground floor was a row of shops, and there people could not always be running through.

One evening the stranger sat out on the balcony. The light burnt in the room behind him; and thus it was quite natural that his shadow should fall on his opposite neighbour's wall. Yes! There it sat, directly opposite, between the flowers on the balcony; and when the stranger moved, the shadow also moved: for that it always does.

'I think my shadow is the only living thing one sees over there,' said the learned man. 'See, how nicely it sits between the flowers. The door stands half-open: now the shadow should be cunning, and go into the room, look about, and then come and tell me what it had seen. Come, now! Be useful, and do me a service,' said he, in jest. 'Have the kindness to step in. Now! Art thou going?' and then he nodded to the shadow, and the shadow nodded again. 'Well then, go! But don't stay away.'

The stranger rose, and his shadow on the opposite neighbour's balcony rose also; the stranger turned round and the shadow also turned round. Yes! If anyone had paid particular attention to it, they would have seen, quite distinctly, that the shadow went in through the half-open balcony door of their opposite neighbour, just as the stranger went into his own room, and let the long curtain fall down after him.

Next morning, the learned man went out to drink coffee and read the newspapers.

'What is that?' said he, as he came out into the sunshine.

'I have no shadow! So then, it has actually gone last night, and not come again. It is really tiresome!'

This annoyed him: not so much because the shadow was gone, but because he knew there was a story about a man without a shadow. It was known to everybody at home, in the cold lands; and if the learned man now came there and told his story, they would say that he was imitating it, and that he had no need to do. He would, therefore, not talk about it at all; and that was wisely thought.

In the evening he went out again on the balcony. He had placed the light directly behind him, for he knew that the shadow would always have its master for a screen, but he could not entice it. He made himself little; he made himself great: but no shadow came again. He said, 'Hem! Hem!' but it was of no use.

It was vexatious; but in the warm lands everything grows so

quickly; and after the lapse of eight days he observed, to his great joy, that a new shadow came in the sunshine. In the course of three weeks he had a very fair shadow, which, when he set out for his home in the northern lands, grew more and more in the journey, so that at last it was so long and so large, that it was more than sufficient.

The learned man then came home, and he wrote books about what was true in the world, and about what was good and what was beautiful; and there passed days and years—yes! Many years passed away.

One evening, as he was sitting in his room, there was a gentle knocking at the door.

'Come in!' said he; but no one came in; so he opened the door, and there stood before him such an extremely lean man, that he felt quite strange. As to the rest, the man was very finely dressed— he must be a gentleman.

'Whom have I the honour of speaking?' asked the learned man.

'Yes! I thought as much,' said the fine man. 'I thought you would not know me. I have got so much body. I have even got flesh and clothes. You certainly never thought of seeing me so well off. Do you not know your old shadow? You certainly thought I should never more return. Things have gone on well with me since I was last with you. I have, in all respects, become very well off. Shall I purchase my freedom from service? If so, I can do it'; and then he rattled a whole bunch of valuable seals that hung to his watch, and he stuck his hand in the thick gold chain he wore around his neck—nay! How all his fingers glittered with diamond rings; and then all were pure gems.

'Nay; I cannot recover from my surprise!' said the learned man.

'What is the meaning of all this?'

'Something common, is it not,' said the shadow. 'But you yourself do not belong to the common order; and I, as you know well, have from a child followed in your footsteps. As soon as you found I was capable to go out alone in the world, I went my own way. I am in the most brilliant circumstances, but there came a sort of desire over me to see you once more before you die; you will die, I suppose? I also wished to see this land again—for you know we always love our native land. I know you have got another shadow again; have I anything to pay to it or you? If so, you will oblige me by saying what it is.'

'Nay, is it really thou?' said the learned man. 'It is most remarkable: I never imagined that one's old shadow could come again as a man.'

'Tell me what I have to pay,' said the shadow; 'for I don't like to be in any sort of debt.'

'How canst[31] thou talk so?' said the learned man. 'What debt is there to talk about? Make thyself as free as anyone else. I am extremely glad to hear of thy good fortune: sit down, old friend, and tell me a little how it has gone with thee, and what thou hast[32] seen at our opposite neighbour's there—in the warm lands.'

'Yes, I will tell you all about it,' said the shadow, and sat down: 'but then you must also promise me, that, wherever you may meet me, you will never say to anyone here in the town that I have been your shadow. I intend to get betrothed, for I can provide for more than one family.'

'Be quite at thy ease about that,' said the learned man; 'I shall not say to anyone who thou actually art: here is my hand—I promise it, and a man's bond is his word.'

'A word is a shadow,' said the shadow, 'and as such it must speak.'

It was really quite astonishing how much of a man it was. It was dressed entirely in black, and of the very finest cloth; it had patent leather boots, and a hat that could be folded together, so that it was bare crown and brim; not to speak of what we already know it had—seals, gold neck chain, and diamond rings; yes, the shadow was well-dressed, and it was just that which made it quite a man.

'Now I shall tell you my adventures,' said the shadow; and then he sat, with the polished boots, as heavily as he could, on the arm of the learned man's new shadow, which lay like a poodle dog at his feet. Now this was perhaps from arrogance; and the shadow on the ground kept itself so still and quiet, that it might hear all that passed: it wished to know how it could get free, and work its way up, so as to become its own master.

'Do you know who lived in our opposite neighbour's house?' said the shadow. 'It was the most charming of all beings, it was Poesy! I was there for three weeks, and that has as much effect as if one had lived three thousand years, and read all that was composed and written; that is what I say, and it is right. I have seen everything and I know everything!'

'Poesy!' cried the learned man. 'Yes, yes, she often dwells a recluse in large cities! Poesy! Yes, I have seen her—a single short moment, but sleep came into my eyes! She stood on the balcony and shone as the Aurora Borealis shines. Go on, go on—thou wert[33] on the balcony, and went through the doorway, and then—'

'Then I was in the antechamber,' said the shadow. 'You always sat and looked over to the antechamber. There was no light;

there was a sort of twilight, but the one door stood open directly opposite the other through a long row of rooms and saloons, and there it was lighted up. I should have been completely killed if I had gone over to the maiden; but I was circumspect, I took time to think, and that one must always do.'

'And what didst[34] thou then see?' asked the learned man.

'I saw everything, and I shall tell all to you: but—it is no pride on my part—as a free man, and with the knowledge I have, not to speak of my position in life, my excellent circumstances—I certainly wish that you would say YOU to me!'

'I beg your pardon,' said the learned man; 'it is an old habit with me. YOU are perfectly right, and I shall remember it; but now you must tell me all YOU saw!'

'Everything!' said the shadow. 'For I saw everything, and I know everything!'

'How did it look in the furthest saloon?' asked the learned man. 'Was it there as in the fresh woods? Was it there as in a holy church? Were the saloons like the starlit firmament when we stand on the high mountains?'

'Everything was there!' said the shadow. 'I did not go quite in, I remained in the foremost room, in the twilight, but I stood there quite well; I saw everything, and I know everything! I have been in the antechamber at the court of Poesy.'

'But WHAT DID you see? Did all the gods of the olden times pass through the large saloons? Did the old heroes combat there? Did sweet children play there, and relate their dreams?'

'I tell you I was there, and you can conceive that I saw everything there was to be seen. Had you come over there, you would not have been a man; but I became so! And besides, I learned to know my inward nature, my innate qualities, the relationship I had with Poesy. At the time I was with you, I thought not of that, but always—you know it well—when the sun rose, and when the sun went down, I became so strangely great; in the moonlight I was very near being more distinct than yourself; at that time I did not understand my nature; it was revealed to me in the antechamber! I became a man! I came out matured; but you were no longer in the warm lands; as a man I was ashamed to go as I did. I was in want of boots, of clothes, of the whole human varnish that makes a man perceptible. I took my way—I tell it to you, but you will not put it in any book—I took my way to the cake woman—I hid myself behind her; the woman didn't think how much she concealed. I went out first in the evening; I ran about the streets in the moonlight; I made myself long up the walls—it tickles the back so delightfully! I ran up, and ran down, peeped into the highest windows, into the saloons, and on the roofs, I peeped in where no one could peep, and I saw what no one else saw, what no one else should see! This is, in fact, a base world! I would not be a man if it were not now once accepted and regarded as something to be so! I saw the most unimaginable things with the women, with the men, with parents, and with the sweet, matchless children; I saw,' said the shadow, 'what no human being must know, but what they would all so willingly know—what is bad in their neighbour. Had I written a newspaper, it would have been read! But I wrote direct to the persons themselves, and there was consternation in all the towns where I came. They were so afraid of me, and yet they were so excessively fond of me. The professors made a professor of me; the tailors gave me new clothes—I am well furnished; the master of the mint struck new coin for me, and the women said I was so handsome! And so I became the man I am. And I now bid you farewell. Here is my card—I live on the sunny side of the street, and am always at home in rainy weather!' And so away went the shadow.

'That was most extraordinary!' said the learned man. Years and days passed away, then the shadow came again. 'How goes it?' said the shadow.

'Alas!' said the learned man. 'I write about the true, and the good, and the beautiful, but no one cares to hear such things; I am quite desperate, for I take it so much to heart!'

'But I don't!' said the shadow. 'I become fat, and it is that one wants to become! You do not understand the world. You will become ill by it. You must travel! I shall make a tour this summer; will you go with me? I should like to have a travelling companion! Will you go with me, as shadow? It will be a great pleasure for me to have you with me; I shall pay the travelling expenses!'

'Nay, this is too much!' said the learned man.

'It is just as one takes it!' said the shadow. 'It will do you much good to travel! Will you be my shadow? You shall have everything free on the journey!'

'Nay, that is too bad!' said the learned man.

'But it is just so with the world!' said the shadow, 'and so it will be!' and away it went again.

The learned man was not at all in the most enviable state; grief and torment followed him, and what he said about the true, and the good, and the beautiful, was, to most persons, like roses for a cow! He was quite ill at last.

'You really look like a shadow!' said his friends to him; and the learned man trembled, for he thought of it.

'You must go to a watering place!' said the shadow, who came and visited him. 'There is nothing else for it! I will take you with me for old acquaintance' sake; I will pay the travelling expenses, and you write the descriptions—and if they are a little amusing for me on the way! I will go to a watering place—my beard does not grow out as it ought—that is also a sickness—and one must have a beard! Now you be wise and accept the offer; we shall travel as comrades!'

And so they travelled; the shadow was master, and the master was the shadow; they drove with each other, they rode and walked together, side by side, before and behind, just as the sun was; the shadow always took care to keep itself in the master's place. Now the learned man didn't think much about that; he was a very kind-hearted man, and particularly mild and friendly, and so he said one day to the shadow: 'As we have now become companions, and in this way have grown up together from childhood, shall we not drink "thou" together, it is more familiar?'

'You are right,' said the shadow, who was now the proper master. 'It is said in a very straightforward and well-meant manner. You, as a learned man, certainly know how strange nature is. Some persons cannot bear to touch grey paper, or they become ill; others shiver in every limb if one rub a pane of glass with a nail: I have just such a feeling on hearing you say thou to me; I feel myself as if pressed to the earth in my first situation with you. You see that it is a feeling; that it is not pride: I cannot allow you to say THOU to me, but I will willingly say THOU to you, so it is half done!'

So the shadow said THOU to its former master.

'This is rather too bad,' thought he, 'that I must say YOU and he say THOU,' but he was now obliged to put up with it.

So they came to a watering place where there were many strangers, and amongst them was a princess, who was troubled with seeing too well; and that was so alarming!

She directly observed that the stranger who had just come was quite a different sort of person to all the others;—'He has come here in order to get his beard to grow, they say, but I see the real cause, he cannot cast a shadow.'

She had become inquisitive; and so she entered into conversation directly with the strange gentleman, on their promenades. As the daughter of a king, she needed not to stand upon trifles, so she said, 'Your complaint is, that you cannot cast a shadow?'

'Your Royal Highness must be improving considerably,' said the shadow, 'I know your complaint is, that you see too clearly, but it has decreased, you are cured. I just happen to have a very unusual shadow! Do you not see that person who always goes with me? Other persons have a common shadow, but I do not like what is common to all. We give our servants finer cloth for their livery than we ourselves use, and so I had my shadow trimmed up into a man: yes, you see I have even given him a shadow. It is somewhat expensive, but I like to have something for myself!'

'What!' thought the princess. 'Should I really be cured! These baths are the first in the world! In our time water has wonderful powers. But I shall not leave the place, for it now begins to be amusing here. I am extremely fond of that stranger: would that his beard should not grow, for in that case he will leave us!'

In the evening, the princess and the shadow danced together in the large ballroom. She was light, but he was still lighter; she had never had such a partner in the dance. She told him from what land she came, and he knew that land; he had been there, but then she was not at home; he had peeped in at the window, above and below—he had seen both the one and the other, and so he could answer the princess, and make insinuations, so that she was quite astonished; he must be the wisest man in the whole world! She felt such respect for what he knew! So that when they again danced together she fell in love with him; and that the shadow could remark, for she almost pierced him through with her eyes. So they danced once more together; and she was about to declare herself, but she was discreet; she thought of her country and kingdom, and of the many persons she would have to reign over.

'He is a wise man,' said she to herself—'It is well; and he dances delightfully—that is also good; but has he solid knowledge? That is just as important! He must be examined.' So she began, by degrees, to question him about the most difficult things she could think of, and which she herself could not have answered; so that the shadow made a strange face.

'You cannot answer these questions?' said the princess.

'They belong to my childhood's learning,' said the shadow. 'I really believe my shadow, by the door there, can answer them!'

'Your shadow!' said the princess. 'That would indeed be marvellous!'

'I will not say for a certainty that he can,' said the shadow, 'but I think so; he has now followed me for so many years, and listened to my conversation—I should think it possible. But your royal highness will permit me to observe, that he is so proud of passing himself off for a man, that when he is to be in a proper humour— and he must be so to answer well—he must be treated quite like a man.'

'Oh! I like that!' said the princess.

So she went to the learned man by the door, and she spoke to him about the sun and the moon, and about persons out of and in the world, and he answered with wisdom and prudence.

'What a man that must be who has so wise a shadow!' thought she. 'It will be a real blessing to my people and kingdom if I choose him for my consort—I will do it!'

They were soon agreed, both the princess and the shadow; but no one was to know about it before she arrived in her own kingdom.

'No one—not even my shadow!' said the shadow, and he had his own thoughts about it!

Now they were in the country where the princess reigned when she was at home.

'Listen, my good friend,' said the shadow to the learned man. 'I have now become as happy and mighty as anyone can be; I will, therefore, do something particular for thee! Thou shalt[35] always live with me in the palace, drive with me in my royal carriage, and have ten thousand pounds a year; but then thou must submit to be called SHADOW by all and everyone; thou must not say that thou hast[36] ever been a man; and once a year, when I sit on the balcony in the sunshine, thou must lie at my feet, as a shadow shall do! I must tell thee: I am going to marry the king's daughter, and the nuptials are to take place this evening!'

'Nay, this is going too far!' said the learned man. 'I will not have it; I will not do it! It is to deceive the whole country and the princess too! I will tell everything! That I am a man, and that thou art a shadow—thou art only dressed up!'

'There is no one who will believe it!' said the shadow. 'Be

reasonable, or I will call the guard!'

'I will go directly to the princess!' said the learned man.

'But I will go first!' said the shadow. 'And thou wilt[37] go to prison!' and that he was obliged to do—for the sentinels obeyed him whom they knew the king's daughter was to marry.

'You tremble!' said the princess, as the shadow came into her chamber. 'Has anything happened? You must not be unwell this evening, now that we are to have our nuptials celebrated.'

'I have lived to see the most cruel thing that anyone can live to see!' said the shadow. 'Only imagine—yes, it is true, such a poor shadow skull cannot bear much—only think, my shadow has become mad; he thinks that he is a man, and that I—now only think—that I am his shadow!'

'It is terrible!' said the princess; 'but he is confined, is he not?'

'That he is. I am afraid that he will never recover.'

'Poor shadow!' said the princess. 'He is very unfortunate; it would be a real work of charity to deliver him from the little life he has, and, when I think properly over the matter, I am of opinion that it will be necessary to do away with him in all stillness!'

'It is certainly hard,' said the shadow, 'for he was a faithful servant!' and then he gave a sort of sigh.

'You are a noble character!' said the princess.

The whole city was illuminated in the evening, and the cannons went off with a bum! Bum! And the soldiers presented arms. That was a marriage! The princess and the shadow went out on the balcony to show themselves, and get another hurrah!

The learned man heard nothing of all this—for they had deprived him of life.

19

# The Pea Blossom

There were once five peas in one shell, they were green, the shell was green, and so they believed that the whole world must be green also, which was a very natural conclusion. The shell grew, and the peas grew, they accommodated themselves to their position, and sat all in a row. The sun shone without and warmed the shell, and the rain made it clear and transparent; it was mild and agreeable in broad daylight, and dark at night, as it generally is; and the peas as they sat there grew bigger and bigger, and more thoughtful as they mused, for they felt there must be something else for them to do.

'Are we to sit here forever?' asked one; 'shall we not become hard by sitting so long? It seems to me there must be something outside, and I feel sure of it.'

And as weeks passed by, the peas became yellow, and the shell became yellow.

'All the world is turning yellow, I suppose,' said they,—and perhaps they were right.

Suddenly they felt a pull at the shell; it was torn off, and held in human hands, then slipped into the pocket of a jacket in company with other full pods.

'Now we shall soon be opened,' said one,—just what they all wanted.

'I should like to know which of us will travel furthest,' said the smallest of the five; 'we shall soon see now.'

'What is to happen will happen,' said the largest pea.

'Crack' went the shell as it burst, and the five peas rolled out into the bright sunshine. There they lay in a child's hand. A little boy was holding them tightly, and said they were fine peas for his peashooter. And immediately he put one in and shot it out.

'Now I am flying out into the wide world,' said he; 'catch me if you can;' and he was gone in a moment.

'I,' said the second, 'intend to fly straight to the sun, that is a shell that lets itself be seen, and it will suit me exactly;' and away he went.

'We will go to sleep wherever we find ourselves,' said the two next, 'we shall still be rolling onwards;' and they did certainly fall on the floor, and roll about before they got into the peashooter; but they were put in for all that. 'We shall go further than the others,' said they.

'What is to happen will happen,' exclaimed the last, as he was shot out of the peashooter; and as he spoke he flew up against an old board under a garret window, and fell into a little crevice, which was almost filled up with moss and soft earth. The moss closed itself round him, and there he lay, a captive indeed, but not unnoticed by God.

'What is to happen will happen,' said he to himself.

Within the little garret lived a poor woman, who went out to clean stoves, chop wood into small pieces and perform suchlike hard work, for she was strong and industrious. Yet she remained always poor, and at home in the garret lay her only daughter, not quite grown up, and very delicate and weak. For a whole year she

had kept her bed, and it seemed as if she could neither live nor die.

'She is going to her little sister,' said the woman; 'I had but the two children, and it was not an easy thing to support both of them; but the good God helped me in my work, and took one of them to Himself and provided for her. Now I would gladly keep the other that was left to me, but I suppose they are not to be separated, and my sick girl will very soon go to her sister above.' But the sick girl still remained where she was, quietly and patiently she lay all the day long, while her mother was away from home at her work.

Spring came, and one morning early the sun shone brightly through the little window, and threw its rays over the floor of the room. Just as the mother was going to her work, the sick girl fixed her gaze on the lowest pane of the window—'Mother,' she exclaimed, 'what can that little green thing be that peeps in at the window? It is moving in the wind.'

The mother stepped to the window and half opened it. 'Oh!' she said, 'there is actually a little pea which has taken root and is putting out its green leaves. How could it have got into this crack? Well now, here is a little garden for you to amuse yourself with.'

So the bed of the sick girl was drawn nearer to the window, that she might see the budding plant; and the mother went out to her work.

'Mother, I believe I shall get well,' said the sick child in the evening, 'the sun has shone in here so brightly and warmly today, and the little pea is thriving so well: I shall get on better, too, and go out into the warm sunshine again.'

'God grant it!' said the mother, but she did not believe it would be so. But she propped up with the little stick the green plant which had given her child such pleasant hopes of life, so that it might not be broken by the winds; she tied the piece of string to the windowsill and to the upper part of the frame, so that the pea tendrils might twine round it when it shot up. And it did shoot up, indeed it might almost be seen to grow from day to day.

'Now really here is a flower coming,' said the old woman one morning, and now at last she began to encourage the hope that her sick daughter might really recover. She remembered that for some time the child had spoken more cheerfully, and during the last few days had raised herself in bed in the morning to look with sparkling eyes at her little garden which contained only a single pea plant. A week after, the invalid sat up for the first time a whole hour, feeling quite happy by the open window in the warm sunshine, while outside grew the little plant, and on it a pink pea blossom in full bloom. The little maiden bent down and gently kissed the delicate leaves. This day was to her like a festival.

'Our heavenly Father Himself has planted that pea, and made it grow and flourish, to bring joy to you and hope to me, my blessed child,' said the happy mother, and she smiled at the flower, as if it had been an angel from God.

But what became of the other peas? Why the one who flew out into the wide world, and said, 'Catch me if you can,' fell into a gutter on the roof of a house, and ended his travels in the crop of a pigeon. The two lazy ones were carried quite as far, for they also were eaten by pigeons, so they were at least of some use; but the fourth, who wanted to reach the sun, fell into a sink and lay there in the dirty water for days and weeks, till he had swelled to a great size.

'I am getting beautifully fat,' said the pea, 'I expect I shall burst at last; no pea could do more than that, I think; I am the most remarkable of all the five which were in the shell.' And the sink confirmed the opinion.

But the young maiden stood at the open garret window, with sparkling eyes and the rosy hue of health on her cheeks, she folded her thin hands over the pea blossom, and thanked God for what He had done.

'I,' said the sink, 'shall stand up for *my* pea.'

# 20

# She Was Good for Nothing

The mayor stood at the open window. He looked smart, for his shirt frill, in which he had stuck a breastpin, and his ruffles, were very fine. He had shaved his chin uncommonly smooth, although he had cut himself slightly, and had stuck a piece of newspaper over the place. 'Hark'ee[38], youngster!' cried he.

The boy to whom he spoke was no other than the son of a poor washerwoman, who was just going past the house. He stopped, and respectfully took off his cap. The peak of this cap was broken in the middle, so that he could easily roll it up and put it in his pocket. He stood before the mayor in his poor but clean and well-mended clothes, with heavy wooden shoes on his feet, looking as humble as if it had been the king himself.

'You are a good and civil boy,' said the mayor. 'I suppose your mother is busy washing the clothes down by the river, and you are going to carry that thing to her that you have in your pocket. It is very bad for your mother. How much have you got in it?'

'Only half a quartern,' stammered the boy in a frightened voice.

'And she has had just as much this morning already?'

'No, it was yesterday,' replied the boy.

'Two halves make a whole,' said the mayor. 'She's good for nothing. What a sad thing it is with these people. Tell your mother she ought to be ashamed of herself. Don't you become a drunkard, but I expect you will though. Poor child! There, go now.'

The boy went on his way with his cap in his hand, while the wind fluttered his golden hair till the locks stood up straight. He turned round the corner of the street into the little lane that led to the river, where his mother stood in the water by her washing bench, beating the linen with a heavy wooden bar. The floodgates at the mill had been drawn up, and as the water rolled rapidly on, the sheets were dragged along by the stream, and nearly overturned the bench, so that the washerwoman was obliged to lean against it to keep it steady. 'I have been very nearly carried away,' she said; 'it is a good thing that you are come[39], for I want something to strengthen me. It is cold in the water, and I have stood here six hours. Have you brought anything for me?'

The boy drew the bottle from his pocket, and the mother put it to her lips, and drank a little.

'Ah, how much good that does, and how it warms me,' she said; 'it is as good as a hot meal, and not so dear. Drink a little, my boy; you look quite pale; you are shivering in your thin clothes, and autumn has really come. Oh, how cold the water is! I hope I shall not be ill. But no, I must not be afraid of that. Give me a little more, and you may have a sip too, but only a sip; you must not get used to it, my poor, dear child.' She stepped up to the bridge on which the boy stood as she spoke, and came on shore. The water dripped from the straw mat which she had bound round her body, and from her gown. 'I work hard and suffer pain with my poor hands,' said she, 'but I do it willingly, that I may be able to bring you up honestly and truthfully, my dear boy.'

At the same moment, a woman, rather older than herself, came towards them. She was a miserable-looking object, lame of one leg, and with a large false curl hanging down over one of her eyes, which was blind. This curl was intended to conceal the blind eye, but it made the defect only more visible. She was a friend of the laundress, and was called, among the neighbours, 'Lame Martha, with the curl.' 'Oh, you poor thing; how you do work, standing there in the water!' she exclaimed. 'You really do need something to give you a little warmth, and yet spiteful people cry out about the few drops you take.' And then Martha repeated to the laundress, in a very few minutes, all that the mayor had said to her boy, which she had overheard; and she felt very angry that any man could speak, as he had done, of a mother to her own child, about the few drops she had taken; and she was still more angry because, on that very day, the mayor was going to have a dinner party, at which there would be wine, strong, rich wine, drunk by the bottle. 'Many will take more than they ought, but they don't call that drinking! They are all right, you are good for nothing indeed!' cried Martha indignantly.

'And so he spoke to you in that way, did he, my child?' said the washerwoman, and her lips trembled as she spoke. 'He says you have a mother who is good for nothing. Well, perhaps he is right, but he should not have said it to my child. How much has happened to me from that house!'

'Yes,' said Martha; 'I remember you were in service there, and lived in the house when the mayor's parents were alive; how many years ago that is. Bushels of salt have been eaten since then, and people may well be thirsty,' and Martha smiled. 'The mayor's great dinner party today ought to have been put off, but the news came too late. The footman told me the dinner was already cooked, when a letter came to say that the mayor's younger brother in Copenhagen is dead.'

'Dead!' cried the laundress, turning pale as death.

'Yes, certainly,' replied Martha; 'but why do you take it so much to heart? I suppose you knew him years ago, when you were in service there?'

'Is he dead?' she exclaimed. 'Oh, he was such a kind, good-hearted man, there are not many like him,' and the tears rolled down her cheeks as she spoke. Then she cried, 'Oh, dear me; I feel quite ill: everything is going round me, I cannot bear it. Is the bottle empty?' and she leaned against the plank.

'Dear me, you are ill indeed,' said the other woman. 'Come, cheer up; perhaps it will pass off. No, indeed, I see you are really ill; the best thing for me to do is to lead you home.'

'But my washing yonder?'

'I will take care of that. Come, give me your arm. The boy can stay here and take care of the linen, and I'll come back and finish the washing; it is but a trifle.'

The limbs of the laundress shook under her, and she said, 'I have stood too long in the cold water, and I have had nothing to eat the whole day since the morning. O kind Heaven, help me to get home; I am in a burning fever. Oh, my poor child,' and she burst into tears. And he, poor boy, wept also, as he sat alone by the river, near to and watching the damp linen.

The two women walked very slowly. The laundress slipped and tottered through the lane, and round the corner, into the street where the mayor lived; and just as she reached the front of his house, she sank down upon the pavement. Many persons came round her, and Lame Martha ran into the house for help. The mayor and his guests came to the window.

'Oh, it is the laundress,' said he; 'she has had a little drop too much. She is good for nothing. It is a sad thing for her pretty little son. I like the boy very well; but the mother is good for nothing.'

After a while the laundress recovered herself, and they led her to her poor dwelling, and put her to bed. Kind Martha warmed a mug of beer for her, with butter and sugar—she considered this the best medicine—and then hastened to the river, washed and rinsed, badly enough, to be sure, but she did her best. Then she drew the linen ashore, wet as it was, and laid it in a basket. Before evening, she was sitting in the poor little room with the laundress. The mayor's cook had given her some roasted potatoes and a beautiful piece of fat for the sick woman. Martha and the boy enjoyed these good things very much; but the sick woman could only say that the smell was very nourishing, she thought. By and by the boy was put to bed, in the same bed as the one in which his mother lay; but he slept at her feet, covered with an old quilt made of blue and white patchwork. The laundress felt a little better by this time. The warm beer had strengthened her, and the smell of the good food had been pleasant to her.

'Many thanks, you good soul,' she said to Martha. 'Now the boy is asleep, I will tell you all. He is soon asleep. How gentle and sweet he looks as he lies there with his eyes closed! He does not know how his mother has suffered; and Heaven grant he never may know it. I was in service at the counsellor's, the father of the mayor, and it happened that the youngest of his sons, the student, came home. I was a young wild girl then, but honest; that I can declare in the sight of Heaven. The student was merry and gay, brave and affectionate; every drop of blood in him was good and honourable; a better man never lived on earth. He was the son of the house, and I was only a maid; but he loved me truly and honourably, and he told his mother of it. She was to him as an angel upon earth; she was so wise and loving. He went to travel, and before he started he placed a gold ring on my finger; and as soon as he was out of the house, my mistress sent for me. Gently and earnestly she drew me to her, and spake as if an angel were speaking. She showed me clearly, in spirit and in truth, the difference there was between him and me. "He is pleased now," she said, "with your pretty face; but good looks do not last long. You have not been educated like he has. You are not equals in mind and rank, and therein lies the misfortune. I esteem the poor," she added. "In the sight of God, they may occupy a higher place than many of the rich; but here upon earth we must beware of entering upon a false track, lest we are overturned in our plans, like a carriage that travels by a dangerous road. I know a worthy man, an artisan, who wishes to marry you. I mean Eric, the glovemaker. He is a widower, without children, and in a good position. Will you think it over?" Every word she said pierced my heart like a knife; but I knew she was right, and the thought pressed heavily upon me. I kissed her hand, and wept bitter tears, and I wept still more when I went to my room, and threw myself on the bed. I passed through a dreadful night; God knows what I suffered, and how I struggled. The following Sunday I went to the house of God to pray for light to direct my path. It seemed like a providence that as I stepped out of church Eric came towards me; and then there remained not a doubt in my mind. We were suited to each other in rank and circumstances. He was, even then, a man of good means. I went up to him, and took his hand, and said, "Do you still feel the same for me?" "Yes; ever and always," said he. "Will you, then, marry a maiden who honours and esteems you, although she cannot offer you her love? But that may come." "Yes, it will come," said he; and we joined our hands together, and I went home to my mistress. The gold ring which her son had given me I wore next to my heart. I could not place it on my finger during the daytime, but only in the evening, when I went to bed. I kissed the ring till my lips almost bled, and then I gave it to my mistress, and told her that the banns were to be put up for me and the glovemaker the following week. Then my mistress threw her arms round me, and kissed me. She did not say that I was "good for nothing;" very likely I was better then than I am now; but the misfortunes of this world, were unknown to me then. At Michaelmas we were married, and for the first year everything went well with us. We had a journeyman and an apprentice, and you were our servant, Martha.'

'Ah, yes, and you were a dear, good mistress,' said Martha, 'I shall never forget how kind you and your husband were to me.'

'Yes, those were happy years when you were with us, although we had no children at first. The student I never met again. Yet

I saw him once, although he did not see me. He came to his mother's funeral. I saw him, looking pale as death, and deeply troubled, standing at her grave; for she was his mother. Sometime after, when his father died, he was in foreign lands, and did not come home. I know that he never married, I believe he became a lawyer. He had forgotten me, and even had we met he would not have known me, for I have lost all my good looks, and perhaps that is all for the best.' And then she spoke of the dark days of trial, when misfortune had fallen upon them.

'We had five hundred dollars,' she said, 'and there was a house in the street to be sold for two hundred, so we thought it would be worth our while to pull it down and build a new one in its place; so it was bought. The builder and carpenter made an estimate that the new house would cost ten hundred and twenty dollars to build. Eric had credit, so he borrowed the money in the chief town. But the captain, who was bringing it to him, was shipwrecked, and the money lost. Just about this time, my dear sweet boy, who lies sleeping there, was born, and my husband was attacked with a severe lingering illness. For three quarters of a year I was obliged to dress and undress him. We were backward in our payments, we borrowed more money, and all that we had was lost and sold, and then my husband died. Since then I have worked, toiled, and striven for the sake of the child. I have scrubbed and washed both coarse and fine linen, but I have not been able to make myself better off; and it was God's will. In His own time He will take me to Himself, but I know He will never forsake my boy.' Then she fell asleep. In the morning she felt much refreshed, and strong enough, as she thought, to go on with her work. But as soon as she stepped into the cold water, a sudden faintness seized her;

she clutched at the air convulsively with her hand, took one step forward, and fell. Her head rested on dry land, but her feet were in the water; her wooden shoes, which were only tied on by a wisp of straw, were carried away by the stream, and thus she was found by Martha when she came to bring her some coffee.

In the meantime a messenger had been sent to her house by the mayor, to say that she must come to him immediately, as he had something to tell her. It was too late; a surgeon had been sent for to open a vein in her arm, but the poor woman was dead.

'She has drunk herself to death,' said the cruel mayor. In the letter, containing the news of his brother's death, it was stated that he had left in his will a legacy of six hundred dollars to the glovemaker's widow, who had been his mother's maid, to be paid with discretion, in large or small sums to the widow or her child.

'There was something between my brother and her, I remember,' said the mayor; 'it is a good thing that she is out of the way, for now the boy will have the whole. I will place him with honest people to bring him up, that he may become a respectable working man.' And the blessing of God rested upon these words. The mayor sent for the boy to come to him, and promised to take care of him, but most cruelly added that it was a good thing that his mother was dead, for 'she was good for nothing.' They carried her to the churchyard, the churchyard in which the poor were buried. Martha strewed sand on the grave and planted a rose tree upon it, and the boy stood by her side.

'Oh, my poor mother!' he cried, while the tears rolled down his cheeks. 'Is it true what they say, that she was good for nothing?'

'No, indeed, it is not true,' replied the old servant, raising her eyes to heaven; 'she was worth a great deal; I knew it years ago, and since the last night of her life I am more certain of it than ever. I say she was a good and worthy woman, and God, who is in heaven, knows I am speaking the truth, though the world may say, even now she was good for nothing.'

# 21

# Jack the Dullard

Far in the interior of the country lay an old baronial hall, and in it lived an old proprietor, who had two sons, which two young men thought themselves too clever by half. They wanted to go out and woo the King's daughter; for the maiden in question had publicly announced that she would choose for her husband that youth who could arrange his words best.

So these two geniuses prepared themselves a full week for the wooing—this was the longest time that could be granted them; but it was enough, for they had had much preparatory information, and everybody knows how useful that is. One of them knew the whole Latin dictionary by heart, and three whole years of the daily paper of the little town into the bargain, and so well, indeed, that he could repeat it all either backwards or forwards, just as he chose. The other was deeply read in the corporation laws, and knew by heart what every corporation ought to know; and accordingly he thought he could talk of affairs of state, and put his spoke in the wheel in the council. And he knew one thing more: he could embroider suspenders with roses and other flowers, and with arabesques, for he was a tasty, light-fingered fellow.

'I shall win the Princess!' So cried both of them. Therefore their old papa gave to each of them a handsome horse. The youth who knew the dictionary and newspaper by heart had a black horse, and he who knew all about the corporation laws received a milk-white steed. Then they rubbed the corners of their mouths with fish oil, so that they might become very smooth and glib. All the servants stood below in the courtyard, and looked on while they mounted their horses; and just by chance the third son came up. For the proprietor had really three sons, though nobody counted the third with his brothers, because he was not so learned as they, and indeed he was generally known as 'Jack the Dullard.'

'Hallo!' said Jack the Dullard, 'where are you going? I declare you have put on your Sunday clothes!'

'We're going to the King's court, as suitors to the King's daughter. Don't you know the announcement that has been made all through the country?' And they told him all about it.

'My word! I'll be in it too!' cried Jack the Dullard; and his two brothers burst out laughing at him, and rode away.

'Father, dear,' said Jack, 'I must have a horse too. I do feel so desperately inclined to marry! If she accepts me, she accepts me; and if she won't have me, I'll have her; but she **shall** be mine!'

'Don't talk nonsense,' replied the old gentleman. 'You shall have no horse from me. You don't know how to speak—you can't arrange your words. Your brothers are very different fellows from you.'

'Well,' quoth Jack the Dullard, 'If I can't have a horse, I'll take the billy goat, who belongs to me, and he can carry me very well!'

And so said, so done. He mounted the billy goat, pressed his heels into its sides, and galloped down the high street like a hurricane.

'Hei, houp! That was a ride! Here I come!' shouted Jack the Dullard, and he sang till his voice echoed far and wide.

But his brothers rode slowly on in advance of him. They spoke not a word, for they were thinking about the fine extempore speeches they would have to bring out, and these had to be cleverly prepared beforehand.

'Hallo!' shouted Jack the Dullard. 'Here am I! Look what I have found on the high road.' And he showed them what it was, and it was a dead crow.

'Dullard!' exclaimed the brothers, 'what are you going to do with that?'

'With the crow? Why, I am going to give it to the Princess.'

'Yes, do so,' said they; and they laughed, and rode on.

'Hallo, here I am again! Just see what I have found now: you don't find that on the high road every day!'

And the brothers turned round to see what he could have found now.

'Dullard!' they cried, 'that is only an old wooden shoe, and the upper part is missing into the bargain; are you going to give that also to the Princess?'

'Most certainly I shall,' replied Jack the Dullard; and again the brothers laughed and rode on, and thus they got far in advance of him; but—

'Hallo—hop rara!' and there was Jack the Dullard again. 'It is getting better and better,' he cried. 'Hurrah! It is quite famous.'

'Why, what have you found this time?' inquired the brothers.

'Oh,' said Jack the Dullard, 'I can hardly tell you. How glad the Princess will be!'

'Bah!' said the brothers; 'that is nothing but clay out of the ditch.'

'Yes, certainly it is,' said Jack the Dullard; 'and clay of the finest sort. See, it is so wet, it runs through one's fingers.' And he filled his pocket with the clay.

But his brothers galloped on till the sparks flew, and consequently they arrived a full hour earlier at the town gate than could Jack. Now at the gate each suitor was provided with a number, and all were placed in rows immediately on their arrival, six in each row, and so closely packed together that they could not move their arms; and that was a prudent arrangement, for they would certainly have come to blows, had they been able, merely because one of them stood before the other.

All the inhabitants of the country round about stood in great crowds around the castle, almost under the very windows, to see the Princess receive the suitors; and as each stepped into the hall, his power of speech seemed to desert him, like the light of a candle that is blown out. Then the Princess would say, 'He is of no use! Away with him out of the hall!'

At last the turn came for that brother who knew the dictionary by heart; but he did not know it now; he had absolutely forgotten it altogether; and the boards seemed to re-echo with his footsteps, and the ceiling of the hall was made of looking glass, so that he saw himself standing on his head; and at the window stood three clerks and a head clerk, and everyone of them was writing down every single word that was uttered, so that it might be printed in the newspapers, and sold for a penny at the street corners. It was a terrible ordeal, and they had, moreover, made such a fire in the stove, that the room seemed quite red hot.

'It is dreadfully hot here!' observed the first brother.

'Yes,' replied the Princess, 'my father is going to roast young pullets today.'

'Baa!' there he stood like a baa-lamb. He had not been prepared for a speech of this kind, and had not a word to say, though he intended to say something witty. 'Baa!'

'He is of no use!' said the Princess. 'Away with him!'

And he was obliged to go accordingly. And now the second brother came in.

'It is terribly warm here!' he observed.

'Yes, we're roasting pullets today,' replied the Princess.

'What—what were you—were you pleased to ob—' stammered he—and all the clerks wrote down, 'pleased to ob—'

'He is of no use!' said the Princess. 'Away with him!'

Now came the turn of Jack the Dullard. He rode into the hall on his goat.

'Well, it's most abominably hot here.'

'Yes, because I'm roasting young pullets,' replied the Princess.

'Ah, that's lucky!' exclaimed Jack the Dullard, 'for I suppose you'll let me roast my crow at the same time?'

'With the greatest pleasure,' said the Princess. 'But have you anything you can roast it in? For I have neither pot nor pan.'

'Certainly I have!' said Jack. 'Here's a cooking utensil with a tin handle.'

And he brought out the old wooden shoe, and put the crow into it.

'Well, that is a famous dish!' said the Princess. 'But what shall we do for sauce?'

'Oh, I have that in my pocket,' said Jack; 'I have so much of it that I can afford to throw some away;' and he poured some of the clay out of his pocket.

'I like that!' said the Princess. 'You can give an answer, and you have something to say for yourself, and so you shall be my husband. But are you aware that every word we speak is being taken down, and will be published in the paper tomorrow? Look yonder, and you will see in every window three clerks and a head clerk; and the old head clerk is the worst of all, for he can't understand anything.'

But she only said this to frighten Jack the Dullard; and the clerks gave a great crow of delight, and each one spurted a blot out of his pen on to the floor.

'Oh, those are the gentlemen, are they?' said Jack; 'then I will give the best I have to the head clerk.' And he turned out his pockets, and flung the wet clay full in the head clerk's face.

'That was very cleverly done,' observed the Princess. 'I could not have done that; but I shall learn in time.'

And accordingly Jack the Dullard was made a king, and received a crown and a wife, and sat upon a throne. And this report we have wet from the press of the head clerk and the corporation of printers—but they are **not** to be depended upon in the least.

# 22

# The Bottle Neck

Close to the corner of a street, among other abodes of poverty, stood an exceedingly tall, narrow house, which had been so knocked about by time that it seemed out of joint in every direction. This house was inhabited by poor people, but the deepest poverty was apparent in the garret lodging in the gable. In front of the little window, an old bent birdcage hung in the sunshine, which had not even a proper water glass, but instead of it the broken neck of a bottle, turned upside down, and a cork stuck in to make it hold the water with which it was filled. An old maid stood at the window; she had hung chickweed over the cage, and the little linnet which it contained hopped from perch to perch and sang and twittered merrily.

'Yes, it's all very well for you to sing,' said the bottle neck: that is, he did not really speak the words as we do, for the neck of a bottle cannot speak; but he thought them to himself in his own mind, just as people sometimes talk quietly to themselves.

'Yes, you may sing very well, you have all your limbs uninjured; you should feel what it is like to lose your body, and only have a neck and a mouth left, with a cork stuck in it, as I have: you wouldn't sing then, I know. After all, it is just as well that there are some who can be happy. I have no reason to sing, nor could I sing now if I were ever so happy; but when I was a whole bottle, and they rubbed me with a cork, didn't I sing then? I used to be called a complete lark. I remember when I went out to a picnic with the furrier's family, on the day his daughter was betrothed,—it seems as if it only happened yesterday. I have gone through a great deal in my time, when I come to recollect: I have been in the fire and in the water, I have been deep in the earth, and have mounted higher in the air than most other people, and now I am swinging here, outside a birdcage, in the air and the sunshine. Oh, indeed, it would be worthwhile to hear my history; but I do not speak it aloud, for a good reason—because I cannot.'

Then the bottle neck related his history, which was really rather remarkable; he, in fact, related it to himself, or, at least, thought it in his own mind. The little bird sang his own song merrily; in the street below there was driving and running to and fro, everyone thought of his own affairs, or perhaps of nothing at all; but the bottle neck thought deeply. He thought of the blazing furnace in the factory, where he had been blown into life; he remembered how hot it felt when he was placed in the heated oven, the home from which he sprang, and that he had a strong inclination to leap out again directly; but after a while it became cooler, and he found himself very comfortable. He had been placed in a row, with a whole regiment of his brothers and sisters all brought out of the same furnace; some of them had certainly been blown into champagne bottles, and others into beer bottles, which made a little difference between them. In the world it often happens that a beer bottle may contain the most precious wine, and a champagne bottle be filled with blacking, but even in decay it may always be seen whether a man has been well born. Nobility remains noble, as a champagne bottle remains the same, even with blacking in its interior. When the bottles were packed our bottle was packed amongst them; it little expected then to finish its career as a bottle neck, or to be used as a water glass to a bird's cage, which is, after all, a place of honour, for it is to be of some use in the world. The bottle did not behold the light of day again, until it was unpacked with the rest in the wine merchant's cellar, and, for the first time, rinsed with water, which caused some very curious sensations. There it lay empty, and without a cork, and it had a peculiar feeling, as if it wanted something it knew not what. At last it was filled with rich and costly wine, a cork was placed in it, and sealed down. Then it was labelled 'first quality,' as if it had carried off the first prize at an examination; besides, the wine and the bottle were both good, and while we are young is the time for poetry. There were sounds of song within the bottle, of things it could not understand, of green sunny mountains, where the vines grow and where the merry vinedressers laugh, sing, and are merry. 'Ah, how beautiful is life.' All these tones of joy and song in the bottle were like the working of a young poet's brain, who often knows not the meaning of the tones which are sounding within him. One morning the bottle found a purchaser in the furrier's apprentice, who was told to bring one of the best bottles of wine. It was placed in the provision basket with ham and cheese and sausages. The sweetest fresh butter and the finest bread were put into the basket by the furrier's daughter herself, for she packed it. She was young and pretty; her brown eyes laughed, and a smile lingered round her mouth as sweet as that in her eyes. She had delicate hands, beautifully white, and her neck was whiter still. It could easily be seen that she was a very lovely girl, and as yet she was not engaged. The provision basket lay in the lap of the young girl as the family drove out to the forest, and the neck of the bottle peeped out from between the folds of the white napkin. There was the red wax on the cork, and the bottle looked straight at the young girl's face, and also at the face of the young sailor who sat near her. He was a young friend, the son of a portrait painter. He had lately passed his examination with honour, as mate, and the next morning he was to sail in his ship to a distant coast. There had been a great deal of talk on this subject while the basket was being packed, and during this conversation the eyes and the mouth of the furrier's daughter did not wear a very joyful expression. The young people wandered away into the green wood, and talked together. What did they talk about? The bottle could not say, for he was in the provision basket.

It remained there a long time; but when at last it was brought forth it appeared as if something pleasant had happened, for everyone was laughing; the furrier's daughter laughed too, but she said very little, and her cheeks were like two roses. Then her father took the bottle and the corkscrew into his hands. What a strange sensation it was to have the cork drawn for the first time! The bottle could never after that forget the performance of that moment; indeed there was quite a convulsion within him as the cork flew out, and a gurgling sound as the wine was poured forth into the glasses.

'Long life to the betrothed,' cried the papa, and every glass was emptied to the dregs, while the young sailor kissed his beautiful bride.

'Happiness and blessing to you both,' said the old people— father and mother, and the young man filled the glasses again.

'Safe return, and a wedding this day next year,' he cried; and when the glasses were empty he took the bottle, raised it on high, and said, 'Thou hast been present here on the happiest day of my

life; thou shalt never be used by others!' So saying, he hurled it high in the air.

The furrier's daughter thought she should never see it again, but she was mistaken. It fell among the rushes on the borders of a little woodland lake. The bottle neck remembered well how long it lay there unseen. 'I gave them wine, and they gave me muddy water,' he had said to himself, 'but I suppose it was all well meant.' He could no longer see the betrothed couple, nor the cheerful old people; but for a long time he could hear them rejoicing and singing. At length there came by two peasant boys, who peeped in among the reeds and spied out the bottle. Then they took it up and carried it home with them, so that once more it was provided for. At home in their wooden cottage these boys had an elder brother, a sailor, who was about to start on a long voyage. He had been there the day before to say farewell, and his mother was now very busy packing up various things for him to take with him on his voyage. In the evening his father was going to carry the parcel to the town to see his son once more, and take him a farewell greeting from his mother. A small bottle had already been filled with herb tea, mixed with brandy, and wrapped in a parcel; but when the boys came in they brought with them a larger and stronger bottle, which they had found. This bottle would hold so much more than the little one, and they all said the brandy would be so good for complaints of the stomach, especially as it was mixed with medical herbs. The liquid which they now poured into the bottle was not like the red wine with which it had once been filled; these were bitter drops, but they are of great use sometimes—for the stomach. The new large bottle was to go, not the little one: so the bottle once more started on its travels. It was taken on board (for Peter Jensen was one of the crew) the very same ship in which the young mate was to sail. But the mate did not see the bottle: indeed, if he had he would not have known it, or supposed it was the one out of which they had drunk to the felicity of the betrothed and to the prospect of a marriage on his own happy return. Certainly the bottle no longer poured forth wine, but it contained something quite as good; and so it happened that whenever Peter Jensen brought it out, his messmates gave it the name of 'the apothecary,' for it contained the best medicine to cure the stomach, and he gave it out quite willingly as long as a drop remained. Those were happy days, and the bottle would sing when rubbed with a cork, and it was called a 'great lark,' 'Peter Jensen's lark.'

Long days and months rolled by, during which the bottle stood empty in a corner, when a storm arose—whether on the passage out or home it could not tell, for it had never been ashore. It was a terrible storm, great waves arose, darkly heaving and tossing the vessel to and fro. The main mast was split asunder, the ship sprang a leak, and the pumps became useless, while all around was black as night. At the last moment, when the ship was sinking, the young mate wrote on a piece of paper, 'We are going down: God's will be done.' Then he wrote the name of his betrothed, his own name, and that of the ship. Then he put the leaf in an empty bottle that happened to be at hand, corked it down tightly, and threw it into the foaming sea. He knew not that it was the very same bottle from which the goblet of joy and hope had once been filled for him, and now it was tossing on the waves with his last greeting, and a message from the dead. The ship sank, and the crew sank with her; but the bottle flew on like a bird, for it bore within it a loving letter from a loving heart. And as the sun rose and set, the bottle felt as at the time of its first existence, when in the heated glowing stove it had a longing to fly away. It outlived the storms and the calm, it struck against no rocks, was not devoured by sharks, but drifted on for more than a year, sometimes towards the north, sometimes towards the south, just as the current carried it. It was in all other ways its own master, but even of that one may get tired. The written leaf, the last farewell of the bridegroom to his bride, would only bring sorrow when once it reached her hands; but where were those hands, so soft and delicate, which had once spread the tablecloth on the fresh grass in the green wood, on the day of her betrothal? Ah, yes! Where was the furrier's daughter? And where was the land which might lie nearest to her home?

The bottle knew not, it travelled onward and onward, and at last all this wandering about became wearisome; at all events it was not its usual occupation. But it had to travel, till at length it reached land—a foreign country. Not a word spoken in this country could the bottle understand; it was a language it had never before heard, and it is a great loss not to be able to understand a language. The bottle was fished out of the water, and examined on all sides. The little letter contained within it was discovered, taken out, and turned and twisted in every direction; but the people could not understand what was written upon it. They could be quite sure that the bottle had been thrown overboard from a vessel, and that something about it was written on this paper: but what was written? That was the question,—so the paper was put back into the bottle, and then both were put away in a large cupboard of one of the great houses of the town. Whenever any strangers arrived, the paper was taken out and turned over and over, so that the address, which was only written in pencil, became almost illegible, and at last no one could distinguish any letters on it at all. For a whole year the bottle remained standing in the cupboard, and then it was taken up to the loft, where it soon became covered with dust and cobwebs. Ah! How often then it thought of those better days—of the times when in the fresh, green wood, it had poured forth rich wine; or, while rocked by the swelling waves, it had carried in its bosom a secret, a letter, a last parting sigh. For full twenty years it stood in the loft, and it might have stayed there longer but that the house was going to be rebuilt. The bottle was discovered when the roof was taken off; they talked about it, but the bottle did not understand what they said—a language is not to be learnt by living in a loft, even for twenty years. 'If I had been downstairs in the room,' thought the bottle, 'I might have learnt it.' It was now washed and rinsed, which process was really quite necessary, and afterwards it looked clean and transparent, and felt young again in its old age; but the paper which it had carried so faithfully was destroyed in the washing. They filled the bottle with seeds, though it scarcely knew what had been placed in it. Then they corked it down tightly, and carefully wrapped it up. There not even the light of a torch or lantern could reach it, much less the brightness of the sun or moon. 'And yet,' thought the bottle, 'men go on a journey that they may see as much as possible, and I can see nothing.' However, it did something quite as important; it travelled to the place of its destination, and was unpacked.

'What trouble they have taken with that bottle over yonder!' said one, 'and very likely it is broken after all.' But the bottle was not broken, and, better still, it understood every word that was said: this language it had heard at the furnaces and at the wine merchant's; in the forest and on the ship,—it was the only good old language it could understand. It had returned home, and the language was as a welcome greeting. For very joy, it felt ready to jump out of people's hands, and scarcely noticed that its cork had been drawn, and its contents emptied out, till it found itself carried to a cellar, to be left there and forgotten. 'There's no place like home, even if it's a cellar.' It never occurred to him to think that he might lie there for years, he felt so comfortable. For many long years he remained in the cellar, till at last some people came to carry away the bottles, and ours amongst the number.

Out in the garden there was a great festival. Brilliant lamps hung in festoons from tree to tree; and paper lanterns, through which the light shone till they looked like transparent tulips. It was a beautiful evening, and the weather mild and clear. The stars twinkled; and the new moon, in the form of a crescent, was surrounded by the shadowy disc of the whole moon, and looked like a grey globe with a golden rim: it was a beautiful sight for those who had good eyes. The illumination extended even to the most retired of the garden walks, at least not so retired that anyone need lose himself there. In the borders were placed bottles, each containing a light, and among them the bottle with which we are acquainted, and whose fate it was, one day, to be only a bottle neck, and to serve as a water glass to a bird's cage. Everything here appeared lovely to our bottle, for it was again in the green wood, amid joy and feasting; again it heard music and song, and the noise and murmur of a crowd, especially in that part of the garden where the lamps blazed, and the paper lanterns displayed their brilliant colours. It stood in a distant walk certainly, but a place pleasant for contemplation; and it carried a light; and was at once useful and ornamental. In such an hour it is easy to forget that one has spent twenty years in a loft, and a good thing it is to be able to do so. Close before the bottle passed a single pair, like the bridal pair—the mate and the furrier's daughter—who had so long ago wandered in the wood. It seemed to the bottle as if he were living that time over again. Not only the guests but other people were walking in the garden, who were allowed to witness the splendour and the festivities. Among the latter came an old maid, who seemed to be quite alone in the world. She was thinking, like the bottle, of the green wood, and of a young betrothed pair, who were closely connected with herself; she was thinking of that hour, the happiest of her life, in which she had taken part, when she had herself been one of that betrothed pair; such hours are never to be forgotten, let a maiden be as old as she may. But she did not recognise the bottle, neither did the bottle notice the old maid. And so we often pass each other in the world when we meet, as did these two, even while together in the same town.

The bottle was taken from the garden, and again sent to a wine merchant, where it was once more filled with wine, and sold to an aeronaut, who was to make an ascent in his balloon on the following Sunday. A great crowd assembled to witness the sight; military music had been engaged, and many other preparations made. The bottle saw it all from the basket in which he lay close to a live rabbit. The rabbit was quite excited because he knew that he was to be taken up, and let down again in a parachute. The bottle, however, knew nothing of the 'up,' or the 'down;' he saw only that the balloon was swelling larger and larger till it could swell no more, and began to rise and be restless. Then the ropes which held it were cut through, and the aerial ship rose in the air with the aeronaut and the basket containing the bottle and the rabbit, while the music sounded and all the people shouted 'Hurrah.'

'This is a wonderful journey up into the air,' thought the bottle; 'it is a new way of sailing, and here, at least, there is no fear of striking against anything.'

Thousands of people gazed at the balloon, and the old maid who was in the garden saw it also; for she stood at the open window of the garret, by which hung the cage containing the linnet, who then had no water glass, but was obliged to be contented with an old cup. In the windowsill stood a myrtle in a pot, and this had been pushed a little on one side, that it might not fall out; for the old maid was leaning out of the window, that she might see. And she did see distinctly the aeronaut in the balloon, and how he let down the rabbit in the parachute, and then drank to the health of all the spectators in the wine from the bottle. After doing this, he hurled it high into the air. How little she thought that this was the very same bottle which her friend had thrown aloft in her honour, on that happy day of rejoicing, in the green wood, in her youthful days. The bottle had no time to think, when raised so suddenly; and before it was aware, it reached the highest point it had ever attained in its life. Steeples and roofs lay far, far beneath it, and the people looked as tiny as possible. Then it began to descend much more rapidly than the rabbit had done, made somersaults in the air, and felt itself quite young and unfettered, although it was half full of wine. But this did not last long. What a journey it was! All the people could see the bottle; for the sun shone upon it. The balloon was already far away, and very soon the bottle was far away also; for it fell upon a roof, and broke in pieces. But the pieces had got such an impetus in them, that they could not stop themselves. They went jumping and rolling about, till at last they fell into the courtyard, and were broken into still smaller pieces; only the neck of the bottle managed to keep whole, and it was broken off as clean as if it had been cut with a diamond.

'That would make a capital bird's glass,' said one of the cellarmen; but none of them had either a bird or a cage, and it was not to be expected they would provide one just because they had found a bottle neck that could be used as a glass. But the old maid who lived in the garret had a bird, and it really might be useful to her; so the bottle neck was provided with a cork, and taken up to her; and, as it often happens in life, the part that had been uppermost was now turned downwards, and it was filled with fresh water. Then they hung it in the cage of the little bird, who sang and twittered more merrily than ever.

'Ah, you have good reason to sing,' said the bottle neck, which was looked upon as something very remarkable, because it had been in a balloon; nothing further was known of its history. As it hung there in the bird's cage, it could hear the noise and murmur of the people in the street below, as well as the conversation of the old maid in the room within. An old friend had just come to visit her, and they talked, not about the bottle neck, but of the myrtle in the window.

'No, you must not spend a dollar for your daughter's bridal bouquet,' said the old maid; 'you shall have a beautiful little bunch for a nosegay, full of blossoms. Do you see how splendidly the tree has grown? It has been raised from only a little sprig of myrtle that you gave me on the day after my betrothal, and from which I was to make my own bridal bouquet when a year had passed: but that day never came; the eyes were closed which were to have been my light and joy through life. In the depths of the sea my beloved sleeps sweetly; the myrtle has become an old tree, and I am a still older woman. Before the sprig you gave me faded, I took a spray, and planted it in the earth; and now, as you see, it has become a large tree, and a bunch of the blossoms shall at last appear at a wedding festival, in the bouquet of your daughter.'

There were tears in the eyes of the old maid, as she spoke of the beloved of her youth, and of their betrothal in the wood. Many thoughts came into her mind; but the thought never came, that quite close to her, in that very window, was a remembrance of those olden times,—the neck of the bottle which had, as it were shouted for joy when the cork flew out with a bang on the betrothal day. But the bottle neck did not recognise the old maid; he had not been listening to what she had related, perhaps because he was thinking so much about her.

# 23

# The Last Dream of the Old Oak

In the forest, high up on the steep shore, and not far from the open seacoast, stood a very old oak tree. It was just three hundred and sixty-five years old, but that long time was to the tree as the same number of days might be to us; we wake by day and sleep by night, and then we have our dreams. It is different with the tree; it is obliged to keep awake through three seasons of the year, and does not get any sleep till winter comes. Winter is its time for rest; its night after the long day of spring, summer, and autumn. On many a warm summer, the Ephemera, the flies that exist for only a day, had fluttered about the old oak, enjoyed life and felt happy and if, for a moment, one of the tiny creatures rested on one of his large fresh leaves, the tree would always say, 'Poor little creature! Your whole life consists only of a single day. How very short. It must be quite melancholy.'

'Melancholy! What do you mean?' the little creature would always reply. 'Everything around me is so wonderfully bright and warm, and beautiful, that it makes me joyous.'

'But only for one day, and then it is all over.'

'Over!' repeated the fly; 'what is the meaning of all over? Are you all over too?'

'No; I shall very likely live for thousands of your days, and my day is whole seasons long; indeed it is so long that you could never reckon it out.'

'No? Then I don't understand you. You may have thousands of my days, but I have thousands of moments in which I can be merry and happy. Does all the beauty of the world cease when you die?'

'No,' replied the tree; 'it will certainly last much longer,— infinitely longer than I can even think of.' 'Well, then,' said the little fly, 'we have the same time to live; only we reckon differently.' And the little creature danced and floated in the air, rejoicing in her delicate wings of gauze and velvet, rejoicing in the balmy breezes, laden with the fragrance of clover fields and wild roses, elder blossoms and honeysuckle, from the garden hedges, wild thyme, primroses, and mint, and the scent of all these was so strong that the perfume almost intoxicated the little fly. The long and beautiful day had been so full of joy and sweet delights, that when the sun sank low it felt tired of all its happiness and enjoyment. Its wings could sustain it no longer, and gently and slowly it glided down upon the soft waving blades of grass, nodded its little head as well as it could nod, and slept peacefully and sweetly. The fly was dead.

'Poor little Ephemera!' said the oak; 'what a terribly short life!' And so, on every summer day the dance was repeated, the same questions asked, and the same answers given. The same thing was continued through many generations of Ephemera; all of them felt equally merry and equally happy.

The oak remained awake through the morning of spring, the noon of summer, and the evening of autumn; its time of rest, its night drew nigh—winter was coming. Already the storms were singing, 'Good-night, good-night.' Here fell a leaf and there fell a leaf. 'We will rock you and lull you. Go to sleep, go to sleep. We will sing you to sleep, and shake you to sleep, and it will do your old twigs good; they will even crackle with pleasure. Sleep sweetly, sleep sweetly, it is your three-hundred-and-sixty-fifth night. Correctly speaking, you are but a youngster in the world. Sleep sweetly, the clouds will drop snow upon you, which will be quite a coverlid, warm and sheltering to your feet. Sweet sleep to you, and pleasant dreams.' And there stood the oak, stripped of all its leaves, left to rest during the whole of a long winter, and to dream many dreams of events that had happened in its life, as in the dreams of men. The great tree had once been small; indeed, in its cradle it had been an acorn. According to human computation, it was now in the fourth century of its existence. It was the largest and best tree in the forest. Its summit towered above all the other trees, and could be seen far out at sea, so that it served as a landmark to the sailors. It had no idea how many eyes looked eagerly for it. In its topmost branches the wood pigeon built her nest, and the cuckoo carried out his usual vocal performances, and his well-known notes echoed amid the boughs; and in autumn, when the leaves looked like beaten copper plates, the birds of passage would come and rest upon the branches before taking their flights across the sea. But now it was winter, the tree stood leafless, so that everyone could see how crooked and bent were the branches that sprang forth from the trunk. Crows and rooks came by turns and sat on them, and talked of the hard times which were beginning, and how difficult it was in winter to obtain food.

It was just about holy Christmas time that the tree dreamed a dream. The tree had, doubtless, a kind of feeling that the festive time had arrived, and in his dream fancied he heard the bells ringing from all the churches round, and yet it seemed to him to be a beautiful summer's day, mild and warm. His mighty summits was crowned with spreading fresh green foliage; the sunbeams played among the leaves and branches, and the air was full of fragrance from herb and blossom; painted butterflies chased each other; the summer flies danced around him, as if the world had been created merely for them to dance and be merry in. All that had happened to the tree during every year of his life seemed to pass before him, as in a festive procession. He saw the knights of olden times and noble ladies ride by through the wood on their gallant steeds, with plumes waving in their hats, and falcons on their wrists. The hunting horn sounded, and the dogs barked. He saw hostile warriors, in coloured dresses and glittering armour, with spear and halberd, pitching their tents, and anon striking them. The watchfires again blazed, and men sang and slept under the hospitable shelter of the tree. He saw lovers meet in quiet happiness near him in the moonshine, and carve the initials of their names in the greyish-green bark on his trunk. Once, but long years had intervened since then, guitars and Eolian harps had been hung on his boughs by merry travellers; now they seemed to hang there again, and he could hear their marvellous tones. The wood pigeons cooed as if to explain the feelings of the tree, and the cuckoo called out to tell him how many summer days he had yet to live. Then it seemed as if new life was thrilling through every fibre of root and stem and leaf, rising even to the highest branches. The tree felt itself stretching and spreading out, while through the root beneath the earth ran the warm vigour of life. As he grew higher and still higher, with increased strength, his topmost boughs became broader and fuller; and in proportion to his growth, so was his self-satisfaction increased, and with it arose a joyous longing to grow higher and higher, to reach even to the warm, bright sun itself. Already had his topmost branches pierced the clouds, which floated beneath them like troops of birds of passage, or large white swans; every leaf seemed gifted with sight, as if it possessed eyes to see. The stars became visible in broad daylight, large and sparkling, like clear and gentle eyes. They recalled to the memory the well-known look in the eyes of a child, or in the eyes of lovers who had once met beneath the branches of the old oak. These were wonderful and happy moments for the old tree, full of peace and joy; and yet, amidst all this happiness, the tree felt a yearning, longing desire that all the other trees, bushes, herbs, and flowers beneath him, might be able also to rise higher, as he had done, and to see all this splendour, and experience the same happiness. The grand, majestic oak could not be quite happy in the midst of his enjoyment, while all the rest, both great and small, were not with him. And this feeling of yearning trembled through every branch, through every leaf, as warmly and fervently as if they had been the fibres of a human heart. The summit of the tree waved to and fro, and bent downwards as if in his silent longing he sought for something. Then there came to him the fragrance of thyme, followed by the more powerful scent of honeysuckle and violets; and he fancied he heard the note of the cuckoo. At length his longing was satisfied. Up through the clouds came the green summits of the forest trees, and beneath him, the oak saw them rising, and growing higher and higher. Bush and herb shot upward, and some even tore themselves up by the roots to rise more quickly. The birch tree was the quickest of all. Like a lightning flash the slender stem shot upwards in a zigzag line, the branches spreading around it like green gauze and banners.

Every native of the wood, even to the brown and feathery rushes, grew with the rest, while the birds ascended with the melody of song. On a blade of grass, that fluttered in the air like a long, green ribbon, sat a grasshopper, cleaning his wings with his legs. May beetles hummed, the bees murmured, the birds sang, each in his own way; the air was filled with the sounds of song and gladness.

'But where is the little blue flower that grows by the water?' asked the oak, 'and the purple bellflower, and the daisy?' You see the oak wanted to have them all with him.

'Here we are, we are here,' sounded in voice and song.

'But the beautiful thyme of last summer, where is that? And the lilies of the valley, which last year covered the earth with their bloom? And the wild apple tree with its lovely blossoms, and all the glory of the wood, which has flourished year after year? Even what may have but now sprouted forth could be with us here.'

'We are here, we are here,' sounded voices higher in the air, as if they had flown there beforehand.

'Why this is beautiful, too beautiful to be believed,' said the oak in a joyful tone. 'I have them all here, both great and small;

not one has been forgotten. Can such happiness be imagined?' It seemed almost impossible.

'In heaven with the Eternal God, it can be imagined, and it is possible,' sounded the reply through the air.

And the old tree, as it still grew upwards and onwards, felt that his roots were loosening themselves from the earth.

'It is right so, it is best,' said the tree, 'no fetters hold me now. I can fly up to the very highest point in light and glory. And all I love are with me, both small and great. All—all are here.'

Such was the dream of the old oak: and while he dreamed, a mighty storm came rushing over land and sea, at the holy Christmas time. The sea rolled in great billows towards the shore. There was a cracking and crushing heard in the tree. The root was torn from the ground just at the moment when in his dream he fancied it was being loosened from the earth. He fell—his three hundred and sixty-five years were passed as the single day of the Ephemera. On the morning of Christmas Day, when the sun rose, the storm had ceased. From all the churches sounded the festive bells, and from every hearth, even of the smallest hut, rose the smoke into the blue sky, like the smoke from the festive thanks offerings on the Druids' altars. The sea gradually became calm, and on board a great ship that had withstood the tempest during the night, all the flags were displayed, as a token of joy and festivity. 'The tree is down! The old oak,—our landmark on the coast!' exclaimed the sailors. 'It must have fallen in the storm of last night. Who can replace it? Alas! No one.' This was a funeral oration over the old tree; short, but well-meant. There it lay stretched on the snow-covered shore, and over it sounded the notes of a song from the ship—a song of Christmas joy, and of the redemption of the soul of man, and of eternal life through Christ's atoning blood.

'Sing aloud on the happy morn, All is fulfilled, for Christ is born; With songs of joy let us loudly sing, "Hallelujahs to Christ our King." '

Thus sounded the old Christmas carol, and everyone on board the ship felt his thoughts elevated, through the song and the prayer, even as the old tree had felt lifted up in its last, its beautiful dream on that Christmas morn.

# 24

# Children's Prattle

At a rich merchant's house there was a children's party, and the children of rich and great people were there. The merchant was a learned man, for his father had sent him to college, and he had passed his examination. His father had been at first only a cattle dealer, but always honest and industrious, so that he had made money, and his son, the merchant, had managed to increase his store. Clever as he was, he had also a heart; but there was less said of his heart than of his money. All descriptions of people visited at the merchant's house, well born, as well as intellectual, and some who possessed neither of these recommendations.

Now it was a children's party, and there was children's prattle, which always is spoken freely from the heart. Among them was a beautiful little girl, who was terribly proud; but this had been taught her by the servants, and not by her parents, who were far too sensible people.

Her father was groom of the Chambers, which is a high office at court, and she knew it. 'I am a child of the court,' she said; now she might just as well have been a child of the cellar, for no one can help his birth; and then she told the other children that she was well-born, and said that no one who was not well-born could rise in the world. It was no use to read and be industrious, for if a person was not well-born, he could never achieve anything.

'And those whose names end with "sen," ' said she, 'can never be anything at all. We must put our arms akimbo, and make the elbow quite pointed, so as to keep these "sen" people at a great distance.' And then she stuck out her pretty little arms, and made the elbows quite pointed, to show how it was to be done; and her little arms were very pretty, for she was a sweet-looking child.

But the little daughter of the merchant became very angry at this speech, for her father's name was Petersen, and she knew that the name ended in 'sen,' and therefore she said as proudly as she could, 'But my papa can buy a hundred dollars' worth of bonbons, and give them away to children. Can your papa do that?'

'Yes; and my papa,' said the little daughter of the editor of a paper, 'my papa can put your papa and everybody's papa into the newspaper. All sorts of people are afraid of him, my mamma says, for he can do as he likes with the paper.' And the little maiden looked exceedingly proud, as if she had been a real princess, who may be expected to look proud.

But outside the door, which stood ajar, was a poor boy, peeping through the crack of the door. He was of such a lowly station that he had not been allowed even to enter the room. He had been turning the spit for the cook, and she had given him permission to stand behind the door and peep in at the well-dressed children, who were having such a merry time within; and for him that was a great deal. 'Oh, if I could be one of them,' thought he, and then he heard what was said about names, which was quite enough to make him more unhappy. His parents at home had not even a penny to spare to buy a newspaper, much less could they write in one; and worse than all, his father's name, and of course his own, ended in 'sen,' and therefore he could never turn out well, which was a very sad thought. But after all, he had been born into the world, and the station of life had been chosen for him, therefore he must be content.

And this is what happened on that evening.

Many years passed, and most of the children became grown-up persons.

There stood a splendid house in the town, filled with all kinds of beautiful and valuable objects. Everybody wished to see it, and people even came in from the country round to be permitted to view the treasures it contained.

Which of the children whose prattle we have described, could call this house his own? One would suppose it very easy to guess. No, no; it is not so very easy. The house belonged to the poor little boy who had stood on that night behind the door. He had really become something great, although his name ended in 'sen,'—for it was Thorwaldsen.

And the three other children—the children of good birth, of money, and of intellectual pride,—well, they were respected and honoured in the world, for they had been well provided for by birth and position, and they had no cause to reproach themselves with what they had thought and spoken on that evening long ago, for, after all, it was mere *'children's prattle.'*

# 25

# What the Old Man Does
# Is Always Right

I will tell you a story that was told me when I was a little boy. Every time I thought of this story, it seemed to me more and more charming; for it is with stories as it is with many people— they become better as they grow older.

I have no doubt that you have been in the country, and seen a very old farmhouse, with a thatched roof, and mosses and small plants growing wild upon it. There is a stork's nest on the ridge of the gable, for we cannot do without the stork. The walls of the house are sloping, and the windows are low, and only one of the latter is made to open. The baking oven sticks out of the wall like a great knob. An elder tree hangs over the palings; and beneath its branches, at the foot of the paling, is a pool of water, in which a few ducks are disporting themselves. There is a yard dog too, who barks at all corners. Just such a farmhouse as this stood in a country lane; and in it dwelt an old couple, a peasant and his wife. Small as their possessions were, they had one article they could not do without, and that was a horse, which contrived to live upon the grass which it found by the side of the high road. The old peasant rode into the town upon this horse, and his neighbours often borrowed it of him, and paid for the loan of it by rendering some service to the old couple. After a time they thought it would be as well to sell the horse, or exchange it for something which might be more useful to them. But what might this something be?

'You'll know best, old man,' said the wife. 'It is fair-day today; so ride into town, and get rid of the horse for money, or make a good exchange; whichever you do will be right to me, so ride to the fair.'

And she fastened his neckerchief for him; for she could do that better than he could, and she could also tie it very prettily in a double bow. She also smoothed his hat round and round with the palm of her hand, and gave him a kiss. Then he rode away upon the horse that was to be sold or bartered for something else. Yes, the old man knew what he was about. The sun shone with great heat, and not a cloud was to be seen in the sky. The road was very dusty; for a number of people, all going to the fair, were driving, riding, or walking upon it. There was no shelter anywhere from the hot sunshine. Among the rest a man came trudging along, and driving a cow to the fair. The cow was as beautiful a creature as any cow could be.

'She gives good milk, I am certain,' said the peasant to himself. 'That would be a very good exchange: the cow for the horse. Hallo there! You with the cow,' he said. 'I tell you what; I dare say a horse is of more value than a cow; but I don't care for that,—a cow will be more useful to me; so, if you like, we'll exchange.'

'To be sure I will,' said the man.

Accordingly the exchange was made; and as the matter was settled, the peasant might have turned back; for he had done the business he came to do. But, having made up his mind to go to the fair, he had determined to do so, if only to have a look at it; so on he went to the town with his cow. Leading the animal, he strode on sturdily, and, after a short time, overtook a man who was driving a sheep. It was a good fat sheep, with a fine fleece on its back.

'I should like to have that fellow,' said the peasant to himself. 'There is plenty of grass for him by our palings, and in the winter we could keep him in the room with us. Perhaps it would be more profitable to have a sheep than a cow. Shall I exchange?'

The man with the sheep was quite ready, and the bargain was quickly made. And then our peasant continued his way on the high road with his sheep. Soon after this, he overtook another man, who had come into the road from a field, and was carrying a large goose under his arm.

'What a heavy creature you have there!' said the peasant; 'it has plenty of feathers and plenty of fat, and would look well tied to a string, or paddling in the water at our place. That would be very useful to my old woman; she could make all sorts of profits out of it. How often she has said, "If now we only had a goose!" Now here is an opportunity, and, if possible, I will get it for her. Shall we exchange? I will give you my sheep for your goose, and thanks into the bargain.'

The other had not the least objection, and accordingly the exchange was made, and our peasant became possessor of the goose. By this time he had arrived very near the town. The crowd on the high road had been gradually increasing, and there was quite a rush of men and cattle. The cattle walked on the path and by the palings, and at the turnpike gate they even walked into the tollkeeper's potato field, where one fowl was strutting about with a string tied to its leg, for fear it should take fright at the crowd, and run away and get lost. The tail feathers of the fowl were very short, and it winked with both its eyes, and looked very cunning, as it said 'Cluck, cluck.' What were the thoughts of the fowl as it said this I cannot tell you; but directly our good man saw it, he thought, 'Why that's the finest fowl I ever saw in my life; it's finer than our parson's brood hen, upon my word. I should like to have that fowl. Fowls can always pick up a few grains that lie about, and almost keep themselves. I think it would be a good exchange if I could get it for my goose. Shall we exchange?' he asked the tollkeeper.

'Exchange,' repeated the man; 'well, it would not be a bad thing.'

And so they made an exchange,—the tollkeeper at the turnpike gate kept the goose, and the peasant carried off the fowl. Now he had really done a great deal of business on his way to the fair, and he was hot and tired. He wanted something to eat, and a glass of ale to refresh himself; so he turned his steps to an inn. He was just about to enter when the ostler came out, and they met at the door. The ostler was carrying a sack. 'What have you in that sack?' asked the peasant.

'Rotten apples,' answered the ostler; 'a whole sackful of them. They will do to feed the pigs with.'

'Why that will be terrible waste,' he replied; 'I should like to take them home to my old woman. Last year the old apple tree by the grassplot only bore one apple, and we kept it in the cupboard till it was quite withered and rotten. It was always property, my old woman said; and here she would see a great deal of property—a whole sackful; I should like to show them to her.'

'What will you give me for the sackful?' asked the ostler.

'What will I give? Well, I will give you my fowl in exchange.'

So he gave up the fowl, and received the apples, which he carried into the inn parlour. He leaned the sack carefully against the stove, and then went to the table. But the stove was hot, and he had not thought of that. Many guests were present—horse dealers, cattle drovers, and two Englishmen. The Englishmen were so rich that their pockets quite bulged out and seemed ready to burst; and they could bet too, as you shall hear. 'Hiss-s-s, hiss-s-s.' What could that be by the stove? The apples were beginning to roast. 'What is that?' asked one.

'Why, do you know'—said our peasant. And then he told them the whole story of the horse, which he had exchanged for a cow, and all the rest of it, down to the apples.

'Well, your old woman will give it to you well when you get home,' said one of the Englishmen. 'Won't there be a noise?'

'What! Give me what?' said the peasant. 'Why, she will kiss me, and say, "what the old man does is always right."'

'Let us lay a wager on it,' said the Englishmen. 'We'll wager you a ton of coined gold, a hundred pounds to the hundredweight.'

'No; a bushel will be enough,' replied the peasant. 'I can only set a bushel of apples against it, and I'll throw myself and my old woman into the bargain; that will pile up the measure, I fancy.'

'Done! Taken!' and so the bet was made.

Then the landlord's coach came to the door, and the two Englishmen and the peasant got in, and away they drove, and soon arrived and stopped at the peasant's hut. 'Good evening, old woman.' 'Good evening, old man.' 'I've made the exchange.'

'Ah, well, you understand what you're about,' said the woman. Then she embraced him, and paid no attention to the strangers, nor did she notice the sack.

'I got a cow in exchange for the horse.'

'Thank Heaven,' said she. 'Now we shall have plenty of milk, and butter, and cheese on the table. That was a capital exchange.'

'Yes, but I changed the cow for a sheep.'

'Ah, better still!' cried the wife. 'You always think of everything; we have just enough pasture for a sheep. Ewe's milk and cheese, woollen jackets and stockings! The cow could not give all these, and her hair only falls off. How you think of everything!'

'But I changed away the sheep for a goose.'

'Then we shall have roast goose to eat this year. You dear old man, you are always thinking of something to please me. This is delightful. We can let the goose walk about with a string tied to her leg, so she will be fatter still before we roast her.'

'But I gave away the goose for a fowl.'

'A fowl! Well, that was a good exchange,' replied the woman. 'The fowl will lay eggs and hatch them, and we shall have chickens; we shall soon have a poultry yard. Oh, this is just what I was wishing for.'

'Yes, but I exchanged the fowl for a sack of shrivelled apples.'

'What! I really must give you a kiss for that!' exclaimed the wife. 'My dear, good husband, now I'll tell you something. Do you know, almost as soon as you left me this morning, I began to think of what I could give you nice for supper this evening, and then I thought of fried eggs and bacon, with sweet herbs; I had eggs and bacon, but I wanted the herbs; so I went over to the schoolmaster's: I knew they had plenty of herbs, but the schoolmistress is very mean, although she can smile so sweetly. I begged her to lend me a handful of herbs. "Lend!" she exclaimed, "I have nothing to lend; nothing at all grows in our garden, not even a shrivelled apple; I could not even lend you a shrivelled apple, my dear woman." But now I can lend her ten, or a whole sackful, which I'm very glad of; it makes me laugh to think about it,' and then she gave him a hearty kiss.

'Well, I like all this,' said both the Englishmen; 'always going down the hill, and yet always merry; it's worth the money to see it.' So they paid a hundredweight of gold to the peasant, who, whatever he did, was not scolded but kissed.

Yes, it always pays best when the wife sees and maintains that her husband knows best, and whatever he does is right.

That is a story which I heard when I was a child; and now you have heard it too, and know that 'What the old man does is always right.'

# 26

# The Snail and the Rose Tree

Round about the garden ran a hedge of hazel bushes; beyond the hedge were fields and meadows with cows and sheep; but in the middle of the garden stood a Rose Tree in bloom, under which sat a Snail, whose shell contained a great deal—that is, himself.

'Only wait till my time comes,' he said; 'I shall do more than grow roses, bear nuts, or give milk, like the hazel bush, the cows and the sheep.'

'I expect a great deal from you,' said the rose tree. 'May I ask when it will appear?'

'I take my time,' said the snail. 'You're always in such a hurry. That does not excite expectation.'

The following year the snail lay in almost the same spot, in the sunshine under the rose tree, which was again budding and bearing roses as fresh and beautiful as ever. The snail crept half out of his shell, stretched out his horns, and drew them in again.

'Everything is just as it was last year! No progress at all; the rose tree sticks to its roses and gets no further.'

The summer and the autumn passed; the rose tree bore roses and buds till the snow fell and the weather became raw and wet; then it bent down its head, and the snail crept into the ground.

A new year began; the roses made their appearance, and the snail made his too.

'You are an old rose tree now,' said the snail. 'You must make haste and die. You have given the world all that you had in you; whether it was of much importance is a question that I have not had time to think about. But this much is clear and plain, that you have not done the least for your inner development, or you would have produced something else. Have you anything to say in defence? You will now soon be nothing but a stick. Do you understand what I say?'

'You frighten me,' said the rose tree. 'I have never thought of that.'

'No, you have never taken the trouble to think at all. Have you ever given yourself an account why you bloomed, and how your blooming comes about—why just in that way and in no other?'

'No,' said the rose tree. 'I bloom in gladness, because I cannot do otherwise. The sun shone and warmed me, and the air refreshed me; I drank the clear dew and the invigorating rain. I breathed and I lived! Out of the earth there arose a power within me, whilst from above I also received strength; I felt an ever-renewed and ever-increasing happiness, and therefore I was obliged to go on blooming. That was my life; I could not do otherwise.'

'You have led a very easy life,' remarked the snail.

'Certainly. Everything was given me,' said the rose tree. 'But still more was given to you. Yours is one of those deep-thinking natures, one of those highly gifted minds that astonishes the world.'

'I have not the slightest intention of doing so,' said the snail. 'The world is nothing to me. What have I to do with the world? I have enough to do with myself, and enough in myself.'

'But must we not all here on earth give up our best parts to others, and offer as much as lies in our power? It is true, I have only given roses. But you—you who are so richly endowed—what have you given to the world? What will you give it?'

'What have I given? What am I going to give? I spit at it; it's good for nothing, and does not concern me. For my part, you may go on bearing roses; you cannot do anything else. Let the hazel bush bear nuts, and the cows and sheep give milk; they have each their public. I have mine in myself. I retire within myself and there I stop. The world is nothing to me.'

With this the snail withdrew into his house and blocked up the entrance.

'That's very sad,' said the rose tree. 'I cannot creep into myself, however much I might wish to do so; I have to go on bearing roses. Then they drop their leaves, which are blown away by the wind. But I once saw how a rose was laid in the mistress's hymn book, and how one of my roses found a place in the bosom of a young beautiful girl, and how another was kissed by the lips of a child in the glad joy of life. That did me good; it was a real blessing. Those are my recollections, my life.'

And the rose tree went on blooming in innocence, while the snail lay idling in his house—the world was nothing to him.

Years passed by.

The snail had turned to earth in the earth, and the rose tree too. Even the souvenir rose in the hymn book was faded, but in the garden there were other rose trees and other snails. The latter crept into their houses and spat at the world, for it did not concern them.

Shall we read the story all over again? It will be just the same.

# 27

# The Silver Shilling

There was once a shilling, which came forth from the mint springing and shouting, 'Hurrah! Now I am going out into the wide world.' And truly it did go out into the wide world. The children held it with warm hands, the miser with a cold and convulsive grasp, and the old people turned it about, goodness knows how many times, while the young people soon allowed it to roll away from them. The shilling was made of silver, it contained very little copper, and considered itself quite out in the world when it had been circulated for a year in the country in which it had been coined. One day, it really did go out into the world, for it belonged to a gentleman who was about to travel in foreign lands. This gentleman was not aware that the shilling lay at the bottom of his purse when he started, till he one day found it between his fingers. 'Why,' cried he, 'here is a shilling from home; well, it must go on its travels with me now!' and the shilling jumped and rattled for joy, when it was put back again into the purse.

Here it lay among a number of foreign companions, who were always coming and going, one taking the place of another, but the shilling from home was always put back, and had to remain in the purse, which was certainly a mark of distinction. Many weeks passed, during which the shilling had travelled a long distance in the purse, without in the least knowing where he was. He had found out that the other coins were French and Italian; and one coin said they were in this town, and another said they were in that, but the shilling was unable to make out or imagine what they meant. A man certainly cannot see much of the world if he is tied up in a bag, and this was really the shilling's fate. But one day, as he was lying in the purse, he noticed that it was not quite closed, and so he slipped near to the opening to have a little peep into society. He certainly had not the least idea of what would follow, but he was curious, and curiosity often brings its own punishment. In his eagerness, he came so near the edge of the purse that he slipped out into the pocket of the trousers; and when, in the evening, the purse was taken out, the shilling was left behind in the corner to which it had fallen. As the clothes were being carried into the hall, the shilling fell out on the floor, unheard and unnoticed by anyone. The next morning the clothes were taken back to the room, the gentleman put them on, and started on his journey again; but the shilling remained behind on the floor. After a time it was found, and being considered a good coin, was placed with three other coins. 'Ah,' thought the shilling, 'this is pleasant; I shall now see the world, become acquainted with other people, and learn other customs.'

'Do you call that a shilling?' said someone the next moment. 'That is not a genuine coin of the country,—it is false; it is good for nothing.'

Now begins the story as it was afterwards related by the shilling himself.

' "False! Good for nothing!" said he. That remark went through and through me like a dagger. I knew that I had a true ring, and that mine was a genuine stamp. These people must at all events be wrong, or they could not mean me. But yes, I was the one they called 'false, and good for nothing.'

' "Then I must pay it away in the dark," said the man who had received me. So I was to be got rid of in the darkness, and be again insulted in broad daylight.

' "False! Good for nothing!" Oh, I must contrive to get lost, thought I. And I trembled between the fingers of the people every time they tried to pass me off slyly as a coin of the country. Ah! Unhappy shilling that I was! Of what use were my silver, my stamp, and my real value here, where all these qualities were worthless. In the eyes of the world, a man is valued just according to the opinion formed of him. It must be a shocking thing to have a guilty conscience, and to be sneaking about on account of wicked deeds. As for me, innocent as I was, I could not help shuddering before their eyes whenever they brought me out, for I knew I should be thrown back again up the table as a false pretender. At length I was paid away to a poor old woman, who received me as wages for a hard day's work. But she could not again get rid of me; no one would take me. I was to the woman a most unlucky shilling. "I am positively obliged to pass this shilling to somebody," said she; "I cannot, with the best intentions, lay by a bad shilling. The rich baker shall have it,—he can bear the loss better than I can. But, after all, it is not a right thing to do."

' "Ah!" sighed I to myself, "am I also to be a burden on the conscience of this poor woman? Am I then in my old days so completely changed?" The woman offered me to the rich baker, but he knew the current money too well, and as soon as he received me he threw me almost in the woman's face. She could get no bread for me, and I felt quite grieved to the heart that I should be cause of so much trouble to another, and be treated as a cast-off coin. I who, in my young days, felt so joyful in the certainty of my own value, and knew so well that I bore a genuine stamp. I was as sorrowful now as a poor shilling can be when nobody will have him. The woman took me home again with her, and looking at me very earnestly, she said, "No, I will not try to deceive anyone with thee again. I will bore a hole through thee, that everyone may know that thou art a false and worthless thing; and yet, why should I do that? Very likely thou art a lucky shilling. A thought has just struck me that it is so, and I believe it. Yes, I will make a hole in the shilling," said she, "and run a string through it, and then give it to my neighbour's little one to hang round her neck, as a lucky shilling." So she drilled a hole through me.

'It is really not at all pleasant to have a hole bored through one, but we can submit to a great deal when it is done with a good intention. A string was drawn through the hole, and I became a kind of medal. They hung me round the neck of a little child, and the child laughed at me and kissed me, and I rested for one whole night on the warm, innocent breast of a child.

'In the morning the child's mother took me between her fingers, and had certain thoughts about me, which I very soon

found out. First, she looked for a pair of scissors, and cut the string.

' "Lucky shilling!" said she, "certainly this is what I mean to try." Then she laid me in vinegar till I became quite green, and after that she filled up the hole with cement, rubbed me a little to brighten me up, and went out in the twilight hour to the lottery collector, to buy herself a ticket, with a shilling that should bring luck. How everything seemed to cause me trouble. The lottery collector pressed me so hard that I thought I should crack. I had been called false, I had been thrown away,—that I knew; and there were many shillings and coins with inscriptions and stamps of all kinds lying about. I well knew how proud they were, so I avoided them from very shame. With the collector were several men who seemed to have a great deal to do, so I fell unnoticed into a chest, among several other coins.

'Whether the lottery ticket gained a prize, I know not; but this I know, that in a very few days after, I was recognised as a bad shilling, and laid aside. Everything that happened seemed always to add to my sorrow. Even if a man has a good character, it is of no use for him to deny what is said of him, for he is not considered an impartial judge of himself.

'A year passed, and in this way I had been changed from hand to hand; always abused, always looked at with displeasure, and trusted by no one; but I trusted in myself, and had no confidence in the world. Yes, that was a very dark time.

'At length one day I was passed to a traveller, a foreigner, the very same who had brought me away from home; and he was simple and true-hearted enough to take me for current coin. But would he also attempt to pass me? And should I again hear the outcry, "False! Good-for-nothing!" The traveller examined me attentively, "I took thee for good coin," said he; then suddenly a smile spread all over his face. I have never seen such a smile on any other face as on his. "Now this is singular," said he, "it is a coin from my own country; a good, true, shilling from home. Someone has bored a hole through it, and people have no doubt called it false. How curious that it should come into my hands. I will take it home with me to my own house."

'Joy thrilled through me when I heard this. I had been once more called a good, honest shilling, and I was to go back to my own home, where each and all would recognise me, and know that I was made of good silver, and bore a true, genuine stamp. I should have been glad in my joy to throw out sparks of fire, but it has never at any time been my nature to sparkle. Steel can do so, but not silver. I was wrapped up in fine, white paper, that I might not mix with the other coins and be lost; and on special occasions, when people from my own country happened to be present, I was brought forward and spoken of very kindly. They said I was very interesting, and it was really quite worthwhile to notice that those who are interesting have often not a single word to say for themselves.

'At length I reached home. All my cares were at an end. Joy again overwhelmed me; for was I not good silver, and had I not a genuine stamp? I had no more insults or disappointments to endure; although, indeed, there was a hole through me, as if I were false; but suspicions are nothing when a man is really true, and everyone should persevere in acting honestly, for a will be made right in time. That is my firm belief,' said the shilling.

# 28

# The Teapot

There was once a proud teapot; it was proud of being porcelain, proud of its long spout, proud of its broad handle. It had something before and behind,—the spout before and the handle behind,—and that was what it talked about. But it did not talk of its lid, which was cracked and riveted; these were defects, and one does not talk of one's defects, for there are plenty of others to do that. The cups, the cream pot, and the sugar bowl, the whole tea service, would think much oftener of the lid's imperfections—and talk about them—than of the sound handle and the remarkable spout. The teapot knew it.

'I know you,' it said within itself. 'I know, too, my imperfection, and I am well aware that in that very thing is seen my humility, my modesty. Imperfections we all have, but we also have compensations. The cups have a handle, the sugar bowl a lid; I have both, and one thing besides, in front, which they can never have. I have a spout, and that makes me the queen of the tea table. I spread abroad a blessing on thirsting mankind, for in me the Chinese leaves are brewed in the boiling, tasteless water.'

All this said the teapot in its fresh young life. It stood on the table that was spread for tea; it was lifted by a very delicate hand, but the delicate hand was awkward. The teapot fell, the spout snapped off, and the handle snapped off. The lid was no worse to speak of; the worst had been spoken of that.

The teapot lay in a swoon on the floor, while the boiling water ran out of it. It was a horrid shame, but the worst was that everybody jeered at it; they jeered at the teapot and not at the awkward hand.

'I never shall forget that experience,' said the teapot, when it afterward talked of its life. 'I was called an invalid, and placed in a corner, and the next day was given to a woman who begged for victuals. I fell into poverty, and stood dumb both outside and in. But then, just as I was, began my better life. One can be one thing and still become quite another.

'Earth was placed in me. For a teapot, this is the same as being buried, but in the earth was placed a flower bulb. Who placed it there, who gave it, I know not; but given it was, and it became a compensation for the Chinese leaves and the boiling water, a compensation for the broken handle and spout.

'And the bulb lay in the earth, the bulb lay in me; it became my heart, my living heart, such as I had never before possessed. There was life in me, power and might. The heart pulsed, and the bulb put forth sprouts; it was the springing up of thoughts and feelings which burst forth into flower.

'I saw it, I bore it, I forgot myself in its delight. Blessed is it to forget oneself in another. The flower gave me no thanks; it did not think of me. It was admired and praised, and I was glad at that. How happy it must have been! One day I heard someone say that the flower deserved a better pot. I was thumped hard on my back, which was a great affliction, and the flower was put into a better pot. I was thrown out into the yard, where I lie as an old potsherd. But I have the memory, and that I can never lose.'

# 29

# The Candles

There was once a big wax candle which knew its own importance quite well.

'I am born of wax and moulded in a shape,' it said 'I give better light and burn longer than other candles. My place is in a chandelier or on a silver candlestick!'

'That must be a lovely existence!' said the tallow candle. 'I am only made of tallow, but I comfort myself with the thought that it is always a little better than being a farthing dip: that is only dipped twice, and I am dipped eight times to get my proper thickness. I am content! It is certainly finer and more fortunate to be born of wax instead of tallow, but one does not settle one's own place in this world. You are placed in the big room in the glass chandelier, I remain in the kitchen, but that is also a good place; from there the whole house gets its food.'

'But there is something which is more important than food,' said the wax candle. 'Society! To see it shine, and to shine oneself! There is a ball this evening, and soon I and all my family[40] will be fetched.'

Scarcely was the word spoken, when all the wax candles were fetched, but the tallow candle also went with them. The lady herself took it in her dainty hand, and carried it out to the kitchen: a little boy stood there with a basket, which was filled with potatoes; two or three apples also found their way there. The good lady gave all this to the poor boy.

'There is a candle for you as well, my little friend,' said she. 'Your mother sits and works till late in the night; she can use it!'

The little daughter of the house stood close by, and when she heard the words 'late in the night,' she said with great delight, 'I also shall stay up till late in the night! We shall have a ball, and I shall wear my big red sash!' How her face shone! That was with joy! No wax candle can shine like two childish eyes!

'That is a blessing to see,' thought the tallow candle; 'I shall never forget it, and I shall certainly never see it again.'

And so it was laid in the basket, under the lid, and the boy went away with it.

'Where shall I go now?' thought the candle; 'I shall go to poor people, and perhaps not even get a brass candlestick, while the wax candle sits in silver and sees all the grand people. How lovely it must be to shine for the grand people! But it was my lot to be tallow and not way!'

And so the candle came to poor people, a widow with three children, in a little, low room, right opposite the rich house.

'God bless the good lady for her gifts,' said the mother, 'what a lovely candle that is! It can burn till late in the night.'

And then the candle was lighted.

'Fut, foi,' it said, 'what a horrid-smelling match that was she lighted me with! The wax candle over in the rich house would not have such treatment offered to it.'

There also the candles were lighted: they shone, out across the street; the carriages rolled up with the elegant ball guests and the music played.

'Now they begin across there,' the tallow candle noticed, and thought of the beaming face of the rich little girl, more sparkling than all the wax lights. 'That sight I shall never see again!'

Then the smallest of the children in the poor house, a little girl, came and took her brother and sister round the neck: she had something very important to tell them, and it must be whispered. 'Tonight we shall have just think!—Tonight we shall have hot potatoes!'

And her face shone with happiness: the tallow candle shone right into it, and it saw a gladness, a happiness as great as over in the rich house, where the little girl said, 'We shall have a ball tonight, and I shall wear my big red sash!'

'It is just as much to get hot potatoes,' thought the candle. 'Here there is just as much joy amongst the children.' And it sneezed at that; that is to say, it spattered; a tallow candle can do no more.

The table was laid, and the potatoes eaten. Oh, how good they tasted! It was a perfect feast, and each one got an apple besides, and the smallest child said the little verse:

'Thou good God, I give thanks to Thee
That Thou again hast nourished me. Amen!'

'Was that not nicely said, Mother?' broke out the little one.

'You must not ask that again,' said the mother; 'you must think only of the good God who has fed you.'

The little ones went to bed, got a kiss and fell asleep at once, and the mother sat and sewed late into the night to get the means of support for them and for herself. And over from the big house the lights shone and the music sounded. The stars shone over all the houses, over the rich and over the poor, equally clear and blessed.

'This has really been a delightful evening!' thought the tallow candle. 'I wonder if the wax candles had it any better in the silver candlestick? I would like to know that before I am burn burned out.'

And it thought of the two happy ones, the one lighted by the wax candle, and the other by the tallow candle.

Yes, that is the whole story!

# 30

# What Old Johanne Told

The wind whistles in the old willow tree. It is as if one were hearing a song; the wind sings it; the tree tells it. If you do not understand it, then ask old Johanne in the poorhouse; she knows about it; she was born here in the parish.

Many years ago, when the King's Highway still lay along here, the tree was already large and conspicuous. It stood, as it still stands, in front of the tailor's whitewashed timber house, close to the ditch, which then was so large that the cattle could be watered there, and where in the summertime the little peasant boys used to run about naked and paddle in the water. Underneath the tree stood a stone milepost cut from a big rock; now it is overturned, and a bramble bush grows over it.

The new King's Highway was built on the other side of the rich farmer's manor house; the old one became a field path; the ditch became a puddle overgrown with duckweed; if a frog tumbled down into it, the greenery was parted, and one saw the black water; all around it grew, and still grow, 'muskedonnere[41],' buckbean, and yellow iris.

The tailor's house was old and crooked; the roof was a hotbed for moss and houseleek. The dovecot had collapsed, and starlings built their nests there. The swallows hung nest after nest on the house gable and all along beneath the roof; it was just as if luck itself lived there.

And once it had; now, however, this was a lonely and silent place. Here in solitude lived weak-willed 'Poor Rasmus,' as they called him. He had been born here; he had played here, had leaped across meadow and over hedge, had splashed, as a child, in the ditch, and had climbed up the old tree. The tree would raise its big branches with pride and beauty, just as it raises them yet, but storms had already bent the trunk a little, and time had given it a crack. Wind and weather have since lodged earth in the crack, and there grow grass and greenery; yes, and even a little serviceberry has planted itself there.

When in spring the swallows came, they flew about the tree and the roof and plastered and patched their old nests, while Poor Rasmus let his nest stand or fall as it liked. His motto was, 'What good will it do?'—and it had been his father's, too.

He stayed in his home. The swallows flew away, but they always came back, the faithful creatures! The starling flew away, but it returned, too, and whistled its song again. Once Rasmus had known how, but now he neither whistled nor sang.

The wind whistled in the old willow tree then, just as it now whistles; indeed, it is as if one were hearing a song; the wind sings it; the tree tells it. And if you do not understand it, then ask old Johanne in the poorhouse; she knows about it; she knows about everything of old; she is like a book of chronicles, with inscriptions and old recollections.

At the time the house was new and good, the country tailor, Ivar Ölse, and his wife, Maren, moved into it—industrious, honest folk, both of them. Old Johanne was then a child; she was the daughter of a wooden shoemaker—one of the poorest in the parish. Many a good sandwich did she receive from Maren, who was in no want of food. The lady of the manor house liked Maren, who was always laughing and happy and never downhearted. She used her tongue a good deal, but her hands also. She could sew as fast as she could use her mouth, and, moreover, she cared for her house and children; there were nearly a dozen children—eleven altogether; the twelfth never made its appearance.

'Poor people always have a nest full of youngsters,' growled the master of the manor house. 'If one could drown them like kittens, and keep only one or two of the strongest, it would be less of a misfortune!'

'God have mercy!' said the tailor's wife. 'Children are a blessing from God; they are such a delight in the house. Every child is one more Lord's prayer. If times are bad, and one has many mouths to feed, why, then a man works all the harder and finds out ways and means honestly; our Lord fails not when we do not fail.'

The lady of the manor house agreed with her; she nodded kindly and patted Maren's cheek; she had often done so, yes, and had kissed her as well, but that had been when the lady was a little child and Maren her nursemaid. The two were fond of each other, and this feeling did not wane.

Each year at Christmastime winter provisions would arrive at the tailor's house from the manor house—a barrel of meal, a pig, two geese, a tub of butter, cheese, and apples. That was indeed an asset to the larder. Ivar Ölse looked quite pleased, too, but soon came out with his old motto, 'What good will it do?'

The house was clean and tidy, with curtains in the windows, and flowers as well, both carnations and balsams. A sampler hung in a picture frame, and close by hung a love letter in rhyme, which

Maren Ölse herself had written; she knew how to put rhymes together. She was almost a little proud of the family name Ölse; it was the only word in the Danish language that rhymed with **pölse** (sausage). 'At least that's an advantage to have over other people,' she said, and laughed. She always kept her good humour, and never said, like her husband, 'What good will it do?' Her motto was, 'Depend on yourself and on our Lord.' So she did, and that kept them all together. The children thrived, grew out over the nest, went out into the world, and prospered well.

Rasmus was the smallest; he was such a pretty child that one of the great portrait painters in the capital had borrowed him to paint from, and in the picture he was as naked as when he had come into this world. That picture was now hanging in the King's palace. The lady of the manor house saw it, and recognised little Rasmus, though he had no clothes on.

But now came hard times. The tailor had rheumatism in both hands, on which great lumps appeared. No doctor could help him—not even the wise Stine, who herself did some 'doctoring.'

'One must not be downhearted,' said Maren. 'It never helps to hang the head. Now that we no longer have father's two hands to help us, I must try to use mine all the faster. Little Rasmus, too, can use the needle.' He was already sitting on the sewing table, whistling and singing. He was a happy boy. 'But he should not sit there the whole day long,' said the mother; 'that would be a shame for the child. He should play and jump about, too.'

The shoemaker's Johanne was his favourite playmate. Her folks were still poorer than Rasmus'. She was not pretty. She went about barefooted, and her clothes hung in rags, for she had no one to mend them, and to do it herself did not occur to her—she was a child, and as happy as a bird in our Lord's sunshine.

By the stone milepost, under the large willow tree, Rasmus and Johanne played. He had ambitious thoughts; he would one day become a fine tailor and live in the city, where there were master tailors who had ten workmen at the table; this he had heard from his father. There he would be an apprentice, and there he would become a master tailor, and then Johanne could come to visit him; and if by that time she knew how to cook, she could prepare the meals for all of them and have a large apartment of her own. Johanne dared not expect that, but Rasmus believed it could happen. They sat beneath the old tree, and the wind whistled in the branches and leaves; it seemed as if the wind were singing and the tree talking.

In the autumn every single leaf fell off; rain dripped from the bare branches. 'They will be green again,' said Mother Ölse.

'What good will it do?' said her husband. 'New year, new worries about our livelihood.'

'The larder is full,' said the wife. 'We can thank our good lady for that. I am healthy and have plenty of strength. It is sinful for us to complain.'

The master and lady of the manor house remained there in the country over Christmas, but the week after the new year, they were to go to the city, where they would spend the winter in festivity and amusement. They would even go to a reception and ball given by the King himself. The lady had bought two rich dresses from France; they were of such material, of such fashion, and so well sewn that the tailor's Maren had never seen such magnificence. She asked the lady if she might come up to the house with her husband, so that he could see the dresses as well. Such things had surely never been seen by a country tailor, she said. He saw them and had not a word to say until he returned home, and what he did say was only what he always said, 'What good will it do?' And this time he spoke the truth.

The master and lady of the manor house went to the city, and the balls and merrymaking began. But amid all the splendour the old gentleman died, and the lady then, after all, did not wear her grand dresses. She was so sorrowful and was dressed from head to foot in heavy black mourning. Not so much as a white tucker was to be seen. All the servants were in black; even the state coach was covered with fine black cloth.

It was an icy-cold night; the snow glistened and the stars twinkled. The heavy hearse brought the body from the city to the country church, where it was to be laid in the family vault. The steward and the parish bailiff were waiting on horseback, with torches, in front of the cemetery gate. The church was lighted up, and the pastor stood in the open church door to receive the body. The coffin was carried up into the chancel; the whole congregation followed. The pastor spoke, and a psalm was sung. The lady was present in the church; she had been driven there in the black-draped state coach, which was black inside as well as outside; such a carriage had never before been seen in the parish.

Throughout the winter, people talked about this impressive display of grief; it was indeed a 'nobleman's funeral.'

'One could well see how important the man was,' said the village folk. 'He was nobly born and he was nobly buried.'

'What good will it do him?' said the tailor. 'Now he has neither life nor goods. At least we have one of these.'

'Don't speak such words!' said Maren. 'He has everlasting life in the kingdom of heaven.'

'Who told you that, Maren?' said the tailor. 'A dead man is good manure, but this man was too highborn to even do the soil any good; he must lie in a church vault.'

'Don't speak so impiously!' said Maren. 'I tell you again he has everlasting life!'

'Who told you that, Maren?' repeated the tailor. And Maren threw her apron over little Rasmus; he must not hear that kind of talk. She carried him off into the peathouse and wept.

'The words you heard over there, little Rasmus, were not your father's; it was the evil one who was passing through the room and took your father's voice. Say your Lord's Prayer. We'll both say it.' She folded the child's hands. 'Now I am happy again,' she said. 'Have faith in yourself and in our Lord.'

The year of mourning came to an end. The widow lady dressed in half mourning, but she had whole happiness in her heart. It was rumoured that she had a suitor and was already thinking of marriage. Maren knew something about it, and the pastor knew a little more.

On Palm Sunday, after the sermon, the banns of marriage for the widow lady and her betrothed were to be published. He was a wood carver or a sculptor; just what the name of his profession was, people did not know; at that time not many had heard of Thorvaldsen and his art. The future master of the manor was not a nobleman, but still he was a very stately man. His was one profession that people did not understand, they said; he cut out images, was clever in his work and young and handsome. 'What good will it do?' said Tailor Ölse.

On Palm Sunday the banns were read from the pulpit; then

followed a psalm and Communion. The tailor, his wife, and little Rasmus were in church; the parents received Communion, while Rasmus sat in the pew, for he was not yet confirmed. Of late there had been a shortage of clothes in the tailor's house; the old ones had been turned, and turned again, stitched and patched. Now they were all three dressed in new clothes, but of black material—as at a funeral. They were dressed in the drapery from the funeral coach. The man had a jacket and trousers of it; Maren, a high-necked dress, and Rasmus, a whole suit to grow in until confirmation time. Both the outside and inside cloth from the funeral carriage had been used. No one needed to know what it had been used for before, but people soon got to know.

The wise woman, Stine, and a couple of other equally wise women, who did not live on their wisdom, said that the clothes would bring sickness and disease into the household. 'One cannot dress oneself in cloth from a funeral carriage without riding to the grave.' The wooden shoemaker's Johanne cried when she heard this talk. And it so happened that the tailor became more and more ill from that day on, until it seemed apparent who was going to suffer that fate. And it proved to be so.

On the first Sunday after Trinity, Tailor Ölse died, leaving Maren alone to keep things together. She did, keeping faith in herself and in our Lord.

The following year Rasmus was confirmed. He was then ready to go to the city as an apprentice to a master tailor—not, after all, one with ten assistants at the table, but with one; little Rasmus might be counted as a half. He was happy, and he looked delighted indeed, but Johanne wept; she was fonder of him than she had realized. The tailor's wife remained in the old house and carried on the business.

It was at that time that the new King's Highway was opened, and the old one, by the willow tree and the tailor's, became a field path, with duckweed growing over the water left in the ditch there; the milepost tumbled over, for it had nothing to stand for, but the tree kept itself strong and beautiful, the wind whistling among its branches and leaves.

The swallows flew away, and the starlings flew away, but they came again in the spring. And when they came back the fourth time, Rasmus, too, came back to his home. He had served his apprenticeship, and was a handsome but slim youth. Now he would buckle up his knapsack and see foreign countries; that was what he longed for. But his mother clung to him; home was the best place! All the other children were scattered about; he was the youngest, and the house would be his. He could get plenty of work if he would go about the neighbourhood—be a travelling tailor, and sew for a fortnight at this farm and a fortnight at that. That would be travelling, too. And Rasmus followed his mother's advice.

So again he slept beneath the roof of his birthplace. Again he sat under the old willow tree and heard it whistle. He was indeed good-looking, and he could whistle like a bird and sing new and old songs.

He was well liked at the big farms, especially at Klaus Hansen's, the second richest farmer in the parish. Else, the daughter, was like the loveliest flower to look at, and she was always laughing. There were people who were unkind enough to say that she laughed simply to show her pretty teeth. She was happy indeed, and always in the humour for playing tricks; everything suited her.

She was fond of Rasmus, and he was fond of her, but neither

of them said a word about it. So he went about being gloomy; he had more of his father's disposition than his mother's. He was in a good humour only when Else was present; then they both laughed, joked, and played tricks; but although there was many a good opportunity, he did not say a single word about his love. 'What good will it do?' was his thought. 'Her parents look for profitable marriage for her, and that I cannot give her. The wisest thing for me to do would be to leave.' But he could not leave. It was as if Else had a string fastened to him; he was like a trained bird with her; he sang and whistled for her pleasure and at her will.

Johanne, the shoemaker's daughter, was a servant girl at the farm, employed for common work. She drove the milk cart in the meadow, where she and the other girls milked the cows; yes, and she even had to cart manure when it was necessary. She never came into the sitting room and didn't see much of Rasmus or Else, but she heard that the two were as good as engaged.

'Now Rasmus will be well off,' she said. 'I cannot begrudge him that.' And her eyes became quite wet. But there was really nothing to cry about.

There was a market in the town. Klaus Hansen drove there, and Rasmus went along; he sat beside Else, both going there and coming home. He was numb from love, but he didn't say a word about it.

'He ought to say something to me about the matter,' thought the girl, and there she was right. 'If he won't talk, I'll have to frighten him into it.'

And soon there was talk at the farm that the richest farmer in the parish had proposed to Else; and so he had, but no one knew what answer she had given.

Thoughts buzzed around in Rasmus' head.

One evening Else put a gold ring on her finger and then asked Rasmus what that signified.

'Betrothal,' he said.

'And with whom do you think?' she asked.

'With the rich farmer?' he said.

'There, you have hit it,' she said, nodding, and then slipped away.

But he slipped away, too; he went home to his mother's house like a bewildered man and packed his knapsack. He wanted to go out into the wide world; even his mother's tears couldn't stop him.

He cut himself a stick from the old willow and whistled as if he were in a good humour; he was on his way to see the beauty of the whole world.

'This is a great grief to me,' said the mother. 'But I suppose it is wisest and best for you to go away, so I shall have to put up with it. Have faith in yourself and in our Lord; then I shall have you back again merry and happy.'

He walked along the new highway, and there he saw Johanne come driving with a load of rubbish; she had not noticed him, and he did not wish to be seen by her, so he sat down behind the hedge; there he was hidden—and Johanne drove by.

Out into the world he went; no one knew where. His mother thought, 'He will surely come home again before a year passes. Now he will see new things and have new things to think about, but then he will fall back into the old folds; they cannot be ironed out with any iron. He has a little too much of his father's disposition; I would rather he had mine, poor child! But he will surely come home again; he cannot forget either me or the house.'

The mother would wait a year and a day. Else waited only a month and then she secretly went to the wise woman, Stine Madsdatter, who, besides knowing something about 'doctoring,' could tell fortunes in cards and coffee and knew more than her Lord's Prayer. She, of course, knew where Rasmus was; she read it in the coffee grounds. He was in a foreign town, but she couldn't read the name of it. In this town there were soldiers and beautiful ladies. He was thinking of either becoming a soldier or marrying one of the young ladies.

This Else could not bear to hear. She would willingly give her savings to buy him back, but no one must know that it was she.

And old Stine promised that he would come back; she knew of a charm, a dangerous charm for him; it would work; it was the ultimate remedy. She would set the pot boiling for him, and then, wherever in all the world he was, he would have to come home where the pot was boiling and his beloved was waiting for him. Months might pass before he came, but come he must if he was still alive. Without peace or rest night and day, he would be forced to return, over sea and mountain, whether the weather were[42] mild or rough, and even if his feet were ever so tired. He would come home; he had to come home.

The moon was in the first quarter; it had to be for the charm to work, said old Stine. It was stormy weather, and the old willow tree creaked. Stine, cut a twig from it and tied it in a knot. That would surely help to draw Rasmus home to his mother's house. Moss and houseleek were taken from the roof and put in the pot, which was set upon the fire. Else had to tear a leaf out of the psalmbook; she tore out the last leaf by chance, that on which the list of errata appeared. 'That will do just as well,' said Stine, and threw it into the pot.

Many sorts of things went into the stew, which had to boil and boil steadily until Rasmus came home. The black cock in old Stine's room had to lose its red comb, which went into the pot. Else's heavy gold ring went in with it, and that she would never get again, Stine told her beforehand. She was so wise, Stine. Many things that we are unable to name went into the pot, which stood constantly over the flame or on glowing embers or hot ashes. Only she and Else knew about it.

Whenever the moon was new or the moon was on the wane, Else would come to her and ask, 'Can't you see him coming?'

'Much do I know,' said Stine, 'and much do I see, but the length of the way before him I cannot see. Now he is over the first mountains; now he is on the sea in bad weather. The road is long, through large forests; he has blisters on his feet, and he has fever in his bones, but he must go on.'

'No, no!' said Else. 'I feel so sorry for him.'

'He cannot be stopped now, for if we stop him, he will drop dead in the road!'

A year and a day had gone. The moon shone round and big, and the wind whistled in the old tree. A rainbow appeared across the sky in the bright moonlight.

'That is a sign to prove what I say,' said Stine. 'Now Rasmus is coming.'

But still he did not come.

'The waiting time is long,' said Stine.

'Now I am tired of this,' said Else. She seldom visited Stine now and brought her no more gifts. Her mind became easier, and one fine morning they all knew in the parish that Else had said 'yes' to the rich farmer. She went over to look at the house and grounds, the cattle, and the household belongings. All was in good order, and there was no reason to wait with the wedding.

It was celebrated with a great party lasting three days. There was dancing to the clarinet and violins. No one in the parish was forgotten in the invitations. Mother Ölse was there, too, and when the party came to an end, and the hosts had thanked the guests, and the trumpets had blown, she went home with the leavings from the feast.

She had fastened the door only with a peg; it had been taken out, the door stood open, and in the room sat Rasmus. He had returned home—come that very hour. Lord God, how he looked! He was only skin and bone; he was pale and yellow.

'Rasmus!' said his mother. 'Is it you I see? How badly you look! But I am so happy in my heart to have you back.'

And she gave him the good food she had brought home from

the party, a piece of the roast and of the wedding cake.

He had lately, he said, often thought of his mother, his home, and the old willow tree; it was strange how often in his dreams he had seen the tree and the little barefooted Johanne. He did not mention Else at all. He was ill and had to go to bed.

But we do not believe that the pot was the cause of this, or that it had exercised any power over him. Only old Stine and Else believed that, but they did not talk about it.

Rasmus lay with a fever—an infectious one. For that reason no one came to the tailor's house, except Johanne, the shoemaker's daughter. She cried when she saw how miserable Rasmus was.

The doctor wrote a prescription for him to have filled at the pharmacy. He would not take the medicine. 'What good will it do?' he said.

'You will get well again then,' said his mother. 'Have faith in yourself and in our Lord! If I could only see you get flesh on your body again, hear you whistle and sing; for that I would willingly lay down my life.'

And Rasmus was cured of his illness, but his mother contracted it. Our Lord summoned her, and not him.

It was lonely in the house; he became poorer and poorer. 'He is worn out,' they said in the parish. 'Poor Rasmus.' He had led a wild life on his travels; that, and not the black pot that had boiled, had sucked out his marrow and given him pain in his body. His hair became thin and grey. He was too lazy to work. 'What good will it do?' he said. He would rather visit the tavern than the church.

One autumn evening he was staggering through rain and wind along the muddy road from the tavern to his house; his mother had long since gone and been laid in her grave. The swallows and starlings were also gone, faithful as they were. Johanne, the shoemaker's daughter, was not gone; she overtook him on the road and then followed him a little way.

'Pull yourself together, Rasmus.'

'What good will it do?' he said.

'That is an awful saying that you have,' said she. 'Remember your mother's words, "Have faith in yourself and in our Lord." You do not, Rasmus, but you must, and you shall. Never say, "What good will it do?" for then you pull up the root of all your doings.'

She followed him to the door of his house, and there she left him. He did not stay inside; he wandered out under the old willow tree and sat on a stone from the overturned milepost.

The wind whistled in the tree's branches; it was like a song: it was like talk.

Rasmus answered it; he spoke aloud but no one heard him except the tree and the whistling wind.

'I am getting so cold. It is time to go to bed. Sleep, sleep!'

And he walked away, not toward the house, but over to the ditch, where he tottered and fell. Rain poured down, and the wind was icy cold, but he didn't feel this. When the sun rose, and the crows flew over the bulrushes, he awoke, deathly ill. Had he laid his head where he put his feet, he would never have arisen; the green duckweed would have been his burial sheet.

Later in the day Johanne came to the tailor's house. She helped him; she managed to get him to the hospital.

'We have known each other since we were little,' she said. 'Your mother gave me both ale and food; for that I can never repay her. You will regain your health; you will be a man with a will to live!'

And our Lord willed that he should live. But he had his ups

and downs, both in health and mind.

The swallows and the starlings returned, and flew away, and returned again. Rasmus became older than his years. He sat alone in his house, which deteriorated more and more. He was poor, poorer now than Johanne.

'You have no faith,' she said, 'and if we do not believe in God, what have we? You should go to Communion,' she said; 'you haven't been since your confirmation.'

'What good will it do?' he said.

'If you say that and believe it, then let it be; the Master does not want an unwilling guest at His table. But think of your mother and your childhood. Once you were a good, pious boy. Let me read a psalm to you.'

'What good will it do?' he said.

'It always comforts me,' she answered.

'Johanne, you have surely become one of the saints.' And he looked at her with dull, weary eyes.

And Johanne read the psalm, but not from a book, for she had none; she knew it by heart.

'Those were beautiful words,' he said, 'but I could not follow you altogether. My head feels so heavy.'

Rasmus had become an old man. But Else, if we may mention her, was no longer young, either; Rasmus never mentioned her. She was a grandmother. Her granddaughter was an impudent little girl.

The little one was playing with the other children in the village. Rasmus came along, supporting himself on his stick. He stopped, watched the children play, and smiled to them, old times were in his thoughts. Else's granddaughter pointed at him. 'Poor

Rasmus!' she shouted. The other little girls followed her example. 'Poor Rasmus!' they shouted, and pursued the old man with shrieks. It was a grey, gloomy day, and many others followed. But after grey and gloomy days, there comes a sunshiny day.

It was a beautiful Whitsunday morning. The church was decorated with green birch branches; there was a scent of the woods within it, and the sun shone on the church pews. The large altar candles were lighted, and Communion was being held. Johanne was among the kneeling, but Rasmus was not among them. That very morning the Lord had called him.

In God are grace and mercy.

Many years have since passed. The tailor's house still stands there, but no one lives in it. It might fall the first stormy night. The ditch is overgrown with bulrush and buck bean. The wind whistles in the old tree; it is as if one were hearing a song; the wind sings it; the tree tells it. If you do not understand it, ask old Johanne in the poorhouse.

She still lives there; she sings her psalm, the one she read for Rasmus. She thinks of him, prays to our Lord for him—she, the faithful soul. She can tell of bygone times, of memories that whistle in the old willow tree.

# 31

# The Gardener and the Manor

A bout one Danish mile from the capital stood an old manor house, with thick walls, towers, and pointed gable ends. Here lived, but only in the summer season, a rich and courtly family. This manor house was the best and the most beautiful of all the houses they owned. It looked outside as if it had just been cast in a foundry, and within it was comfort itself. The family arms were carved in stone over the door; beautiful roses twined about the arms and the balcony; a grassplot extended before the house with red thorn and white thorn, and many rare flowers grew even outside the conservatory. The manor kept also a very skilful gardener. It was a real pleasure to see the flower garden, the orchard, and the kitchen garden. There was still to be seen a portion of the manor's original garden, a few box tree hedges cut in shape of crowns and pyramids, and behind these two mighty old trees almost always without leaves. One might almost think that a storm or waterspout had scattered great lumps of manure on their branches, but each lump was a bird's nest. A swarm of rooks and crows from time immemorial had built their nests here. It was a townful of birds, and the birds were the manorial lords here. They did not care for the proprietors, the manor's oldest family branch, nor for the present owner of the manor, —these were nothing to them; but they bore with the wandering creatures below them, notwithstanding that once in a while they shot with guns in a way that made the birds' backbones shiver, and made every bird fly up, crying 'Rak, Rak!'

The gardener very often explained to the master the necessity of felling the old trees, as they did not look well, and by taking them away they would probably also get rid of the screaming birds, which would seek another place. But he never could be induced either to give up the trees or the swarm of birds the manor could not spare them, as they were relics of the good old times, that ought always to be kept in remembrance.

'The trees are the birds' heritage by this time!' said the master. 'So let them keep them, my good Larsen.' Larsen was the gardener's name, but that is of very little consequence in this story. 'Haven't you room enough to work in, little Larsen? Have you not the flower garden, the greenhouses, the orchard and the kitchen garden!' He cared for them, he kept them in order and cultivated them with zeal and ability, and the family knew it; but they did not conceal from him that they often tasted fruits and saw flowers in other houses that surpassed what he had in his garden, and that was a sore trial to the gardener, who always wished to do the best, and really did the best he could. He was good-hearted, and a faithful servant.

The owner sent one day for him, and told him kindly that the day before, at a party given by some friends of rank, they had eaten apples and pears which were so juicy and well-flavored that all the guests had loudly expressed their admiration. To be sure, they were not native fruits, but they ought by all means to be introduced here, and to be acclimatised if possible. They learned that the fruit was bought of one of the first fruit dealers in the city, and the gardener was to ride to town and find out about where they came from, and then order some slips for grafting. The gardener was very well acquainted with the dealer, because he was the very person to whom he sold the fruit that grew in the manor garden, beyond what was needed by the family. So the gardener went to town and asked the fruit dealer where he had found those apples and pears that were praised so highly.

'They are from your own garden,' said the fruit dealer, and he showed him, both the apples and pears, which he recognised. Now, how happy the gardener felt! He hastened back to his master, and told him that the apples and pears were all from his own garden. But he would not believe it.

'It cannot be possible, Larsen. Can you get a written certificate of that from the fruit-dealer?' And that he could; and brought him a written certificate.

'That is certainly wonderful!' said the family.

And now every day were set on the table great dishes filled with beautiful apples and pears from their own garden; bushels and barrels of these fruits were sent to friends in the city and country, nay, were even sent abroad. It was exceedingly pleasant;

but when they talked with the gardener they said that the last two seasons had been remarkably favourable for fruits, and that fruits had done well all over the country.

Some time passed. The family were at dinner at court. The next day the gardener was sent for. They had eaten melons at the royal table which they found very juicy and well-flavored; they came from his Majesty's greenhouse. 'You must go and see the court gardener, and let him give you some seeds of those melons.'

'But the gardener at the court got his melon-seeds from us,' said the gardener, highly delighted.

'But then that man understands how to bring the fruit to a higher perfection,' was the answer. 'Each particular melon was delicious.'

'Well; then, I really may feel proud,' said the gardener. 'I must tell your lordship that the gardener at the court did not succeed very well with his melons this year, and so, seeing how beautiful ours looked, he tasted them and ordered from me three of them for the castle.'

'Larsen, do not pretend to say that those were melons from our garden.'

'Really, I dare say as much,' said the gardener, who went to the court gardener and got from him a written certificate to the effect that the melons on the royal table were from the manor. That was certainly a great surprise to the family, and they did not keep the story to themselves. Melon seeds were sent far and wide, in the same way as had been done with the slips, which they were now hearing had begun to take, and to bear fruit of an excellent kind. The fruit was named after the manor, and the name was written in English, German, and French.

This was something they never had dreamed of.

'We are afraid that the gardener will come to think too much of himself,' said they; but he looked on it in another way: what he wished was to get the reputation of being one of the best gardeners in the country, and to produce every year something exquisite out of all sorts of garden stuff, and that he did. But he often had to hear that the fruits which he first brought, the apples and pears, were after all the best. All other kinds of fruits were inferior to these. The melons, too, were very good, but they belonged to quite another species. His strawberries were very excellent, but by no means better than many others; and when it happened one year that his radishes did not succeed, they only spoke of them, and not of other good things he had made succeed.

It really seemed as if the family felt some relief in saying 'It won't turn out well this year, little Larsen!' They seemed quite glad when they could say 'It won't turn out well!'

The gardener used always twice a week to bring them fresh flowers, tastefully arranged, and the colours by his arrangements were brought out in stronger light.

'You have good taste, Larsen,' said the owner, 'but that is a gift from our Lord, not from yourself.'

One day the gardener brought a great crystal vase with a floating leaf of a white water lily, upon which was laid, with its long thick stalk descending into the water, a sparkling blue flower as large as a sunflower.

'The sacred lotos[43] of Hindostan[44]!' exclaimed the family. They had never seen such a flower; it was placed every day in the sunshine, and in the evening under artificial light. Everyone who saw it found it wonderfully beautiful and rare; and that said the most noble young lady in the country, the wise and kind-hearted princess. The lord of the manor deemed it an honour to present her with the flower, and the princess took it with her to the castle. Now the master of the house went down to the garden to pluck another flower of the same sort, but he could not find any. So he sent for the gardener, and asked him where he kept the blue lotos. 'I have been looking for it in vain,' said he. 'I went into the conservatory, and round about the flower garden.'

'No, it is not there!' said the gardener. 'It is nothing else than a common flower from the kitchen garden, but do you not find it beautiful? It looks as if it was the blue cactus, and yet it is only a kitchen herb. It is the flower of the artichoke!'

'You should have told us that at the time!' said the master. 'We supposed of course that it was a strange and rare flower. You have made us ridiculous in the eyes of the young princess! She saw the flower in our house and thought it beautiful. She did not know the flower, and she is versed in botany, too, but then that has nothing to do with kitchen herbs. How could you take it into your head, my good Larsen, to put such a flower up in our drawing room? It makes us ridiculous.'

And the magnificent blue flower from the kitchen garden was turned out of the drawing room, which was not at all the place for it. The master made his apology to the princess, telling her that it was only a kitchen herb which the gardener had taken into his head to exhibit, but that he had been well reprimanded for it.

'That was a pity,' said the princess, 'for he has really opened our eyes to see the beauty of a flower in a place where we should not have thought of looking for it. Our gardener shall every day, as long as the artichoke is in bloom, bring one of them up into the drawing room.'

Then the master told his gardener that he might again bring them a fresh artichoke flower. 'It is, after all, a very nice flower,' said he, 'and a truly remarkable one.' And so the gardener was praised again. 'Larsen likes that,' said the master; 'he is a spoiled child.'

In the autumn there came up a great gale, which increased so violently in the night that several large trees in the outskirts of the wood were torn up by the roots; and to the great grief of the household, but to the gardener's delight, the two big trees blew down, with all their birds' nests on them. In the manor house they heard during the storm the screaming of rooks and crows, beating their wings against the windows.

'Now I suppose you are happy, Larsen,' said the master: 'the storm has felled the trees, and the birds have gone off to the woods; there is nothing left from the good old days; it is all gone, and we are very sorry for it.'

The gardener said nothing, but he thought of what he long had turned over in his mind, how he could make that pretty sunny spot very useful, so that it could become an ornament to the garden and a pride to the family. The great trees which had been blown down had shattered the venerable hedge of box, that was cut into fanciful shapes.

Here he set out a multitude of plants that were not to be seen in other gardens. He made an earthen wall, on which he planted all sorts of native flowers from the fields and woods. What no other gardener had ever thought of planting in the manor garden he planted, giving each its appropriate soil, and the plants were in sunlight or shadow according as each species required. He cared tenderly for them, and they grew up finely. The juniper tree from the heaths of Jutland rose in shape and colour like the Italian cypress; the shining, thorny Christ-thorn, as green in the winter's cold as in the summer's sun, was splendid to see. In the foreground grew ferns of various species: some of them looked as if they were children of the palm tree; others, as if they were parents of the pretty plants called 'Venus's golden locks' or 'Maiden hair.' Here stood the despised burdock, which is so beautiful in its freshness that it looks well even in a bouquet. The burdock stood in a dry place, but below in the moist soil grew the colt's foot, also a despised plant, but yet most picturesque, with its tall stem and large leaf. Like a candelabrum with a multitude of branches six feet high, and with flower over against flower, rose the mullein, a mere field plant. Here stood the woodroof and the lily of the valley, the wild calla and the fine three-leaved wood sorrel. It was a wonder to see all this beauty!

In the front grew in rows very small peartrees from French soil, trained on wires. By plenty of sun and good care they soon bore as juicy fruits as in their own country. Instead of the two old leafless trees was placed a tall flagstaff, where the flag of Dannebrog was displayed; and near by[45] stood another pole, where the hop tendril in summer or harvest time wound its fragrant flowers; but in wintertime, after ancient custom, oat sheaves were fastened to it, that the birds of the air might find here a good meal in the happy Christmastime.

'Our good Larsen is growing sentimental as he grows old,' said the family; 'but he is faithful, and quite attached to us.'

In one of the illustrated papers there was a picture at New Year's of the old manor, with the flagstaff and the oat sheaves for the birds of the air, and the paper said that the old manor had preserved that beautiful old custom, and deserved great credit for it.

'They beat the drum for all Larsen's doings,' said the family. 'He is a lucky fellow, and we may almost be proud of having such a man in our service.'

But they were not a bit proud of it. They were very well aware that they were the lords of the manor; they could give Larsen warning, in fact, but they did not. They were good people, and fortunate it is for every Mr Larsen that there are so many good people like them.

Yes, that is the story of the gardener and the manor. Now you may think a little about it.

# Notes

1   a variant spelling of 'hello'
2   an obsolete variant of 'three times'
3   a variant spelling of 'plough'
4   don't have
5   an old-fashioned, dialect word for 'no'
6   need
7   a contraction of 'God be with ye', same as 'good-bye'
8   a variant spelling of 'axe'
9   an old-fashioned, dialect word for 'over there'
10  lovelier
11  more pleasant
12  an old-fashioned, literary word for 'where'
13  fitter
14  thought about
15  his
16  given to
17  an old-fashioned, poetic word for 'yours', used when speaking to one person and before a vowel sound or the letter 'h'
18  an old-fashioned, poetic word for 'yourself', used when speaking to one person
19  an old-fashioned, poetic word for 'you', used as the object of a verb of preposition and when speaking to one person
20  Do you have
21  an old-fashioned, poetic word for 'you', used when talking to one person
22  an old-fashioned, literary word for 'where'
23  enough flowers
24  Don't I have
25  an old-fashioned, literary variant spelling of 'nothing'
26  cleverer
27  Hush
28  look
29  the objective form of 'whosoever', same as 'whoever'
30  the archaic, poetic word for 'ever' or 'always'
31  an archaic word for 'can'
32  an old-fashioned second person singular form of 'have'
33  an archaic second person singular form of the past tense of 'be'
34  an archaic form of the past tense of 'do'
35  an old-fashioned form of 'shall'
36  an old-fashioned second person singular form of 'have'
37  an archaic singular form of the present tense of 'will'
38  an old-fashioned word for 'listen'

39  have come
40  All my family and I
41  of French origin 'mousqueton', which means 'short musket'
42  was
43  lotus
44  Hindustan
45  nearby

# 安徒生童話

# Preface to the Chinese Translation
## 中文譯本序

世界上有一些書，真可以從小讀到老，丹麥偉大作家漢斯·克里斯汀·安徒生（1805—1875）的童話就是這樣。這個奧妙，其實作者本人早就道破。

安徒生在寫他的早期童話之一《美人魚》時說過，在他收有《美人魚》的那個小集子裏，"其他童話比這一篇更是兒童故事，而這一篇含義更深，只有大人能夠理解。但是我相信，孩子光是看故事也會喜歡它：故事情節本身就足以吸引住孩子"。

我們談京劇不是有一句"外行看熱鬧，內行看門道"嗎？孩子們看書也是先看個熱鬧，要看情節能吸引住他們的故事。安徒生童話是講給孩子們聽的，當然都很熱鬧，這裏說的熱鬧，指的是有趣，但其中這樣既熱鬧又有更深含義的作品也不少。就拿我們最熟悉的《國王的新衣》來說，它的故事情節實在有趣，孩子們愛看，那個光着身體而自以為穿着最美麗的新衣的皇帝實在愚蠢，這個道理他們也懂，他們就很滿足了，而這篇童話更深刻的含義，他們未必能夠領會。等到他們長大起來，懂事了，再讀一次，或者再想一想那故事，也會回味無窮。也許因為安徒生童話是眾所周知的兒童文學作品，人大了往往就不去讀，這很可惜。我年逾七十，有機會又讀了安徒生童話一次，頗有以前沒有過的感受。因此我深深領悟到，安徒生童話真是可以從小讀到老的書。

而說到兒童文學，安徒生的確做了文學這一新領域的開創性工作。在他以前，有過著名的法國佩羅的《鵝媽媽的故事》、德國的《格林童話》，但它們都是根據民間流傳的童話和故事編寫或收集記錄而成。安徒生最初也給孩子們講這種故事。不過他在講述時也加進了自己的東西。例如《國王的新衣》原是一個西班牙民間故事，連西班牙大作家塞萬提斯也根據它寫過戲，而安徒生寫出來的童話截然不同，成了很有特色的安徒生童話。然而安徒生很快又從改寫民間故事轉入童話創作。他繼承了神仙故事和民間故事這一古老文學樣式並發展了它，創作出新的童話和故事，這就有了我們今天的兒童文學。

　　安徒生在當時恐怕還不知道他開創兒童文學這一新興文學領域的重大意義。他一心一意要寫的是傳統的長篇小說、詩歌、劇本等“嚴肅”文學作品，而對於寫兒童文學作品有過猶豫。倒是他的好朋友——丹麥大物理學家奧斯忒，看到了他的才能。他對安徒生說，如果他的長篇小說能使他出名，那麼，他的童話將使他不朽。這句話應驗了，他的其他作品不出國門，而他的童話傳遍了全世界，已經流傳了一百多年，還在一代一代流傳下去。

　　安徒生童話的成就也不是偶然的。我們知道，安徒生的父親是個鞋匠，母親是個洗衣婦，他小時候生活貧窮，十四歲到了首都哥本哈根，想當演員，不成，想當歌唱家，也不成，於是發奮學習文學，要當作家寫出大作品。他豐富的生活經歷、對丹麥老百姓的熱愛、對生活的思索、對文學和藝術的刻苦鑽研，可以說都結晶在他說給孩子們聽的童話裏。這就使他曾認為是“小玩意”的童話成了真正的“大作品”。

安徒生是一個多世紀以前的人，是位古人，我們自然很容易認為他的作品也很古老，然而事實不然，他的作品讀起來會給人一種新鮮感。他說："多年來，我已試着走過童話圓周裏的每一條半徑。因此，如果碰到一個想法或者題材會帶我回到嘗試過的形式，我常常不是放棄它，而是試一試給予它另一種形式。"安徒生一直在求新，他有一些寫法到今天來看還是很有啟發性。比方那篇《影子》，寫影子成了它的主人的主人，不是很容易讓我們想起現代派大小說家卡夫卡的作品嗎？也許因為它是童話，過去不太為人注意，而現在小說發展到和魔幻結合，這作品就使人覺得新鮮。對於"內行"，其中也是有些"門道"可看的。

所以我說，安徒生童話可以讓人從小讀到老。

任溶溶

# 1
# 打火盒

公路上有一個大兵，正邁着大步走來："左，右 —— 左，右。"他背着一個包，腰間佩着一把劍。他身經百戰，現在回到了家

他這樣走着走着，在路上遇見一個樣子十分嚇人的老巫婆。她下唇都快下垂到胸口了。她叫住他說："晚上好，當兵的。你有一把非常厲害的劍，還有一個大背包，你是一個地道的士兵。因此，你要多少錢就有多少錢。"

"謝謝你，老巫婆，"大兵說。

"你看見那棵大樹啦，"巫婆指着他們旁邊一棵大樹說。"聽我說，它裏面是空的，你先要爬到樹頂，在那裏你會看見一個窟窿，鑽進這個窟窿，你可以一直下到樹底。我用一根繩子拴住你的身體，這樣，你一叫我，我就可以重新拉你上來了。"

"但是我到樹底裏面做甚麼？"大兵問道。

"拿錢啊，"巫婆回答說。"因為到了樹底下你就來到一個大廳，裏面點着三百盞燈，然後你會看到三扇門，門很容易開，因為鑰匙都在鎖上面。打開第一扇門走進第一個房間，你就看到地板中間有個大箱。箱上蹲着一隻狗，兩隻眼睛大得像茶杯。但你完全不用怕牠，我給你這條藍格子圍裙，你必須鋪它在地上，然

後放膽抓住那隻狗，放牠在圍裙上面。然後你可以打開箱子，從裏面愛拿多少錢就拿多少錢，但它們都只是些銅幣。如果你想要銀幣，你就到第二個房間。在這個房間裏，你會看到另一隻狗，眼睛大得像水車輪，但你不用擔心。你還是放牠在我的圍裙上，然後愛拿多少銀幣就拿多少。不過你最喜歡的還是金幣吧，那麼你進第三個房間，那裏有個滿載金幣的箱。蹲在這個箱上的狗非常可怕，牠的眼睛大得像座塔，但是別理牠。只要放牠在我的圍裙上，牠就不能傷害你，你從箱裏愛拿多少金幣就拿多少。"

"這聽起來很好，"大兵説，"不過我要給你甚麼呢，老巫婆？因為你不會白白告訴我這些事情。"

"不，"老巫婆説，"我一個硬幣也不要。只要你答應為我取回一個舊打火盒，那是我奶奶上次下去時留在那裏的。"

"很好，我答應你。現在繞繩子在我身上吧。"

"繩子給你，"巫婆説，"再給你我這條藍格子圍裙。"

繩子一拴好，大兵就爬上樹，從那個窟窿通過空心樹身跳到下面的地上。正如巫婆告訴他，他來到了一個大廳，裏面幾百盞燈全都點亮了。於是他打開了第一扇門。"啊！"面前蹲着一隻狗，眼睛大得像茶杯，正在盯着他看。

"你真漂亮，"大兵説着，抓住了牠，放在巫婆的圍裙上，同時他從箱裏拿出銅幣塞進衣袋裏，它們能裝多少就塞多少，把幾個衣袋裝得滿滿的。然後他蓋上箱蓋，重新放狗回箱子上，再到第二個房間去。果然一點不假，那裏蹲着的狗，眼睛大得像水車輪。

"你最好別那樣看着我，"大兵説，"這樣你會流眼淚。"接着他也放牠在圍裙上，打開箱子。當他看到裏面裝着那麼多銀幣時，他趕緊扔掉剛才拿的銅幣，把幾個衣袋加上背包全裝滿了銀幣。

接着他走進第三個房間，裏面那隻狗真是可怕，牠的眼睛確確實實大得像座塔，它們在牠的頭上像輪子般咕嚕嚕轉。

"早上好，"大兵把手舉到帽檐行了個禮，因為他一輩子還沒有見過一隻這樣的狗。但是他更靠近點看過牠後，覺得已經夠禮貌了，就放牠在地上，打開箱子。天啊，裏面有多少金幣啊！足夠買下賣糖果女人的所有糖果，足夠買下天底下的小錫兵、馬鞭和木馬，甚至買下整個城。金幣實在多極了。於是大兵這一回扔掉他剛裝上的所有銀幣，所有衣袋和背包他全換成了金幣，不但裝滿他的衣袋和背包，連帽子和靴子都裝滿了，因此使他不容易走路。

現在他真的有錢了，於是他重新放那隻狗回箱子上，關上門，往樹外叫。"現在拉我上去吧，老巫婆。"

"你拿到那打火盒沒有？"巫婆問。

"沒有，老實說，我真把它忘得一乾二淨了。"於是他回去拿打火盒，接着巫婆拉他上來，他下了樹，又站在公路上了，衣袋裏、背包裏、帽子裏和靴子裏全都塞滿了金幣。

"你要這打火盒來做甚麼呢？"大兵問道。

"這不關你的事，"巫婆回答說，"你有錢了，現在給我打火盒吧。"

"我告訴你，"大兵說，"如果你不告訴我你要拿它來做甚麼，我就拔出劍來，砍下你的頭。"

"不告訴你，"巫婆説。

大兵馬上砍下了她的頭，她就這樣躺在地上。接着大兵用巫婆的圍裙包起他所有的錢，像個包袱一樣搭在背上，放打火盒進衣袋，就向最近的城走去。那是個非常漂亮的城，他住進最好的旅館，點各種他最愛吃的菜，因為他現在發達了，錢多的是。

給他擦靴子的僕人想，這雙靴子給這麼有錢的一位紳士穿，實在是太寒酸了，因為大兵還沒來得及去買新靴子。第二天他終於買了新衣服、像樣的靴子，於是我們這位大兵很快就成了一位聞名的漂亮紳士，人們來拜訪他，告訴他城裏值得看的種種了不起的東西，還講到了國王美麗的女兒。

"我在甚麼地方能夠看到她呢？"大兵問道。

"你根本不可能看到她，"他們説。"她住在一座大銅城堡裏，四周圍着高牆和尖塔。只有國王一個人可以進出，因為曾經有過一個預言，説她將要嫁給一個普通大兵，國王一想到這門婚事就受不了。"

"我倒真想看看她，"大兵心裏説，但是他不可能得到允許。不過不管怎樣，他度過了一段十分快樂的時光：去看戲，在御花園裏坐馬車，施捨了一大筆錢給窮人，他這樣做是非常好的，他想起了自己當初一個錢也沒有的時候，日子是怎麼過。現在他有錢了，有漂亮衣服了，還有了許多朋友，個個説他是了不起的人物、真正的紳士，這一切使他感到飄飄然。但是他的錢不能一直沒完沒了地花下去，他每天這樣大把大把地花錢、施捨，卻又只出不進，最後他只剩下兩個硬幣了。於是他不得不搬出他漂亮的房間，住到屋頂底下一間小閣樓裏，他在那裏得自己擦靴子，甚至用粗針縫補它們。再也沒有朋友來看他，上閣樓梯級也太多了。一個漆黑的晚上，他連一個銅幣也沒有，不能去買蠟燭。他忽然想起，還有一根蠟燭放在打火盒裏，就是從巫婆幫他進去的那棵老樹裏面拿來的打火盒。

他找出打火盒來，但當他用火石和鐵剛擦出幾點火星，房門就一下子打開了，他在樹底下見過的那隻兩眼大得像茶杯的狗，站到他面前來，說：“有甚麼吩咐，主人？”

“你好，”大兵說。“如果我要甚麼，這打火盒就能給我帶來甚麼，它倒是個稱心如意的打火盒。”

“給我弄些錢來，”他對狗說。

狗轉眼就不見了，很快叼着一袋銅幣回來。從這件事情開始，大兵馬上發現這打火盒是個寶。他只要擦一下火石，坐在那箱銅幣上的狗就出現；擦兩下，坐在那箱銀幣上的狗就來了；擦三下，來的就是眼睛像塔、守着金幣的那隻狗。大兵如今又有許多錢了，他回到那個漂亮的房間，重新穿上那些華麗衣服出現在大家面前，於是他那些朋友又立刻認得他，吹捧他。

過了不久他想，沒有人能看到公主一眼，這太奇怪了。“大家都説她美麗非凡，”他心裏説，“但是她被關在一座圍着那麼多塔樓的銅堡裏，那又有甚麼意思呢。我能有甚麼辦法去看看她嗎？等一等！我的打火盒在哪裏？”於是他擦了一下火石，眼睛大得像茶杯的那隻狗一下子站在他面前。

“現在是半夜，”大兵説，“但是我很想見見公主，哪怕看一眼也好。”

狗馬上不見了，大兵還沒來得及轉眼，牠已經背着公主回來。公主躺在狗的背上睡着了，看起來那麼美麗，讓人一看就知道她是個真正的公主。連他這樣一個老實的大兵也忍不住吻了她一下。狗隨即背着公主跑回去了。但是到了早晨，當公主跟國王和皇后一起吃早餐的時候，她告訴他們昨夜做了一個怪夢，夢到一隻狗和一個大兵，她躺在狗的背上，那大兵吻了她一下。

"那的確是一個非常美麗的故事，"皇后說。於是在第二天夜裏派了一個老宮女守在公主床邊，看這真是一個夢呢，抑或是怎麼一回事。

大兵很想再見公主一次，於是夜裏又派那隻狗去把她接來，帶着她有多快跑多快。但是老宮女穿上水靴，跑得和狗一樣快，在後面緊緊地追，發現牠把公主背進了一座大屋。她想，只要用粉筆在這座大屋的門上畫上一個大十字，就能幫助她認出這個地方。接着她回去睡覺了，狗很快就背着公主回來。但是狗看到了大兵住的大屋門上畫了個十字，牠也用粉筆在全城所有的門上畫上十字，這一來，老宮女也就沒有辦法找到原先那扇門了。

第二天大清早，國王和皇后在那老宮女和所有皇室官員陪同下去看公主曾經到過哪裏。

"就在這裏，"他們來到畫了十字的第一扇門時，國王說道。

"不對，我親愛的丈夫，一定是那一扇門，"皇后指着畫了十字的第二扇門說。

"這裏有一個，那裏有一個！"所有人都叫起來，因為四面八方所有的門上都畫了十字。

於是他們覺得，再這樣找下去也沒有用處。但是皇后是一個非常聰明的女人，不僅會坐馬車，她會做的事情有很多。她拿起她那把金做的大剪刀，把一塊絲綢剪成幾個方塊，縫成一個精緻的小袋子。她在袋子裏裝滿蕎麥粉，把這袋蕎麥粉掛在公主的頸上。接着她在袋子上剪一個小洞，這樣，公主一路走時，蕎麥粉就會一路撒落。夜裏那狗又來把公主背在背上，背着她跑到大兵那裏去。大兵太愛她了，恨不得自己是一個王子，這樣就可以娶她做妻子。這一回，狗沒有留意到蕎麥粉從袋子裏一路上漏下來，從城堡的牆一直漏到大兵住的房子，甚至漏到牠背着公主爬過的窗。因此，在早晨，國王和皇后就查出了他們的女兒到過甚麼地方，大兵被抓起來關進了監牢。噢，他坐在那裏是多麼黑，多麼難受啊，人們對他說：“明天你就要被吊死了。”這不是個令人愉快的消息，再說，他把打火盒留在旅館裏了。到了早晨，他透過小窗的鐵欄杆，看到人們急急忙忙出城去準備看他被吊死。他聽到鼓聲咚咚敲響，他看見士兵們邁大步走。人人跑出來看他們，一個圍着皮圍裙、穿着拖鞋的鞋匠小學徒飛快地跑過，因為跑得太快了，一隻拖鞋飛了出去，正好撞在大兵透過鐵欄杆朝外看的那堵牆上。“喂，小鞋匠，你不用那麼急急忙忙啊，”大兵對他叫道。“在我還未到場以前沒甚麼可看。但是你如果跑到我原先住的房子，給我把我的打火盒拿來，我可以給你四塊錢，不過你得有多快跑多快。”

那鞋匠小學徒很想得到那四塊錢，於是飛也似的跑去拿來了打火盒，交它給大兵。現在我們就有好戲看了。城外已經豎起大絞刑架，絞刑架周圍站着士兵和幾千人。國王和皇后坐在法官和全體顧問官對面的華麗寶座上。大兵已經站在梯級上面，但就在他們要把絞索套到他的脖子上時，他說在犯人臨死之前，通常總是恩准他一個不違禁的請求。他非常想抽煙，這將是他在世上最後一次抽煙了。國王不能拒絕他的請求，於是大兵拿起他的打火盒，擦他的火石，一下，兩下，三下——一下子三隻狗都出現了——眼睛大得像茶杯的，眼睛大得像水車輪的，眼睛大得像塔的。"快救我，讓我不要被吊死，"大兵叫道。

三隻狗向法官和所有顧問官們撲上去，咬住這個的腿，咬住那個的鼻，拋他們上許多尺高的半空，因此他們落下來都跌得粉身碎骨。

"不許碰我，"國王說。但是最大的那隻狗咬住他，又咬住皇后，和扔其他人一樣扔上去。這時候士兵們和所有人都嚇壞了，哇哇大叫："好大兵，你做我們的國王吧，你娶那位美麗的公主吧。"

於是他們讓大兵坐上國王的馬車，三隻狗跑在前面大呼"萬歲！"小孩子們用手指吹口哨，士兵們持槍敬禮。公主從銅堡裏出來，當上了皇后，這使她十分高興。婚禮慶祝了整整一個禮拜，那三隻狗也參加了婚禮，瞪大了牠們的眼睛盯着看。

# 2
# 小克勞斯和大克勞斯

從前，一個村子裏有兩個同名的人。他們都叫克勞斯。一個有四匹馬，一個只有一匹馬。人們為了區別他們兩個，有四匹馬的叫他做"大克勞斯"，只有一匹馬的叫他做"小克勞斯"。現在我們就來聽聽他們發生了甚麼事吧，因為這事情是真的。

一個星期六天，小克勞斯都要替大克勞斯犁地，自己的一匹馬也要給他用；一個星期的一天，那是星期日，大克勞斯卻總是在假日借他那四匹馬給小克勞斯用。

"萬歲！"小克勞斯把鞭子在五匹馬的頭頂上抽得劈劈啪啪響。在這一天，這五匹馬幾乎都像是他自己的。

太陽照耀得明亮，教堂鐘敲出快活的鐘聲，人們穿着他們最好的衣服，夾着他們的祈禱書走過。他們正要去聽牧師佈道。他們看到小克勞斯用他那五匹馬犁地，揚揚得意地把鞭子抽得劈劈啪啪響，嘴裏叫着："快跑啊，我的駿馬。"

"你不能這樣說，"大克勞斯說，"因為只有一匹是你的。"

但是小克勞斯很快就忘記了他該怎麼叫，一有人走過，他就大聲叫起來："快跑啊，我的駿馬！"

"我真的要求求你不要再這麼叫了，"大克勞斯經過時說，"你再這麼叫，我就給你的馬當頭砍一下，讓牠當場倒地死掉，那牠就完了。”

“我向你保證，我一定不再這麼叫了，”小克勞斯說。但是只要有人走過，向他點點頭，說聲“你好”，他一下子得意忘形，覺得有五匹馬犁自己的地有多麼神氣，於是又叫起來：“快跑啊，我所有的馬！”

“我來幫你讓你的馬跑快些，”大克勞斯說着，拿起一把錘子，給小克勞斯那僅有的一匹馬當頭砍一下，馬立即倒地死了。

“噢，我現在連一匹馬也沒有了！”小克勞斯哭着說。過了一會，他剝下死馬的皮，掛在風裏吹乾。

然後他把乾馬皮裝進一個袋，搭在肩上，拿到隔壁城鎮去賣。他要走很遠的路，路上還要穿過一片陰暗的大樹林。很快他就遇上暴風雨，迷了路，等到找到路，已經黃昏了，但是到城裏還有很長的路要走，回家又太遠了，入夜前趕不到回去。

路旁正好有一座農莊大宅。窗外面的百葉窗關着，但是百葉窗的頂上和縫隙漏出了亮光。“他們也許能讓我在裏面過一夜吧，”小克勞斯想。於是他上前去敲門。農戶的妻子打開門，但是一聽到他想過夜，就叫他走開，因為她的丈夫不在家，她不可讓陌生人進來。

小克勞斯想：“那我就只好睡在外面了。”農民的妻子隨即關上門。

靠近這農舍附近有一個很大的乾草堆，在乾草堆和農舍之間有一個棚子，棚頂是茅草造的。“我可以躺在上面睡，”他看到這棚頂時說，“那當床睡還不錯，只希望那隻鸛鳥不要飛下來咬我的腿。"棚頂上正站着一隻鸛鳥，牠的巢就在棚頂上。

於是小克勞斯爬到棚頂上，當他轉動身體想睡得舒服點時，他發現關着的百葉窗沒有遮蔽宅子的玻璃窗，窗頂上露出一道夾縫，因此他可以看到屋子裏面。裏面是個房間，房間裏有一張大桌子，上面擺着酒、烤肉和肥美的魚。農民的妻子和教堂司事雙雙坐在桌旁，農民的妻子給教堂司事的酒杯斟滿了酒，教堂司事夾了許多魚，他看來最喜歡吃這道菜。

"如果我也能吃上一點就好了，"小克勞斯想。他向窗戶伸長了脖子，又看到一個漂亮的蛋糕。天啊！他們面前擺着一桌盛宴。

就在這時候，他聽到路上有人騎着馬向這農舍過來了。原來農民正好回家來。他是個好人，但是有個非常古怪的偏見 —— 看不順眼任何教堂司事。只要有教堂司事出現在他面前，他就會勃然大怒。由於他這樣討厭教堂司事，這位教堂司事只好趁他不在家的時候去看他的妻子，而這個女人把家裏最好的東西端到他面前來給他吃。

這時候他們聽到農民回家的聲音，嚇壞了，農民的妻子連忙求教堂司事鑽到房間角落一個空的大箱子裏去躲起來。教堂司事只好照辦，匆忙躲起來，因為他知道她丈夫看不順眼任何教堂司事。那女人趕緊把酒和所有好吃的東西都藏到烤爐裏，因為她的丈夫看到它們，就會問為甚麼把它們擺出來。

"噢，天啊！"小克勞斯在棚頂看到所有這些好吃的東西一下子沒有了，不禁歎氣說。

"喂！上面有人嗎？"農民抬頭看見了小克勞斯，問道。"你在上面做甚麼？下來吧，到我屋裏來。"

於是小克勞斯爬下來，告訴農民他怎樣迷了路，並請求借宿一宵。

"沒問題，"農民説，"不過我們先要吃點東西。"

那女人非常殷勤地侍候他們兩個，在大桌子上鋪上枱布，在他們面前放好一大碗粥。農民已經很餓，津津有味地大吃他的粥，但是小克勞斯不禁想起那些好吃的烤肉、魚和蛋糕，他知道它們在烤爐裏。

桌子底下，就在他的腳旁放着袋子，裏面裝着他打算進城去賣的那袋馬皮，我們要謹記他是要去賣馬皮的。小克勞斯根本不喜歡吃粥，所以用腳踩桌子底下那袋馬皮，乾馬皮被踩得發出很響的嘎吱聲。

"噓！"小克勞斯一面對他那袋馬皮説，一面又踩它，踩得它吱吱嘎嘎響得更厲害。

"喂！你那袋子裏裝的是甚麼東西啊？"農民問他説。

"哦，是個魔法師，"小克勞斯説，"他在説我們不用吃粥，因為他已經變出了滿滿一烤爐的烤肉、魚和蛋糕。"

"是嗎？"農民叫道，匆匆站起身去打開爐門。果然，爐子裏滿是他妻子藏起來的好吃東西，不過他以為是桌子底下那個魔法師為優待他們變出來的。

他妻子一句話也不敢説，只好把這些東西全端到他們面前來，他們兩個就吃了頓大餐，有魚，有肉，有蛋糕。這時候小克勞斯又踩他的袋子，它又吱吱嘎嘎響起來。

"這一回他又説甚麼呢？"那農民問道。

"他是説，"小克勞斯立刻回答他，"他已經給我們變出了三瓶酒，就在爐子旁邊那個角落裏。"於是那女人又只好把她藏起來的酒端上來，農民和小克勞斯喝得心裏高興。農民真想有小克勞斯那袋子裏裝着的這麼一個魔法師。

"他能變出一個魔鬼嗎？"農民問道。"趁我現在高興，我倒很想見見魔鬼。"

"噢，當然可以！"小克勞斯回答說。"我要我的魔法師做甚麼，他就能夠做甚麼。"他一面說，一面踩那袋馬皮，直踩得它吱吱嘎嘎響。"你聽到了嗎？他在回答說：'我能。只是魔鬼太醜陋，你最好不要看到那魔鬼。'"

"噢，我不怕。那魔鬼會是甚麼樣子呢？"

"這個嘛，他會以教堂司事的形象出現。"

"哈！"農民說。"那麼他一定很醜。你知道我就是受不了教堂司事。不過，沒關係，我知道他是魔鬼，因此我不在乎。我已經鼓起了勇氣，只是不要讓他離我太近。"

"等一等，我必須先問問我的魔法師，"小克勞斯說，於是他踩他那袋馬皮，把耳朵靠到下面。

"他說甚麼？"

"他說你可以去打開牆角上那個大箱子，就能看到那魔鬼蜷縮在裏面，但是你必須抓緊箱蓋，不讓他溜走。"

"你來幫我抓住箱蓋好嗎？"農民說着，朝箱子走去。他妻子藏了那位教堂司事在箱裏，司事這時候嚇得顫抖。

農民稍為打開箱蓋一點，朝箱子裏窺看。"噢！"他大叫一聲，向後一跳，"我看見他了，他和我們那個教堂司事一模一樣。多麼可怕啊！"

接下來他們不得不再喝點酒，於是他們兩個坐下來喝酒，直喝到深夜。

"你怎麼也要賣你的魔法師給我，"農民說，"隨便你要甚麼我都願意給。說實在的，我可以馬上給你整整一斗錢。"

"不行，我不能給你，"小克勞斯說，"你要想想，我能從這魔法師身上得到多大好處啊。"

"但是我實在很想得到他，"農民說，並極力請求。

"好吧，"小克勞斯最後說，"你對我這麼好，讓我住一晚，我絕不能拒絕你。就一斗錢吧，不過我要十十足足的一斗錢。"

"沒問題，"農民說，"但你一定要帶走那箱子，我不想它留在家裏多一分鐘，誰知道魔鬼還在不在裏面。"

於是小克勞斯把那袋乾馬皮給了農民，換來了一斗錢——十十足足的一斗錢。農民還給了他一輛手推車，好把那箱子和錢推走。

"再見，"小克勞斯說了一聲，就推着他的錢和那個大箱子走了，教堂司事還關在那個箱子裏。

樹林另一邊有一條河，又寬又深，水流太急，沒有人能游過去。河上剛造好一座大橋，小克勞斯到了橋的中間停下來，大聲說話，好讓教堂司事聽見："現在我怎樣處理這個討厭的舊箱子好呢。它重得像裏面裝滿了石頭，我不想再把它往前推，我可要累壞了，我還是扔它到河裏去算了。如果它能跟着我漂回家，那當然好；如果不漂，也沒甚麼關係，我不在乎。"於是他抓住箱子，把它提起一點，像是要扔它到河裏去的樣子。

"不不不，放下，"教堂司事叫道，"先放我出來。"

"噢，"假裝嚇壞了的小克勞斯説，"他還在裏面，怎麼會這樣？我必須扔他到河裏淹死他。"

"噢，不要。噢，不要，"教堂司事在箱裏叫。"如果你放了我，我一定給你整整一斗錢。"

"是嗎，那又當別論了，"小克勞斯説着，打開了箱。教堂司事爬出來後，小克勞斯推空箱到河裏去，跟教堂司事回家，量了整整一斗錢給小克勞斯。小克勞斯本來已經拿到農民給他的一斗錢，因此他現在有了滿滿一輛手推車的錢。

"我那匹馬賣了個好價錢，"他回家走進自己的房間，自言自語，又倒所有錢在地板上堆成一堆。"大克勞斯如果發現，我就靠我的一匹馬，竟變得這麼有錢，他會多怒啊，但我不能如實告訴他整件事情。"接着他派了一個孩子到大克勞斯家去借一個量斗。

"他要量斗做甚麼呢？"大克勞斯想。於是他在這個斗的底下塗上焦油，這樣，不管小克勞斯放甚麼東西到量斗器裏，都會黏住一些留在上面。的確如此，還量斗的時候，上面黏着三個嶄新的三元銀幣。

"這到底是怎麼回事！"大克勞斯説。他直接跑到小克勞斯那裏去問："這麼多錢你是從哪裏弄來的？"

"噢，是我的馬皮換來的，我昨天早上賣了它。"

"這麼説，賣的價錢確實不錯，"大克勞斯説。於是他跑回家，抓起一把斧頭，把他的四匹馬全都當頭一砍，然後剝下牠們的皮，拿它們到城裏去賣。

"皮啊，賣皮啊，誰要買皮啊？"他沿着一條條街叫賣。

所有鞋匠和製革匠跑來問他要賣多少錢。

"一斗錢一張，"大克勞斯回答説。

"你瘋了嗎？"他們都叫了起來。"你以為我們有整斗的錢嗎？"

"皮啊，賣皮啊，"他又吆喚起來，"誰要買皮啊？"鞋匠拿起他們的皮條，製革匠拿起他們的皮圍裙打大克勞斯。

"皮啊，皮啊！"他們學他的腔調叫着取笑他。"一點不錯，我們剝你的皮，拿你的皮製革，趕他出城去，"他們大喊。大克勞斯只好拔腿逃走，能跑多快就跑多快，他一輩子還沒有挨過這麼厲害的痛打。

"唉，"他回家後説，"小克勞斯得償我這筆債，我非打死他不可。"

正好這時候，小克勞斯的老祖母死了。她生前很兇惡，很不好，對小克勞斯實在壞透了。但是小克勞斯還是非常難過，把她的遺體放在他自己溫暖的床上，看能不能使她活過來。他決定讓她躺一個通宵，而他自己則打算一整晚坐在房間角落，他以前也是這樣睡覺的。

夜裏當他坐在那裏的時候，門開了，大克勞斯拿着一把斧頭進來。他很清楚小克勞斯的床在哪裏，因此他一直走到床前，一斧頭砍在老祖母的頭上，他以為床上這個人一定就是小克勞斯。

"好，"他説，"你現在再也不能戲弄我了。"然後他就回家了。

"那傢伙太壞了"小克勞斯想，"他是要殺我。幸虧我的老祖母已經死了，要不然他就要了她的命。"

於是他給老祖母穿上她最好的衣服，又向鄰居借了一匹馬，繫牠到一輛馬車上。然後他放老祖母在後座，好讓她在他趕車時不會跌出去，接着他就趕車穿過樹林。太陽出來時他們到了一家大客棧，小克勞斯停下車，進去弄點東西吃。

店老闆是個有錢人，也是個好人，不過脾氣急躁，就好像他這個人是胡椒和鼻煙做的一樣。"早安，"他對小克勞斯說，"你今天一早就來了，而且穿了你最好的衣服。"

"不錯，"小克勞斯說，"我和我的老奶奶要進城去，她在外面坐在車子裏，我不能帶她進店。你能給她一杯啤酒嗎？不過你得大聲說話，因為她耳朵不靈。"

"行，當然可以，"店老闆回答說。他倒了一杯啤酒拿出去給那死了的祖母，祖母在車上坐得筆直。

"你孫子給你要的一杯啤酒來了，"店老闆說。死了的老太太一聲也不回答，坐着一動不動。

"你沒聽見嗎？"店老闆有多響叫多響，"你孫子給你要的一杯啤酒來了。"

他叫了又叫，但是看見她連動也不動，他的急躁脾氣來了，一發火，把那杯啤酒向她的臉上扔過去。她向後一倒，摔到車外去了，因為她只是坐在那裏，沒有綁好。

"唉！"小克勞斯叫着，從門裏衝出來，掐住店老闆的喉嚨。"你害死了我的奶奶。看，她的前額上有個大窟窿。"

"噢，多麼倒霉啊，"店老闆哭着說。"都是我的火爆脾氣誤事。親愛的小克勞斯，我給你一斗錢，我要像安葬我的親祖母一樣把你的祖母安葬。只要你別出聲，否則他們會殺我的頭，那就糟糕了。"

於是小克勞斯又到手一斗錢，店老闆把他的老祖母像自己的祖母一樣給安葬了。

小克勞斯一回到家，又馬上派一個孩子到大克勞斯家去借個量斗。

"這又是怎麼回事啊？"大克勞斯想。"我沒有殺死他嗎？我得去親眼看一看。"於是他帶着量斗上小克勞斯家去。

"你怎麼弄到這些錢？"大克勞斯睜大眼睛看着他鄰居那一大堆錢，問道。

"你殺死的不是我，而是我的奶奶，"小克勞斯說，"我拿她賣了一斗錢。"

"不管怎麼說，這是一個好價錢，"大克勞斯說。於是他趕回家，拿起斧頭，一下就把他自己的老祖母砍死了。

他接着放她到板車上，趕車進城，來到藥劑師那裏，問他要不要買個死人。

"那是誰，你從哪裏弄來？"藥劑師問他。

"那是我的奶奶，"他回答說，"我一斧頭就砍死了她，好拿她賺一斗錢。"

"我的天啊！"藥劑師叫道，"你瘋了。這種話可不能說，否則你要人頭落地。"接着藥劑師嚴厲地對他解釋他做了甚麼樣的壞事，告訴他這樣的壞人一定要受到懲罰。大克勞斯聽了嚇得衝出藥房，跳上馬車，用鞭抽馬，趕車穿過樹林回家去。藥劑師和所有人都以為他瘋了，就任由他趕車離開。

"你得償還這筆債！"大克勞斯一到公路上就說，"不由你不償，小克勞斯！"

一回到家裏，他找出最大的麻袋，到小克勞斯那裏去。

"你又耍了我一次，"他說，"第一次我殺了我所有的馬，這一次殺了我的老奶奶，全都怪你，不過你再也不能耍弄我了。"於是他抱起小克勞斯，塞他進麻袋，搭上肩頭說："現在我要讓你在河裏淹死。"

去河邊要走很遠的路，他扛着小克勞斯可不輕。路上要經過一座教堂，走過時正好聽到裏面風琴鳴響，人們唱得很好聽。大克勞斯靠近教堂門口放下麻袋，想進去聽聽詩篇再走。小克勞斯反正在口麻袋裏出不來，所有人又在教堂裏，於是他進去了。

"噢，天啊！噢，天啊！"小克勞斯在麻袋歎着氣，把身體左扭右扭，可是他發覺沒辦法弄鬆紮着袋口的繩子。正在這時候走過一個趕牛的老人，頭髮雪白，手裏握着一根大棒，用它趕着面前一大羣母牛和公牛。牠們被裝着小克勞斯的那個麻袋絆了一下，踢翻了它。

"噢，天啊，"小克勞斯又歎氣說，"我還很年輕，卻很快要上天堂了。"

"可我這可憐人呢，"趕牛的老人說，"我已經這麼老了，卻去不了那裏。"

"打開麻袋吧，"小克勞斯叫起來，"爬進來代替我，你很快就到那裏了。"

"我真心願意，"趕牛的老人說着，解開麻袋，小克勞斯趕快跳出來。"你照顧我的牛羣好嗎？"老人一面鑽進麻袋，一面說。小克勞斯紮好麻袋，然後趕着所有母牛和公牛走了。

不一會，大克勞斯從教堂裏出來，把麻袋扛到肩上，覺得它好像輕了，因為趕牛的老人只有小克勞斯一半重。

"他現在多麼輕啊，"大克勞斯説，"啊，一定是因為我進教堂聽了詩篇。"

於是他走到那條又深又寬的河邊，把裝着趕牛老人的麻袋扔到水裏，自以為扔進去的是小克勞斯。"你就躺在那裏吧！"他説，"現在你再不能作弄我了。"

接着他回家，可是剛走到十字路口的地方，看見小克勞斯趕着那羣牛。

"怎麼回事？"大克勞斯大叫。"我不是剛把你淹死了嗎？"

"不錯，"小克勞斯説，"大約半個鐘頭以前，你把我扔到河裏去了。"

"可是你從哪裏弄來這些漂亮的牛呢？"大克勞斯問道。

"這些牛是海牛，"小克勞斯回答説，"我來把事情原原本本告訴你吧，並且要謝謝你把我扔到了河裏：現在我比你強了。我的的確確非常有錢。説實在的，我被裝在麻袋裏，蜷縮着，被扔進水裏，我可是嚇壞了。我馬上就沉到水底，但是我一點也沒有受傷，因為我掉在那極其柔軟的草上。麻袋一下子打開，一個美艷絕倫的女孩向我走來。她穿着雪白的衣裳袍子，濕頭髮上戴着綠葉織成的花環。她拉着我的手説：'你終於來了，小克勞斯，這裏我先送你一些牛。在路上再走上一里，還有一羣牛在等着你。'

"這時候我看到這條河是海中居民走的一條大路。他們在河底上行走，從大海走到地面，直到河的盡頭。河底鋪滿了最美麗的花和鮮嫩的草。魚在我旁邊游過，快得像小鳥在空中飛。

那裏所有人多麼漂亮，還有多麼好的牛羣在山崗上和山谷裏吃草啊！"

"如果下面那麼好，"大克勞斯説，"你為甚麼又這麼快就上來呢？叫我就不上來了！"

"這個嘛，"小克勞斯説，"正是我的妙計。你剛才聽我説過了，那海女孩説，我在河路上再走一里就會找到一大羣牛。但是我知道河是彎彎曲曲的，路很長，因此我選了一條捷徑。我先上陸地來，穿過田地，然後再回到河裏去，這樣我就可以少走一半路，能夠更快地把我的牛羣弄到手。"

"你這個傢伙真幸運！"大克勞斯説，"你認為如果我到河底，也能得到一些海牛嗎？"

"對，我認為能，"小克勞斯説。"但是我不能放你在麻袋裏扛到河邊，你太重了。不過你如果先到那裏再鑽進麻袋，我倒很樂意扔你到河裏去。"

"那太謝謝你了，"大克勞斯説，"只是記住啊，如果我到下面得不到海牛，我上來可要給你狠狠一頓痛打。"

"別這樣，好了，不要太兇！"

小克勞斯説着，他們一起向河走去。當那些牛看見河流就連忙跑過去。"你看牠們多麼着急，"小克勞斯説，"牠們渴望重新回到水下面去。"

"來，快來幫幫我，"大克勞斯説，"不然你就要挨揍。"於是他趕緊鑽進一個大麻袋，那個麻袋一直搭在一頭母牛的背上。"再放塊大石頭進來，"大克勞斯説，"要不然我可能沉不下去。"

"噢，這個你不用擔心，"小克勞斯回答説。不過他還是照他說的在麻袋裏放了一塊大石頭，然後紮緊袋口，把麻袋一推。"撲通！"大克勞斯掉到水裏，馬上沉到河底去了。

"我怕他找不到甚麼牛羣，"小克勞斯説，接着就趕着自己的那羣牛回家了。

# 3
# 豌豆公主

從前有一個王子，他想娶一位公主，但必須是一位真正的公主。他周遊世界去找，但是哪裏也找不到他所想找的公主。公主多的是，只是很難知道她們是不是真的。她們身上總有些甚麼地方不對勁。因此他只好又回到家裏來，愁眉不展，因為他實在很想要一位真正的公主。

一天晚上忽然來了可怕的暴風雨。一時間雷鳴電閃，傾盆大雨，是個令人害怕的晚上。

忽然傳來敲城門的聲音，老國王親自開門。

外面站着的是一位公主。可是天啊，風雨把她弄成狼狽不堪的樣子。雨水從她的頭髮和衣服上嘩嘩地往下直淌，從她的鞋面淌進鞋裏，又從鞋跟淌出來。然而她說她是一個真公主。

"好吧，這一點我們很快就能弄清楚，"老皇后心裏說。但是她一聲不響，走進睡房，拿走床上所有寢具，在底下放上一顆豌豆。然後她拿來二十張床褥放在這顆豌豆上，再在二十張床褥上放二十張羽毛褥墊。公主得在這二十張床褥加二十張羽毛褥上睡一整夜。第二天早晨他們問她睡得怎麼樣。

"噢，睡得糟透了！"她說。"我簡直通宵沒有合過眼。只有天知道床上到底有甚麼，我躺在一樣硬繃繃的東西上面，弄得我渾身青一塊紫一塊。真可怕！”

現在大家知道了，她是一位真正的公主，因為她在二十張床褥和二十張羽毛褥墊上還能感覺到那顆豌豆。只有真正的公主的皮膚才能這樣嬌嫩。

於是王子娶她為妻，因為現在他知道了，他找到了一位真正的公主。而那顆豌豆呢，被陳列在博物館裏，如果沒有人偷走它的話，大家仍可以看到它。

看，這是一個真實的故事。

# 4
# 小伊達的花

"**我**那些可憐的花都死了，"小伊達說，"它們昨天晚上還那麼漂亮，可現在所有葉子都垂了下來，枯萎了。它們為甚麼這樣呢？"她問坐在沙發上的那個學生。她很喜歡這個學生，因為他會給她講最美麗的故事，會在紙上剪出最有趣的畫：有女士在裏面跳舞的心、門能開能關的皇宮。他是一個快樂的學生。"今天的花為甚麼看起來這樣憔悴呢？"她指着一束枯萎了的花，再問一遍。

"你不知道為甚麼嗎？"學生說。"這些花昨晚參加舞會，因此它們現在都累得垂下了頭呢。"

"怎麼可能！花不會跳舞啊！"小伊達叫起來。

"它們當然都會跳舞，"學生回答。"天一黑，等所有人都睡覺以後，它們就快快活活地跳來跳去。幾乎每晚都開舞會。"

"那它們的小孩子可以參加這些舞會嗎？"

"可以，"學生說，"山谷的小雛菊和小百合也參加舞會。"

"這些美麗的花在甚麼時候跳舞呢？"小伊達問道。

"你不是常常看到城門外那個大花園嗎？就在國王夏天住的城堡旁，那裏開滿了美麗的花。你不是用麵包屑餵過那裏的天鵝嗎，當牠們向你游過來的時候？對，那些花就在那裏開盛大舞會，相信我的話好了。”

“昨天我才跟我媽媽到過那花園，”伊達說，“但是所有樹葉都落下來了，花一朵也沒有剩下。它們到哪裏去了？夏天時那裏一向有很多花。”

“它們都在皇宮裏，”學生回答說。“你必須知道，國王和所有臣僕一回城裏，這些花就離開花園跑進皇宮，你真該看看它們有多快活！兩朵最美麗的玫瑰花坐在王位上，獲尊為國王和皇后，然後所有高高的紅雞冠花排列在兩旁，向它們鞠躬，這些紅雞冠花是侍臣。接着那些漂亮的花進來了，盛大的舞會於是開始。藍色的紫羅蘭是海軍學員，它們和風信子以及藏紅花小姐跳舞。鬱金香和虎皮百合老貴婦坐在一旁監視着它們，這樣它們就會規規矩矩，合乎禮儀。”

“不過，”小伊達說，“這些花斗膽在皇宮裏跳舞，沒有人來收拾它們嗎？”

“它們在那裏跳舞，根本沒有人知道，”學生說。“當然，皇宮的看守老人夜裏有時要到那裏巡查，但是他帶着一大串鑰匙，那些花一聽到鑰匙哐啷響，都跑到長長的絲做簾子後面躲起來，或站在原地一動不動，只探出頭來偷看。看守老人只是說：‘我在這裏不是聞到花香嗎？’但是他看不到它們。”

“噢，真有趣，”伊達拍着手高興地說。“但我是不是不能看到這些花跳舞？”

“當然可以，”學生說，“下次再去皇宮的時候，你只要記住偷偷往窗裏看，你一定能看到它們。今天我就這麼做了，我看到一朵長長的黃百合花伸展着身體躺在沙發上。它是宮廷的貴婦。”

"植物園的花離皇宮那麼遠，也可以去參加這些舞會嗎？"伊達問道。

"噢，當然，"學生說，"它們甚麼時候要去都可以去，因為它們會飛。你沒有見過那些樣子很像花的美麗的紅、黃蝴蝶嗎？它們曾經是花。它們離開它們的莖飛起來，搧動着它們的花瓣，就好像這些花瓣是使它們飛起來的小翅膀。如果它們品行端正，它們就得到允許在白天也可以飛，而不必留在莖上一動不動，到時候花瓣也就變成了真正的翅膀，你自己也看過的。

不過，植物園的花可能從來沒有到過皇宮，因此完全不知道每天晚上在那裏舉行的快樂舞會。我來告訴你怎樣做，你下次到植物園的時候，悄悄告訴其中一朵花，說皇宮裏要舉行盛大舞會，這一來，消息以花傳花，它們將全部都飛到皇宮去。等教授走進他的花園，那裏一朵花也沒有。他將會大吃一驚，不知道這些花出甚麼事了？"

"不過花怎麼能相互轉告呢？我肯定花不會說話。"

"不會，當然不會，"學生回答，"不過它們能夠做動作。你有沒有看過，風輕吹的時候它們互相點頭和簌簌地搖動它們的綠葉嗎？它們這樣就能溝通，就好像我們說話那樣。"

"教授能夠明白這種動作嗎？"伊達問道。

"對，他一定能夠，最少懂一部份。他有一天早晨走進他的花園，看見一棵有刺的蕁麻用葉子對一棵美麗的紅康乃馨示意。那動作是說：'你那麼漂亮，我非常愛你。'但是教授不喜歡這種無聊的事，因此他拍拍蕁麻的葉子阻止它。其實這時候它的葉子，那就是它的手指，狠狠地刺了他一下，刺得他從此不敢再去摸蓴麻了。"

"噢，多麼有趣啊！"伊達説着，大笑起來。

"怎麼可以灌輸這種東西到一個孩子的頭腦裏？"一位來做客的討厭的市議員坐在沙發上説。他不喜歡這學生，看見他用紙皮剪出滑稽的人偶就會責備他。那學生剪出來的，有時候是一個人吊在絞刑架上，手裏捧着一顆心，表示他是偷心的人；有時候是一個騎着掃帚在天上飛的老女巫，用她的鼻子載着她的丈夫。但是市議員不喜歡這種開玩笑的東西，看到了就會像剛才説的那樣説："怎麼可以灌輸這種胡鬧的東西到一個孩子的頭腦裏？都是些多麼荒唐的幻想啊！"

但是對伊達來説，學生講給她的所有這些關於花的故事都非常滑稽有趣，她對它們想了很多。她現在確信那些花垂着頭，是因為它們通宵跳舞，累壞了，極可能是病了。於是她放它們到一張有她的玩具的桌子上。她的玩偶蘇菲在床上睡覺，小伊達對她説："你真的要起來了，蘇菲，今天夜裏你只好睡在抽屜裏。這些可憐的花病了，必須睡在你的床上，這樣它們也許明天會好起來。"

於是她拿出玩偶，玩偶看起來很不高興，一句話也不説，因為從床上被搬走，心裏很生氣。

伊達放那些花在玩具床上，用被子蓋在它們上面。接着她叫它們乖乖地躺着不要動，她去拿些茶來給它們，好讓它們明天早晨可以起床。她拉上床四周的床幔，不讓太陽照到它們的眼睛。

伊達整晚都在想學生跟她説的事。她自己回臥室上床之前，還走到窗旁看她媽媽在那裏種的風信子和鬱金香。她輕輕對它們説："我知道你們今天夜裏要去參加舞會。"但是那些花假裝不明白她的意思，葉子也沒動一動，不過伊達依然知道這一切。

她躺下了很久也沒睡着，想着如果能看見花在國王的城堡跳舞，那該多好。"我不知道我的花是不是真的到過那裏，"她心裏説，接着就睡着了。

半夜裏她醒來。她在夢裏見到那些花和那位學生，還見到那位市議員，他告訴伊達，她被花兒們戲弄了。伊達的臥室非常靜，夜燈靜靜地在桌子上燃燒着，她的爸爸媽媽都睡了。

"我不知道我那些花是不是還躺在蘇菲的床上，"她心裏想，"我太想知道了！"她起身，望向一扇半開的門，裏面有她的花和所有玩具。她仔細聽着，好像有人在那房間裏彈鋼琴，彈得很輕，但比她過去聽過的都彈得動聽。

"所有花這一刻一定都在裏面跳舞，"她想，"噢，我多麼想看看它們啊！"但是她不敢起來，怕吵醒她的父母。"如果它們能到這裏來就好了，"她又想。但是它們沒有來，只是琴聲仍是那麼好聽，那麼美。她再也忍不住了，就從她的小床上爬下來，很輕地走到房門口，朝那房間裏偷看。噢，那真是多麼美麗的景象啊！

房裏沒有點夜燈，但是很亮，因為月光透進窗戶照在地板上，就像日光那樣。所有風信子和鬱金香在房間裏站成長長的兩行，窗臺上一朵花也沒有了，所有花盆都是空的。所有花正在地板上翩翩起舞，旋轉着，轉身時互相用它們綠色的長葉子摟着對方。鋼琴前坐着一朵大黃百合，小伊達記得夏天曾經見過它，因為她記得學生説過它非常像伊達的朋友勞拉小姐，當時大家都在笑他的話。但是現在小伊達覺得這朵長長的黃花的確像那位年輕小姐。它彈起鋼琴來正是同樣的姿態，它的黃色長臉一會側向這邊，一會側向那邊，合着音樂的節拍點着頭。

接着伊達看見一朵藍色的大藏紅花往前跳到放着玩具的桌子上，走到玩具床那裏，拉開床幔。床上躺着那些生病的花，但是它們馬上起來，跟其他花打招呼，示意說它們想要和大家一起跳舞。它們現在看起來一點病也沒有了。

這時候好像有甚麼東西從桌上掉了下來，伊達朝那方向看，看見一根她於"懺悔星期二"在床上找到的細長彩棒，它好像也想成為花中的一員。彩棒很漂亮，頭上有一個蠟製的小玩偶，樣貌跟那位市議員一模一樣。

彩棒開始跳舞，忽然彩棒頭上的那個蠟製玩偶好像越變越大，越變越高，就像市議員本人。它呼喊道："你們怎麼可以灌輸這樣的東西到一個孩子的頭腦裏？"這太好玩了，伊達忍不住哈哈大笑。彩棒繼續跳舞，那市議員也不得不跳舞。儘管他仍舊可以變大變高，或者變回蠟製小玩偶，但都沒有用，他還是得跳。最後，其他的花，特別是曾經在玩具床上睡過的花為他說情，彩棒這才停止跳舞。

就在這時候，伊達的玩偶蘇菲和許多玩具所在的抽屜裏響起了敲擊聲。那玩偶伸出頭，驚訝地說："在舉行舞會嗎？為甚麼沒有誰告訴過我？"她坐在桌上，心想有些花會來邀請她共舞，但是它們一朵也沒有來邀請她。蘇菲於是把自己甩到地板上，發出很大的響聲。所有花馬上圍住她，問她有沒有跌傷，很有禮貌，特別是那些在她的床上睡過的花。

但是她根本沒有受傷，那些花感謝她讓它們睡她舒服的床，帶她到月光照着的房間中央，和她一起跳舞，其他的花組成圓圈圍住她們。於是蘇菲十分開心，說它們可以繼續睡她的床，並且睡在抽屜裏她一點也無所謂。

　　但是那些花回答說：“我們衷心感謝你的善意，但我們活不久了。明天早晨我們就差不多要死，你告訴小伊達埋我們在花園裏，靠近金絲雀的墳墓。這樣，到了下個夏天我們便將醒來，那時候會比今年更美麗。”

　　“不，你們不可以死，”蘇菲吻着這些花說，然後許多美麗的花跳着舞進來。伊達無法想像它們是從哪裏來的，除非是從國王的花園裏來。首先進來的是兩朵美麗的玫瑰花，頭上戴着金冠。它們後面跟着美麗的壁花和石竹花，向每一位在場的鞠躬行禮。它們也帶來了樂隊。野風信子和白色小雪花蓮叮嚀叮嚀搖響它們鈴鐺形的花，這是一支非凡的管弦樂隊。接着花越來越多：紫羅蘭、雛菊、鈴蘭，還有其他花全都一起跳舞，真是好看極了。

　　最後所有花互道晚安。於是小伊達重新回到她的床，夢見她看到的所有情景。

　　第二天早晨，她一起來，趕緊去小桌子那裏，看那些花是不是還在。她拉開小床的床幔。它們都躺在那裏，但是全都枯萎了，比上一天枯萎得更厲害。蘇菲也躺在抽屜裏，但是她看起來很困倦。

　　“這些花要你告訴我的話，你還記得嗎？”小伊達說。

　　但是蘇菲那副樣子糊裏糊塗，一個字也說不出來。

　　“你一點也不好，”伊達說，“然而它們全都和你跳舞。”

接着她拿來一個上面畫着美麗小鳥的小紙盒，放那些死了的花進去。

"這是為你們做的漂亮棺材，"她說。"等我那些表兄弟來看我，不久他們會幫我埋你們在花園裏。這樣，明年夏天你們又可以生長起來，長得更美麗。"

她的表兄弟是兩個脾氣很好的男孩，一個叫古斯塔夫，一個叫阿多爾夫。他們的父親給了他們一人一張新的十字弓，他們帶弓給伊達看。伊達把那些可憐的死花的事講給他們聽，又說要葬它們在花園。兩個男孩背着弓走在前面，小伊達捧着裝了死花的美麗盒子跟在後面。他們在花園裏挖了一個小墓坑。伊達親親她那些花，然後放它們到泥土裏。古斯塔夫和阿多爾夫在墳上射他們的箭，因為他們既沒有槍，也沒有炮。

# 5

# 拇指姑娘

從前有一個女人，非常希望有一個小孩。她去找一個小仙子，說："我太想有一個小孩了，你能告訴我，我到甚麼地方可以找到一個嗎？""噢，那好辦，"小仙子說。"我給你這顆大麥，它不是農民田地裏種的那種大麥，也不是雞吃的那種大麥。你種它到花盆裏，看看會發生甚麼事情吧。"

"謝謝你，"那女人說，然後給了小仙子十二個銀幣付那顆大麥的價錢。接着她回家種下它，馬上就長出一朵漂亮的大花，樣子有點像鬱金香，但是它的花瓣緊緊地包着，好像還只是一個花蕾。

"這是一朵美麗的花，"那女人說着，親親那些紅色和金色的花瓣，她這麼一親，花就開了，她看到這是一朵真正的鬱金香。在花裏面，在天鵝絨般的綠色雄蕊上，卻坐着一個非常嬌小可愛的女孩。她幾乎還沒有大拇指的一半長，大家就叫她做"小拇指"，或者"拇指姑娘"，因為她實在太小了。

一個擦得很亮的胡桃殼給她作搖籃，她的床褥是藍色的紫羅蘭花瓣，被子是玫瑰花瓣。夜裏她睡在這裏，但是白天她就在桌上玩，那女人在桌上放了一盤水。

沿着盤子放着一圈花環，花莖浸在水裏，水上漂着很大的一片鬱金香花瓣，給拇指姑娘當船玩。拇指姑娘坐在那上面，用白馬鬃做的兩根槳從這一邊划到那一邊，從那一邊划到這一邊，真是好看極了。拇指姑娘還能唱歌，那麼輕柔甜潤，像她那樣的歌聲從來沒有人聽過。

一天夜裏，正當她睡在她漂亮的床上時，一隻濕漉漉的癩蛤蟆，又大又醜，從窗上一塊玻璃破掉的地方爬進來，一跳就跳到蓋着拇指姑娘那玫瑰花瓣被子正在睡覺的桌上。

"這女孩可以給我的兒子做個漂亮的小媳婦啊，"癩蛤蟆說着，捧起睡着拇指姑娘的胡桃殼，跳出窗，到外面花園裏去了。

這癩蛤蟆和她的兒子，就住在花園裏一條寬闊小溪的潮濕岸邊。她的兒子甚至比她還要醜，他一看見睡在精巧小床上的美麗小女孩，只叫得出幾聲："呱呱，呱呱，呱呱！"

"別叫得那麼響，要不然她會醒，"癩蛤蟆說，"這一來她會跑掉，因為她輕得就像一根天鵝毛。我們得放她到小溪上的一片睡蓮葉子上，她又輕又小，對於她來說，那就像一個小島，她就逃不掉了。趁她在那裏，我們趕緊去佈置好爛泥底下那個高級房間，你們結婚以後要住到那裏面去。"

小溪遠處長着不少睡蓮，有寬大的綠葉，好像漂在水面上。這些葉子中最大的一片遠遠離開其他的葉子，老癩蛤蟆就帶着拇指姑娘還在裏面睡着的胡桃殼游到那裏去。

小女孩一大清早醒來，一看見自己在甚麼地方就傷心地哭起來，因為她甚麼也看不到，只看到綠色大葉子的周圍都是水，沒有辦法到陸地上去。

這時候那老癩蛤蟆在濕地底下正忙得不亦樂乎，用燈心草和黃色的野花裝飾房間，要給她的新兒媳婦佈置得漂漂亮亮。接着她帶着她那個醜八怪兒子游到她安置可憐的小拇指姑娘的葉子那裏。她想搬走那張漂亮的床，放到洞房裏去，為她安置好。老癩蛤蟆在水裏對她深深鞠躬説："這就是我的兒子，他將要做你的丈夫，你們將幸福地生活在小溪旁的爛泥裏面。"

"呱呱，呱呱，呱呱，"她兒子説得出的就只有這幾聲。然後癩蛤蟆抬起美麗的小床，帶着它遊走了，剩下拇指姑娘獨自一個在綠色的葉子上，她坐在那裏嚶嚶地哭。她一想到要和那老癩蛤蟆住在一起，並由她那個醜八怪兒子當她的丈夫，心裏就受不了。在下面水裏游來游去的那些小魚見到了癩蛤蟆，聽到了她的話，於是伸出頭來看那小女孩。

他們一望就看到她有多麼美麗，想到她要去跟兩隻醜八怪癩蛤蟆生活在一起，就覺得非常憤怒。

"不行，絕對不可以這樣！"他們於是在水裏聚集起來，圍住小女孩所站的那片葉子的綠莖，用他們的牙齒咬斷它的根。那片葉子隨即順着小溪往下漂，帶拇指姑娘到遠遠的，陸地接觸不到的地方。

拇指姑娘漂過許多城鎮，灌木叢中的小鳥看見她，唱道："多麼可愛的小東西啊！"那葉片載着她越漂越遠，一直來到別的地方。一隻優美的小白蝴蝶一直環繞着她飛，最後停到葉子上。他喜歡拇指姑娘，她也喜歡現在這樣，因為現在癩蛤蟆到不了她這裏來了。她漂過的地方很美麗，太陽照在水上，水面像熔化的黃金那樣閃光。她解下她腰間的緞帶，一頭拴着蝴蝶，另一頭拴在葉子上，葉子載着站在上面的拇指姑娘，現在走得比原先快多了。

這時有一隻大金龜子飛過，他一見拇指姑娘，馬上用他的爪子抓住她纖細的腰，帶着她飛到一棵樹上去。那片綠葉在小溪上漂走了，蝴蝶也跟着它飛走了，因為他被拴在葉子上面，離不開它。

噢，當那隻金龜子抓住拇指姑娘飛到樹上去的時候，她是多麼害怕啊！但是她更為被她拴到葉子上的漂亮白蝴蝶感到難過，因為他如果不能掙脫，就會餓死。但是那金龜子根本不為這件事傷腦筋。他在一片大綠葉上坐到她身邊，給她一些花蜜吃，並對她說，她雖然一丁點也不像金龜子，但是非常漂亮。

過了一會，所有住在樹上的金龜子都來看拇指姑娘，他們盯着她看，然後年輕的雌金龜子豎起她們的觸鬚說："她只有兩條腿！那模樣多醜啊。""她沒有觸鬚，"另外一隻說。"她的腰太細了。呸！她像一個人。"

"噢！她很醜，"所有雌金龜子都說。這時候，抓她來的那隻金龜子聽見大家都說她醜，他也相信了，再不願意跟她說話，只告訴她，她愛到哪裏去就可以到哪裏去。接着他帶着她從樹上飛下來，放她在一朵雛菊上，她想到自己醜得連金龜子都不要跟她說話，不禁哭起來。然而她始終是人們所能想像的最美麗的造物，像一片美麗的玫瑰花瓣那樣嬌嫩。

整個夏天，小拇指姑娘孤苦伶仃地在荒涼的森林裏生活。她用草葉給自己編了一張床，懸掛在一片大葉子底下擋雨。她吮吸花蜜充饑，每天早晨喝花葉上的露水。

就這樣，夏天和秋天過去了，接着冬天來了 —— 漫長寒冷的冬天。曾經那麼甜蜜地對她唱歌的所有鳥兒飛走了，所有樹木和花兒也凋謝了。她曾在下面生活並得到遮蔽的那片大三葉草如今也捲起來，枯萎了，只留下一根黃色的枯莖。她冷得可怕，因為她的衣服已經穿破，她本人又是那麼孱弱嬌嫩，於是可憐的小拇指姑娘幾乎要冷死了。天也開始下雪，一片小雪花落到她身上就如同整鏟的雪落到我們身上一樣，因為我們高大，她卻只有一寸高。她於是用一片乾樹葉裹起自己，可是它在中間裂開，不能使她暖和，她冷得直發抖。

離開她居住的森林不遠有一塊大麥田，但是麥子已經收割了很久，除了光禿禿的枯麥茬露在凍結的地上以外，甚麼也沒有留下。走過這塊麥田，對她來說，就如同艱難地穿過一片大森林。

噢！她冷得發抖成甚麼樣子了啊。她最後來到了一隻田鼠的家門口，這田鼠在一撮麥茬底下有個小洞。田鼠住在洞裏又溫暖又舒服，她有整房間的麥子，有個廚房，還有個漂亮的飯廳。可憐的拇指姑娘站在洞門前就像個討飯的小女孩，請求田鼠施捨給她一小粒大麥，因為她已經兩天沒有吃過一點東西了。

"你這可憐的小東西，"田鼠說，她真是隻好心腸的老田鼠，"到我暖和的房間裏來和我一起吃飯吧。"

她非常喜歡拇指姑娘，因此說："如果你高興的話，歡迎你留下來和我一起過冬。不過你必須把我的房間收拾得乾乾淨淨，整整齊齊，並且給我講故事，因為我非常喜歡聽故事。"拇指姑娘完全照田鼠吩咐她的話做，日子過得十分舒適。

"很快就有一位客人來看我們了，"有一天田鼠說，"我這鄰居一個星期來看我一次。他比我過得好，他有大房間，穿漂亮的黑天鵝絨大衣。如果你能有他這樣一個丈夫就好了，你一定可以吃好穿好。不過他眼睛看不見，因此你必須給他講你最有趣的故事。"

但是拇指姑娘對這位鄰居根本不感興趣，因為他是一隻鼹鼠。不過他的確穿上那件黑天鵝絨大衣來看她們。

"他非常有錢有學問，他的房子要比我的大二十倍，"田鼠說。

他有錢有學問是真的，但是他談到太陽和美麗的花兒總帶着一種輕蔑口氣，因為他從來沒有看過它們。拇指姑娘被迫唱歌給他聽。"瓢蟲瓢蟲，飛回家中"，以及許多好聽的歌。鼹鼠竟愛上她了，因為她有那麼甜潤的嗓子。不過他沒有說出來，因為他十分小心謹慎。不久前，鼹鼠在地底下挖了一條很長的地道，從田鼠的家一直通到他自己的家，他讓田鼠隨時高興就帶着拇指姑娘在地道裏走走。不過他事先提醒她們，萬一在地道裏看見一隻死鳥不必害怕。那是一隻完好的鳥，嘴和羽毛都好好的，死了不會很久，就躺在鼹鼠挖出來的地道裏。鼹鼠嘴巴叼着一塊發出磷光的木片，它在黑暗中像火一樣閃光。然後他在前面帶路，照亮她們穿過又長又黑的地道。當他們來到躺着那隻死鳥的地方時，鼹鼠用他那個寬鼻子往地道的頂上拱，泥土紛紛落下來，於是露出了一個大窟窿，太陽光照進了地道。

地道當中躺着一隻死了的燕子，他美麗的翅膀貼着身體兩邊，腳和頭縮在羽毛底下，這隻可憐的鳥顯然是冷死了。小拇指姑娘看到這情景非常難過，她太愛小鳥了，整個夏天他們那麼悅耳地為她啁啾鳴唱。但是鼹鼠用他彎曲的腿推他到一邊，說："現在他再也不能唱歌了。生為小鳥該多麼悲慘啊！謝天謝地，我沒有一個孩子會是鳥，因為他們除了'唧唧喳喳'地叫就甚麼也不會做，而且在冬天裏總是餓死。"

"對，你真聰明，說得好！"田鼠說道。"唧唧喳喳叫又有甚麼用，冬天一來，他不是餓死就是冷死。不過鳥還是非常高貴的。"

拇指姑娘沒有說話，但是等到他們一轉身，她就彎下腰，撥開蓋着鳥頭的柔軟羽毛，親親他緊閉的眼簾。"也許他就是夏天甜蜜地給我唱歌的小鳥，"她說，"那給了我多麼大的快樂啊，親愛的美麗小鳥。"

現在鼴鼠封住那照進陽光的洞，然後送她們回家。但是到了夜裏拇指姑娘睡不着，於是她下床用乾草編了一塊漂亮的大毯子，帶到死鳥那裏去，蓋在他身上，還蓋上她在田鼠的房間裏找來的一些花絮。它們和羊毛一樣鬆軟，她在鳥的每一側蓋上一些，這樣他躺在寒冷的地上就可以暖和些了。

"永別了，美麗的小鳥，"她說，"永別了，謝謝你在樹木蔥蘢、太陽溫暖並照耀着我們的夏天時所唱的歌，那多麼令人愉快。"接着她把頭靠在鳥的心口上，但她馬上大吃一驚，因為鳥的身體裏好像有甚麼東西在"撲通撲通"地響。那是鳥的心臟，他並沒有當真死掉，只是凍僵了，溫暖已經使他復生。到了秋天，所有燕子都飛到暖和的地方去，誰一耽擱就會被寒冷逮住，凍僵，像死了一樣掉下來，留在掉下的地方，給冰冷的雪覆蓋住。

拇指姑娘這時被嚇壞了，嚇得發起抖來。因為那鳥很大，比她本人大得多 —— 她只有一寸高。但是她鼓起勇氣，在可憐的燕子身上蓋上更厚的花絮，接着拿來她當被子蓋的一片葉子，蓋在可憐的鳥的頭上。

第二天晚上她又偷偷出來看他。他活過來了，但非常虛弱。他只能睜開一會眼睛看看拇指姑娘，她手裏拿着一塊腐朽了發磷光的木片，因為她沒有提燈。"謝謝你，漂亮的小女孩，"生病的燕子說，"我暖和得多了，我會很快恢復體力，重新在暖和的陽光中飛來飛去。"

"噢，"拇指姑娘說，"外面現在很冷。在下雪，四周都結冰了。你在溫暖的床上待着吧，我會照料你的。"

接着她用花瓣給燕子盛來一點水，他喝完以後告訴拇指姑娘，他在荊棘叢裏傷了一隻翅膀，無法和其他燕子飛得一樣快，追不上他們，他們很快就向着溫暖的地方遠遠地飛走了。到後來他掉到了地面上，甚麼都記不起來，也不知道他怎麼會來到這個地方。

整個冬天這燕子留在地底下，拇指姑娘細心溫柔地服侍他。這件事她一點也沒告訴鼴鼠和田鼠，因為他們不喜歡燕子。很快春天就到了，太陽溫暖了大地。於是燕子告別拇指姑娘，拇指姑娘重新打開鼴鼠曾經挖出來的窟窿。和煦的太陽照進來，燕子問她願不願意和他一起走。他說拇指姑娘可以坐在他的背上，他就帶着她飛到蔥蘢的森林裏去。但是拇指姑娘知道，她這樣走會使田鼠非常傷心，因此她說："不，我不能走。"

"那麼再見了，你這善良、漂亮的小女孩，"燕子說，接着他就飛到外面的陽光去了。

拇指姑娘目送着他，眼淚盈眶。她非常喜歡這隻可憐的燕子。

燕子飛進綠色的森林時唧唧喳喳地唱着，拇指姑娘覺得非常難過。田鼠不允許她到外面溫暖的陽光去。種在田鼠家上面麥田裏的麥子已經長得很高，對拇指姑娘來說成了一個濃密的森林，因為拇指姑娘只有一寸高。

"你快要結婚了，拇指姑娘，"田鼠說。"我的那位鄰居已經向你求婚。對於你這樣的可憐孩子，這是多麼大的福氣啊。現在我們得準備你的嫁衣了。羊毛的、麻布的都要有。當鼴鼠的妻子就甚麼都不會缺啊。"

拇指姑娘只好搖起紡車來，田鼠還僱了四隻蜘蛛，日紡夜織。鼴鼠每天晚上來看她，不停地講夏天過去以後的日子。到那時候他就要和拇指姑娘結婚，但現在太陽太曬了，把大地烤得像石頭一樣硬繃繃。只等夏天一過就舉行婚禮。但是拇指姑娘根本不願意結婚，因為她不喜歡那討厭的鼴鼠。

每天早晨太陽一出來，每天晚上太陽一落下，她就爬到門外，這時風吹開麥穗，她可以看到蔚藍的天空，心裏說，外面多麼美麗，多麼明亮啊，同時渴望再見到她那隻親愛的燕子朋友。但是燕子沒有回來過，這時候他已遠遠飛到美麗的翠綠森林去了。

秋天一到，拇指姑娘的嫁衣全準備好了，田鼠對她說："過四個星期婚禮就要舉行。"

拇指姑娘於是哭着說她不要嫁給那討厭的鼴鼠。

"胡說，"田鼠回答道。"現在不要固執了，不然我就用我的白牙齒咬你。他是一隻十分英俊的鼴鼠，就連皇后穿的天鵝絨衣服和裘衣也不會比他的更漂亮，他的廚房和儲藏室塞得滿滿。你交上這樣的好運，就該謝天謝地。"

婚禮日子落實了，當天鼴鼠就會接她到家裏，跟他一起住在地底深處，從此看不到溫暖的陽光，因為他不喜歡陽光。想到要跟美麗的太陽道別，可憐的女孩很不開心。田鼠准許她站在門前，她就再看看太陽一次。

"再見了，光輝的太陽，"她向它伸出雙手叫道，接着她離開房子走了一小段路，因為麥子已經收割，麥田裏只剩下乾枯的麥茬。"再見了，再見了，"她反覆說着，用一隻手臂抱住長在她身邊的一朵小紅花。"如果你看到小燕子，請替我向他問好。"

"唧唧喳喳，"忽然她的頭頂上響起了叫聲。她抬起頭來看，就是那隻燕子在上面不遠處飛過。他看到拇指姑娘，高興極了。拇指姑娘於是告訴他，她多麼不願意嫁給那難看的鼴鼠，永遠住在地底下，再也看不到明亮的太陽。她一面說，一面哭。

"寒冷的冬天就要到了，"燕子說，"我正要飛到溫暖的地方去。你和我一起走好嗎？你可以坐在我的背上，用你的腰帶繫緊自己。然後我們就可以離開那難看的鼴鼠和他那些陰暗的房間，飛得老遠老遠，飛過羣山，飛到溫暖的地方去，那裏的太陽照耀得比這裏更明亮。那裏一年四季是夏天，花也開得更美。現在就和我飛走吧，親愛的拇指姑娘。當我躺在那黑暗、沮喪的地道裏凍僵的時候，是你救了我的命。"

"好，我和你一起走，"拇指姑娘說。她坐到燕子身上，腳放在他伸出來的翅膀上，腰帶繫在他最粗壯的羽毛上。

接着燕子飛上空中，飛過森林，飛過大海，飛得比終年積雪的高山還要高。拇指姑娘在寒冷的空氣中本來會凍僵，但是她鑽到溫暖的羽毛底下，只是一直露出個小頭，欣賞他們正在飛過的美麗土地。終於他們來到了溫暖的地方，這裏太陽照耀得明亮，天空也似乎離地更高。這裏，在樹籬旁和路邊長着紫的、綠的和白的葡萄，檸檬和橙懸在田地裏的樹上。空氣透着香桃木和橙花香。漂亮的孩子們在鄉村路上奔跑，逗着色彩鮮艷的大蝴蝶玩。燕子越飛越遠，一處比一處更好看。

最後他們來到了一個藍色的湖上，湖邊在墨綠的樹木蔭蔽下，有一座耀眼的白色大理石古老宮殿。葡萄藤圍繞着它那些高大圓柱叢生，柱頂有許多燕子的巢，其中一個，就是帶拇指姑娘到這裏來的燕子的家。

"這就是我的家，"燕子說，"不過它不適合你，你住着不會舒服的。你必須給自己在那些美麗的花中挑一朵，我放你到它上面，然後你就可以快快樂樂，想甚麼有甚麼了。"

"那真是太令人高興了，"拇指姑娘快活得拍着手說。

一根大理石大圓柱倒在地上，倒下時它斷成了三段。在這三段圓柱之間長着最美麗的大白花，燕子於是背着拇指姑娘飛下來，放她在其中一片寬大的花瓣上。但是她多麼吃驚啊，因為她看到花當中有一個很細小的人，又白又透明，像是水晶做的。這小人頭戴金冠，肩上長着好看的雙翼，個子比拇指姑娘大不了多少。他是大白花的天使，每朵花裏都住着一個小人，男的或者女的，而這一個是他們大家的國王。

"噢，他多麼英俊啊！"拇指姑娘對燕子悄悄地說。

小王子初時對燕子非常害怕，燕子和他這樣一個嬌嫩的小東西相比，就像是一隻巨鳥。但是等到他看見拇指姑娘，他高興極了，心想她是他見過最美麗的小女孩。他摘下頭上的金冠，放到她的頭上，問她叫甚麼名字，願不願意做他的妻子，也就是做所有花的皇后。

比起癩蛤蟆的兒子，或者穿黑天鵝絨袍的鼴鼠，這自然是完全不同的另一種丈夫。因此她對這英俊的王子説：“我願意。”這時候所有花兒盛放，從每一朵花裏走出一位很細小的女士，或者一位很細小的先生，個個那麼漂亮，看到他們真是賞心悦目。他們每一位都給拇指姑娘帶來一份禮物，但是最好的禮物是一對美麗的翅膀，這對翅膀本來是大白蛾的。他們繫翅膀到拇指姑娘的雙肩上，這樣她就能夠從一朵花飛到另一朵花上。

接着就開始了熱烈的慶祝，住在他們頭頂上的巢的那隻小燕子受到邀請來唱婚禮歌，他盡可能有多好唱多好，但是他的內心感到憂傷，因為他非常喜愛拇指姑娘，真想和她永不分開。

“你不要再叫拇指姑娘了，”花的精靈告訴她。“這名字很醜陋，你這麼漂亮，我們叫你瑪雅吧。”

“再見了，再見了，”燕子離開溫暖的地方飛回丹麥時，懷着沉重的心情地説。他在丹麥一座房子的窗上有一個巢，這座房子裏正好住着一位童話作家。燕子“唧唧喳喳”地唱，從他的歌中就原原本本地出來了這麼一個故事。

# 6
# 調皮的孩子

從前有一位老詩人，是位心地很好的老詩人。有一天晚上他坐在家裏，外面狂風呼嘯，暴雨傾盆，但是老詩人舒舒服服地坐在他的葫蘆形壁爐旁邊，壁爐裏燒着火，烤着蘋果。"這種天氣，今晚在外面的可憐人都成落湯雞了，"他歎氣說。

"噢，開開門！我冷壞了，濕透了，"外面一個孩子叫道。他又叫又使勁拍門，這時雨傾盆而下，所有窗給風吹得砰砰響。

"可憐的小東西！"詩人說着，站起來，走過去打開門。在他面前站着一個小男孩，光着身體，水從他的金髮上往下直流。他冷得渾身發抖，要是不讓他進來，他在暴風雨中一定沒命。

"可憐的小東西！"詩人說着，拉住他的手。"進來吧，坐在爐邊烘乾吧。你可以喝點酒，吃些烤蘋果。你是個那麼好看的孩子！"

他也的確好看。他的眼睛閃亮得像兩顆星星，雖然他的金髮濕了，頭髮依然鬈得非常好看。他看起來像個小天使，儘管冷得面色蒼白，渾身發抖。他手裏拿着一把弓和一些箭，但是完全被雨水打壞了，美麗的箭的顏色濕了以後也混雜在一起。

老詩人坐在火旁，把小男孩抱在膝蓋上，扭乾他頭髮上的水，用自己的手暖和他的手。老人接着給他吃一個烤蘋果和喝加了香料的熱酒。小男孩很快恢復過來，於是他帶着發紅的雙頰跳到地板上，圍着椅子跳舞。

"你是一個活潑的孩子，"老詩人說。"你叫甚麼名字？"

"我叫丘比特，"小男孩回答，"你不認識我嗎？我有弓和箭，我很擅長射箭。看，月亮出來了，天氣好了。"

"但是你的弓壞了，"老詩人說。

"那真糟糕，"小男孩說着，拿起弓來看。"噢，它全乾了，看起來沒事。看，弦繃得很緊，沒有壞。"於是他插上箭，拉開弓，瞄準，一箭射中了老詩人的心！"你現在看到了吧，我的弓沒有壞？"他對着老詩人哈哈大笑地說。一個多麼調皮、不懂感恩的孩子啊，竟然那樣射老詩人，他曾帶他進自己溫暖的家，曾給他香料熱酒和最好的烤蘋果！

老人躺在地上哭，他的心真的被射中了。"噢……噢……"他哭道。"這丘比特是個多調皮的孩子啊！我要把這件事告訴所有好孩子，讓他們小心他，永遠不要去和他玩，否則他會傷害他們。"

所有孩子，不管男孩還是女孩，都受老詩人警告要盡力提防丘比特，但丘比特還是作弄了他們，因為他很狡猾。一個男孩從大學下課時，丘比特在後面跟着他跑。他穿着黑色長袍，手臂夾着一本書。那男孩認不出是丘比特，以為是另一個同學，就挽着他的手臂。然後，丘比特向他的心射了一箭。女孩也不能倖免，甚至在教堂裏接受堅信禮時也不例外。劇院裏，他騎在吊燈上，在燃燒的蠟燭之間，沒有人留意他在上面。但當丘比特的箭射中人們的心時，他們是感覺得到的。丘比特喜歡在你父母愛去散步的各個皇家公園和堤岸跑來跑去。你父母也被丘比特的箭射中過一次。問問他們，看看他們怎麼說。丘比特是個壞蛋！不要跟他有任何瓜葛。

想像一下，他射過你可憐的老祖母，正中心臟。雖然已是很久以前的事，傷口也癒合了，但她仍記得這件事。哎呀！調皮的丘比特！現在你知道了，他是怎樣一個調皮搗蛋的孩子。

# 7
# 美人魚

在很遠很遠的海上，那裏的水像最美麗的矢車菊那麼藍，像水晶那麼清澈，非常非常深，說實在的，深得沒法用錨鍊來測量它的深度。就算把許多教堂的尖塔一個個疊起來，也不能從下面的海底達到上頭的海面。海王和他的臣民就住在那地方。

我們千萬不要以為海底甚麼也沒有，光有一些黃沙。才不是這樣呢，那裏生長着最奇異的花草樹木。它們的葉子和枝幹是那麼柔軟，水哪怕是最輕微地動一動，也會使得它們搖晃起來，好像它們是有生命的。大魚小魚在枝幹間游來游去，就像我們地面上的鳥兒在樹木間飛來飛去那樣。

在最深的地方聳立着海王的城堡。它的牆是用珊瑚砌的，那些哥德式長窗嵌着最明淨的琥珀。屋頂是貝殼鋪的，水在牠們上面流過時，牠們就一開一合，看起來真是美極了，因為每個貝殼裏都有一顆閃閃發亮的珍珠，用它們做皇后的珠冠實在再合適不過。

不過海王的皇后已經去世多年。如今是他年邁的母親替他管家。他的母親是一位非常聰明的女人，但為自己的高貴出身過份自豪。為此她在她的尾巴上戴上十二隻蠔，而別人儘管也是顯貴卻只可以戴六隻。

不過她的確值得大大稱讚，尤其是她對公主們，也就是她的孫女們的愛護。孫女一共六個，個個美麗，而最小的一個是六個當中最美麗的。她的皮膚光潔細嫩得有如玫瑰花瓣，她的眼睛藍得像最深的海水，但是她和其他人一樣沒有腿，她的下半截身體是一條魚尾巴。這六位小公主整天在城堡那些大廳裏，或者在牆上長出來的鮮花之間遊戲，琥珀大窗都敞開着，魚游進來，就像燕子在我們打開窗時飛進來那樣，只是這些魚一直游到公主們身邊吃她們手裏的東西，並且讓她們撫摸自己。

城堡外面是一座美麗的花園，花園裏長着鮮紅和深藍的花，盛開得好像火焰。果子像黃金般閃亮，葉子和枝幹不停來回招搖。地上鋪着最細潔的沙，不過藍得像燃燒着的硫磺火焰。在所有東西上都罩着一層奇異的藍光，好像不管水面還是水底，四處都是藍天，而不是在黑暗的海底。風平浪靜的時候，這裏可以看到上面的太陽，它看起來像一朵紫紅色的花，光線從花萼裏射出來。

在花園裏，每位小公主有一小塊地，可以在上面隨意栽種東西。一位小公主把她的花壇做成鯨魚的形狀；另一位小公主覺得把她的花壇做成美人魚的形狀更好。但最小的那位公主的花壇卻圓得像太陽，裏面的花紅得像晚霞。

她是一個古怪的孩子，文靜，愛沉思。當她那些姐姐從沉船中弄來了珍奇東西感到歡天喜地的時候，她只關心她那些像太陽一樣紅的美麗的花，唯獨一個漂亮的大理石像除外。這是一個英俊少年的石像，用潔白的石頭雕出來，從一艘沉船上落到了海底。

她在石像旁邊種了一棵玫瑰色的垂柳。它長得很好，不久就把它的嫩枝懸在石像上，幾乎垂到了藍色的沙地。樹影帶紫色，和樹枝一樣搖來搖去，看起來就像樹冠和樹根在玩遊戲，想要互相親吻。

　　這位小公主最愛聽海上面那個世界的事情。她要她的老祖母講她所知道關於船和城市、人和動物的一切。她最感新奇和美麗的似乎是聽說陸地上的花有香味，而水底下的花卻沒有。還有樹林裏的樹木是綠色，樹木間的魚會唱歌，唱得悅耳動聽，聽牠們唱歌簡直是一大樂事。她祖母把小鳥說成魚，要不然小公主就聽不懂她的意思了，因為小公主從來沒有看過小鳥。

　　"等你到了十五歲，"老祖母說，"你就可以游上海面，在月光中坐在岩石上，一些大船在你旁邊駛過，到那時你就能看到樹林和城市了。"

　　下一年她的一個姐姐就到十五歲，但是她們幾姊妹是一個比一個小一歲，最小的公主還足足要等上五年，才輪得到她從海底游上去，像我們一樣看世界。不過每個公主都答應，要把她第一次上去看到的，以及她認為最美的東西告訴其他姊妹，因為她們祖母講的不可能讓她們聽夠，她們想知道的東西太多了。

　　不過幾姊妹中誰也不像最小的妹妹那樣渴望輪到自己，因為她要等的時間最長，人又是那麼文靜，又愛沉思。多少個夜裏她站在開着的窗口抬頭望着深藍的海水，看魚用牠們的鰭和尾巴拍水。她能看到月亮和星星微微地發亮，不過透過水，它們看起來比我們的眼睛所看到的要大。當在她和它們之間飄過像一團烏雲那樣的東西時，她知道那不是一條鯨魚在她的頭頂上游過，就是一艘載滿人的船在她頭頂上駛過，船上的人永遠想不到會有一條美人魚正站在他們底下，向他們的船底伸出了她雪白的雙手。

終於，最大的姐姐一到十五歲，就得到允許游到海面上去了。

等到她回來，她有千百件事情可以講。不過她說最美的事情是在月光下，在風平浪靜的海上，貼近海岸躺在沙灘上眺望附近一座燈火像繁星閃爍的城市，傾聽音樂聲、車馬的喧囂和人聲，然後是從教堂尖塔傳出的歡樂鐘聲。由於不能靠近所有這些美妙的東西，她就更渴望它們。

噢，所有對她說的這些話，最小的妹妹能不豎起了耳朵聽嗎？接下來，當她站在打開的窗口透過黑暗的海水朝上看時，她只想着那大城市和它所有鬧哄哄的聲音，甚至想像在海底她能聽見教堂的鐘聲。

第二年輪到第二個姐姐得到准許游到海面上去，愛到哪裏就游到哪裏。她上去的時候正好碰到日落，她說這真是最美麗的景色。整個天空看起來像黃金，她無法形容的紫藍色和玫瑰色的雲朵在她的頭頂上飄過。還有一大羣野天鵝飛得比雲朵還要快，牠們飛向落日，像一條雪白的長紗飄過大海。她也朝太陽游去，但是太陽沉到了波浪中，雲朵和大海的玫瑰色也消失了。

接下來輪到第三個姐姐。她是她們當中膽子最大的一個，一直游到了流進大海的一條寬闊大河那裏。她在河岸上看到覆蓋着美麗葡萄藤的青翠山崗，宮殿和城堡在樹林的雄偉樹木間隱現。她聽到小鳥的鳴唱。太陽的光線是那麼強烈，她不得不時時潛到水下，使自己灼熱的臉涼快一下。在一個小河灣她看到一大羣小人類，光着身體在水裏玩。她也想和他們一起玩，但是他們看見她嚇了一大跳，逃走了。這時候一隻黑色的小動物來到水邊，那是一隻狗，但是她不認識，因為她從來沒有見過狗。這隻動物對她汪汪叫得那麼可怕，她嚇壞了，連忙逃回大海。但是她說她永遠不會忘記那美麗的樹林、那些青翠的山崗和那些會游水的漂亮小人類，儘管他們沒有魚尾巴。

第四個姐姐膽子小一些。她停留在大海當中，但是她說那裏也和靠近岸邊一樣美麗。她可以遙望周圍許多里遠，頭頂上的天空看着就像一口玻璃大鐘。她看到了船，不過離得太遠，它們看起來像些海鷗。海豚在波浪中嬉戲，大鯨的鼻孔會噴水，看起來就像成百個噴泉在牠的四面八方噴水。

第五個姐姐的生日碰上冬天。因此輪到她上去時，她看到幾個大姐姐第一次上去時沒有見過的東西。大海看起來一片碧綠，大冰山在上面漂流，她說每一座冰山像是一顆珍珠，但是比人造出來的教堂還要大還要高。它們奇形怪狀，像鑽石般閃光。她坐到其中最大的一座冰山上，讓風吹拂她的長髮，她注意到所有船急忙駛過，能多快就多快，並且離這座冰山越遠越好，像是害怕這座冰山似的。傍晚太陽下山時，天上一下子烏雲密佈，巨雷滾過，電光閃閃，冰山在洶湧的大海上搖滾，閃着紅光。所有船驚恐萬分地收下了帆，她卻安靜地坐在浮冰上，凝望着藍色的閃電把它的曲折電光射進海裏。

幾個姐姐第一次得到准許游到海面時，個個看到新鮮的美景都高興雀躍，但是她們如今都長大成人，可以愛到哪裏去就到哪裏去，對這些東西不再那麼感興趣了。她們一上去就想回到海下面來，一個月以後，她們説水底下美麗多了，而且在外面哪有在家快活。

不過在黃昏時刻，她們五姊妹還是常常手挽手一排地結伴上海面。她們的嗓子比任何人類中哪一個都好。在風暴到來之前，當她們想到某一艘船會出事的時候，她們就游到這艘船前面，唱出在海底可以找到的快樂的迷人歌曲，請海員們萬一沉下海底時不要害怕。但是海員們聽不懂她們的歌，把它當作風暴的嗚咽聲。沉下海底這種事對他們來說永遠不可能是美好的，因為船一沉，人就要淹死，他們的屍體便會到達海王的宮殿。

當姐姐們這樣手挽着手穿過海水上去的時候，她們那位最小的妹妹孤零零一個人站在下面目送她們，都要哭出來了。不過人魚沒有眼淚，因此她更加難受。

"噢，我有十五歲就好了，"她說，"我知道我會愛上上面那個世界，愛生活在那個世界上的所有人。"

她終於到十五歲了。

"好，現在你長大了，"她的祖母老皇太后說，"因此你必須讓我像打扮你那些姐姐那樣把你打扮起來。"她在小公主的頭髮上戴上白百合花環，百合花的每塊花瓣是半顆珍珠。接着皇太后吩咐八隻大蠔貼到小公主的尾巴上去顯示她的高貴身份。

"但是牠們弄得我太痛了，"美人魚說。

"當然，要氣派就得吃苦頭，"皇太后回答說。

噢，小公主多麼想甩掉所有這些高貴的裝飾，摘下那個沉重的花環啊！她自己花園裏的紅花會更適合她，但是她不能自己做主，因此她說了聲"再見"，就像個小氣泡那麼輕盈地游到海面上去了。

當她把頭伸出海浪時，太陽剛下山，但是雲朵還染着緋紅色和金色的光彩，昏星透過閃爍的暮色美麗地照耀着。大海很平靜，空氣溫和新鮮。一艘三桅大船隻掛着一張帆停在海上，因為沒有一絲風，海員們懶洋洋地坐在甲板上或者索具之間。船上有音樂和歌聲。隨着天黑下來，上百盞五顏六色的燈籠點亮，就像世界各國的國旗飄揚在空中。

美人魚游近船艙的窗口。海浪不時托起她來，她可以透過清澈的窗玻璃望進去，看見不少穿着考究的人。

其中一個是年輕的王子，他是所有人中最漂亮的，長着一雙黑色大眼睛。他十六歲了，正在慶祝他的生日，隆重得很。海員們在甲板上跳着舞，但是當王子走到外面甲板上時，一百多個煙火噼嚦啪啦放到空中，使天空亮得如同白晝。美人魚一下子嚇得鑽到了水底下，等到她重新伸出頭來，只覺得好像滿天的星星正在她周圍落下來。

她還沒有看到過這樣的煙火。許多大太陽噴出火焰，無數璀璨的螢火蟲飛上藍色的天空，這一切反映在下面明淨的大海上。船本身被照得那麼亮，所有人，甚至連最細的繩子都可以看得清清楚楚。年輕的王子看起來是多麼英俊啊，他和所有在場的人一一握手，向他們微笑，而音樂聲響徹明淨的夜空！

夜已經很深了，然而美人魚沒有辦法把眼睛從那船、從美麗的王子身上移開。彩色燈籠已經熄滅，再也沒有煙火放上空中，禮炮也已經不再鳴放，但是大海變得很不平靜，從波浪底下可以聽到嗡嗡聲和隆隆聲。美人魚仍舊逗留在船艙窗口旁邊，在水上一起一伏，這使她能看到船艙裏面。過了一會，幾張帆很快地張開，豪華的船繼續前進了。但是不久波浪越來越高，沉重的雲使整個天空暗了下來，遠處閃起了電光。可怕的風暴來了，船帆再一次收起，大船在洶湧的海上隨風疾駛。浪頭湧上來像山那麼高，好像要蓋過船桅。船像隻天鵝一樣鑽到波浪中間，接着又在浪花四濺的高聳浪頭上冒出來。對於美人魚來說，這像是一個好玩的遊戲，但對於海員們來說就完全不是這麼回事。最後船發出悶響，還有折裂聲。海浪沖擊甲板，厚木板在其抽打下頂不住斷裂開來，主桅則像一棵蘆葦那樣劈劈啪啪折成幾段。船向一邊側倒，水頓時嘩嘩地湧進去。

直到這時候美人魚才知道，船上的人遇到危險了，連她自己也不得不小心避開失事的船的船樑和木板，這些東西如今在水面上到處都是。天一度變得漆黑，她甚麼也看不見，但是一道電光照出了整個慘相。她看見了所有曾經在船上的人，只是看不到王子。當船折裂的時候，她曾看見他沉落到大浪裏，她一時高興，以為他現在可以和她在一起了。但是她馬上想起，人是不能活在水中，等到他落到她父王的宮殿，他早已經死了。

但是他怎麼也不能死！於是她在漂滿海面的船樑和木板之間游來游去，也忘記了它們會把她撞得粉身碎骨。接着她深深潛到黑暗的深水海裏，隨着波浪起伏，直到最後終於來到年輕的王子身邊，他在刮着風暴的大海中已經完全失去游泳的能力。他的手腳不聽使喚，美麗的眼睛閉上，如果不是美人魚來救他，他必死無疑。美人魚把他的頭托出水面，任憑波浪帶他們到甚麼地方去。

到了早晨，風暴停了。那艘船卻連一點碎片也看不到。燦爛的紅太陽從海上升起來，它的光使王子的臉重新紅潤起來，但是他依然兩眼緊閉。美人魚吻他高挺光滑的前額，向後梳抹他的濕頭髮。她覺得他很像她小花園裏那座大理石像，又吻了吻他，希望他能醒來。

這時候他們來到了能看見陸地的地方。她看到青色的高山，山頂積雪，像棲息着一羣天鵝。靠近海岸是青翠的美麗樹林，附近有一座高大建築物，她説不出是教堂還是修道院。它的花園裏長着橙樹和香橼樹，門前有一些高大的棕櫚樹。這裏的海洋形成一個小海灣，海灣裏的水靜止不動，但非常深。於是她托着英俊的王子游到鋪着潔白細沙的海灘上，把他放在溫暖的陽光中，小心地抬高他的頭，比他的身體高一些。這時候那座白色大建築物響起了鐘聲，幾個年輕女孩到花園來了。美人魚游得離岸遠些，躲到露出水面的高大岩石之間，然後她讓海水的泡沫遮住她的頭和脖子，不叫人看見她那張小臉，她就這樣等着看可憐的王子會怎麼樣。

沒過多久，她就看見一個年輕女孩來到王子躺着的地方。那女孩最初似乎大吃一驚，但這只是一轉眼的事。接着她叫來了幾個人，美人魚看到王子重新醒過來了，對站在他周圍的人微笑。但是他沒有對她微笑過，他根本就不知道是她救了他，這使她十分傷心。當王子被大家送進那大建築物時，她難過地潛進海裏，回到她父親的城堡。

她一向沉默和愛沉思，現在就更加沉默和愛沉思了。她的姐姐們問她，這頭一回到海面上看到了甚麼。她甚麼也沒有對她們説。許多個夜晚和早晨，她游去留下王子的地方。她看到花園裏的果子成熟了，被採摘了，山頂上的雪融化了，但是她再也沒有看過王子，因此她回家總是一次比一次難過。

她唯一的安慰就是坐在她自己的小花園裏，抱着那個像王子的美麗大理石像。但是她不再照料她那些花了，它們在小徑上胡亂生長，它們的長葉子和枝幹纏繞着樹枝，因此，這整塊地方變得又陰又暗。

最後她再也忍不住，把這件事全告訴了她的一個姐姐，接着其他幾個姐姐也聽説了，不久有幾個人魚也知道了，她們其中一個有一個知己朋友正好知道這王子是誰。這個好友也見過船上的歡慶場面，於是告訴她們，這王子是從哪裏來，他的皇宮在哪裏。

“來吧，小妹妹，”其他幾位公主説。於是她們手挽手一長排地游到水面，游近她們所知的王子的皇宮。這皇宮是用光亮的淡黃色石頭砌成的，有一座座大理石高臺階，其中一座一直通到海邊。皇宮頂上高聳着華麗燦爛的鍍金圓頂，環繞整座皇宮的圓柱之間矗立着和真人一樣的大理石雕像。透過高大窗戶的清澈玻璃可以看到富麗堂皇的房間，裏面有貴重的絲綢簾子和掛毯，牆上滿是美麗的圖畫。在最大的廳堂中央，一個噴泉把閃爍發光的水柱高高噴到玻璃圓屋頂上，太陽透過玻璃圓屋頂照到下面的水上和噴水池周圍的美麗花木上。

如今美人魚知道王子住在甚麼地方，許多個傍晚和夜裏她總在那皇宮附近的海裏。她比誰都更大膽地游近岸邊。真的，有一次她甚至一直來到大理石陽臺底下的小河裏，大理石陽臺在這裏的水面上投下了很大的倒影。她會坐在這裏盯着年輕王子看，王子卻還以為只有他一個人在這明朗的月下呢。

她看見他好多個晚上坐着一隻舒適的船遊玩，船上奏着音樂，飄着旗子。她從綠色的燈心草間向外窺看，如果風吹起她銀白色的長面紗，看見的人會相信這只是一隻天鵝在展開雙翅。

還有許多個夜裏，當漁民們帶着火把出海的時候，她聽見他們講了年輕王子做的那麼多好事，她感到很高興，在他被巨浪拋來拋去都已經快死的時候救了他的命。她想起他的頭曾經靠在她的懷裏，她當時又是怎樣熱情地吻他，但是所有這些他都一無所知，甚至做夢也不會想到她。

她越來越喜歡人類了，也越來越希望能和他們在一起玩，人的天地比她自己的天地看起來要大得多。他們能乘船飛渡大海，能攀登聳入雲端的高山。他們所擁有的土地、他們的森林和田野，她看都看不到盡頭。她希望知道的東西太多了，她的姐姐們沒有辦法回答她所有的問題。於是她去問她的老祖母，她知道"上面的世界"的所有事，非常恰當地用這個名稱來稱呼海上面的陸地。

"如果人類不淹死的話，"美人魚問道，"他們能夠永遠活下去嗎？他們能夠永遠不死，不像我們在這裏那樣嗎？"

"不，"老夫人回答說，"他們也要死，他們的壽命甚至比我們的還短。我們有時候能活到三百歲，不過我們生命結束的時候只是變成水面上的泡沫，在下面這裏甚至沒有一個我們所愛的人的墳墓。我們沒有不滅的靈魂，我們永遠不會再活。我們就像綠色的海草，一旦被割掉就再也不能生長。人類卻相反，他們有永遠不滅的靈魂，肉體化成塵土了，它依然活着。靈魂通過純淨的空氣升到閃爍的星星上面。就像我們升到水面看到整個大地一樣，他們升到我們永遠無法看到的那個光輝的未知世界。"

"為甚麼我們沒有不滅的靈魂呢？"美人魚悲哀地問。"哪怕只要能夠做一天人，能夠知道星星上面那個光輝世界的快樂，我心甘情願少活我能夠活的幾百年。"

"你可絕不要那麼想，"老祖母說，"比起人類，我們要快活得多也好得多。"

"那麼我就得死去了，"美人魚說，"我將成為海上的泡沫被吹來吹去，再也聽不見波浪的音樂聲，再也看不到美麗的花或者鮮紅的太陽了。我有辦法能贏得一個不滅的靈魂嗎？"

"沒有辦法，"老祖母說，"除非有一個人是那樣地愛你，你對於他比他的父母還重要；除非他所有的心思和全部的愛都傾注到你身上，牧師把這人的右手放到你的手上，這人答應從此以後對你忠實。那麼，這時候他的靈魂就轉移到你的體內，你才能在未來分享到人類的快樂。他將給你一個靈魂，同時保留着他自己的，但這種事永遠不會有。你那條魚尾巴在我們看來是如此美麗，但在陸地上卻被認為非常難看。他們不懂得任何更美的東西，以為要美就要有兩條粗壯的支撐棍，他們稱它們做腿。"

美人魚聽着，歎了口氣，難過地看着她的魚尾巴。"讓我們高興起來吧，"老祖母說，"讓我們在我們將要活的三百年中蹦蹦跳跳吧，那時間實在是夠長的了，那以後我們就可以好好地休息。今天晚上我們要開一個宮廷舞會。"

這是我們在陸地上永遠看不到的壯麗場面之一。大舞廳的牆上和頂上鑲鋪着很厚但是透明的水晶。每一邊排列着千百個巨型貝殼，有深紅的，有草綠的，貝殼裏燃着藍色火焰，照亮整個大廳，光穿透過透明的牆壁，也照亮了海。無數的魚，有大有小，游過水晶牆。魚鱗有閃着紫光的，有閃着銀光和金光的。一條寬寬的小溪流過一個個廳，溪中男人魚和女人魚與他們自己甜美的歌聲跳着舞。

　　陸地上沒有人有他們那麼美麗的嗓子，而美人魚公主唱得比他們所有人魚更優美動聽。整個宮廷的人都向她鼓掌拍尾，有一刻她感到十分快樂，因為她知道自己有陸地上和海裏最美的聲音。但是她很快又想起那個在她上面的世界，因為她忘不了那位迷人的王子，也忘不了她沒有他那種不滅靈魂的悲哀。因此她悄悄地離開了她父親的皇宮，儘管宮內充滿快樂和歌聲，她卻一個人坐在她自己的小花園裏感到又悲傷又孤單。接着她聽見水中傳來號角聲，不禁想："他一定是在上面坐船遊玩了，我的希望都在他身上，我願意把我一生的幸福交給他。為了他，為了贏得一個不滅的靈魂，我要去冒一切的危險，趁我那些姐姐在父親的皇宮裏跳着舞的時候，我要去見海女巫，我一直怕她怕得要命，但是她能給我指點和幫助我。"

　　於是美人魚離開了她的花園，一路上朝那些起着泡沫的漩渦走去，那女巫就住在那些漩渦後面。她以前從未走過這條路，這裏不長花草，只有一大片光禿禿的灰沙一直伸展到漩渦那裏，漩渦的水像激起水花的水車輪，瘋狂旋轉被捲進的東西，轉到無底洞裏去。為了到達海女巫的地方，美人魚不得不穿過這些瘋狂旋轉的漩渦。過了這些漩渦，還要沿着一條穿過一些沸騰滾燙的泥沼的小道，走一段很長的路，女巫叫這個泥沼做她的"地盤"。

　　過了泥沼就是她那座在古怪樹林中央的房子，樹林中所有的花草樹木都是水螅體，半是動物半是植物，看起來像是從地裏長出來的有上百個頭的蛇。樹枝是黏糊糊的長臂，上面有像蠕蟲般彎來彎去的手指，這些長臂從樹根到樹頂相繼不停地擺動。牠們抓住海裏一切能到手的東西，抓得緊緊，不讓它從牠們的爪子裏逃脫。

美人魚看到這種東西嚇得呆住不動，心慌得怦怦直跳，想要轉身回去。但是她想起了王子，想起了她渴望得到的人的靈魂，於是她重新鼓起勇氣。她把她飄動的長髮盤在頭上，這樣水螅體就抓不到它們。她把雙手交叉放在胸前，然後像魚在水中躥過去一樣直衝向前，在兩邊向她伸出來的醜惡水螅體的柔軟手臂和手指之間穿過。她看到每一棵水螅體都用牠無數的鐵箍般的小臂抓住一些已經到手的東西。淹死在水中並沉到海底的人的白骨、陸上動物的殘骸、船槳、船舵和船上的箱子都被緊緊抱在牠們的臂裏，甚至還有一個美人魚，牠們把她抓住和勒死了。對於小公主來說，這可說是最觸目驚心了。

她現在來到了森林中一塊沼澤地，那上面一些又大又粗的水蛇在翻滾，露出牠們黃褐色的難看的身體。就在這塊沼澤地中間有一座房子，用沉船的人的骨頭砌成。海女巫就坐在那裏，讓一隻癩蛤蟆從她的嘴上吃東西，像人們有時候用方糖餵金絲雀的樣子。她叫那些難看的水蛇做小雞，讓牠們在她的胸口上爬來爬去。

"我知道你要甚麼，"海女巫說，"你真是太蠢了，但是你可以隨心而行，不過它將給你帶來痛苦，我美麗的公主。你想去掉你的魚尾巴，換上陸地上的人那兩條支撐棍，好讓年輕的王子愛上你，好讓你可以得到一個不滅的靈魂。"接着女巫哈哈大笑，笑得那麼響那麼難聽，癩蛤蟆和水蛇都掉落到了地上，在那裏扭來扭去。

"不過你來得正是時候，"女巫説，"因為過了明天早晨日出，我就沒有辦法幫助你，要等到下一年的年底了。我會為你煮一服藥，你必須帶着它在明天日出前游上陸地，坐在海岸上把它喝下去。喝了以後你的尾巴便會消失，變成人類稱為腿的東西。

"那時你將感到劇痛，就像一把劍在刺穿你的身體。但是所有見到你的人都會説你是他們見過最美麗的人。你的動作將依舊像游水一樣優美，沒有一個舞蹈家的步伐能這麼輕盈，但是每走一步你都會感到像踩在鋒利的刀刃上，就像要流血那樣。如果所有這些痛苦你都能忍受住，那我就幫助你。"

"是的，我能，"小公主用顫抖的聲音説，她想起了王子和不滅的靈魂。

"不過你再好好想想，"女巫説，"因為你的形狀一旦變成人，你再也不能恢復成人魚了。你將永遠不能穿過水遊回你的姐姐們那裏，也不能再回到你父親的皇宮。萬一你爭取不到王子的愛，使他願意為了你忘卻他的父母，用他的整個靈魂愛你，同意牧師把你們的手放在一起成為夫妻，那你將永遠得不到一個不滅的靈魂。在他和別人結婚以後的第一個早晨，你的心將會破碎，你將成為浪峯上的泡沫。"

"我決定這樣做，"美人魚説，她的臉色變得和死人一樣蒼白。

"但是我也必須得到報酬，"女巫説，"而且我要的不是無謂的東西。你有勝過海底任何一個的最甜美的嗓子，而且你自信能用它迷住王子，但你必須給我這嗓子，我要你所擁有的最好的東西作為我給你的藥的代價。我自己的血必須攪到藥裏，這樣藥就會和雙刃劍一樣鋒利。"

"但是你拿走了我的嗓子,"美人魚説,"我還剩下甚麼呢?"

"你美麗的身姿、你優雅的步態和你動人眼睛啊,用這些你一定能吸引男人的心。怎麼,你已經失去你的勇氣了嗎?伸出來你的小舌頭吧,讓我割掉它作為我的報酬,然後你就能得到那強力的藥了。"

"就這麼辦吧,"美人魚説。

於是女巫把她的大鍋子放在火上,煮那有魔力的藥。

"清潔是一件好事,"她説着,把幾條蛇打成一個大結,用來洗刷大鍋子。接着她刺破自己的胸口,讓黑色的血滴到鍋子裏。冒起來的蒸氣扭結成可怕的形狀,沒有人看着它能不膽戰心驚。女巫不斷往鍋子裏投進不同的東西,等到滾起來時,那聲響就像鱷魚的哭聲。有魔力的藥汁煮好後看起來卻像最清的水。

"給你煮好了,"女巫説。接着她割去了美人魚的舌頭,這樣美人魚就啞了,再也不能説話唱歌。"當你穿過森林回去的時候,如果水螅體抓住你,"女巫説,"只要把這藥汁在牠們身上滴上幾滴,牠們的手指就會粉碎。"但是美人魚沒有必要這樣做,因為那些水螅體一看見她手裏的藥汁像閃爍的星星一樣發光,早嚇得趕緊縮回去了。

於是她很快地穿過了森林、沼澤地和瘋狂地打轉的漩渦。她回去看到在她父親的皇宮裏舞廳的火把已經熄滅,所有人已經睡覺。但是她不敢進去看他們,因為她現在啞了,並且要永遠離開他們,她覺得她的心要碎了。她偷偷溜進花園,從每個姐姐的花壇裏採了一朵花,對着皇宮飛了一千個吻,然後通過深藍的海水游上去。

當她看到王子的皇宮，游近美麗的大理石臺階時，太陽還沒有升起，但是月亮照得清澈明亮。美人魚隨即喝下有魔法的藥汁，一下子像有一把雙刃劍插進她嬌嫩的身體。她昏倒在地，像死了一樣躺着。當太陽升起照耀着大海時，她醒過來了，感到一陣陣劇痛，但就在她面前卻站着那位英俊的年輕王子。

他用烏黑的眼睛那麼真誠地緊緊盯住她看，弄得她不禁垂下了自己的眼睛，這時候才看到她的尾巴已經不見，卻有一雙只有少女會有的雪白的腿和纖細的腳。只是她沒有穿衣服，於是她用她濃密的長髮裹起自己來。王子問她是誰、從哪裏來。她用深藍色的眼睛溫柔和悲哀地看着他，但是她不能說話。他牽着她的手，帶她到皇宮。

她每走一步，正如女巫說過的，便感到像踩在針尖或者鋒利的刀刃上。不過她心甘情願地忍受着痛苦，在王子身邊走得像肥皂泡那麼輕盈，使他和所有看見她的人對她那種婀娜多姿的步伐驚訝不已。很快她就穿上了用絲綢和細紗做的貴重長袍，成為皇宮裏最美麗的人。但她是啞的，既不能說話，也不能唱歌。

穿着絲綢衣服、戴着黃金首飾的漂亮女僕們走上前，在王子和他的父王母后面前唱歌，一個唱得比一個動聽，王子拍着手向美人魚微笑。對美人魚來說這是巨大的悲哀，她知道自己曾經唱得比這不知要好多少，不禁想道："噢，如果他知道就好了！為了和他在一起，我永遠交出了我的嗓子。"

接下來女僕們合着美妙的音樂跳起了仙子般的舞蹈。這時候美人魚舉起她可愛的雪白雙臂，踮起腳尖，在地上飄然而舞，沒有任何人比她跳得好。每跳一步，她的美就愈發流露，她含情脈脈的眼睛比女僕們的歌聲更直接地打動人心。所有人都入了迷，特別是王子，他稱她為他的小棄孩。她欣然地又跳起舞來，要令他高興，雖然每當她的腳碰到地面，就像踩在鋒利的刀刃上。

王子說她應該一直留在他的身邊，讓她睡在他房門口的絲絨墊子上。他給她做了一套見習騎士的衣服，這樣她可以陪他騎馬。他們一起騎馬穿過香氣撲鼻的森林，綠枝拂着他們的肩頭，小鳥在嫩葉間鳴唱。她和王子一起爬到高山頂上。儘管她嬌嫩的腳流血，甚至一步一個血印，她卻只是笑，跟着他走，直到看見雲朵在他們下面像一羣鳥向遠方飛行。在王子的皇宮裏，當大家全都睡了以後，她一個人走出來，坐在寬闊的大理石臺階上，把像火燒那樣痛的腳浸在冷海水裏，使它們舒服些。這時候她想起了在海底的所有人。

有一天夜裏，她的幾個姐姐手挽手地上來，一面在水上游，一面傷心地唱歌。美人魚向她們招手，她們認出了她，姐姐們訴說她使她們多麼傷心。以後她們每夜都到這地方來。有一次她還遠遠看到了她多少年沒上過海面的老祖母，還有她的父親老海王，頭上戴着他的皇冠。他們向她伸出雙手，但是不敢像她的姐姐們那樣游近岸邊。

日子一天天過去，她更愛王子了，王子也愛她，但只像愛一個孩子那麼愛她，從來沒有想到過要娶她為妻。然而，除非王子娶她，不然她就不能得到一個不滅的靈魂，而在他和別人結婚後的第一個早晨，她將化成海上的泡沫。

"在所有人當中，你不是最愛我嗎？"當王子抱着她吻她漂亮的前額時，美人魚的眼睛好像在説。

"是的，你是我的寶貝，"王子説，"因為你有最善良的心，你對我最好，你很像我曾見過的一個年輕女孩，但是我永遠不能再見到她了。那時我的船沉了，海浪把我拋到一座聖殿附近的岸邊，正好有幾個年輕女孩來做禮拜。其中最年輕的一個在岸邊發現了我，救了我的性命。我只見過她兩次，她是我在這世界上唯一能夠愛的人，但是你很像她，你在我的心中幾乎已經取代她了。她屬於那座聖殿，我很幸運有你來代替她，我們將永不分離。"

"啊，他不知道救了他性命的是我，"美人魚想。"是我托着他游過大海，來到那座聖殿所在的森林。我坐在海浪泡沫底下看守，直到有人來救他。我看見那個他愛她勝過愛我的美麗女孩。"美人魚深深地歎氣，但是她不懂流淚。"他説那女孩屬於那聖殿，因此她永遠不會回到這個俗人世界來。他們將不再相會，而我在他身邊，天天看見他。我要關心他，愛他，為他獻出我的生命。"

很快就傳出王子要結婚了，他的妻子將是鄰國國王的美麗女兒，因為一艘美麗的船正在裝備。雖然王子説他只是要去拜訪那位國王，但大家普遍認為他其實是去看他的女兒。一大幫隨員還要跟他一起去。美人魚微笑着搖頭。她比任何人更知道王子的心思。

"我必須坐船去那裏，"他對美人魚説，"我必須去看看這位美麗的公主，我的雙親想要我這麼做，但是他們並不強迫我把她作為我的新娘帶回家。我不可能愛她，她不像聖殿那位美麗女孩，而你像她。如果我不得不選擇一位新娘的話，我情願選你，我的啞巴棄妞，你有那麼一雙會説話的眼睛。"他吻她鮮紅的嘴唇，撫弄她波浪似的長髮，把頭靠在她的心口上，而她在幻想着人的幸福和不滅的靈魂。

"你不怕海，對嗎？我的啞孩子，"當他們站在那艘華麗大船的甲板上時他説，這船正送他們到鄰國的國王那裏去。接着他跟她講起風暴，講平靜的海，講他們底下的深海裏那些奇怪的魚，講潛水的人曾在那裏看見的東西。她對他的話微笑着，因為她比任何人更清楚在海底有甚麼奇妙的東西。

在月夜裏，等到船上所有人都睡了，只餘下一個人在掌舵的時候，她獨自坐在月下的甲板上，透過清澈的海水往底下看。她覺得她能辨認出她父親的城堡，在它頂上，她的老祖母頭戴銀冠，正透過激流凝視着船底。這時候她的姐姐們游到波浪上來，悲哀地看着她，絞着她們雪白的手。她向她們招手，微笑，想告訴她們她有多麼快樂幸福，過得多麼好。但是船員過來了，她的姐姐們連忙潛下去，船員還以為自己看到的只是海水的泡沫。

第二天早晨，船駛進了王子前來拜訪的國王的一個美麗城市的港口。教堂敲響了鐘，許多高塔上喇叭齊鳴，士兵們舉起飄揚的旗子和閃亮的刺刀，排列在他們經過的石路兩旁。天天像過節，舞會、表演一個接着一個不斷舉行。但是公主還沒有露臉。人們説她正在一個修道院裏受教育，在那裏學習各種皇家美德。

最後她來了。美人魚一直急於看看她是不是真的很美，這時候不得不承認，她還從來沒有看過一個更完美的美的形象。她的皮膚細嫩白皙，在她的黑色長睫毛下面，含笑的藍眼睛閃着誠摯和純潔的目光。

"就是你，"王子説，"當我像死了一樣躺在海灘上的時候，是你救了我的性命。"他説着，把他這位漲紅了臉的女孩摟在懷裏。

"噢，我太幸福了！"他對美人魚説，"我最嚮往的希望實現了。你會為我的幸福感到高興，因為你對我的愛是偉大和真誠的。"

美人魚吻他的手，覺得自己的心好像已經碎了。他舉行婚禮後的第一個早晨將帶給她死亡，她會變成海上的泡沫。

所有教堂的鐘響起來，報信人騎着馬在全城宣佈王子結婚的喜訊。在每個祭壇上的貴重銀燈裏燃燒着香油。當新郎和新娘挽着手接受主教的祝福時，牧師們搖着香爐。穿綢衣戴金飾的美人魚捧着新娘的拖紗，但是她的耳朵聽不見歡樂的音樂，她的眼睛看不到神聖的儀式。她只想着自己就在眼前的死亡之夜，想着她在世界上已經失去的一切。

當晚新郎和新娘上了船。禮炮齊鳴，旗幟飄揚，在船中央已經搭起一個紫色和金色的華麗篷帳，裏面有漂亮雅致的睡榻，供新婚夫婦在這裏度過良宵。順風鼓起了船帆，船輕快地開走，平穩地駛在風平浪靜的大海上。

天黑時不少彩燈點亮着，海員們在甲板上興高采烈地跳舞。美人魚不禁想起她第一次到海面上來，當時已經見過類似的歡樂場面。她也進去跳舞，她像追逐獵物的燕子那樣在空中盤旋，所有在場的人全都驚訝地為她喝采。她以前還從來沒有跳得這樣優美過。她嬌嫩的腳只覺得像被鋒利的刀割着，但是她不在乎，她的心正經歷着比這更厲害的刺痛。

她知道這已經是最後一個能看到王子的夜晚，為了他，她拋棄了親人和家，交出了她美麗的嗓子。為了他，她天天忍受着前所未有的痛苦，而他卻一無所知。這已經是最後一個晚上她能和他一起呼吸同樣的空氣，凝視星空和深海。一個沒有思想或者夢的永恆之夜正在等着她，她沒有靈魂，如今她永遠也不能得到一個靈魂了。

　　一直到半夜過去了很久，船上依然一片歡騰。她和其他人一起笑着，跳舞，然而死的念頭存在她心中。王子吻他美麗的新娘，而她撫摸他烏亮的頭髮，直到他們手挽手走進豪華的帳篷歇息。這時候船上的一切靜下來了，唯一醒着的掌舵人站在船舵旁邊。美人魚把她的雪白雙臂靠在船舷上，看着東方，等待着早晨的第一道霞光，等待着將帶給她死亡的黎明第一縷陽光。她突然看到她的幾個姐姐從波濤中浮出來，她們和她自己一樣面色蒼白。然而她們的美麗長髮不再在風中飄舞，已被剪掉了。

　　"我們把我們的頭髮給了女巫，"她們說，"這是為了救你，使你今夜不死。她給了我們一把刀，現在我們把刀給你，你看，它非常鋒利。在太陽出來以前，你必須它紮進王子的心臟，當熱血落到你那雙腳上時，它們將重新合在一起變成一條魚尾巴，這樣你就可以重新成為人魚，回到我們那裏去享盡你的三百年壽命，然後才死去變成海上的鹹泡沫。趕緊吧，日出前不是他死就是你死。我們的老祖母是那樣為你傷心，她悲痛得白髮都掉下來了，就像我們的頭髮給女巫剪下來那樣。刺死王子回來吧，趕快！你沒看見天空最早的紅光嗎？過幾分鐘太陽就要出來了，那時你就非死不可。"

接着她們憂傷地深深歎着氣，沉到波浪下面去了。

美人魚掀開帳篷的深紅色簾子，看到美麗的新娘把頭枕在王子的胸口上。她彎身吻了一下王子美麗的眉頭，接着去看天空，那上面紅色的曙光正在越來越亮。接着她看看那把鋒利的刀，再用眼睛盯住了王子，王子正在夢中喃喃叫着新娘的名字。

她存在於他的腦裏，刀在美人魚的手裏抖動，但她把刀從手中遠遠地扔到波浪裏。在它落下的地方，海水變紅了，濺起來的水滴看起來像是血。她向王子再投去戀戀不捨的、迷迷糊糊的一眼，接着從船上跳進了大海，心想她的身體正在化為泡沫。

太陽升到波浪上面，它的溫暖光線落到美人魚那冰冷的泡沫上，美人魚卻沒有感覺到她在死去。她看到明亮的太陽，看到在她周圍漂浮着的千百個透明的美麗人形。透過她們，她能夠看見那艘船的白帆和天空上的紅色雲朵。她們的話像音樂般悅耳，但是太輕飄了，人的耳朵聽不見，就如同人的眼睛看不見她們一樣。美人魚發現自己也有她們那樣的一個身體，同時離開泡沫升起來，越升越高。"我在哪裏？"她問道，她的聲音也是輕飄飄的，和她在一起的那些人的聲音一樣，沒有人間音樂能夠模仿它。

"在天空的女兒之間，"其中一個回答說。"人魚沒有不滅的靈魂，也沒有辦法得到一個不滅的靈魂，除非她贏得一個凡人的愛情。她永恆的存在要依靠別人的力量。但是天空的女兒，她們雖然也沒有不滅的靈魂，卻能夠通過善行為自己創造一個。我們飛到炎熱的地方，使散佈疫病且毀滅人類的悶熱空氣涼快下來。我們盛載花香，散播健康和康復。

"當我們盡了我們的力量，做上三百年所有這種好事以後，我們就能得到一個不滅的靈魂，分享人類的幸福。你，可憐的美人魚，曾用你的整個心去做我們所正在做的事。你受過苦，堅持下來了，用你的善行使自己升到靈魂的世界。現在，用同樣的方式努力三百年以後，你就可以得到一個不滅的靈魂了。"

美人魚向太陽抬起她增添了光輝的眼睛，感覺到它們 —— 這還是第一次 —— 充滿了淚水。

在她離開了王子的那艘船上，人們在來來去去，喧鬧異常，她看見王子和他美麗的新娘在尋找她。他們悲哀地凝視着珍珠般的浪花，好像知道她已經投身到波濤中去了。看不見的美人魚吻了一下那位新娘的前額，吹拂了一下王子，接着就和其他天空的孩子一起乘上一朵玫瑰色的雲，升到天外之境去了。

"三百年以後我們就可以升入天國，"她說。"我們甚至可能更早一點到達那裏，"她的一個同伴輕輕地說。"別人看不見我們，我們可以進入人們的家，那裏有孩子，如果每天我們能找到一個好孩子，他給他的父母帶來快樂，值得他們愛他，那麼我們的考驗時間就可以縮短。孩子不知道，我們飛過他的房間時對他的好品行高興地微笑，因為這樣我們就能在我們的三百年中減去一年。不過我們如果看到一個頑皮孩子，或者一個壞孩子，我們就會流下傷心的眼淚，而每流下一滴眼淚，我們的考驗時間就得加上一天。"

# 8

# 國王的新衣

很久很久以前有一個國王，他太喜歡新衣服了，錢都花費在做新衣服上面。他不關心他的軍隊，不關心戰場的事，也不關心在森林中巡遊。說實在的，他腦裏只轉着一個念頭，就是坐馬車到外面去炫耀一下他的新衣服。一天裏面，他每一個鐘頭要換一次衣服。因此，其他國家的人們說到本國國王時一般會照例說"他正在他的會議室裏"，而說到他呢，就可以說"國王嗎，他正在他的更衣室裏"。

他所在的那個大城市熱鬧非凡，每天有許多外國人來到這裏。有一天這城市裏來了兩個騙子，他們假扮成織布師，自稱能織出任何可以想像出來的最美麗的布。他們說，他們織出來的布不僅顏色和花樣異常漂亮，而且做出來的衣服有一種奇妙的特點，任何不稱職或者愚蠢得無可救藥的人是看不見的。

"那一定是了不起的布，"國王心裏說。"如果我穿上用這種布做出來的衣服，我就能發現我的國家裏哪些人不稱職，也能辨別出哪些人聰明哪些人愚蠢了。我必須叫他們立刻給我織出這種布來。"於是他按照兩個騙子的要求，預付一大筆錢給他們。

那兩個騙子擺出兩架織布機，裝出工作得很賣力的樣子，但是他們在空空如也的織布機上甚麼也沒有織出來。他們要來不少最好的絲線和最純淨的金線，東西一到手他們就全都收藏起來，整天只是在那兩架空織布機上做到深夜。

"我很想知道他們把布織得怎樣了，"國王心裏説。但是想起愚蠢或不稱職的人看不見那種布，他又覺得很不自在。他相信他自己不用怕甚麼，但又想，還是派個人先去看看織得怎麼樣更穩當些。全城的人都知道織出來的布有何等非凡的特點，都急於知道他們周圍的人有多愚蠢。

"我要派我誠實的老首席大臣到織布工那裏去，"國王想。"看看織出來的布怎麼樣，沒有人比他更能看出來了，因為他聰明，而他的職務，也沒有人比他做得更好。"

這位值得尊敬的老大臣走進房間，只見那兩個騙子坐在空空如也的織布機前面織布。"我的天啊！"他心裏説着，兩隻眼睛瞪得老大。"我根本甚麼也沒有看見，"但是這句話他沒有説出口。

兩個騙子請他走近些，指着空空如也的織布機問他喜不喜歡布上精美的花紋和漂亮的顏色。可憐的老大臣拼命地看，但是甚麼也沒看見，因為本來就沒有東西可以看見嘛。

"噢，天啊，"他想，"我會是那麼愚蠢嗎？我從來沒有這麼想過，也不能讓任何人知道！會是我工作不稱職嗎？不行，不行，我不能説我看不見他們織的布。"

"怎麼，先生，您沒有甚麼要説的嗎？"一個騙子假裝忙着織布，説道。

"噢，布非常漂亮，漂亮極了，"發懵的老大臣透過他的眼鏡看着説。"多麼美麗的花紋啊，多麼鮮豔的顏色啊！我要稟報國王，説我非常喜歡這布。"

"聽到這話我們真高興，"兩個騙子説着，然後向大臣描述顏色，解釋花紋的特徵。老大臣仔細聽着，好把他們的話轉告給國王聽。

現在兩個騙子要求更多錢、絲線和金線，説是用來織布。他們把要來的所有東西都裝進了自己的口袋，一根線也沒有用到織布機上，但是他們繼續照舊在空空如也的織布機上織布。

過了不久，國王又派出一個誠實的大臣到織布工人那裏，看看他們織得怎麽樣，布是不是快織好了。這個大臣和那位老大臣一樣，看了又看，但是甚麽也看不見，因為本來就沒有東西可以看見嘛。

"這塊布不是很美麗嗎？"兩個騙子問道，同時指給他看，並且解釋布上美麗出色的花紋和顏色，其實根本甚麽花紋、甚麽顏色也沒有。

"我知道我並不蠢！"大臣心裏説。"這麽説來，就是我不勝任我現在的好職位了。這太奇怪啦，但是我絕不能讓任何人知道。"於是他對他並沒有看見的布讚不絕口，對鮮豔的顏色和美麗的花紋表示滿心歡喜。"真是出色極了，"他稟告國王説。

全城的人都在談論那華麗貴重的布。最後國王親自去參觀那還在織布機上的布。他帶了一批臣子，都是精挑細選過的，包括已經去過的那兩位。兩個織布工人如常賣足力氣織布，但是一根線也不用。

"這布不是華麗極了嗎？"兩位曾經到過這裏的誠實的大臣説。"陛下！多美的顏色，多美的花紋啊！"他們説完，指着那兩架甚麽也沒有的織布機，因為他們想，那上面的布其他人一定看得見。

"這是怎麼回事？"國王想。"我根本甚麼也沒有看見。太可怕了！是我愚蠢嗎？是我不配當國王嗎？這實在是我遇過最可怕的事情！"

"當真不假，"他大聲對兩個織布工人說，"你們的布深得我心。"他看着那一無所有的織布機滿意地點頭，因為他不願說出他甚麼也沒有看見。

他所有的隨員看了又看，雖然一點也不比別人看到的更多，但也都像國王那樣說："布真是美極了。"大家還勸他在即將舉行的大巡遊中穿上用這種布做的華麗新裝。

"那就真是華麗、漂亮、出色了，"人人聽了都附和。所有人似乎都很高興，很滿意兩個騙子的工藝，國王就封兩個騙子為爵士，給他們各一個勳章，扣在鈕孔，又封他們為"皇家宮廷織布大師傅"。

在舉行大巡遊的前一夜，兩個騙子裝作通宵工作，點了十六支蠟燭。人們該可以看到他們忙於趕製國王的新衣。他們裝出從織布機上拿下布來的樣子，用大剪刀空剪，又用不穿線的針縫個不停，最後終於說："國王的新衣現在做好了。"

國王和他所有的貴族朝臣於是來到騙子那裏。兩個騙子各舉起他們的胳臂，好像手裏拿着甚麼東西，說："這是褲子！""這是上衣！""這是長袍！"等等等等。"它們全輕得像蜘蛛網，穿在身上好像甚麼也沒穿似的，但這正是這件新衣的優點。"

"的確如此！"所有朝臣說。但是他們甚麼也沒有看到，因為本來就沒有東西可以看到嘛。

"陛下是否樂意現在寬衣，"兩個騙子説，"那麼我們可以幫助陛下在大鏡子前面穿上新衣。"

國王脱掉衣服，兩個騙子裝作在他身上一件又一件穿上新衣，又假裝在他的腰上繫上甚麼，然後打結，他們説這是長袍的拖尾。國王在鏡子裏從各個側面看來看去。

"它們看起來多漂亮啊！多合身啊！"所有人輪流大聲説。"多麼華麗的衣服啊！"

典禮官説："陛下，在巡遊中舉華蓋的人已經在外面準備好了。"

"我也準備好了，"國王説。"我這套衣服不是正合適嗎？"接着他對着鏡子又轉了幾次身，這樣大家就會認為他在欣賞他的衣服。

跟在國王身後捧長袍拖尾的內侍把他們的手伸到地上，像是捧起拖尾，再裝出手上捧着甚麼東西的樣子。他們不想讓人知道他們甚麼也沒有看到，甚麼也沒摸到。

就這樣，國王在華麗的華蓋下開始巡遊，所有在街道兩旁看見他的人都説："國王的新衣真是無與倫比！他那件長袍有多麼漂亮的拖尾啊！衣服多麼合身啊！"

沒有一個人希望別人知道他甚麼也沒有看到，因為這樣一來，他不是不稱職就是太愚蠢了。國王的衣服從來沒有得到過如此盛大的稱讚。

"但是他根本甚麼也沒有穿啊，"最後有一個小孩説。

"聽聽純真小孩的話"他的父親説。"他根本甚麼也沒穿啊，有個小孩説他甚麼也沒穿！"小孩的這句話人們一個一個悄悄地傳了開去。

　　"但是他甚麼也沒穿啊！"最後所有人都大喊起來。這話使國王大為震驚，因為他覺得他們説的話是對的。但是他心裏説："現在我必須堅持到底，把巡遊走完。"於是他僵着身體，前所未有如此生硬地走下去，內侍們也走得更加畢恭畢敬，好像是在捧着國王那並不存在的長袍拖尾。

# 9
# 堅定的錫兵

從前有二十五個錫兵，他們都是兄弟，因為他們是由同一把舊錫湯匙鑄出來的。他們肩上佩着刺刀，站得筆直，眼睛直盯着前方，穿着華麗漂亮的軍服，有一半是紅的，有一半是藍的。他們在這個世界上聽到的第一句話是"錫兵！"這是他們躺在一個盒裏時，一個小男孩打開盒蓋後，高興得拍着雙手說出來的。錫兵獲贈送給他作為生日禮物，現在他站在桌子旁邊把他們一個一個站起來。

這些兵全都一模一樣，除了一個，他只有一條腿。他是最後一個被鑄造的，熔化的錫不夠用了，但他用一條腿穩穩站住，跟其他錫兵兩條腿的站得一樣穩，這使他非常顯眼。

錫兵們站着的桌子上還擺了幾件別的玩具，但最引人注目的是一座紙做的美麗小城堡。透過小窗可以看到裏面的大廳。城堡前面有一些小樹圍着一面鏡子，它代表一個清澈的湖。幾隻蠟做的天鵝在湖上游着，它們的影子倒映在湖水裏。

這一切非常好看，但是最好看的是一位小姐，她站在城堡的門口，門是打開的。她也是紙做，穿一身淡雅的薄紗連身裙，肩上圍着一條藍色的細緞帶，就像披着一條披肩。在緞帶中央插着一朵用錫紙做的閃光玫瑰花。這位小姐是個舞者，她張開雙臂，一條腿舉得很高，高得這位獨腳錫兵根本看不見它，以為她也和他一樣只有一條腿。

"她正好給我做妻子，"他想，"但是她太高貴了，住在城堡裏，而我只有一個盒子可以住，而且我們二十五個擠在一起，住不下她了。不過我還是必須試一試去認識她。"桌上正好有一個鼻煙盒，他在鼻煙盒後面平躺下來，偷看那位嬌小玲瓏的小姐，她繼續用一條腿站着而不失去平衡。

等到天晚了，其他錫兵都給放進盒內，小男孩的一家人也上床去睡了。這時候玩偶們就開始玩他們自己的遊戲——聊天、打仗和開舞會。錫兵們在盒裏也吵鬧起來，他們也想出去跟大家一起玩，但是打不開盒蓋。胡桃夾子在翻筋斗，鉛筆在桌子上蹦蹦跳。吵得那麼厲害，金絲鳥給吵醒了，並開始說話，而且出口成詩。只有那個錫兵和那位舞者小姐在原地一動不動。她張開雙臂，豎着腳尖站着，那錫兵同樣用一條腿站穩，他的眼睛連一瞬間也沒有離開過她。

鐘敲響十二點，鼻煙盒的蓋子砰地彈開，但是跳上來的不是鼻煙，而是一個黑色的小妖精。這不是真的鼻煙盒，是個嚇人一跳的玩具。

"錫兵，"小妖精說，"不要望了，不要指望不屬於你的東西。"

但是錫兵假裝沒有聽見他的話。

"那麼，就等到明天吧，"小妖精說。

第二天早晨，孩子們醒來，放這錫兵在窗口。不知是小妖精做的，還是風吹的，窗一下子打開了，錫兵頭朝下腳朝天地從三樓跌落到下面街上。跌得太厲害了！他落地前在空中轉了幾圈，他的軍盔和刺刀牢牢插在鋪石的縫間，那條獨腿豎直朝天。

女僕和那小男孩馬上下樓找他，但是哪裏也看不到他，雖然有一次差點就踩在他身上。如果他叫一聲"我在這裏！"就好了，但是他穿着軍服，太自豪了，不宜大叫救命。

緊接着就下起雨來，雨點越來越密，最後下起了傾盆大雨。雨後恰巧有兩個無家可歸的男孩走過。

其中一個說："看，這裏有個錫兵。他應該坐着船去航行。"

於是他們用一張舊報紙摺成一艘船，放錫兵進去，讓他順着水溝航行，兩個男孩在旁邊跟着他走，一路拍着手。

可是，水溝裏的浪有多麼高啊！水流有多麼急啊！紙船搖來晃去，有時候轉得那麼快，錫兵也頭暈目眩了。然而他保持堅定，臉色不變，筆直地望着前面，緊緊地扛着他的刺刀。

船忽然來到下水道，四周黑得像錫兵在盒子裏時一樣。"我這一刻要到哪裏去呢？"他想。"我斷定這都是那小妖精做的。啊，要是那小姐和我一起在船上就好了，黑不黑我就一點也不在乎。"

忽然出現了一隻很大的水老鼠，牠住在這下水道裏。

"你有通行證嗎？"老鼠問道。"馬上把它給我。"

但是錫兵保持沉默，把刺刀握得更緊。

船繼續漂走，老鼠跟在後面。牠憤怒得咬牙切齒，牠對木棍和乾草大叫："攔住他！攔住他！他還沒有付過路錢！他還沒有出示通行證！"

但是水流得越來越急。錫兵已經看得見下水道的盡頭處有陽光照耀了。這時候他聽見一陣急速的隆隆聲，可怕得足以使最勇敢的人嚇倒。在下水道的盡頭處，水流變成一幅大水簾，猛地瀉入溝渠口，對於他來說，這危險程度就像大瀑布對於我們一樣。

他離它已經太近，沒有辦法停住，船就這樣沖了下去，錫兵盡量挺直身體，眼皮也不動一動，表示他一點也不害怕。船旋轉了三四圈，接着水漲到了船邊，沒有任何辦法能挽救它使它不沉下去了。

現在他站在那裏，水到了他的脖子，而船越沉越深，紙一濕就變軟，最後水淹沒了錫兵的頭頂。他想起了那位再也看不到的嬌美舞者，耳邊響起了一首歌中這樣的話：

狂暴冒險，致死危險，

此為爾命，英勇遊子。

這時候紙船中央已經破開，錫兵沉到水裏去，很快就被一條大魚吞下了。

噢，在魚肚裏是多麼黑啊！比在下水道裏黑得多，也窄得多，但是錫兵繼續保持堅定，平躺在那裏，肩上仍佩着刺刀。

魚游來游去，又轉又扭，做出最奇怪的動作，但最後完全靜止下來。

過了一會，錫兵身上好像掠過一道閃電，接着陽光照下來了，一個聲音叫起來："是個錫兵。"原來那條魚被捉住了，送到市場上賣給了一個女廚師，她拿牠進廚房，用一把大菜刀剖開牠。她夾起錫兵來，用食指和大拇指夾住他的腰送到房間裏。她的家人坐在那裏，都急着要看看這個在魚肚子裏旅行了一趟的了不起的錫兵，但是他一動不動，一點也不覺得自豪。

他們放他在桌子上。可是，世界上真會發生那麼多意想不到的古怪事情嗎？他竟就在原來那個房間裏，孩子們是原來的孩子們，桌子上放着原來的玩具、原來那座美麗的宮殿，嬌美的小舞蹈員就站在玩具之間。她仍舊用一條腿平衡着身體，另一條腿舉起，同樣保持堅定。看到她，錫兵感動得幾乎要流下錫的眼淚來，但這並不合適。他只是看着她，她也看着他，兩個都保持着沉默。

這時候一個小男孩拿起錫兵扔進了火爐。他毫無理由這樣做，但這一定是鼻煙盒裏那個小妖精搞的鬼。

錫兵站在紅紅火光當中，熱得厲害，但是他說不出這是由於周圍的火還是由於愛情的火。接着他看到他軍服上鮮豔的顏色褪掉了，但這是在旅途中被洗得褪去的呢，還是由於傷心而褪去的呢，沒有人能說出來。他看着那位小姐，那位小姐看着他。他感到自己在熔化，但是他肩上仍佩着刺刀，仍保持着堅定。忽然房門打開，風吹起那小舞者來，她像個仙子一樣飄起來，正好飛到火爐裏錫兵的身邊，馬上着火，燒掉了！錫兵熔化成一塊錫，第二天早晨當女僕來倒爐灰的時候，她發現他化成了一顆小小的錫的心。至於那位女舞者，那就甚麼也沒有剩下，只留下了那朵用錫紙做的玫瑰花，燒黑了，像一塊炭。

# 10

# 野天鵝

在燕子每年冬天要飛去的那個遙遠的地方,住着一個國王,他有十一個兒子,還有一個女兒,叫愛莉莎。

那十一個兄弟自然都是王子,每人上學時胸前佩顆星星,腰間佩把劍。他們用鑽石筆在金板上寫字,課業很快就學得好,朗讀起書來那麼流利,因此人人都可以看出來他們是王子。他們的妹妹愛莉莎坐在一張平板玻璃小櫈上,拿着一本價值半個王國的圖畫書。

噢,這些孩子實在是快樂和幸福,但是並不長久。他們的父親,也就是那個國王,娶了一個非常壞的女巫當皇后,她完全不愛這些可憐的孩子。

從第一天起,皇后就顯露出她的刻薄。當時皇宮裏舉行盛大慶祝典禮,孩子們玩招待客人的遊戲,但是他們不是像平時那樣拿到剩下來的蛋糕和蘋果,她只給他們一茶杯沙,叫他們把它當作是好東西。一星期以後,她把小愛莉莎打發到鄉下去給農民夫妻收養,接下來憑空捏造,對國王說了小王子們那麼多壞話,弄得國王再也不關心他們了。

"滾到外面去自己過日子吧,"皇后說。"變成不會說話的大鳥飛走吧。"但是她不能像她想的那樣使他們變醜,因為他們變成了十一隻美麗的野天鵝。

接着他們發出一陣奇怪的叫聲，飛出了皇宮窗口，飛過花園，飛到遠遠的森林那邊去了。他們飛過那個農民的農舍時是大清早，他們的愛莉莎正在她的房間裏睡覺。他們在屋頂上盤旋，扭動長脖子，拍動翅膀，但是沒有人聽見他們或者看見他們，他們最後只好飛走了，高高地飛上雲端。他們飛越廣闊的世界，直至來到一個濃密黑暗的森林，這森林一直遠遠地延伸到海邊。

可憐的小愛莉莎孤零零一個人在她的房間裏玩綠色的葉子，因為她沒有玩具玩。她在葉子上鑽一個洞，透過洞看天上的太陽，看着它就像看到她哥哥們明亮的眼睛，當溫暖的太陽照着她的臉蛋時，她想到他們曾經給她的所有熱吻。

一天又一天毫無變化地過去。有時候風在玫瑰叢的葉子間吹過，對玫瑰花悄悄地說：“還有誰能比你更美麗呢？”玫瑰花會搖搖頭說：“愛莉莎比我們更美麗。”當老太太星期日坐在農舍門口讀她那本讚美詩集時，風吹動書頁，對讚美詩集說：“還有誰能比你更虔誠呢？”讚美詩集會回答說：“愛莉莎。”玫瑰花和讚美詩集說的都是真話。

到十五歲時她回到家裏，皇后一看見她長得多麼漂亮，不禁對她充滿了惡意和怨恨。她恨不得把她也變成一隻天鵝，和她那些哥哥一樣，但是她現在還不敢這樣做，因為她害怕國王。

有一天大清早，皇后走進浴室。它是大理石砌的，裏面有柔軟的墊子，墊子鑲着最美麗的絨繡。她帶進去三隻癩蛤蟆，親親牠們，對其中一隻說：“等愛莉莎來洗澡，你蹲到她的頭上，這樣她就會變得和你一樣愚蠢。”然後她對另一隻說：“你蹲到她的額頭上，這樣她就會變得和你一樣醜，連她的朋友都會不認識她。""還有你，你蹲在她的心窩上，"她悄悄地對第三隻說，"那她就會有邪念，為此痛苦不堪。"就這樣，她把三隻癩蛤蟆放到清水裏，水馬上變成綠色。接着她叫來愛莉莎，幫她脫衣服，然後她走進浴池。

當愛莉莎把頭浸到水裏的時候，一隻癩蛤蟆蹲到她的頭髮上，一隻癩蛤蟆蹲到她的額頭上，一隻癩蛤蟆蹲到她的心窩上，但是她沒有注意到牠們，等她站起來離開了水，水上漂着三朵紅罌粟花。如果牠們沒有毒或者沒有被女巫吻過，牠們本該變成紅玫瑰花。不過牠們還是變成了花，因為牠們在愛莉莎的頭上和心窩上停留過。愛莉莎太善良，太單純了，巫術對她沒有任何效力。

惡毒的皇后看到這一招不成，就用胡桃汁擦她的臉，使她變成深棕色。接着她把她漂亮的頭髮弄得亂蓬蓬的，在上面擦上臭烘烘的油膏，直到美麗的愛莉莎再也沒法被人認出來為止。

愛莉莎的父親看到她時嚇了一大跳，說她不是他的女兒。沒有一個人認出她來，除了看門狗和燕子，然而牠們只是可憐的動物，不會說話。可憐的愛莉莎哭起來，想到全都走掉的十一個哥哥。她傷心地偷偷離開皇宮，穿過田野和沼澤地走了整整一天，最後來到一座大森林。她不知道往哪個方向走好，但是她太難過，太想念跟她一樣被趕到外面的哥哥了，因此決定去找他們。

她進森林才一會天就黑了，她完全迷了路。於是她在柔軟的青苔上躺下來，做晚禱，把頭靠在一棵樹墩上。萬籟俱寂，輕柔的微風吹拂她的前額。幾百點螢火蟲的光在青草和青苔之間閃爍，好像綠色的火星一樣。她用手碰碰一根樹枝，儘管很輕輕地，這些發光的小蟲子就像流星似的在她四周飄下來。

她整夜夢見她那些哥哥。她和他們又變成了小孩子，在一起玩。她看見他們用鑽石筆在金板上寫字，而她在看價值半個王國的美麗圖畫書。他們不像原先那樣寫句子和字母，而是在敘述他們的高尚行為、所有的發現和看過的東西。圖畫書也變了，上面所有的東西都是活生生的。小鳥唱歌，人從書裏走出來跟愛莉莎和她的哥哥們説話。但是書頁一翻，他們又都趕緊回到了原處，使位置不致弄亂。

等到她醒來，太陽已經升得很高，但是她看不到它，因為高大的樹木在她頭頂上濃密地展開了樹枝。但是太陽的光線仍透過樹葉從四面八方射下來，像一片金色的迷霧。清新的草木發出甜蜜的芳香，小鳥幾乎停到她的肩上來了。她聽見幾道泉水的潺潺流水聲，它們全都流進一個鋪着金色沙的湖。環湖長着稠密的灌木叢，其中一處有一個被鹿弄出來的缺口，愛莉莎就穿過這個缺口到湖邊去。

湖水太清澈了，樹枝和灌木叢要不是被風吹得擺動的話，它們真像是畫在湖底上的，因為每一片葉子，不管在陰影裏還是在陽光中，都在水中清楚地反映出來。

愛莉莎一照自己的臉，看見那麼黑那麼醜，簡直嚇壞了。但是當她把她的小手浸濕去擦自己的眼睛和前額時，雪白的皮膚再次閃亮起來。等到她脫掉衣服在清涼的水裏浸過以後，在整個廣闊的世界上就再找不到一個比她更美麗的國王女兒了。

她一穿好衣服，把長頭髮編成了辮子，就到冒着水泡的泉水那裏去，用手捧水喝。接着她繼續往森林深處走，也不知道自己要去甚麼地方。她想到她的父母和那些哥哥，感覺到上帝一定不會遺棄她。是上帝讓野蘋果長在森林中給她充飢，祂如今正引導她走到一棵因水果多得連樹枝都承受不住而彎了下來的樹那裏。她在這裏吃了午餐，靠在大樹枝下休息，然後走進森林最陰暗的深處。

這裏靜得她能聽見自己的腳步聲，以及她腳下每一片枯葉的碎裂聲。一隻鳥也看不到，一線陽光也透不過那些粗大的樹木黑枝。它們高大的枝幹靠得那麼近，當她朝前面看時，只覺得像是被柵欄四面圍住。她以前從來不知道有這樣的孤獨。

夜非常黑。青苔裏連一點螢火蟲的亮光也沒有。她傷心地躺下來睡覺。過了一會，她感到頭頂上的樹枝好像分開了，天使們溫柔的眼睛正從天上向她看下來。

她早晨醒來時，也不知道這是做夢看見抑或真有其事。接着她繼續向前走。但是她走了沒有很多路就遇到了一位老太太，她挽着一籃莓果，還給愛莉莎吃了幾個。愛莉莎於是問她有沒有看過十一位王子騎馬穿過森林。

"沒有，"老太太說。"但是昨天我看過十一隻天鵝，頭上戴着金冠，在附近那條河上游泳。"接着她帶愛莉莎向前走了一小段路，來到一個斜岸，岸下面蜿蜒着一條小河。兩岸的樹木把它們茂盛的葉子長枝伸過河另一面，在一些彼此接觸不到的地方，連樹根都從地面上掙脫出來了。這樣，所有懸在河面上的樹枝就把它們一簇簇的葉子都交織在一起。

愛莉莎告別了老太太以後，順着河向前走，一直來到海邊。在這裏，年輕女孩的眼前是一片茫茫壯麗的大海，但是海面上一片帆也沒有，連一隻小船也看不到。她怎樣繼續前進呢？她注意到海岸上無數的小石子被海水沖得變光滑了，變圓了。那裏玻璃、鐵片和石塊混雜在一起，全都同樣給海水沖成了新的形狀，叫人覺得它們和她纖細的手一樣光滑。

「水不知疲倦地流動，」她説，「直到使所有堅硬的東西都變得光滑，我也要這樣不知疲倦地做我的事。謝謝你的教訓，清亮的流水。我的心告訴我，終有一天，你會領我到我親愛的哥哥們那裏去。」

在冒着泡沫的海藻上有十一根白色的天鵝羽毛，她撿起它們放在一起，然後帶走。它們上面有水珠，是露珠還是淚珠，誰也沒法得知。海邊雖然孤寂，但是她並沒有注意到，因為不停波動的大海在幾個小時內呈現出來的變化，比變化最大的湖在整整一年中發生的變化還要多。如果升起一片沉重的烏雲，就像大海在説：「我也會顯得陰暗和生氣。」這時候風刮起來，海浪洶湧地翻起了白色的浪花。等到風平息下去，雲彩在日落下發出紅色的霞光，這時候大海看起來像一片玫瑰花瓣，有時是綠色，有時是白色。但是不管海面如何平靜如鏡，海岸這裏卻仍舊在波動，海浪像一個睡着嬰兒的胸口那樣在一起一落。

當太陽快要下山時，愛莉莎看到十一隻頭戴金冠的白天鵝，一隻接着一隻，像根白色的長絲帶似的向着陸地飛來。這時候愛莉莎從海岸走下斜坡，躲在灌木叢後面。那些天鵝在離她很近的地方降落，拍動他們雪白的大翅膀。太陽一落到水下消失，天鵝們的羽毛就脱落下來了，站在她面前的是十一位英俊的王子，愛莉莎的十一個哥哥。

她發出一聲驚呼，因為他們雖然變了許多，但她一眼就認出了他們。她撲到他們的懷裏，逐一叫他們的名字。這時候王子們重新見到自己的小妹妹，他們是多麼高興啊，因為她雖然已經長得那麼高，變得那麼美麗，但是他們也一眼就認出了她。他們又是笑又是哭，很快就互相訴說他們的後母對他們大家有多壞。

"我們十一個兄弟，"大哥説，"只要太陽在天上，就要變成野天鵝飛來飛去，但等太陽一落山，我們就又恢復人形。因此在太陽落山之前，我們總是必須靠近一個可以落腳休息的地方，因為在恢復我們天生的人形的時候，如果我們還向雲端飛，就會沉到深海裏去了。

"我們不住在這裏，但住在一個同樣美麗的地方，它在大海的那一邊，我們必須飛很長的路。中途沒有一個小島可以過夜，只有一塊很小的岩石露出海面，我們只能勉強站在它上面，還得緊緊擠在一起。碰到大浪洶湧的時候，水花濺到了我們身上，不過有這塊岩石，我們還是得感謝上帝。我們在那岩石上曾度過多少個長夜啊，如果沒有這塊岩石，我們就永遠回不到我們親愛的祖國了，因為飛越大海要花去一年中最長的兩天。

"我們得到允許一年回家一次，逗留十一天。在逗留的這段時間，我們飛過森林再去看一眼我們父親居住着的、我們自己出生的皇宮，再去看一眼我們母親在那裏長眠的教堂。在這裏，好像連樹木和灌木叢都和我們相親。野馬就跟我們小時候看見的那樣在平原上奔馳。燒炭人唱那些古老的歌，我們小時候曾隨着這些歌的拍子跳舞。這是我們的故土，感情把我們和它連在一起。而我們在這裏找到了你，我們親愛的小妹妹。我們在這裏還可以停留兩天，然後我們就必須飛回那不是我們家鄉的美麗土地了。我們怎麼才能把你一起帶走呢？我們沒有大船也沒有小舟。"

"我怎麼能破解這咒語呢？"他們的小妹妹問道。接着就這件事他們差不多談了一整夜，只睡了幾個小時。

愛莉莎被頭頂上一陣天鵝翅膀的簌簌聲驚醒了。她的哥哥們又變成了天鵝在上空盤旋，圈子越繞越大，最後遠遠飛走了。但其中最小的天鵝留了下來，他把頭枕在他妹妹的膝蓋上，愛莉莎撫摸他的翅膀。他們兩個在一起度過了一整天。

傍晚時候，其他的天鵝也都回來了，太陽一落山，他們又恢復了原形。"明天，"一個哥哥說，"我們就要飛走，過一年才能再回來。但是我們不能把你留在這裏。你有勇氣跟我們一起走嗎？我們的手臂既然有足夠的力氣把你抱過森林，我們的翅膀就沒有足夠的力氣帶着你飛過大海嗎？"

"是的，帶我一起去，"愛莉莎說。他們整晚都在編織一個大而強壯的柳樹和燈心草網。愛莉莎在這個網中躺下睡覺，當太陽升起，她的兄弟再次變成野天鵝，他們用喙抬起網，和他們仍在睡覺的親愛的妹妹一起飛上雲端。當陽光落在她的臉上時，其中一隻天鵝在她的頭上翱翔，這樣他寬闊的翅膀就可以遮擋着她。

當愛莉莎醒來時，他們離地很遠了。她以為她一定還在做夢，感覺自己被高高地懸在海面上空很奇怪。在她身邊躺着一根結滿美麗成熟莓果的樹枝，還有一束甜甜的根，她最小的哥哥收集了它們並將它們放在那裏。愛麗莎向他微笑，感謝他，她知道那是在她四周盤旋並用翅膀為她遮擋陽光的哥哥。他們現在如此之高，以至於他們下面的一艘大船看起來像是一隻掠過海浪的白色海鷗。飄浮在他們後面的大雲像是一座巨大的山峯，在山峯上面，愛莉莎看到了自己的影子和十一隻天鵝的影子，就像巨大的飛行物一樣。這畫面比愛莉莎以往看過的都更美麗。但隨着太陽越升越高，雲層落在後面，畫面消失了。

整整一天，他們像有翅膀的箭一樣在空中飛行，但比平常慢，因為他們要帶着妹妹。天氣越來越差，愛莉莎看着沉沒的太陽，十分焦慮，因為那塊海洋中的小石頭還沒有出現。在她看來，好像天鵝們正在盡最大努力。唉！她是他們無法前進得更快的原因。當太陽落山時，他們會變成人，掉入大海淹死。

然後她在心底最深處祈禱，但那塊石頭仍然沒有出現。烏雲越來越近，一陣陣狂風吹過，風暴即將到來，而一團厚重的雲閃着閃電，閃完又閃。太陽已經到達了大海的邊緣，天鵝們迅速衝下來，快得愛莉莎的心顫抖起來。她相信他們正掉下去，但他們又一次飛起來。

現在，到了這個時候，太陽被海浪遮住了一半，她看到了正下方的石頭。它看起來並不比海豹從水中伸出的頭大。太陽下沉得如此之快，當他們的腳碰到石頭時，它像一顆星星一樣閃耀，最後像一張燒焦的紙上快熄滅的火花一樣消失。她的哥哥們圍在她身邊，靠她很近，手臂挽在一起，因為空間小得不能再小。大海沖向石頭，浪花濺向愛莉莎和她的哥哥們。天空被不斷的閃光照亮，雷聲從雲層中翻滾出來。愛莉莎和她的哥哥們站在一起互相握着手，唱着讚美詩。

黎明初起，空氣變得平靜。在日出時，天鵝們帶着他們的妹妹從石頭上飛走。大海仍然很大浪，從他們的高度看，深綠色海浪上的白色泡沫看起來就像數百萬隻天鵝在水面上游動。隨着太陽越升越高，愛莉莎在她面前看到飄浮在空中的羣山，山峯有很多雪閃耀着。在中心矗立着一座似乎有一英里長的城堡，柱子一排比一排高，而在城堡周圍，棕櫚樹揮動着，和磨輪一樣大的鮮花也盛放着。她問這是否他們正趕往的土地。天鵝們搖搖頭，因為她看到的是美麗且不斷變化的"仙女摩根"浮雲宮殿，沒有凡人可以進入。

愛莉莎仍然凝視着這個場景，山脈、森林和城堡融化了，二十座莊嚴的教堂隨之升起，有高高的塔樓和尖尖的哥德式窗戶。她甚至覺得她能聽到管風琴的聲音，但其實是潺潺大海的聲音。當他們越來越靠近教堂，這些也變得不同了，變成了一支船隊，似乎在她身下航行。但當她再看時，她只看到一片海霧在海洋上滑過。

一個場景化成另一個場景，直到最後她看到了他們要去的真實土地，有青色的山脈、雪松森林、城市和宮殿。早在太陽落山之前，她就坐在一個大洞穴前面的岩石上，洞穴的地上長滿了精緻的綠色攀緣植物，就像刺繡的地毯。

"現在我們要聽聽你今晚想夢見甚麼，"最小的哥哥說，他向愛莉莎展示了她的臥室。

"天保佑我能夢見怎樣解救你們，"她回答說。這種想法一直困擾着她的心，因此她誠心誠意地祈求上帝幫助她，連睡着了也繼續在祈禱。這時候她只覺得她正飛在高空，飛向"仙女摩根"的浮雲宮殿，一位仙女出來接見她。這仙女看起來光彩照人，十分美麗，然而非常像曾在森林中給她吃莓果，並告訴她那些頭戴金冠的天鵝的那位老太太。

"你那些哥哥會得救的，"她說，"只要你有勇氣和毅力。沒錯，水比你嬌嫩的手還要柔軟，然而它能把石頭磨成別的形狀。它不像你的手指那樣會感覺疼痛，它沒有靈魂，不會受到你所必須忍受的那種痛苦和折磨。你看見我手裏握住的這些帶刺蕁麻嗎？在你睡覺的岩洞周圍長着許多這種東西，但是只有長在教堂墳地上的才有用。你必須採集它們，即使它們刺得你的手起泡也不要停。用你的手和腳把它們壓碎，它們就變成一絲絲的麻，你必須紡麻織布，縫成十一件長袖袍子。只要把它們披在十一隻天鵝身上，咒語就解除了。但是要記住一點，從你的工作開始直到結束，即使要佔去你一生中的許多個年頭，你絕不能開口說話。你說出來的第一個字將像致命的短劍那樣刺穿你那些哥哥的心。他們的死活就看你的舌頭了。我對你說的每一句話你都要好好記住。"

她一說完，就用蕁麻輕輕地碰了碰愛莉莎的手，像火燒一樣的痛把愛莉莎痛醒了。

這時候是大白天，靠近她剛才睡覺的地方就有一簇她在夢中見過的蕁麻。她雙膝跪下感謝上帝。接着她離開岩洞，用她嬌嫩的雙手開始去做她的工作。她在難看的蕁麻叢中拔它們，蕁麻在她的手上和手臂上像火燒一樣刺出大泡，但是她決意愉快地忍受住痛苦，只要能把她親愛的哥哥們救出來。於是她光着腳踩碎這些蕁麻，然後紡那些麻。

太陽下山時哥哥們回來，發現妹妹變成了啞巴，都嚇壞了。他們以為這是某種新魔法。但是他們看到她的雙手時，他們馬上明白她為了他們正在做甚麼，最小的哥哥哭了。他的眼淚落在妹妹的手上，沾到眼淚的地方痛就止了，火燒一樣的泡也消失了。她通宵工作，因為不把她親愛的哥哥們解救出來，她就無法休息。接下來整整一天，當她的哥哥們不在的時候，她獨自一個人坐着，但是時間從來沒有過得這樣快。

一件袍子做好了，她開始做第二件，這時候她聽見獵人的號角聲，不禁害怕起來。聲音越來越近，她還聽見了狗叫，馬上驚恐地逃到岩洞裏。她急急忙忙把採集到的蕁麻捆成一捆，坐在它上面。馬上就有一隻大狗從深谷裏向她跳着撲過來，接着是一隻又一隻。牠們狂怒地汪汪大叫，退回去，又回來。一轉眼，所有獵人都站在岩洞前面，其中最英俊的一個是這個國家的國王。當他看見如此美麗的女孩，就向她走上來。"你怎麼到這裏來，我可愛的女孩？"他問道。

但是愛莉莎搖搖頭。她不敢以她哥哥們的救贖和性命為代價說出話來。她把她的雙手藏在圍裙底下，讓國王看不到她是多麼痛苦。

"跟我走吧，"他說，"你不能留在這裏。如果你的心腸和你的容貌一樣美好，我要讓你穿上絲綢的和天鵝絨的衣服，在你的頭上加上金冠，你將住在我最華麗的城堡裏，管理它，在那裏安家。"說着，他把她抱上他的馬。愛莉莎哭着絞她的手，但是國王說："我只是想令你幸福。終有一天，你會為這件事感謝我的。"

接着他讓她坐在他的前面，抱住她，飛馬越過羣山，獵人們跟在他們後面。太陽下山時，他們來到一個美麗的城市，有許多教堂和圓屋頂。到達城堡以後，國王領她步入大理石廳堂，裏面大噴水池在噴水，牆上和天花板上滿是富麗堂皇的繪畫。但是所有這些燦爛奪目的東西她都無心欣賞，而只是傷心哭泣。她耐着性子讓宮女們給她穿上華麗的袍子，把珍珠插進她的秀髮，在她起泡的手指上戴上柔軟的手套。等到她穿戴好了，盛裝站在眾人面前時，她看起來是如此美麗奪目，全宮廷的人不由自主地向她深深鞠躬。

接着國王宣佈要娶她為妻，只有大主教連連搖頭，悄悄地對國王說，這個美麗的女孩只是一個女巫，她蒙住國王的眼睛，用魔法迷住他的心了。但是國王不聽他這一套。他吩咐奏樂，擺出最好的佳餚，請最美麗的少女們跳舞。

隨後他領她走過芳香的花園和高大的廳堂，但是沒有一絲微笑在她的嘴唇上出現，或者在她的眼睛裏閃露。她看起來就像悲哀的化身。接着國王打開作為她睡房的小房間的門，房間裝飾着鮮綠色的絨繡，就像他找到她時那個岩洞的樣子。地上放着她用蕁麻紡成的那捆麻線，天花板下掛着她已經縫好的那件袍子。這些東西是一個獵人當作珍品從岩洞裏搬回來的。

"在這裏你可以重溫在岩洞老家的夢，"國王說，"這些是你埋頭做的工作。如今在所有這些了不起的東西當中想到往事，這可以使你得到消遣。"

愛莉莎一看見所有這些貼心的東西，嘴上露出微笑，鮮紅的血色湧上雙頰。她想到她那些哥哥和他們即將得救，這使她高興得吻了國王的手。他於是把她緊抱在心口。

很快教堂的愉快鐘聲就宣佈婚宴開始，從森林帶回來的啞女孩就要成為國家的皇后了。這時候大主教又對着國王的耳朵悄悄地説出惡毒的話，但這些話沒有進入他的心。婚禮還是舉行了，大主教只好親手把皇冠放在新娘的頭上。出於惡意，他把窄小的帽箍緊緊地壓在她的前額上把她壓痛。但是她的心頭上壓着更重的份量——那就是為她那些哥哥感到的憂傷。她感覺不到肉體上的痛苦。她的嘴緊閉，説出一個字也會送掉她那些哥哥的性命。但是她愛這位善良、英俊的國王，他每天做越來越多的事情使她開心。她全心全意地愛他，她的兩隻眼睛閃露出她不敢説出來的愛。噢！如果她能向他吐露隱情，把她的苦衷告訴他就好了！但是在她的工作完成之前，她必須繼續不開口説話。

因此她夜裏溜進她那個佈置成山洞的小房間，很快地織成一件又一件袍子。但是等到她開始織第七件的時候，她發現麻沒有了。她知道她要用的蕁麻在教堂墓地裏長着，必須親自去那裏採集。她怎麼能走到那裏呢？"噢，比起我的心所忍受的折磨，手指痛又算得上甚麼？"她心裏説。"我必須冒險到那裏去，上天不會拒絕幫助我的。"

於是她好像去做甚麼壞事似的，心顫抖着，偷偷溜進月光照得很亮的花園，穿過狹窄的小路、空無一人的街道，一直來到教堂墓地。這時候她看見一塊大墓碑上有一羣食屍鬼。這些可怕的東西像是要洗澡那樣脱掉它們身上破爛的衣服，接着用它們皮包骨頭的長手指挖開新墳，拖出屍體，吃它們的肉！愛莉莎不得不貼近它們走過，它們用邪惡的眼睛盯住她看，但是她默默地祈禱，只管採集使她像給火燒一樣痛的蕁麻，把它們帶回城堡去。

只有一個人看見了她，那就是大主教——當所有人睡着時他醒着。現在他想，他的看法顯然是對的，皇后完全不對勁，她是一個女巫，用魔法迷住了國王和所有人。他把他看到和擔心的事偷偷告訴了國王，當他這些激憤的言詞從他的舌頭說出來的時候，眾聖徒的雕像搖着頭，像是說：「根本不是這麼一回事。愛莉莎是清白的。」

但是大主教對這件事作另一種解釋。他相信聖徒證明她是壞的，所以對她的邪惡搖頭。兩顆大淚珠滾下國王的臉頰，他心中狐疑着回房。夜裏他假裝睡覺，但是兩眼沒有真的閉上，因為他確實看到愛莉莎每天夜裏起床離開她自己的房間。他的眉頭一天比一天陰沉，愛莉莎看到了，卻不明白是甚麼緣故，但這使她害怕，為她那些哥哥而心中顫抖。她的熱淚在絲絨的衣服上像珍珠和鑽石一樣閃亮，而所有看到她的人都希望自己能夠成為皇后。

這時候她的工作差不多完成了，還只缺一件袍，只是麻已經用得一點不剩，蕁麻又一根也沒有。只得再去一次，去最後一次了，她必須冒險到教堂墓地去採幾把蕁麻回來。她想起單獨一個人走路，想起會遇到那些可怕的食屍鬼就心驚膽戰，但是她的信念是堅定的，她對上帝的信任也是堅定的。愛莉莎去了，國王和大主教跟在她後面。他們看着她走進教堂墓地的小邊門，當他們走近一點時，他們看見了食屍鬼坐在墓石上，就像愛莉莎曾經看見它們時那樣，國王扭轉了頭，因為他以為她和它們是一夥的——而她，那天晚上還曾把她的頭靠在他的胸口上。「人民必須審判她，」他說，而她很快就被每一個人判決燒死。

她從華麗的廳堂被帶到一個陰暗可怕的小牢房，風呼呼地穿過鐵欄杆吹進來。人們不再給她穿絲絨和絲綢的衣服，而是給她披上她自己織的十件蕁麻袍，還給她那捆蕁麻當枕頭，但他們不知道沒有甚麼比這些東西使她更高興了。她喜洋洋地繼續做她的工作，同時向上帝祈求幫助，而這時，街上的孩子在唱嘲笑她的小曲，沒有一個人用好話來安慰她。

傍晚時她聽見鐵窗上天鵝拍翅膀的聲音，那是她最小的哥哥——他終於找到了他的小妹妹，愛莉莎高興得泣不成聲，雖然她知道這很可能是她生命中的最後一夜。但是她依然抱着希望，因為她的工作差不多完成了，她那些哥哥也都來了。

這時候大主教到她這裏，要在她的最後幾小時和她留在一起，他答應了國王。但是她搖頭，用眼睛和手勢求他不要留在這裏，因為她知道這一夜必須完成她的工作，不然的話，她的所有痛苦、眼淚和不眠之夜都白費了。大主教退出去，咕嚕着罵她的惡言惡語，但是可憐的愛莉莎知道自己是清白無辜的，繼續加緊做她的工作。

一些小老鼠在地上跑來跑去，把蕁麻拖到她的腳下，盡力幫助她。有隻鶇鳥蹲在鐵窗外通宵為她唱歌，盡可能唱得悅耳動聽，提起她的精神。

這時候還是曙光熹微，離太陽出來至少還有一個小時，十一個哥哥站在城堡門前求見國王。守門的人告訴他們這是不可能的，現在幾乎還是夜裏，國王在睡覺，不可以打擾他。十一個兄弟又是威脅又是懇求。這時候衛兵來了，連國王本人也來了，問吵些甚麼。就在這時候，太陽升了起來。十一個兄弟不見了，只有十一隻野天鵝從城堡上空飛走。

這時候所有人像潮水般從幾個城門湧來，要看女巫被燒死。一匹老馬拉來一輛大車，車上坐着愛莉莎。他們給她穿上了粗麻布衣服。她美麗的頭髮披散在肩頭上，臉頰蒼白得可怕，雙唇無聲地翕動，而她的手指仍舊在織着綠色的麻。甚至在去死的路上她也不放棄她的工作。十件袍子放在她的腳下，她正在拼命織第十一件，而亂哄哄的人羣嘲笑她説："看這女巫，她在念念有詞呢！她手裏沒有讚美詩集。她坐在那裏擺弄着她難看的妖物。讓我們把它撕碎吧。"

接着他們向她擠過去，真的想把那些蕁麻袍撕碎，但就在這時候，十一隻野天鵝飛到她的上空，落到大車上。他們拍動他們的大翅膀，人羣嚇得退到了一邊。

"這是上天降下來的訊號，説明她是無辜的，"有許多人悄悄地説，但是不敢大聲説出來。

正當劊子手抓住她的一隻手把她從大車上拉下來的時候，她急忙把那十一件蕁麻袍拋到那些天鵝身上，他們馬上變成了十一個英俊的王子。只有最小的一個在本應是手臂的位置留下了一隻天鵝的翅膀，因為她來不及織完這件袍子的最後一個袖子。

"現在我可以開口説話了，"她大聲説。"我是清白無辜的。"

這時親眼目睹此事的人紛紛向她鞠躬致敬，就像對待一位聖徒那樣。但是由於長時期的擔驚受怕，以及精神和肉體的痛苦，她支持不住，昏倒在她的哥哥們的懷裏。

"是的，她是清白無辜的，"最大的哥哥説。於是他説出了全部經過。在他説話的時候，空氣中散發出一股芳香，像是千百萬朵玫瑰花散發出來的一樣。柴堆的每一根木柴已經生了根，長出了樹枝，形成一道密密的樹籬，又大又高，上面蓋滿了玫瑰花，而在所有花之上開着一朵又白又亮的花，它像一顆星星那樣閃閃發光。國王把這朵花摘下來，放在愛莉莎的胸前，這時候她從昏厥中醒來了，心中充滿和平與幸福。所有教堂的鐘自動鳴響，鳥大羣大羣地飛來。一支新婚隊伍返回城堡，這樣的結婚隊伍是以前沒有一個國王看到過的。

## 11
# 天使

“每當一個好孩子死了，上帝的天使就從天上下來，把死去的孩子抱在懷裏，張開他白色的大翅膀，帶着這孩子飛過他活着時喜歡的所有地方。然後他採集一大束花，帶它到上帝那裏，好讓花在天堂比在人間開得更鮮豔。上帝把這些花緊緊地摟在胸前，但是他只吻那朵他最喜歡的花，這朵花就有了聲音，就能和大家一起合唱天堂之歌了。”

這番話是上帝的一個天使帶一個死去的孩子上天時説的，孩子像做夢一樣傾聽着。接着他們飛過那孩子經常玩的熟悉地方，飛過開滿可愛鮮花的美麗花園。

“這麼多花，我們帶哪些移植到天上去呢？”天使問道。

就在他們旁邊長着一棵細長的漂亮小玫瑰樹。但是甚麼人該死的手已經把樹幹折斷，半開的玫瑰花苞在垂下來的樹枝上凋謝了。

“可憐的玫瑰樹！”孩子説。“讓我們帶它到天上去吧，讓它可以在上面上帝的花園裏開花。”

天使拔出那棵玫瑰樹，接着親吻孩子，那小傢伙半張開他的眼睛。天使還採集了一些美麗的花，以及幾朵被人看不起的毛茛和三色菫。

"現在花夠了，"孩子説。但是天使只是點了點頭，沒有向天上飛。

這時候是夜裏，大城鎮靜悄悄的。他們留在這裏，天使盤旋在一條狹小的街道上空，街上有一大堆乾草、塵土和人們搬家時從房子裏掃出來的垃圾。這裏面有盤子的碎片、一塊塊的灰泥、破布、舊帽子和各種難看的破爛東西。在所有這些亂七八糟的東西當中，天使指着一個破花盆的碎片和一團從它裏面掉出來的泥土。那團泥土沒有跌散，因為和其他垃圾一起扔掉的一棵枯萎野花的根把它攀住了。

"我們把這個也一起帶走吧，"天使説。"在我們一路飛的時候，我來告訴你為甚麼。"他們一路飛的時候，天使把這個故事講給他聽。

"在下面那條窄巷的一個低矮地窖裏，曾經住着一個生病的可憐孩子。他從小就病得很苦，即使在最好的時候也只能撐着拐杖在房間裏來回走一兩次。夏天裏有那麼幾天，太陽光可以在地窖的地板上逗留大約半小時。生病的可憐孩子就留在這太陽光照着的一點地方暖和自己的身體，看着鮮紅的血流過他舉在面前的細長手指。然後他就會説他出過去了，然而他對春天青翠的樹林一無所知，直到鄰居一個孩子給他拿來一根山毛櫸的綠枝。他把這樹枝舉在頭頂上，想像着他是在山毛櫸樹林裏，太陽正在照耀着，鳥兒正在快活地歌唱。春天裏有一天，那鄰居孩子帶給他一些野花，其中有一朵還帶着根。他小心地把它種在花盆裏，放在靠近他那張床的窗臺上。這朵花算是遇到了幸運的手栽種，因為它長活了，冒出新芽，年年開花。對這生病的孩子來説，它成了一個美麗的花園，以及在世界上的小寶貝。他給它澆水，愛護它，小心讓它享受好不容易射到地窖的每一線陽光，從早晨的第一線陽光到傍晚的最後一線陽光。這花甚至進入他的夢中——它為他開花，為他散發香氣。它愉悅他的眼睛，甚至當上帝召喚他，在他臨死時，他也回過頭去看這朵花。他已經在上帝那裏過了一年。在這期間，那朵花一直站在窗戶，枯萎了，被遺忘了，直到最後住戶搬家時，它和別的垃圾一起扔到了街上。就是這朵可憐的花，枯萎成這副樣子，我們把它收進我們這束花裏，因為它給予人的真正快樂，遠遠勝過女王花園裏最美麗的花。"

"這一切你是怎麼知道的？"孩子問道。

"我知道，"天使說，"因為我就是撐着拐杖走路的那個生病的可憐孩子，我熟悉我自己的花。"

這時候孩子張大他的眼睛，凝視着天使那張光輝幸福的臉，也就在這時候，他們已經來到天上那個只有幸福和快樂的家。上帝把那死去的孩子緊貼在心口，賜給他翅膀，好讓他和天使一起手拉着手飛翔。接着上帝把所有花緊緊摟在胸前，但是祂只吻了那棵枯萎的野花，於是它有了聲音。它隨即跟着天使們唱起歌來，這些天使或近或遠地圍着上帝的寶座，但他們都一樣快樂。他們合唱着讚美歌，讚美偉大的和渺小的——那好孩子、那可憐的野花，即那曾經枯萎，又被扔到外面黑暗窄巷的一堆垃圾上面的野花。

# 12

# 夜鶯

在中國，你們知道皇帝是中國人，他周圍的人也都是中國人。我現在跟你講的這個故事發生在許多年前，因此最好趁它還沒有被忘記，現在就來聽聽。我要講的這個皇帝，他那皇宮是天底下最美麗的，全由最好的瓷磚砌成，價值連城，但是它太脆弱，誰摸它都得十分小心。在花園裏可以看到最珍奇的花卉，當中最美麗的花朵上面繫着美麗的小銀鈴，叮鈴叮鈴響個不停，人人走過都不由得都會注意到那些花。的確，皇帝的花園裏的每樣東西都是精心擺設出來的。這花園大得連園丁也不知道它到哪裏為止。曾經到過花園的人知道，那裏有一座宏偉的樹林，樹木很高，湖很深。樹林通到蔚藍的深海邊，海深得大船可直接在樹枝下航行。在這些樹當中，有一棵上面住着一隻夜鶯，牠唱歌那麼動聽，連忙碌的漁夫也會躺下來傾聽。有時候他們夜裏出來撒網，聽着牠唱，不禁會說："噢，夜鶯的歌聲多麼美啊！"但是等到他們要打魚時，他們把鳥忘掉了。然而第二天夜裏一聽到牠的歌聲，他們又要說："噢，夜鶯的歌聲多麼美啊！"

世界各國的人來到皇帝的京城，都非常仰慕這個地方，尤其是皇宮和花園。但是一聽到那夜鶯的歌唱，全都說這才是所有東西當中最好的。

這些旅行者回國以後，介紹他們的見聞。有學問的人還寫成書，書中描寫這座京城、皇宮和花園，但是他們沒有忘記那隻夜鶯，說牠才真正是見聞中最大的奇蹟。會寫詩的人寫美麗的詩來歌頌這隻住在海邊樹林中的夜鶯。這些書暢銷全球，一段時間後，其中一些來到了這位皇帝的手裏。他坐在他那把金交椅上，一面讀，一面不時點頭稱讚，因為他看到文章把他這座京城、皇宮和花園描寫得如此美麗，感到十分高興。他讀到"但是其中要數夜鶯最美麗"這句話。

他這時說："這是怎麼回事啊？我根本不知道有甚麼夜鶯。在我的王國裏有這麼一隻鳥嗎？甚至就在我的花園裏？這個我可從來沒有聽說過。我竟然要讀書才知道這回事。"

於是他召來他的一個侍臣。這個侍臣官階是如此高，任何比他地位低的人對他說話，或者問他一件事情，他只會回答一聲"呸"，這個字甚麼意思也沒有。

"這裏提到一隻非常了不起的鳥，這隻鳥叫做夜鶯，"這回是皇帝對他說話。"他們說這是我整個龐大王國裏最好的東西。這件事為甚麼從來沒有人告訴過我？"

"這名字我連聽也沒有聽說過，"這位侍臣回答說。"牠從來沒有被進貢到宮裏來。"

"我要牠今天晚上就送到這裏，為我歌唱，"皇帝說。"我有些甚麼東西，全世界竟然都知道，我卻一無所知。"

"我從來沒有聽說過這隻鳥，"侍臣還是說，"不過我一定會找到牠。"但是這隻夜鶯到哪裏去找呢？這位侍臣又上樓梯又下樓梯，走遍一個個大廳和一條條長廊，但是他遇到的人沒有一個聽説過有這隻鳥。於是他回稟皇帝，説這一定是個神話，是寫書的人編造的。"陛下不能盡信書，"他説，"有時書裏寫的東西純屬虛構，或所謂無中生有。"

"但是我讀到寫有這件事的書，"皇帝説，"是日本天皇送給我的，因此不可能有假。我一定要聽到這隻夜鶯的歌聲，牠今天晚上一定要送到這裏，牠將受到我最仁慈的保護。如果牠送不到來，全宮的人晚飯後都將挨打。"

"是！"侍臣説，然後他又走了，到過所有房間和走廊，在樓梯上上下下。皇宮一半的人都跟着他跑，因為他們都不想挨打。對於這隻夜鶯有很多疑問，全世界所有人都知道牠，但皇宮內卻沒有一個人知道。最後他們問到了廚房裏一個窮苦的小女孩，她説："噢，那隻夜鶯？我很熟悉牠。沒錯，牠很會唱歌。我得到允許，每天晚上把殘羹剩飯送回家去給我生病的可憐母親，她就住在下面海邊。回來的時候，我累了就坐在樹林裏休息，聽那隻夜鶯唱歌。這時候我會熱淚盈眶，就像是我的媽媽在吻我。"

"小女孩，"侍臣説，"我一定會在廚房裏給你一份固定的工作做，而且可以侍候皇上用膳，只要你把我們帶到夜鶯那裏去，因為皇上下令要邀請牠今晚進宮。"

於是她到林中夜鶯唱歌的地方，半個皇宮的人跟在她後面。他們一路走時，一頭母牛哞哞叫起來。

"噢！"一位年輕侍臣説，"現在我們找到牠了。這麼小的一隻動物，中氣多麼驚人啊，叫得那麼響。這聲音我肯定過去聽過。"

"不對，那只是牛叫，"小女孩説，"我們還有很長的路要走呢。”

　　接着沼地裏青蛙呱呱叫起來。

　　“好聽！”有位牧師説，“現在我聽到牠了，清脆得像教堂小鐘的聲音。”

　　“不對，那些是青蛙，”小女孩説，“不過我想現在很快就可以聽到牠的聲音了。”

　　不久，夜鶯唱了起來。

　　“聽啊，聽啊！那就是牠，”女孩説。“牠在那裏！”她指着樹枝上一隻灰色小鳥。

　　“這可能嗎？”那位侍臣説。“我從來沒想到牠會是那樣一隻普普通通、平平凡凡的小東西。牠看到有那麼多顯貴的人圍住牠，一定是大驚失色了吧。”

　　“小夜鶯，”女孩提高嗓子叫道，“我們最仁慈的皇帝希望你在他面前唱歌。”

　　“非常樂意，”夜鶯説着，高興地開始唱得更加悦耳。

　　“牠聽起來像是水晶小鈴鐺，”侍臣説，“看牠的小歌喉多有力量。真奇怪，我們以前竟然沒有聽過這歌聲！牠在皇宮裏一定會大獲讚賞！”

　　“要我在皇帝面前再唱一次嗎？”夜鶯問道，牠以為皇帝在場。

　　“我頂呱呱的小夜鶯，”侍臣説，“我有幸邀請你今晚參加一個宮廷盛會，你在那裏將會用你迷人的歌聲贏得皇上陛下的寵愛。”

　　“我的歌聲在樹林裏唱起來最好聽，”夜鶯説。不過牠聽説是皇帝希望牠去，還是樂意地去了。

皇宮裏為了這件事情佈置得非常考究。瓷磚牆和瓷磚地在上千盞金色燈的亮光中閃耀。走廊上放置掛着小鈴鐺的美麗的花，隨着人們跑來跑去和大風對流，這些鈴鐺叮鈴叮鈴響得連説話也聽不見。大廳當中已經裝好了一根金的棲架，夜鶯可在上面休息。全皇宮的人都出席了，那廚房的小女孩也得到恩准站在門口。她已經被封為正式的宮廷廚師。所有人都衣冠楚楚，當皇帝向夜鶯點點頭讓牠開始歌唱的時候，每一隻眼睛都盯住了這隻灰色小鳥。夜鶯唱得那麼甜潤，眼淚湧上了皇帝的眼睛，等到牠的歌聲變得更加動人，深入到每個人的心中時，淚水滾下了皇帝的臉頰。皇帝太喜歡牠了，傳旨給這夜鶯在脖子上套上他的金絲領巾，但是夜鶯謝絕了，説牠已經得到了足夠的獎賞。

"我已經看到了皇帝的眼淚，"牠説，"那是我最豐厚的獎賞。皇帝的眼淚具有了不起的力量！對我來説，這就是最高的榮譽！"接着牠再次唱出甜美的歌聲。

"真是天賦的美麗歌喉，我從來沒聽過這麼悅耳的歌聲，"女侍臣們説道。從此以後，要對人説話時她們就先含上一點水，好讓説出來的話帶有咯咯的聲音，也就可以自以為是夜鶯了。侍者和宮女也都表示滿意，這種評價來得不簡單，因為要討他們喜歡是極不容易的。説實在話，夜鶯進宮獲得了轟動。如今牠在宮中留下，有自己的鳥籠，可以白天出來兩次，夜裏出來一次。出來時指定十二名僕人侍候牠，每人握住繫在牠腿上的一根絲線。這樣的飛法實在不怎麼快活。

全城都在談論這隻了不起的鳥，兩個人相遇時，這個説"夜"，那個就説"鶯"，然後都歎口氣，他們懂得這箇中的意思，因為大家開口就只談夜鶯。有十一個芝士小販的孩子取名"夜鶯"，但是他們一個也不會唱歌。

有一天皇帝收到一個大包裹，上面寫着"夜鶯"兩個字。

"毫無疑問，這又是一本寫我們這隻名鳥的新書，"皇帝説。但拆開來一看，這不是書，而是一件裝在盒子裏的工藝品，一隻人造的夜鶯，看起來和活的一樣，全身鑲滿鑽石、紅寶石和藍寶石。

給這隻人造夜鶯一上鍊，牠能唱得和真夜鶯一樣，尾巴還能一上一下地跳動，發出銀色和金色的閃光。牠的脖子上掛着一條緞帶，上面寫着："日本天皇的夜鶯比起中國皇帝的差太多。"

"這隻夜鶯美極了！"看見的人都説，而把這人造夜鶯送來的人也被封為"皇家首席夜鶯使者"。

"現在必須讓牠們一起唱，"皇宮裏的人説，"那將是多麼好聽的二重唱啊。"

但是他們配合得不好，因為真夜鶯自由自在地想唱甚麼就唱甚麼，而人造夜鶯只會唱圓舞曲。

"這不能怪它，"樂師説，"它節奏很準，唱得完全符合我的口味。"

於是人造夜鶯只好獨唱，獲得和真夜鶯同樣的成功，而且它看起來漂亮多了，因為它像手鐲和胸針一樣閃閃發光。

它把同一首曲子唱上三十三遍而絲毫不累，人們還樂意聽下去，但是皇帝説也該讓真夜鶯唱唱了。但是牠到哪裏去啦？誰也沒有注意到，牠已經飛出了打開的窗，回到牠自己翠綠的林中去了。

"這是甚麼意思？"發現牠飛走以後，皇帝説。

宮中所有的人都罵牠，説牠忘恩負義。

"不過我們獲得了一隻最好的鳥，"朝臣説，接着大家要這隻鳥再唱，雖然這同一首曲子，他們已經聽到第三十四遍，他們還是沒有把它記住，因為這首曲子很難。

樂師把這隻鳥捧上了天，甚至認為它比真夜鶯還要好，不僅它的外型衣飾和美麗寶石比真夜鶯好，它的音樂才能也比真夜鶯好。

"因為你必須認識到，我的陛下，各位先生、女士，對於一隻真夜鶯，我們永遠説不出牠接下來將唱甚麼，但是對於這隻鳥，一切都是安排好了！所以它一定要留下來，必須這樣。可以打開它，一切都能解釋清楚：人們的才智是如何安排圓舞曲的結構、舞曲是怎樣展開、一個音符是如何跟着另一個音符。"

"這正是我們所想要的，"大家回答説。接着樂師得到許可，下星期日要向公眾展示這隻鳥，皇帝命令大家必須到場聽它唱歌。人們一聽到它的歌唱都變得醉醺醺，不過這一定是由於喝了茶，因為喝茶是地道的中國習慣。

他們都説："噢！"舉起他們的食指並點頭，但是聽過真夜鶯唱歌的窮漁夫説："它聽起來的確動聽，很像真夜鶯，但是同時好像還缺了點甚麼，我也説不清楚到底缺了甚麼。"

真夜鶯被驅逐出了這個王國。

這隻人造夜鶯被放在皇帝床邊一個絲綢墊子上，周圍都是金銀珠寶，這些都是給它的禮物，它現在被封為"皇帝御用龍床首席小歌手"，等級是左邊第一等，因為皇帝認為心房在左邊，左邊是較重要的一邊。即使是皇帝，他的心房也和普通老百姓的心房在同一個位置上。關於這隻人造鳥，樂師寫了一部巨著，達二十五卷之多，寫得淵博高深，篇幅又長，全是用最難的中文字寫出來的。但是所有人卻都説讀過了，讀懂了，因為怕被人認為愚蠢而挨打。

就這樣，一年過去了，人造鳥唱的歌的每一小節，皇帝、全皇宮的人和所有其他中國人都能背出來，因此大家更喜歡它。他們能和它一起唱，也常常和它一起唱。連街上的孩子也唱"吱吱吱，咯咯咯"，皇帝本人也會唱"吱吱吱，咯咯咯"這實在是好玩極了。

有一天晚上，人造鳥正唱得最精彩，皇帝躺在床上正聽得出了神的時候，鳥的內部忽然發出"喊喊"聲。接着一根鍊子斷了，所有齒輪"嗚嗚"一陣亂轉，音樂隨即停止。皇帝馬上跳下床，召來他的御醫，但是御醫有甚麼辦法呢？接着召來鐘錶匠，經過好大一番討論和檢查，鳥總算是勉強修好。不過鐘錶匠說以後必須小心使用它，因為磨損已經很嚴重，如果裝上新的部件，勢必會影響音準。這是多麼沉重的打擊！現在他們只敢讓這鳥一年唱一次，甚至連這樣也會對整個內部機器有危險，這真是太叫人傷心了。接着樂師作了一次小演講，充滿難懂的字眼，説這鳥和原先一樣好，所以它就和以前一樣好，那自然沒有一個人反對他。

五年過去，這時候國土上降臨了真正的悲哀。中國人確實喜愛他們這個皇帝，然而他現在患了重病，沒有希望了。雖然新的皇帝已經選定，但是站在街上的人還是問那侍臣，老皇帝怎麼樣了。

而他只是"呸！"一聲，搖搖頭。

皇帝躺在他的龍床上，身體冰涼，臉色蒼白，整個皇宮的人都以為他死了，個個跑去朝覲新皇帝。侍者們出去談論這件事，宮女們則找伴喝咖啡。各個大廳和所有走廊都鋪上了布，不讓聽到一點腳步聲，周圍一片死寂。但是皇帝還沒有死，雖然他躺在他那張掛着絲絨簾幔、垂着沉重金絲流蘇的華麗床上，臉色蒼白，身體僵直。上方的窗開着，月亮照在皇帝和那隻人造鳥身上。

可憐的皇帝只覺得胸前被壓得出奇地沉重，連氣也喘不過來，於是睜開眼睛，看到死神正坐在那裏。他戴上了皇帝的金冠，一隻手握着皇帝的金劍，一隻手握着皇帝的旗子。床的四周有許多奇怪的臉孔從長長的絲絨床幔間窺探進來，有些非常醜陋，有些好看溫柔。這些臉孔代表皇帝做過的好事和壞事，現在死神已經坐在皇帝的心口上，它們盯着皇帝的臉看。

"你記得這件事嗎？""你想起了那件事嗎？"它們接二連三地低語問道，這就使他回想起許多往事，使他的臉上冒出了冷汗。

"這種事我一點也不知道，"皇帝說。"音樂！音樂！"他叫道。"快敲堂鼓啊！讓我不要聽到它們說的話。"但是它們仍舊說下去，死神對它們說的每件事都像中國人那樣點頭。

"音樂！音樂！"皇帝大叫。"你這隻珍貴的小金鳥，唱歌啊，求求你唱歌啊！我給了你那麼多黃金和貴重的禮物，我甚至把我的金絲領巾掛在你的脖子上。唱啊！唱啊！我叫你唱啊！"

但是這鳥一聲不響。沒有人給它上鍊，因此它一個音也唱不出來。死神繼續用他凹陷的冰冷眼睛看着皇帝，房間裏靜得可怕。

忽然之間，開着的窗戶傳進來甜美的歌聲。外面，在一棵樹的樹枝上停着那隻真夜鶯。牠聽到皇帝呼救，因此為他帶來希望和慰藉。牠一唱，周圍的臉孔越來越淡，越來越淡，皇帝血管裏的血流得更快，給他虛弱的四肢帶來了活力。連死神自己也邊聽邊説："唱吧，小夜鶯，唱下去。"

"那麼，你肯把那把美麗的金劍和那面華麗的皇室旗子給我嗎？你肯把那頂皇冠給我嗎？"夜鶯説。

於是死神為了一支曲子交出了這些財寶，夜鶯繼續唱牠的歌。牠歌唱那安靜的教堂墓地，那裏玫瑰綻放，那裏接骨木樹在微風中散發着芳香，鮮嫩的草再次被哀悼者的眼淚滋潤。於是死神渴望着去看看他的花園，化成一股寒冷的灰霧，從窗口飄了出去。

"謝謝，謝謝，你這神聖的小鳥。我認得你。我曾經驅逐你出我的王國，然而你用你甜蜜的歌聲從我的床邊驅走那些鬼臉，從我的心上趕跑死神。我該怎麼回報你呢？"

"你已經獎賞過我了，"夜鶯説。"我永遠不會忘記，我第一次對你唱歌的時候引得你流下了眼淚。這些眼淚是使唱歌者的心充滿喜悅的珠寶。不過現在你睡吧，養好身體，恢復健康。我要再為你歌唱。"

在牠的歌聲中，皇帝沉入甜美的酣睡中。這一覺是多麼安寧和解乏啊！等到他恢復了體力和精力醒來時，太陽明亮地照進窗，但是他的僕人一個也沒有回來 —— 他們都相信他已經死了，只有那隻夜鶯依然蹲在他的身邊，歌唱着。

"你必須永遠留下來和我在一起，"皇帝説。"你喜歡唱就唱，我要把那人造鳥砸個粉碎！"

“不，不要這樣做，”夜鶯回答説，“這隻鳥在它還能唱的時候盡全力唱得非常好。仍舊保存它在這裏吧。我不能住在這個皇宮裏，不能在這裏築我的巢，但是在我願意來的時候就讓我來好了。我晚上將在你窗外的樹枝上給你唱歌，讓你高興，也讓你沉思。我要給你歌唱幸福的人、受苦的人的故事。這些故事都被人隱瞞，你並不知道。我這小小的鳴禽要遠離你和你的皇宮，飛到漁夫的家和農民的農舍去。我愛你的心勝過愛你的皇冠，然而皇冠也存在着它神聖之處。我會來的，我會為你歌唱的，但是你必須答應我一件事。”

“每一件事我都答應，”皇帝説，這時候他已經穿好了他的皇袍，站在那裏，用握着那把沉重的金劍的手按着他的心口。

“我只請求一件事，”夜鶯回答，“不要讓任何人知道你有一隻告訴你所有事情的小鳥。最好把這件事隱瞞起來。”

夜鶯説完這句話，就飛走了。

僕人們現在進來料理死了的皇帝。一下子，看啊！他站在那裏，向他們説：“你們早！”

# 13
# 醜小鴨

鄉間這時候正是可愛的夏天，黃澄澄的小麥，綠油油的燕麥，加上牧場上的乾草堆，看起來真是美極了。鸛鳥邁着他紅色的長腿踱來踱去，喋喋不休說着埃及話，這是他從媽媽那裏學來的。

麥地和牧場被大樹林包圍着，樹林中央有個深湖。在這鄉間走走實在叫人心曠神怡。

就在這裏一處陽光照到的地方，有一座舒適的舊農宅，周邊包圍着深水運河，從農宅牆壁到河邊密密麻麻地長滿了牛蒡的大葉子，葉子都長得很高，那些最高的，小孩甚至可以直着腰站在它們底下。這地方荒涼得像是在密林中央。

就在這樣一個幽靜舒服的地方，一隻母鴨正蹲在她的窩裏等着她的小鴨子孵出來。她開始不認為這是樂事，已經孵得不耐煩，覺得很厭倦，因為小鴨子出殼要很長時間，又很少有誰來探望她。其他鴨子都寧願在運河裏游泳，而不願意爬上滑溜溜的河岸，蹲在牛蒡葉子底下跟她聊天。要她自己留着，時間很漫長。

不過到最後，一個蛋殼終於裂開了，接着又是一個，一個接一個，從每個蛋殼裏出來一隻活生生的小鴨子，抬起頭來叫"唧唧，唧唧"。

"嘎嘎，嘎嘎！"母鴨說，於是他們也跟着盡可能像樣地嘎嘎叫，朝周圍綠色的大葉子東張西望。鴨媽媽讓他們看個夠，因為綠色對眼睛有好處。

"世界多麼大啊，"小鴨子們說，他們發現現在的天地比蛋殼裏的大多了。

"你們以為這就是整個世界嗎？"鴨媽媽問道。"等你們看到花園就知道了，它伸展到很遠很遠的地方，一直伸展到牧師的田地裏去，不過連我自己也沒敢去那麼遠。你們全都出來了嗎？"她一邊說，一邊站起來看看。"還沒有，最大的那隻蛋還在那裏一動不動。我不知道還得等多久，我真是厭煩透了。"她說着，又在窩裏蹲下來。

"唉，孵得怎麼樣啊？"一隻來看她的老母鴨問道。

"有一隻蛋還沒有孵出來，"母鴨蹲在窩裏繼續說，"殼很硬，它不肯裂開。可是看看其他那些吧。我這一家不是很漂亮嗎？他們不是你見過最漂亮的小鴨子嗎？他們像透了他們的爸爸。那傢伙太壞了，一次也沒來看過我。"

"讓我來看看那隻不肯裂開的蛋，"老母鴨說。"我覺得它毫無疑問是隻珍珠雞的蛋。有一次我也上了當，孵過幾個這種蛋，我為那些小傢伙受夠了苦，他們竟然見水就怕。我又是咯咯地叫又是嘎嘎地叫，但是一點用處也沒有。我沒法讓他們放膽下水。讓我來看看這蛋吧。沒錯，這是一隻珍珠雞的蛋。聽我的話吧，不要再孵化它了，你教其他的小鴨子去游泳吧。"

"我想我還是再孵一會，"母鴨說，"我都已經孵了那麼久，再孵一兩天也沒甚麼。"

"那就隨便你吧，"老母鴨説着，起來走了。

那大蛋終於裂開，一隻小東西爬了出來，叫着："唧唧，唧唧。"他長得又大又醜！母鴨盯着他，一臉愕然説："這也實在太大了，一點也不像其他的小鴨子。我有點懷疑，他會不會真是一隻珍珠雞。不過到了水邊就知道了。在水邊他非下水不可，我推也要把他推下去。"

第二天天氣非常好，太陽明亮地照在綠色的牛蒡葉子上，於是鴨媽媽帶着她那些小鴨子到水邊去，她自己首先撲通一聲跳下去，水花四濺。"嘎嘎，嘎嘎，"她叫道，小鴨子一隻接一隻也跳到了水裏。水淹沒他們的頭，但是他們馬上又冒出來，腿在水底下輕鬆自然地划着，游得棒極了，醜小鴨也在水裏和大家一起游。

"噢，"鴨媽媽説，"他不是一隻珍珠雞，他的腿划得多麼俐落，身體多麼挺啊！他是我的孩子，仔細看，他也不是那麼醜得不成樣子。嘎嘎，嘎嘎！現在跟我來，我帶你們到大園子裏去，讓你們認識農場內那些親戚朋友，但是你們一定要緊貼着我，要不然，你們會被踩。還有最要緊的是，當心那隻貓。"

當他們來到農場的時候，那裏正在大吵大鬧，兩家的鴨子正在爭奪一個鱔魚頭，到頭來，那鱔魚頭卻被那隻貓搶走了。"看見了嗎，孩子們，世界就是這樣！"鴨媽媽呷着嘴説，因為她自己也想吃那個鱔魚頭。"好，走吧，邁開你們的腿，讓我看看你們有多規矩。對那邊那位鴨老婆婆你們必須深深地鞠躬，她是所有鴨子當中出身最高貴的，有西班牙血統，因此她最闊氣。你們沒看見嗎，她的一條腿上纏着一條紅布，那是非常了不起的東西，是鴨子能夠得到的最高榮譽。它顯示誰都希望不要失去她，有了這紅布，人和動物就都能注意到她。好，現在來吧，不要扭動你們的腳趾，一隻有教養的小鴨子會把腳張得開開，就像他爸爸和媽媽的這個樣子。現在鞠躬，說一聲‘嘎嘎’。”

小鴨子們照着吩咐做，但是其他鴨子盯着他們，說：“看，這裏又來了一家，好像我們鴨子還不夠多似的！噢，天啊，他們當中一個是甚麼醜八怪啊，我們不要他在這裏。”接着一隻鴨子飛出來啄他的脖子。

“不要啄他，”鴨媽媽說，“他不妨礙誰啊。”

“對，但是他那麼大那麼醜，嚇壞我了，”那懷有惡意的鴨子說，“因此必須趕走他，啄一啄對他有好處。”

“其他的小鴨子都很漂亮，”腿上纏着布條的老母鴨說，“就除了那一隻。我希望他的媽媽能把他變得好看些，他真的很醜。”

“那是辦不到的，老夫人，”鴨媽媽回答說，“他是不漂亮，但是他的性情非常善良，游泳也和其他小鴨子一樣好，甚至還要好些。我想他長大起來會漂亮的，也許會變得小一些。他在蛋裏留得太久了，因此他的體型不大正常。”接着她撫摸他的脖子，抹平他的羽毛，說：“他是一隻公鴨，因此關係不大。我想他會長得健壯，能夠照顧好好自己。”

“別的小鴨子都很可愛，”老母鴨說。“好，那你們就留下來吧，當自己的家就好，如果能找到個鱔魚頭，就送來給我。”

於是他們在這裏安頓下來，但是那隻最後出殼、樣子又醜得可憐的小鴨子卻常常挨啄，被推來搡去，讓人取笑，不但鴨子對他這樣，其他家禽也對他這樣。

“他長得太大了，”他們都說。有一隻生來腳上就有後爪的雄火雞，自以為真是個國王，趾高氣揚得像一艘船帆鼓滿了風的船，他向醜小鴨飛過來，激動得滿面通紅，因此可憐的小傢伙不知躲到哪裏去才好，只覺得萬分悲哀，因為他長得那麼醜，被整個農場取笑。

一天一天這樣過去，後來情況越來越糟。他不但被大夥趕來趕去，連他那些哥哥姐姐也對他不客氣，竟對他說：「哼，你這個醜八怪。我恨不得貓把你抓走。」聽說他的媽媽也說，要是沒生下他就好了。鴨子啄他，雞打他，連餵家禽的女孩也用腳踢他。因此他最後逃走了，在飛撲過籬笆時，還把樹籬上的小鳥們嚇了一大跳。「他們怕我是因為我長得醜，」他說。因此他不停地向前飛，直至來到一片住着野鴨的沼澤地。他在這裏過了整整一夜，覺得非常難過。

早晨野鴨們飛起來，看到他們這個新朋友。「你是一隻甚麼鴨子啊？」他們圍上來問他。

他向他們鞠躬，盡可能地彬彬有禮，但是沒有回答他們的問題。「你醜得出奇，」野鴨們說，「但是只要你不打算和我們家哪一個結婚，這沒有甚麼關係。」

可憐的小傢伙根本沒有想過結婚，他想的只是允許躺在燈心草叢中，喝點沼澤的水。他在沼澤地過了兩天後，這裏來了兩隻大雁，或者不如說他們是兩隻小大雁，因為他們剛出殼不久，非常無禮。「聽我說，朋友，」其中一隻對小鴨子說，「你醜得叫我們十分喜歡。你要和我們一起走，去當一隻候鳥嗎？離開這裏不遠還有一片沼澤地，那裏有一些大雁，全都未結婚。這是你找老婆的好機會。你醜成這個樣子，也可能會交好運弄到一個。」

"啪，啪"，空中響了兩聲，那兩隻大雁落到燈心草叢中死了，水被血染得鮮紅。"啪，啪"的槍聲又響起來，遠遠地迴蕩，整羣整羣的大雁從燈心草叢中飛起來。

槍聲從四面八方響個不停，因為獵人包圍了沼澤地，有些人甚至坐在樹枝上俯視着燈心草叢。槍的藍煙像雲一樣瀰漫在黑樹上空，等到它在水面上飄走，幾條獵犬就衝進燈心草叢，在每個他們所到之處，燈心草都倒在他們身下。他們嚇壞了可憐的小鴨子！小鴨子扭過頭來藏到翅膀底下，這時正好有一條可怕的大狗很近地從他身邊走過。那條狗張大了嘴，舌頭從嘴裏垂下來，眼睛嚇人地發出閃光。他的鼻子都快頂到小鴨子的身上了，露出了尖牙齒，接着只聽見"嘩啦，嘩啦"，他碰也沒碰小鴨子就涉水走了。

"噢，"小鴨子歎了口氣，"我這麼醜真是謝天謝地，連狗都不要咬我。"

於是他躺着一動不動，這時燈心草叢間響起了槍聲，子彈在他頭頂上一發接着一發飛過。直到天很晚了一切才平靜下來，但就是到這時候這可憐的小傢伙仍舊不敢動。他靜靜地又等了幾個鐘頭，然後小心地向四周看了一看，才拼命地跑離這片沼澤地。他跑過田野，跑過草場，直到刮起了暴風雨，他幾乎捱不過。

天快黑的時候他來到一間可憐的小農舍，它看起來好像已經準備倒下來，它之所以還沒有倒下來，只是因為拿不定主意先往哪一邊倒。暴風雨一直不停，小鴨子無法前進。他在農舍旁邊蹲下來，接着看到門沒有關好，因為一個門鉸鍊已經脫落，靠近門腳有一條窄縫，大小正好夠他鑽進去，他就靜悄悄地鑽進去了，弄到個地方過一夜。這農舍裏住着一位老太太、一隻雄貓和一隻母雞。女主人叫雄貓做"我的小兒子"，他真是一個寵兒，能拱起背，能咕嚕叫，如果逆掃他的毛，他的毛還會迸出火花。母雞腿短，因此叫她"短腳雞"。她下的蛋很好，女主人愛她就像愛自己的孩子。第二天早晨那陌生來客被發現了，雄貓開始咕嚕叫，母雞開始咯咯喊。

"你們吵甚麼啊？"老太太環顧着房間說，但是她眼睛不大好，所以她看到小鴨子，以為一定是隻迷路的肥鴨。"噢，多大的意外收穫啊！"她說，"我希望那不是一隻公鴨，那麼我就有鴨蛋了。我必須等着看看。"於是小鴨子得到允許留下來三個星期接受考驗，但是一隻蛋也沒有下來。

現在雄貓是這房子的主人，母雞是女主人，他們開口閉口總是說："我們和這世界。"因為他們認為他們就是半個世界，而且是那好的一半。小鴨子認為對這個問題別人可能有不同的意見，但是母雞對這種懷疑聽都不要聽。

"你會下蛋嗎？"她問道。"不會。""那你最好閉上你的嘴。""你會拱起背，或者咕嚕叫，或者射出火花嗎？"雄貓說。"不會。""那麼當聰明人說話的時候你沒有權利發表意見。"於是小鴨子獨自蹲在角落裏，覺得沒精打采，直到陽光和新鮮空氣通過打開的門透進房間，他開始感覺到很渴望到水裏去游泳，忍不住把這話說了出來。

"多麼荒唐的念頭，"母雞說。"你沒事可幹悶慌了，所以才會有這種愚蠢的幻想。如果你能咕嚕叫或者下蛋，這種念頭就不會有。"

"但是在水裏游泳太快活了，"小鴨子説，"潛到水底，感覺到水淹沒你的頭，那太舒服了。"

"快活，真的？一定是古怪的快活。"母雞説。"你一定是瘋了！去問問貓吧，他是我所認識的最聰明的動物，你問問他喜不喜歡在水裏游泳或者潛到水下面去，因為我不想發表我自己的意見。要不然你就去問問我們的女主人，那位老太太 —— 世界上沒有比她更聰明的人了。你想她會喜歡游泳，或者讓水淹沒她的頭嗎？"

"你們不了解我，"小鴨子説。

"我們不了解你？我想，甚麼人能了解你呢？你以為你比貓，或者比老太太更聰明嗎？我就不説我自己了。不要這樣胡鬧啦，小傢伙，你在這裏得到收留，就該謝謝你的好運氣了。你不是留在溫暖的屋裏嗎？這裏還能讓你學到點東西，但你是一個多嘴鬼，和你在一起真不痛快。相信我的話吧，我這只是為了你好。我可能跟你講了些不中聽的大實話，但那是我把你當朋友的證明。因此我勸你下蛋，並且盡快地學會咕嚕咕嚕叫。"

"我認為我必須重新到外面的世界去，"小鴨子説。

"好，去吧，"母雞説。於是小鴨子離開農舍，很快就找到他能游泳和下潛的水域，但是所有動物都避開他，因為他長得醜。

秋天到了，樹林裏的葉子變成橙色和金色。接着冬天來了，葉子一落下來，風就接住它們，讓它們在寒冷的空中打轉。載着冰雹和雪花的雲沉沉的，在空中懸得低低的，烏鴉站在蘆葦上大叫："呱，呱！"看着他都會叫人冷得發抖。對於可憐的小鴨子來説，這一切都十分難受。

一天晚上，正當太陽落到絢爛的雲間時，從灌木叢中飛出來一大羣美麗的鳥，小鴨子從來沒有看過這樣的鳥。他們是天鵝，優美的長頸彎彎的，蓬鬆的羽毛白得耀眼。他們張開光輝的翅膀，從寒冷的地區飛越大海到更溫暖的地方去，同時發出一陣奇妙的叫聲。當他們在空中越飛越高時，醜小鴨看着他們有一種十分奇怪的感覺。他向他們伸長了脖子，在水中像車輪一樣打轉，發出古怪得連自己也害怕的叫聲。他能忘掉那些美麗、快活的鳥嗎？當他們最後消失了以後，他潛到水下，等到重新上來的時候他興奮不已。他不知道這些鳥的名字，也不知道他們飛到哪裏去，但是他對他們的感覺，是對世界上其他任何一種鳥都還沒有過的感覺。

　　他不是妒忌這些美麗的鳥，而和他們一樣漂亮的想法他從沒有過。可憐的醜小鴨，若是跟鴨子留在一起，獲得友善的對待和鼓勵，他就已經可以快樂地生活了。

　　這時候冬天越來越冷，他不得不在水上不停地游來游去，好讓水不會結冰，但是一夜一夜下來，他游泳的範圍越來越小。最後冷得太厲害，他只要動一動水上的冰就會碎裂，小鴨子不得不用腿拼命去踩它們，使留下的一點水面不致冰封。最後他筋疲力竭，躺在那裏一動不動，無助得很，他很快就在冰裏凍住了。

　　一個農夫大清早經過，看到出了甚麼事情。他用木鞋把冰敲碎，帶小鴨子回家去給他的妻子。溫暖使可憐的小東西甦醒過來，但是當孩子們要和他玩時，小鴨子卻以為他們要傷害他，嚇得跳到了牛奶盤裏，牛奶四面八方濺到了房間。這時候農婦不禁拍手呼喝，這使他更加害怕。他先是飛進牛油桶，接着又跳進磨粉盆，然後再跳出來。他落到了甚麼地步啊！農婦哇哇大叫，用火鉗打他。孩子們尖聲叫嚷，想要捉住他，卻接連跌成一團，但是小鴨子幸運地逃了出去。門開着，可憐的小東西立刻鑽進灌木叢，筋疲力竭地躺在新下的雪上。

如果我把這可憐的小鴨子在嚴寒的冬天所經歷的災難和不幸一一說出來，那就太悲慘了。但是等到冬天過去，一天早晨他發現自己正躺在一片沼澤地裏，在燈心草叢中。他感覺到溫暖的太陽在照耀，他聽到百靈鳥在歌唱，他看見周圍已是美麗的春天。

接着這年輕鴨子用翅膀拍拍身體，覺得他的翅膀強壯了，於是高高地飛到空中。翅膀托着他一直向前飛，他還不知道是怎麼回事，卻已經來到一座大花園。這裏蘋果樹盛開着花，芳香的接骨木把長長的綠枝垂到環繞平坦草地的小溪上。在初春的清新氣息中，樣樣看去都是那麼美麗。從附近的叢灌木中來了三隻美麗的白天鵝，羽毛簌簌響着，輕盈地遊在光滑的水面上，小鴨子看到了這些漂亮的鳥，感到更說不出的難過。

"我要飛到那些高貴的鳥那裏去，"他說，"他們會殺死我的，因為我太醜了，竟敢接近他們，但這都無所謂。被他們殺死總比被鴨子啄，被雞打，被餵雞鴨的女僕趕來趕去，或者在冬天餓死好。"

於是他飛到水上，向這些美麗的天鵝游去。這些天鵝一看到這陌生者，馬上展開翅膀向他迎過來。

"殺死我吧，"可憐的小鴨子說，接着他把頭垂在水面上等死。

但是在下面清澈的溪水上他看見甚麼？他看到了自己的倒影，他不再是一隻叫人看了討厭的深灰色醜小鴨，而是一隻優雅美麗的天鵝。

他是從天鵝蛋中孵出來的，生在農場的鴨窩又有甚麼關係呢。他曾經經歷悲哀和苦難，如今他為此感到高興，因為這使他更能體會到如今圍繞着他的喜悅和快樂，因為碩大的天鵝們圍着這新來的天鵝遊着，用他們的嘴撫摸他的頸表示歡迎。

這時候幾個小孩走進花園，扔麵包和糕餅到水上。

"看，"最小的一個叫道，"有一隻新來的。"其他孩子都很高興，向他們的爸爸媽媽跑去，又是跳舞又是拍手，快活地大叫："又來了一隻天鵝，來了一隻新的。"

接着他們扔更多麵包和糕餅到水上，說："新來的一隻最美麗，他又年輕又漂亮。"那些老天鵝向他鞠了躬。

這時候他覺得非常難為情，把頭藏到他的翅膀底下，因為他不知道怎麼辦好，他太高興了，但是一點也不驕傲。他曾經因醜而受到虐待和譏笑，現在卻聽到他們說他是所有鳥中最美麗的。連接骨木也在他前面把樹枝垂到水裏，太陽照耀得溫暖明亮。接着他簌簌地抖動羽毛，彎起他細長的脖子，從心底裏快活地叫道："當我是一隻被看不起的醜小鴨的時候，我做夢也沒有想過這樣的幸福。"

# 14

# 祖母

祖母很老了，她的臉上都是皺紋，她的頭髮很白。但是她的眼睛像兩顆星星，當它們看着你的時候，有一種溫和慈祥的神情，這使你覺得很舒服。她穿一身厚綢子做的裙子，上面有大朵大朵的花，她走動時裙子簌簌響。她還會講最好聽的故事。祖母知道的東西真多，因為爸爸媽媽還沒生下來她就活着了，這是絕對不會錯的。她有一本帶大銀扣子的讚美詩集，她經常讀它。書頁中夾着一朵玫瑰花，乾了，壓得很平。它沒有插在玻璃杯裏的玫瑰花漂亮，但是她對它流露出最親切的微笑，甚至流下眼淚。「我不知道祖母為甚麼那樣看那本舊書裏的這朵乾花，你知道嗎？」是這樣的，當祖母的眼淚落到玫瑰花上，而眼睛看着玫瑰花的時候，玫瑰花復活了，使整個房間充滿了它的芳香。四面牆壁像在迷霧中消失，她四周是那片美麗的綠樹林，這時候正當夏天，陽光從濃密的葉叢中透進來，而祖母，她又變年輕了，變成一個可愛的女孩，和玫瑰花一樣鮮嫩，有一張紅紅的圓臉，一頭光亮秀麗的長鬈髮，體態美麗優雅。但是那雙眼睛，那雙溫柔聖潔的眼睛還是一樣，它們給祖母保留下來了。在她的身邊坐着一個年輕男子，高大強壯。他送給她一朵玫瑰花，她微笑着。祖母現在再不能像那個樣子微笑了。是的，她如今只是對那天的回憶、對過去事情的思念和回想在微笑。但是那英俊的年輕男子已經不在，那朵玫瑰花已在舊書中乾枯，祖母仍舊坐在那裏，重新變回一位老太太，低頭看着書中那朵乾枯的玫瑰花。

祖母如今已經去世了。當時她一直坐在她那把扶手椅上給我們講一個又美又長的故事。等到故事講完，她說她很累，把頭向後靠到椅背上睡一會。我們聽到她睡着後平和的呼吸聲，呼吸聲越來越輕，越來越安靜，在她的臉上洋溢着幸福和寧靜的神情。它就像被一線陽光照亮了。她又微笑了一下，接着人們說她已經死了。她被放進一副黑色棺材，在罩布的白色褶層中，她看起來是那麼慈祥美麗，雖然兩眼已經閉上，但是每一道皺紋都消失了，她的頭髮銀白，嘴上留着甜蜜的微笑。我們根本不害怕看她的遺體，她曾經是那麼可愛的一位好祖母。裏面依然夾着那朵玫瑰花的讚美詩集放在她的頭下，因為她曾經這樣希望過，接着他們埋葬了祖母。

在靠近教堂墓地牆邊的墳上，他們種了一棵玫瑰樹，很快它就開滿了玫瑰花，夜鶯停在花叢中，在墓上歌唱。教堂裏響起了風琴的音樂聲和美麗的讚美詩，這些讚美詩就在去世的祖母頭下那本舊詩集裏面寫着。

月亮照在墳墓上，但祖母不在那裏。即使在晚上，每個孩子都可以安全走到那裏，在教堂墓地的牆旁摘下一朵玫瑰。逝者比我們活着的知道得多。若發生我們看到死去的人出現這樣古怪的事，逝者會知道我們有多恐懼。他們比我們過得好，逝者不再歸來了。泥土已經堆積在棺材上，棺材裏面亦只有泥土。讚美詩集的書頁也是塵土。至於那玫瑰，亦帶着所有回憶化成塵土。但是，鮮嫩的玫瑰在墳墓上綻放，夜鶯唱着，風琴奏着，人們仍在緬懷年邁的祖母，她有着慈愛的、溫柔的眼睛，那雙眼睛看起來總是很年輕。眼睛可以不逝。而我們的眼睛也將再次看到親愛的祖母，她年輕而美麗，就像她第一次親吻了那鮮嫩的紅玫瑰時一樣年輕，而那紅玫瑰現在已是墳墓裏的塵土。

# 15

# 牧羊女和掃煙囱的人

你看過這樣一個舊木櫃嗎？舊得都發黑了，上面雕着葉子和古怪的人形的。好，正是這麼一個櫃子站在客廳裏，是這一家的曾祖母遺留下來的。這個櫃子從頭到腳雕着玫瑰花和鬱金香，它上面有最古怪的渦卷形花紋，從花紋中露出一些帶角的小鹿頭。櫃門中間雕着一個全身人像，一看就叫人覺得荒唐可笑。他對着你齜牙咧嘴，因為誰也不能說這是在笑。他下面有山羊的腿，頭上長着小角，下巴有把長鬍子，房間裏的孩子們通常叫他"少將、陸軍中士、公羊腿指揮官"。這實在是個十分難唸的頭銜，這個頭銜也沒有人得到過，那麼他怎麼會雕在這上面就怪了。反正他就是雕在那裏，眼睛老盯着鏡子下面的桌子看，那裏站着一個異常美麗的瓷做的小牧羊女。她的鞋子鍍成金色，連衣裙上有一朵紅玫瑰花，或是甚麼裝飾。她頭上戴着帽子，手裏拿着一根曲柄杖，這兩樣東西也都鍍成金色，又明亮又好看。她旁邊站着一個小小的掃煙囱的人，黑得像炭，也是瓷做的。不過他乾淨整齊得就像其他任何一個瓷人，他只是被做成掃煙囱的人，瓷器工人如果高興，也可以把他做成王子。他站在那裏很熟練地拿着一把梯子，他的臉很俊秀，紅紅的，像一張女孩的臉，這確實可算是一個錯誤，臉上該加上一些黑漬才對。他和那牧羊女並排放在一起。這樣放,他們兩個就訂婚了,因為他們十分匹配,都是一種瓷做的,亦都同樣易碎。靠近他們站着另一個人像,有他們三倍大,也是瓷做的。這是一位中國老人,能點頭,總自稱是牧羊女的祖父,雖然他提不出甚麼證明。不過他認為他有權管她,因此當"少將、陸軍中士、公羊腿指揮官"向小牧羊女求婚時,他點頭表示同意。"你要有一個丈夫了,"中國老人對她說,"我完全相信他是桃花心木做的。他會使你成為'少將、陸軍中士、公羊腿指揮官'夫人。他有滿滿一櫃子銀盤子,鎖在那些秘密的抽屜裏。"

"我不要到那黑暗的櫃子裏去,"小牧羊女說。"我聽説他裏面已經有十一個瓷做的妻子了。"

"那麼你做第十二個,"中國老人説。"今天夜裏你一聽到那舊櫃子裏格格響,你就要結婚了,這和我是一個中國人一樣千真萬確。"接着他點點頭,就睡着了。

於是小牧羊女哭起來,看着她心愛的瓷做掃煙囪人。"我必須求求你,帶我到外面廣闊的世界去,"她說,"因為我們在這裏留不下去了。"

"你要我做甚麼,我就一定做甚麼,"小掃煙囪人説,"讓我們馬上走吧,我想我做我的工作能養活你的。"

"只要我們能平安離開這張桌子就好了!"她説。"我只有真的到了外面的世界才會開心。"

於是掃煙囪人安慰她,告訴她怎樣把她的小腳踩在桌子雕花的邊上和貼金的葉子上。他搬來他的小梯子幫助她,於是他們到了下面地板上。但是他們一看那舊櫃子,只見它整個大吵大鬧。雕出來的鹿伸出它們的頭，翹起它們的犄角，扭動它們的脖子。少將跳得半天高，向中國老人大叫："他們逃走了！他們逃走了！"這一對情人看到這情景十分害怕，於是跳進了靠近窗臺的大抽屜裏。這裏面有三四副不完整的撲克牌，還有一座造得十分精巧的玩偶劇場。劇場正在上演一齣喜劇。所有方塊、梅花、紅心和黑桃皇后坐在第一排，用鬱金香當扇子搧着，她們後面站着所有傑克，讓人看到他們上下都有頭，就像撲克牌上那樣。戲裏講一對情人不能成為眷屬，牧羊女看了哭起來，因為和她自己的事太相似了。"我受不了，"她說，"我必須離開這抽屜。"但是當他們來到地板上抬頭向桌上看時，中國老人醒了，全身搖來搖去，突然"咕咚"的一聲，他掉到地上。"中國老人來了，"牧羊女嚇得大叫，跪倒在地上。

"我有一個主意，"掃煙囪人說，"讓我們到牆角那個放乾花瓣和鹽的大罈裏去。我們可以躺在玫瑰花瓣和薰衣草上面，如果他靠近我們，我們就向他的眼睛撒鹽。"

"不，那不行，"她說，"因為我知道，那中國人和那罈子曾經相愛，相愛過總是有點感情。不，我們沒有別的辦法，只能逃到外面廣闊的世界去。"

"你真的有足夠的勇氣和我一起到外面廣闊的世界去嗎？"掃煙囪人說，"你有沒有想過它有多大，而且我們再也不能回到這裏來嗎？"

"是的，我想過，"她回答說。

掃煙囪的人看到她十分堅決，說："我的走法是鑽過爐子爬上煙囪。你有勇氣和我一起爬過爐膛和鐵管嗎？只要到煙囪那裏，我就有辦法了。很快我們就爬得高高的，誰也追不到我們，然後我們就通過頂上一個洞鑽到外面廣闊的世界去。"於是他帶她到爐門那裏。

"裏面真黑，"她説，但她還是和他一起進去了，穿過爐膛，穿過鐵管，那裏漆黑一片。

"現在我們在煙囱裏了，"他説，"看，煙囱的上空有一顆美麗的星星在閃耀着。"那是一顆真正的星星在照下來，照着他們，像是給他們指路。於是他們爬上煙囱，爬啊爬啊，這地方陡得嚇人，但是掃煙囱的人幫助她，攙扶她，他們越爬越高。他指給她看，在哪些地方落腳最穩妥，於是他們最後來到了煙囱頂，坐下來，因為他們非常累了，他們也早知道會這樣。他們頭頂上是星空，他們下面是滿城的屋頂。他們可以看得很遠，看到廣闊的世界，可憐的小牧羊女把頭靠在她的掃煙囱人的肩上，直哭到她彩帶上的金色都被淚水洗掉了，世界和她原先想的是那麼大不相同。"這叫我受不了，"她説，"我真受不了啦，世界太大了。噢，我希望重新回到桌子上，回到鏡子底下，安安穩穩的。我不重新回到那裏去，我是永遠不會快樂的。現在我已經跟着你來到外面廣闊的世界，如果你愛我，你就帶我回去吧。"

掃煙囱的人於是試圖勸説她，提到中國老人，提到"少將、陸軍中士、公羊腿指揮官"。但是她哭得那麼傷心，吻她的小掃煙囱人，他最後不得不照她要求的做，儘管這樣做太傻了。於是他們花了很大功夫爬下煙囱，接着爬過鐵管和爐子，這些自然都不是很舒服的地方。然後他們站在漆黑的爐膛裏，豎起了耳朵在爐門後面聽房間裏的動靜。聽到外面一切靜悄悄，他們才探出頭去看。天啊！中國老人躺在地板上。他想追他們的時候從桌子上掉下來，碎成了三塊，他的背整個和身體分開了，他的頭滾到了房間角落。少將站在老地方，像是在想心事。

"太可怕了，"小牧羊女說。"我可憐的老祖父跌碎了，全都怪我們，我再也沒法活了。"她絞着她的兩隻小手。

"他可以補好的，"掃煙囪的人說，"他可以補好的。不要那麼着急。只要黏起他的背，用釘子把他的頭好好地釘上去，他又會完好如新，能夠照舊對我們嘰哩咕嚕個沒完。"

"你真的這麼想嗎？"她說。於是他們重新爬上桌子，站在他們的老地方。

"既然我們白白走了一趟，"掃煙囪的人說，"我們還是留在這裏，不要那麼煩了。"

"我希望祖父會補好，"牧羊女說。"我不知道這是不是要花許多錢。"

她的希望實現了。這家人補好中國人的背，在他的脖子上釘上一根結實的釘子。他看起來完好如新，但是他再也不能點頭了。

"自從你跌碎過以後，你變得驕傲了，""少將、陸軍中士、公羊腿指揮官"說。"你沒有理由擺出那麼一副架子，把她給我還是不給？"

掃煙囪的人和小牧羊女可憐地看着這位中國老人，因為他們很怕他會點頭，但是他不可能點頭。而且老是告訴陌生人他的頸後釘着一顆釘子，也太累人了。

於是這一對小瓷人還是留在一起，很高興祖父有這麼一顆釘子。他們繼續相愛，直到破碎變心為止。

# 16
# 賣火柴的小女孩

除夕夜冷得厲害，天已經差不多黑了，雪下得很大。在嚴寒和黑暗中，一個光着頭赤着腳的可憐小女孩流浪街頭。不錯，她離家時穿着一雙拖鞋，但是它們沒有多大用處。它們非常大，太大了，說實在的，它們本來是她媽媽穿的。這小傢伙為了躲開飛馳而過的兩輛馬車，急急忙忙穿過街道，弄丟了它們。一隻拖鞋她沒能找到，另一隻被一個男孩搶走，他一邊跑開，一邊說，等他有了自己的孩子，可以用它做搖籃。

於是小女孩只好赤着她的小腳一路上走，它們都冷成青紫色了。她圍着一條舊圍裙，裏面兜着幾束火柴，而且手裏還拿着一束。整整一天沒有人買過她的火柴，也沒有人給過她一個錢。

她又冷又餓，瑟瑟發抖，一步一步地向前走。可憐的小女孩，她看起來十分悲苦。

雪片落在她捲曲着的披在肩上的長長淡黃的秀髮上，但是她的心不在這頭秀髮上面，也不在這寒冷上面。每一個窗戶都射出亮光，只聞到一股烤鵝的香味，因為今天是除夕夜。不錯，她在想的是今天是除夕夜。

在一座比另一座突出一點的兩座房子之間的角落裏，她坐下來，縮成一團，她已經把她的兩隻小腳縮在身體下面，但還是不能禦寒。她不敢回家，因為她連一根火柴也沒有賣出去，連一個錢也沒法帶回家。她的爸爸準要打她。再説，家裏也冷得和這裏差不多，因為他們只能算是有個屋頂遮遮頭，風還是呼呼吹進來，儘管最大的一些窟窿已經用乾草和破布堵住了。

她的兩隻小手幾乎已經凍僵。啊！如果她從那束火柴裏抽出一根在牆上劃燃，一根燃燒的火柴也許會有點用處，哪怕暖和一下手指也好！她於是抽出一根，嚓！火柴閃過一道光便燃燒起來！她把手放到火柴上面，它發出溫暖明亮的光，像一支小蠟燭。這光真叫人愉快。小女孩只覺得像是坐在一個大鐵火爐旁邊，這鐵火爐還有擦亮了的黃銅爐腳、黃銅鏟子和黃銅鉗子。火燃燒得多麼旺啊！而且好像暖和得那麼舒服，小女孩不禁伸出她的腳去取暖，可就在這時候，看！火柴的火焰滅了，火爐消失了，她手裏只有燒剩的一點火柴。

她在牆上又劃一根火柴。它冒出了明亮的火焰，它的光投在牆上的地方變得和薄紗一樣透明，她能夠看到房間裏面。桌上鋪着雪白的枱布，上面擺着漂亮的瓷製餐具，有一隻熱氣騰騰的塞着蘋果和梅乾的烤鵝，蒸得很好，香噴噴的。更叫人驚訝的是，這鵝從盤子上跳下來，胸口插着餐刀和餐叉，一搖一晃地在地板上向小女孩走過來。

就在這時候火柴又熄滅了，她面前剩下的，只有那濕冷的厚牆。

她又劃一根火柴，這一回她發現自己正坐在一棵最美麗的聖誕樹下。它比她透過那個大老闆的玻璃門所看到的那棵還要大，裝飾得也更美麗。綠枝上點着幾百支細蠟燭，一些就像她在店鋪櫥窗裏見過的顏色鮮艷的小人從上面望下來，看她。小女孩向它們伸出手去，但是火柴熄滅了。

聖誕樹的燭光越升越高，越升越高，最後她覺得它們像天上的星星。這時候她看見一顆星星落下來，在後面留下明亮的一道長長的火光。

"有一個人正在死去，"小女孩想，因為她的老祖母——唯一曾經愛過她的人，但現在已經去世了——告訴過她，天上一顆星星落下來，地上一個靈魂就升到上帝那裏去。

她在牆上又劃一根火柴，光照亮了她的周圍。在亮光中站着她那位親愛的老祖母，看得清清楚楚，全身閃閃發亮，樣子和藹可親，生前她從未如此開心過。

"噢，奶奶，"小女孩叫道，"你帶走我吧。我知道火柴一點完你就要走掉，你將和溫暖的火爐、烤鵝、漂亮的聖誕樹一樣消失不見。"她趕緊劃亮整束火柴，因為她要留住她的老祖母。

火柴燃燒着，那光照得四周比中午還亮，她的祖母從來沒有那麼高大，或者那麼美麗過。她抱小女孩在懷裏，她們雙雙在光明和歡樂中向上飛升，飛到遠離地球的地方，那裏沒有寒冷，沒有饑餓，也沒有痛苦，因為她們和上帝在一起。

第二天天剛亮時，那可憐的小女孩靠在牆上，臉蛋紅紅的，嘴帶微笑。她在昨晚的除夕夜冷死了。小女孩冰冷的身體僵硬了，她依然坐着，手裏拿着火柴，一束火柴都燒光了。

"她想溫暖自己，可憐的小女孩。"有人說。沒有人會想到她曾看見多麼美麗的東西，也沒有人會想到在新年裏，她和她的祖母一起進入了多麼美好的天國。

# 17
# 老路燈

你聽過老路燈的故事嗎？它並不特別有趣，但也不妨一聽。那是盞最可敬的老燈，已經服務了許多許多年，如今要領退休金了。今天晚上是它最後一次在路燈柱上照亮這條路。它的心情有點像劇院裏的老舞蹈女演員作最後一次舞蹈演出，並且知道第二天就要留在她的閣樓上，從此孤孤單單，被人忘掉。老路燈對這第二天感到極其焦慮，因為它知道第二天不得不有生以來第一次到市政廳去，由市長和市議會們審查，決定它是不是適合繼續服務——它還可不可以用來照亮市郊某住宅區的居民，或者用到鄉下某家工廠去。如果都不行，它馬上就會送進鑄鐵廠去熔掉。遇到後面這種情況，熔掉的鐵可能就變成別的東西，它很想知道到那時候它是不是還會記得它曾是一盞路燈，這使它感到極其苦惱。不管可能發生甚麼事，有一點看來是肯定的，就是它要和守夜人夫婦分開了，它把這家人看作自己的家人。路燈第一次掛上去的那天晚上，守夜人那時候還是個強壯小伙子，也正好開始做他的守夜人工作。啊，它成為路燈，而他當上守夜人，說起來已經很久很久了。他的妻子那時候有點驕傲，很難得才賞臉朝路燈看一眼，除了晚上走過的時候，白天是從來不看的。可是近年來，他們大家——那就是守夜人、他的妻子和這盞路燈都老了，守夜人的妻子照料它，擦洗它，給它添油。這兩位老人家極其忠厚老實，供應路燈的油他們一滴也不少。

這是路燈在這條街上的最後一夜了，明天它就得上市政廳去，是兩件想想就叫人異常難過的事情，這就怪不得它燃燒得不大亮了。許多別的念頭也湧上了它的心，它曾照亮過多少過路的人啊，它曾看到過多少事情啊，很可能和市長及其市政委員會所看到的一樣多！不過所有這些念頭，它一個也沒有說出來，因為它是一盞善良可敬的老路燈，它不想傷害任何人，特別是那些當權的人。由於心中勾起許多事，它的光會突然間閃亮。在這種時候，它確信它會被人記住。"從前有一個英俊的小伙子，"它想，"不用說，那是很久以前了，但是我記得他有一張小字條，寫在一張鑲金邊的粉紅色紙上，字跡清秀，顯然出自一位小姐之手。他把字條從頭到尾讀了兩遍，親親它，然後抬頭看我，那雙眼睛簡單直接地說：'我是所有男人中最幸福的！'只有他和我知道，他心愛的那位小姐的第一封信寫着甚麼。啊，對了，我記得還有另一雙眼睛——真是奇怪，思想怎麼會從一件事一下子跳到另一件事！一支送葬隊伍在街上走過，一位年輕貌美的女子躺在棺材架上，鋪着花圈，伴隨着火把，這些火把蓋過了我的光。整條街都站着從各家房子裏出來的人，一羣一羣的，準備參加送葬隊伍。但是當那些火把在我面前經過以後，我轉臉看看，看到一個人孤零零地靠在我的路燈柱上站着在哭。我永遠忘不了那雙抬起來看我的悲哀眼睛。"在老路燈的光最後一次照耀的時候，它滿腦子都是這樣的和類似這樣的回憶。下崗的哨兵至少知道誰來接班，可以對接班的人輕輕說句話，但是老路燈不知道接班的是誰，不然可以給它指點一下雨和霧的事，告訴它月光在行人路上會照到多遠，風一般從哪一邊吹來等等。

在水渠上的橋上有三樣東西想向老路燈自薦，因為它們以為老路燈能把位置讓給它自己挑選的東西。第一個是鯡魚頭，它在黑暗中會發光。它說如果安置它在路燈柱上，可以省掉許多油。第二個是一塊爛木頭，它在黑暗中也會發光。它自稱來自一個古樹幹，這古樹曾是森林的驕傲。第三個是一隻螢火蟲，牠是怎麼到這裏來的，老路燈想不出來，然而牠就是在這裏，也當真和其他兩個一樣能發光。但是爛木頭和鯡魚頭極其神聖莊嚴地發誓說，螢火蟲只在一定的時候發光，絕不能讓螢火蟲跟它們競爭。老路燈老實對它們說，它們中沒有一個能發出足夠的光來頂替一盞路燈的位置，但是它們一點也不相信老路燈說的話。等到它們知道路燈並沒有權力指定它的繼承者，它們說它們聽到這一點很高興，因為老路燈太過腐朽了，已經作不出正確的選擇。

正在這時候，風呼呼地從街角吹來，吹進老路燈的氣孔。"我聽見的這是甚麼話？"風說。"你明天要走啦？今晚是我們最後一次見面嗎？那麼我一定要送你一樣告別禮物。我要吹進你的腦裏，這樣你將來不但能夠記住你過去的所見所聞，而且你內心的光將如此明亮，以後別人在你面前所說或所做的一切你都可以明白。"

"噢，那真是一份非常、非常了不起的禮物，"老路燈說。"我衷心地感謝你。我但願不會被熔掉。"

"那很可能不會，"風說，"我還要把記憶吹進你的腦裏。這樣，如果類似的禮物你再多幾件，你的老年生活就可以過得非常愉快了。"

"那是如果我不被熔掉的話，"老路燈說。"但是萬一熔掉了，我還能保持我的記憶嗎？"

"要理智一點，老路燈，"風説着，吹起來。

這時候月亮從雲中出來。"你送甚麼給老路燈呢？"風問她。

"我甚麼也送不出，"月亮回答説。"我常常用光照燈，現在我月缺，卻沒有燈曾給過我光。"月亮説着，又躲到雲後面去了，這樣可以省得別人再硬向她要甚麼。就在這時候，屋頂上有一滴水落到老路燈上，但是那滴水解釋説，它是那些烏雲送的禮物，也許是所有禮物中最好的。"我將徹底滲透你，"它説，"使你具有生鏽的力量，萬一你需要，可以在一夜之間化為塵土。"

但是老路燈覺得這是非常壞的禮物，風也這麼想。"沒有誰再送禮物了嗎？沒有誰再送禮物了嗎？"風呼呼地有多響吼多響。這時候一顆很亮的流星掉下來，在後面留下一道寬闊的光帶。

"那是甚麼？"鯡魚頭叫道。"一顆星不是掉下來了嗎？我斷定它落到燈裏去了。當然，出身這樣高貴的人物來求那個位置，我們最好是説聲'晚安'就回家去吧。"

它們三個説完就這樣做，而老路燈在它周圍投出驚人強烈的亮光。

"這是一件極好的禮物，"它説，"閃亮的星星一直是我的快樂，它發的光一直比我發的亮，雖然我已經用盡力氣了。而現在它們注意到我，一盞可憐的老路燈，送給我一份禮物，使我能看清楚我記得的每一件事情，好像它仍舊在眼前一樣，並且讓所有愛我的人都看見它們。最真實的快樂就在這裏，因為不能和別人分享的快樂，只能算是享受到一半的快樂。”

“這種想法使你受到尊敬，”風説，“但是要達到這個目的，蠟燭是必需的。如果不在你裏面點上蠟燭，你就一點也不能照亮別人。星星沒有想到這一點，它們以為你和每一樣會發光的東西都一定是支蠟燭，但是我現在必須歇一會了。”於是它躺下來休息。

“蠟燭，一點也不錯！”老路燈説。“我從來沒有過這種東西，看來也不會有了。只要我能確定我不被熔掉就好！”

第二天。但也許最好省掉第二天白天的事。晚上來了，老路燈在一把老人椅上休息，猜猜它在哪裏？是這樣的，老路燈在老守夜人的家。守夜人求市長和市政委員會，説他二十四年前做這份工的第一天，也是老路燈掛上去、燃亮起來的第一天，念在它多年來忠心耿耿的服務，就讓他保管這盞老路燈吧。守夜人幾乎像看自己的孩子一樣看着老路燈，他沒有孩子，所以這盞燈給了他。老路燈躺在靠近溫暖爐子的大扶手椅上，看起來好像它變大了，因為它佔了整把椅子。老人們坐着吃晚餐，友好地瞥了一眼老路燈，他們願意讓老路燈坐到餐桌去。他們住在地下兩碼深的地窖裏，不得不穿過一條石道進入他們的房子，但是房子內是溫暖舒適的，一條條布條圍着門口釘着。床有床幔，小窗有窗簾，一切看起來整齊清潔。在窗戶上放着兩個奇怪的花盆，是一個叫克里信的水手從東印度群島或西印度群島帶來的。它們是陶土做的，做成大象的形狀，沒有背脊。它們是空心的，裏面都是泥土，花在象背裏盛開。其中一頭大象種了細香蔥或者韭蔥，他們叫它做“廚房花園”。另一頭大象種了一朵美麗的天竺葵，他們稱之為“鮮花花園”。牆上掛着一幅大彩色畫，是維也納會議，所有國王和皇帝都在上面。牆上掛着一個鐘，重得很。鐘“滴答滴答”，節奏有致。然而，它總是走得快，但守夜人夫婦說快總比慢好。他們正在吃晚餐，而老路燈，正如剛才所說，躺在爐子附近的老人扶手椅上。老路燈似乎覺得整個世界都倒轉過來。但過了一會，老守夜人看着燈，說着他們一起經歷的事 —— 雲雨霧露；或夏天明亮而短暫的夜晚；又或是刮着暴風雪，他渴望回到地窖裏的家的漫長冬夜。然後老路燈感覺它沒事了，發生過的一切它都看到很清楚，彷彿就在它面前經過。當然，風給它的禮物很好。守夜人夫婦很活躍、很勤奮，他們連一小時也沒有閒着。星期天下午，他們會拿出一些書，通常是一本他們非常喜歡的旅行書。老守夜人會大聲朗讀關於非洲的東西，有大森林和野大象，而他的妻子會專注地聽，不時偷看一下大象花盆。

“我幾乎可以想像我看見了這一切，”她說。這時候老路燈多麼希望它裏面點着一支小蠟燭啊，這樣老太太就能像它那樣清楚地看到最細微的地方了。樹枝密密交叉的高大樹木啦，騎在馬背上光着身體的黑人啦，用寬大沉重的腳踩倒竹林的成羣大象啦。

“沒有蠟燭，我有一身本領又有甚麼用，”老路燈歎氣說。“他們這裏只有食油和動物油脂，但是這些又不好用。”有一天地窖裏弄來了一大堆蠟燭頭。大的蠟燭頭拿來點燃，小的老太太留下來蠟她的線。因此，這時候蠟燭是夠多了，但是誰也沒有想到在燈裏放一支。

“現在我就這樣帶着少有的本領留在這裏，”老路燈想。“我有本領，但是我無法施展出來。他們不知道我能把這些白牆蒙上美麗的掛毯，或者把它們變成宏偉的森林，又或者變成他們希望的任何東西。”不過燈總是被擦得乾乾淨淨，在角落裏亮晶晶地吸引着所有眼睛。外人把它看作木材，但是老夫婦不在乎，他們愛這燈。有一天──那是守夜人的生日──老太太拿出燈來，暗自微笑着説：“為了慶賀我的老頭子生日，今天我要把燈點亮。”燈在它的鐵皮框裏格格響，因為它想：“現在我裏面終於可以有光了。”但終究她沒有放蠟燭到燈裏，只是照常加了油。燈燃燒了整個晚上，開始清楚地認識到，星星的禮物只好成為它一生秘密珍藏的寶貝了。接着它做了一個夢，因為對於一個有本領的東西來説，做夢是不難的。它夢見老夫婦都死了，它被送到了鑄鐵所去熔掉。這使它和被送到市政廳見市長及市議員那天一樣焦慮。它雖然獲賦予了隨時可以生鏽化為灰塵的法力，但是它沒有用它。因此它被投進熔爐，變成了一個美麗得你都會想看看的鐵燭臺，插蠟燭用的。燭臺的形狀是一個天使拿着一個花束，花束的中心可以放蠟燭。燭臺放到一個非常舒適的房間裏的一張綠色寫字枱上，周圍散佈着許多書，牆上掛着精美的畫。房間的主人是個詩人，一個有知識的人，他想的或者寫的每一樣東西在他周圍顯現出來。大自然有時候向詩人呈現出黑暗的森林，有時候呈現出鸛鳥在昂首漫步的快活草原，有時候呈現出在浪花飛濺的大海上、晴朗蔚藍的天空下航行的輪船的甲板，或者是在繁星閃爍的夜晚。“我擁有甚麼樣的本領啊！”燈説着，從夢中醒來。“我幾乎想要被熔掉了，但是不行，老夫婦活着的時候絕對不行。他們愛我僅僅是因為我是我。他們一直把我擦亮，給我添油。我的境遇和那幅維也納會議的畫一樣好，他們從中可以得到那麼大的樂趣。"從此它感到內心平安，一盞如此忠厚老實的老路燈，真正應該享有的就莫過於此了。

# 18

# 影子

在太陽威力很大的熱帶，人們的皮膚通常棕黑得像紅木。在最熱的地方，他們就曬成黑人。有一次，一位學者從寒帶來到熱帶，他本想像在家鄉那樣到處漫遊，但是很快就改變了主意。

他像所有有頭腦的人那樣整天留在房子裏，關緊每一扇門窗，因此那些房子像是屋裏所有的人都睡着了，或者裏面根本沒有人。

他住的那條小街上的房子都很高，太陽從早曬到晚，叫人實在受不了。

這位寒帶來的年輕學者看起來很聰明。他覺得好像是坐在火爐裏，這使他變得筋疲力竭，渾身無力，消瘦得連他的影子也縮小了，因為太陽連這點剩下的影子也不給留下，他要到晚上太陽下山以後才能看到它。

在熱帶，每個窗都有一個陽臺，人們在這上面呼吸新鮮空氣，這是他們十分需要的，哪怕他們已習慣了使他們的皮膚棕黑得有如紅木的這種炎熱！因此，這條街一下子就顯得生氣蓬勃起來。鞋匠、裁縫和各式各樣的人走到街上。在下面街上，人們端出桌子和椅子，點上幾千支蠟燭，又聊天又唱歌，十分快活。人們走路，教堂鐘聲響起，驢子一面跑，韁具上的鈴鐺一面叮鈴叮鈴響！孩童一面尖叫大笑，一面射擊爆炸球。此時來了扶靈的人和衣服有兜帽的人，因為這是有讚美詩的葬禮，然後聽見馬車駛過、人群抵達。這的確是這條街的眾生相，生氣勃勃的。只有一座房子，就在那位外國學者住的房子對面，是寂靜無聲的。然而那裏住着人，因為陽臺上擺着花，在烈日下開得很漂亮。如果不是有人細心澆水，它們是不可能這樣的。因此，這房子裏一定有人。晚上對面的門亦開着，雖然前面的房間是黑漆漆的，後面的也可能是這樣，卻能聽到房子內部傳出音樂聲。那位外國學者認為這音樂很美妙，但這也許只是他的想像，因為在這些炎熱的國家裏樣樣令他高興，只除了太陽的熱力。外國學者的房東說他也不知道對面房子住的是誰，因為沒有見過那裏有人。至於音樂，他認為單調乏味透了。"就像是甚麼人在練習一首他彈奏不了的曲子，老是一個曲子。我想他自以為最後能行，不過我認為不管他練習多久，也辦不到。"

有一次外國學者半夜醒來。他開着陽臺門睡覺，風吹起了門簾，他看到對面房子的陽臺整個十分亮，亮得奇怪。花像是色彩鮮艷的火焰般閃耀，在花叢中站着一位苗條的美麗女孩。他只覺得她也在發光，耀花了他的眼睛。他睜大眼，因為他已經從睡夢中醒來。他一下子跳下床，輕輕地爬到門簾後面。但是女孩不見了，花也不再閃耀，雖然它們美麗如常。門半開着，從裏面遠處響起音樂，那麼輕柔，那麼悅耳，它產生最迷人的思想，使人感到入迷。誰會住在那裏呢？真正的入口在哪裏呢？下面整層是店鋪，人們是不能隨便進到那裏面去的。

一天晚上，這位外國學者坐在陽臺上。他自己的房間裏點着燈，就在他後面。因此很自然，他的影子就落到對面房子的牆的正對面，在陽臺上的花叢間。人一動，影子也跟着動，每每如是。

　　"我想，我的影子是對面能看到會動的唯一東西，"學者說，"看它在花叢間坐得多麼愉快。門半開着，影子該聰明一點走進去看看，回來告訴我看到了甚麼。去吧！現在！這樣你也有點用處，幫我一個忙，"他開玩笑說。"拜託你這就走進去好不好？你不去嗎？"他說着，向影子點點頭，影子也向他點點頭。"現在去吧！不過別一去不回來。"

　　接着外國學者站起來，對面陽臺的影子也站起來；外國學者轉身，影子也轉身。如果這時候有人在看，他們就會明顯看到影子一直走進對面陽臺上那扇半開着的門，就像學者走進他自己的房間，放下了門簾。

　　第二天早晨，他出來喝咖啡讀報紙。

　　"這是怎麼回事？"他站在陽光中叫起來。

　　"我丟掉了我的影子。這麼說，它昨天晚上真的一去不回了。這太糟糕啦。"

　　這真正使他十分苦惱，倒不是因為他的影子不見了，而是因為他知道一個故事，正是講一個人沒有了影子。在他寒冷的本國，這個故事人盡皆知。等到他回去講他自己的親身遭遇，大家只會說他是抄那個故事，他可不希望人家這樣說他。因此，他決定乾脆不說出這件事，這個決定十分明智。

　　晚上他又到外面陽臺上，預先把燈放在背後，因為他知道一個影子總是要隨着它的主人，但是他沒有辦法引它出來。他把身體縮小，把身體伸直，但是沒有影子出現。他拼命說："嘿，嘿"，要叫影子出來，但是完全沒有用處。

這真是太惱人了。不過在炎熱的國家，一切長得非常快。八天一過，他很高興地看到，當他在陽光裏行走時，一個新的影子已經生出來了。過了三星期，他已經有一個和他相稱的影子。在他回北方家鄉時，這影子還在長大，最後大到、長到已超出所需。

這位學者回到家，就寫書在這個世界上的真善美。就這樣，一天天一年年過去，許多許多年過去了。

有一天晚上，他正坐在書房裏，聽見有人很輕地敲門。

"進來，"他說，但是沒有人進來。他於是走去打開房門，只見面前站着一個人，瘦得叫他吃驚。不過那人穿着講究，像位紳士。

"請問閣下是哪一位？"學者說。

"啊！早就猜到了，我猜您不認識我，"那高雅的陌生人說。"我得到了那麼多，我連肉體都有了，衣服也穿上了。您永遠沒想過會看見我過得這麼好吧。您不認識您的舊影子了嗎？您永遠沒想過我會再回來。自從我離開您以後，我發達了。我非常富有，想不再做事，享享清福，這一點我很容易就能做到。"他一面說，一面把掛在手錶上的整串值錢飾物弄得嗒嗒響，一面用手指把戴在脖子上很粗的一根金鍊弄得吁吁響。他的全部手指上都戴着鑽戒，閃閃發光，全是真正的寶石。

"我吃驚得糊裏糊塗了，"學者說。"這是怎麼一回事啊？"

"事情很不尋常，"影子說。"不過您本人就是一位不尋常的人，您知道得很清楚，從您小時候起我就跟着您的腳印走。等到您覺得我已經有足夠的經歷，相信我可以單獨生活了，我這才離開了您，走我自己的路。如今我正處於飛黃騰達的頂峯，但是我覺得我有一種渴望，要在您死前再見您一次，您快死了，我猜。我要再看看這個地方，因為一個人對自己的故土總會懷念。我知道您如今有另外一個影子。我欠您或是這個新影子甚麼嗎？如果有，請勞駕說出來是甚麼吧。"

"不！這真是你嗎？"學者說。"這真是再驚人不過了，我永遠沒想過一個人的舊影子會變成一個人。"

"告訴我，我欠了您甚麼，"影子說，"因為我不想欠任何人的債。"

"你怎麼能這樣說呢？"學者說。"我們之間能有甚麼債不債的問題嗎？你和任何人一樣自由自在。我極想聽聽你的好運氣。坐下吧，老朋友，告訴我這到底是怎麼一回事，而且在那熱帶國家，你在我對面那座房子裏看到了甚麼吧？"

"好，我都告訴您，"影子坐下說，"但是您必須答應我，在這個城市，不管在甚麼地方碰到我，不要跟人說我曾經是您的影子。我正想訂婚，因為我要維持一個家庭真是綽綽有餘。"

"你放心吧，"學者說，"我不會跟任何人說你實際上是誰。我答應，在人與人之間一句話就足夠了。"

"在人與影子之間，"影子說，他忍不住要這麼說一句。

他竟變成了一個人，這真正是再驚人不過了。他穿着一套最漂亮的黑西裝、一雙擦亮了的皮靴，戴一頂可以壓扁得只剩帽頂和帽邊的大禮帽，再有就是剛才已經提到過的金鍊、墜子和鑽戒。說實在的，正是這影子穿着十分考究，這使他成為一個人。

"現在我來告訴您我經歷了甚麼，"影子説着，把一隻穿上擦亮了的皮靴的腳牢牢踩在學者新影子的一隻手臂上，那新影子躺在他的腳下像一隻貴婦狗。他這樣做也許是出於驕傲，但是地上的影子還是那樣安安靜靜地躺着，好聽得仔細，因為它也想知道一個影子怎麼能獲得自由，努力變成一個人。

"您知道嗎，"影子説，"您知道住在您對面的是誰嗎？在您對面那房子裏住着世界上最了不起的人物，那是詩神。我在那裏留了三星期，卻像留了三千年，因為我讀了詩神用詩歌和散文寫的一切。説實在的，我可以説，我見過了一切，無所不知。"

"詩神！"學者叫起來。"不錯，她常隱居在一些大城市裏！詩神！我見過她一次，只有一轉眼的時間，但我眼睏了。她出現在陽臺上，像燦爛的北極光在我眼前發亮。告訴我，那天晚上你在陽臺上，進了門，看見甚麼了？"

"我發覺自己進了一個前廳，"影子説。"您還坐在我對面，朝前廳裏看。那裏沒有燈，或者有些許暮光，然而有一房間的門是開着的，這扇門和在另一端的一列房間和大廳一扇門正對着，燈火輝煌。要是我走得離那女孩太近的話，我早就死了。但是我很謹慎小心，等候時機，這是每個人都應該做的。"

"你到底看到甚麼了？"學者問道。

"我甚麼都看到了，我這就説給您聽。不過，完全不是由於我驕傲，但身為一個自由人，又擁有我所擁有的知識，更不要説我所擁有的財富了，我希望您稱呼我做'您'，而不是'你'。"

"請您原諒，"學者説，"這是個老習慣，不容易改。您説得很對，我要謹記這一點。不過現在告訴我您看到的一切吧。"

"當然，一切，"影子説，"因為我看到並且知道了一切。"

"裏面最遠的大廳是甚麼樣子的？"學者問道。"裏面像一片清新的樹林，還是像一座教堂？那些大廳像從高山頂上看到的星空嗎？"

"裏面正如您説的一切！"影子説。"不過我沒有完全走進去，我仍舊留在前廳的暮光中，但是我的位置非常好，我能夠看到和知道詩宮前廳裏所發生的一切。"

"但是您究竟看到甚麼啦？古代的神在那些大廳穿來穿去嗎？古代的英雄們在戰鬥嗎？有可愛的孩子們在玩，講述他們的夢嗎？"

"我告訴您，我到過那裏，因此您不用懷疑，可以看到的一切我都看到了。如果您到過那裏，您就不會再是一個人，然而我卻變成了一個人。與此同時，我開始發現我的內在本質、我對詩歌的天生愛好。真的，我過去和您在一起的時候，我不大想到這一點，但是您會記得，在日出和日落的時候我總是大得多，在月光中我甚至比您本人還清晰，只是當時我並不明白我的內在本質，但在前廳裏我就發現了！我變成了一個人！我出來時完全成形了，但是您已經離開了這熱帶國家。身為一個人，不穿靴子，不穿衣服，沒有人的外表，我覺得這樣真不好意思走來走去。於是我用了我的辦法，我可以告訴您，因為您不可寫它到書裏去。我躲到一個賣糕餅女人的背後，但是她一點也不知道她遮蔽了一個人。我到晚上才敢出來，在月光裏跑過一條條街。我貼着牆伸直我的身體，這使我的背癢癢的，舒服得很。我跑上跑下，我望進最高的窗、大廳，我從屋頂上望下去，我看到了別人看不到的地方、別人看不到的東西！事實上，這是一個醜惡的世界！要不是做人有點了不起，我還真不願意做一個人呢！我看到在男人、女人、父母和可愛無比的孩子之間發生的最想像不到的事。我看到了沒有人能知道，但都會很高興知道的事 —— 他們鄰居的惡行。如果我寫出來在報紙上發表，大家會多麼起勁地看啊！但是我卻直接給那些人親身寫信，於是我所到的城市弄得全城大恐慌。他們太怕我了，然而又太喜歡我。教授推選我為教授，裁縫送給我新衣服。這樣一來，我得到了充足的供給。造幣廠長為我造幣。女人們說我英俊。於是我就成了您現在所看到的這樣一個人。現在我必須說再見了。這是我的名片。我住在街上有太陽的一邊，雨天總留在家裏。"影子告別了。

"這一切太驚人了，"學者說。

一天天一年年過去，許多年過去，影子又來了。"您現在過得好嗎？"他問道。

"啊！"學者說。"我在寫論述真善美的書，但是這種事沒有人要聽。我感到十分失望，因為我對這件事是很認真的。"

"我正好從來不這樣做，"影子說。"所以我變胖，人人都想如此。您不懂得這個世界。您這樣會生病。您應該去旅行！夏天我要去旅行，您和我一起去好嗎？我很高興有個旅伴！您肯做我的影子和我一起去旅行嗎？有您在會給我極大的樂趣，一切費用全由我付。"

"這不是太過份了嗎？"學者問道。

"這只是個看法問題，"影子回答說。"不管怎麼說，旅行對您是有好處的！如果您肯當我的影子，您去旅行不花一個錢。"

"我覺得這很奇怪，"學者說。

"但是世界就是這個樣子，"影子回答說，"而且永遠是這個樣子。"於是他走了。

學者沒有一點叫人羨慕的地方。使他傷心和痛苦的事接連而來，他所論述的真善美對於大多數人來說，其價值猶如牛吃牡丹。最後他病倒了。

"你那副樣子真像個影子，"朋友對他說。他聽了不由得渾身一個冷顫，因為他們這話正好說中了他的心事。

"您真的需要去溫泉療養院，"影子又來看他時說。"您沒有別的機會了。看在老相識的份上，我帶您去。您的一切路費我包了，您可以寫遊記供我在路上消遣。我會去溫泉療養院，我的鬍子不能按規矩長出來，這也是病，人必須有鬍子。現在明智一點接受我的建議吧，我們將像親密朋友一樣旅行。"

最後他們一起出發了。如今影子做了主人，主人成了影子。他們一起坐馬車、騎馬和步行，或是肩並肩，或是一前一後，這要看太陽的位置如何而定。影子總是確保自己走在主人的位置，但是學者毫不在意，因為他有一顆善良的心，極其溫和客氣。所以有一天他對影子說："因為我們現在已成為同伴，我們從小就一起長大都結伴而行，不如我們都不說'您'，這樣會更熟絡？"

"您說得對，"影子說道，他現在是正式的主人。"這樣說更直接，但好心不一定做到好事。您是有學問的人，當然知道人的本性有多奇怪。有些人碰不得灰紙，不然會生病；有些人聽到指甲刮玻璃的聲音，會全身發抖。我聽到您對我說'你'就是這種感覺，我覺得自己彷彿就像最初被壓在地上一樣。您看，這是感覺，不是驕傲。您不准跟我説'你'，但我樂意對您説'你'，所以也成功了一半！"

所以影子對前主人説"你"。

"這太糟糕了，"學者想，"我必須説'您'，他就可説'你'。"但他現在不得不按捺住。

最後他們來到了溫泉療養院，那裏有許多外國人，其中有一位公主，她的毛病是眼睛有過份敏鋭的視力，看得人不舒服！

她一下子看到這位新來的人全然與眾不同。"大家説他到這裏來是為了使他的鬍子長出來，"她想，"但是我知道他來的真正原因，他不能投射出一個影子。"

於是她對這件事十分好奇，有一天散步時她和這位奇怪的外國紳士説起話來。身為一位公主，她不必太拘禮，因此她直截了當對他説："您的毛病在於不能投射出一個影子？"

"公主殿下的病一定快要康復了，"他説，"我知道您抱怨眼睛有過份敏鋭的視力，但在這件事情上這毛病完全沒有了。我正好有一個最不尋常的影子，您沒看見有一個人老是在我身邊嗎？別人的影子都很普通，但我不喜歡普通的東西。人們常常用比自己的衣服更好的衣料來給他們的僕人做制服，我就是這樣把我的影子打扮得像一個人。不僅如此，我還給他一個他自己的影子。這很花錢，不過我喜歡我的東西與眾不同。"

"這是怎麼回事？"公主想。"我的毛病真的好了嗎？這一定是世界上最好的溫泉療養院。我們這裏的溫泉有真正神奇的威力。不過我先不離開這裏，因為它開始使我感興趣了。我非常喜歡這位外國人。我只希望他的鬍子不要長出來，不然他馬上要離開了。"

　　晚上公主和影子一起在大舞廳跳舞。她體態輕盈，但是他體態更輕盈，她以前從未遇過這樣好的舞伴。她告訴他自己來自甚麼國家，發現他知道並且到過這個國家，但那時候她不在國內。他曾從窗外看過她父親的皇宮，上面看過，下面也看過。他看到了許多東西，因此公主說甚麼他都能回應，還隱約說出一些事情使她大為吃驚。她想他一定是天下第一聰明人，對他的知識尊敬得五體投地。當她再度和他共舞時，她愛上了他，這一點影子馬上發覺了，因為她盯着看，快把他看出個洞來。他們又跳了一支舞，她差不多要告訴他她愛上他了，但是她比較慎重，她想到了她的國家、她的王位，她有一天要統治的許多百姓。

　　"他是一個聰明人，"她心裏說，"這是一件好事，他跳起舞來令人佩服，這也非常好。但是他有紮實的學問嗎？這也是一個重要問題，我必須先考考他。"於是她問他一些難題，從最容易的開始，連她本人也無法回答，影子聽後做了一個古怪的鬼臉。

　　"您回答不出來？"公主說。"這個問題我小時候就略知一二，"他回答說。"我相信連我的影子，就站在門那邊，也能夠回答。"

　　"您的影子！"公主說。"這的確非常驚人！"

　　"我不說得那麼肯定，"影子說，"不過我想他能回答。他跟隨我多年，聽我說過那麼多話，我想他大致上能做到。不過公主殿下務必讓我說明，他對被當作人看待感到十分自豪，要讓他心情好，這樣他就會正確回答，必須把他作為一個人看待。"

　　"我很樂意這樣做，"公主說。

於是她走到站在門口的學者面前，跟他談太陽，談月亮，談世界上遠遠近近的人，學者謹慎而聰明地對答如流。

"他有一個這樣聰明的影子，他本人一定是個多麼了不起的人啊！"她想。"如果我選擇他做丈夫，這對我的國家和我的百姓來說真是一種福氣啊，我一定要這麼辦。"

於是公主和影子很快就訂了婚，但是在她回國以前，對誰一個字也不說。

"誰也不會知道，"影子說，"連我自己的影子也不知道。"他說這話是有他特殊道理的。

不久，公主回到她統治的國家，影子陪着她回去。

"聽我說，我的好朋友，"影子對學者說，"現在我無比高興，有權有勢，我要對你做一件異常好的事。你可以住在我的皇宮裏，和我一起乘坐皇家馬車，一年有十萬元收入。不過你必須讓每個人稱你做影子，永遠不要斗膽說你曾經是一個人。一年一度，當我在陽光中坐在陽臺上，你必須躺在我的腳下，像影子應做的那樣！我必須告訴你，我要和公主結婚了，我們的婚禮將在今晚舉行！"

"不過這真是太荒唐了！"學者說。"我不能，也絕不屈服於這種傻事。這將是欺騙整個國家，也將是欺騙公主！我要揭發一切，說我是一個人，而你只是一個穿上人衣服的影子！"

"沒有人會相信你的話，"影子說，"現在理智一點吧，不然我就叫衛兵。"

"我直接去見公主，"學者說。

"但是我會比你先去，"影子說，"你會被關進監獄。"結果就是如此，因為衛兵們一知道他要和國王的女兒結婚，都服從他。

"您在發抖，"影子一出現在公主面前，公主說。"出甚麼事了嗎？您今天絕對不能生病，因為今天晚上我們要舉行婚禮。"

"我遇到了最可怕的事，"影子說。"想一想吧，我的影子瘋了，真的。想一想吧，這樣一個淺薄的可憐頭腦承受不了多少東西。他以為他已經變成一個真正的人，而我成了他的影子。"

"太可怕了，"公主叫道，"關起他了嗎？"

"噢，是的，當然，因為我怕他再也好不起來。"

"可憐的影子！"公主說。"他太不幸了。把他從卑微的生命中解脫出來會是一件好事，但當我認真想過這件事，我認為悄悄殺掉他會是上策。"

"這樣對他實在太嚴厲了，因為他曾經是一個忠實的僕人，"影子說着，假裝歎了一口氣。

"您品格真高尚！"公主說。

晚上全城燈火通明，禮炮轟轟鳴響，兵士們持槍行禮。這確實是一個隆重的婚禮！公主和影子步出陽臺露面，接受再一次的歡呼！

所有這些歡慶的聲音，學者一概沒有聽見，因為他已經被處死了。

# 19

# 一個豆莢裏的五顆豆

從前有五顆豌豆住在一個豆莢裏，它們是綠色的，豆莢也是綠色的，因此它們相信整個世界也一定是綠色的，它們得到這個結論十分自然。豆莢長大，這些豌豆也長大，它們按照自己的位置坐成一排。太陽在外面照着，曬暖了豆莢，雨水把它洗得乾淨透明。大白天溫暖舒適，但夜裏黑沉沉，就跟平時一樣。豌豆們坐在那裏越長越大，整天坐着想事情就變得更有腦筋，因為它們覺得它們一定有甚麼別的事可以做。

"我們就這樣永遠坐着嗎？"一顆豌豆問。"坐這麼久我們不會受不了嗎？我覺得外面一定有些甚麼事。"

一個星期又一個星期過去，這些豌豆變黃了，豆莢也變黃了。

"我想是整個世界變黃了，"它們說，也許它們是對的。

忽然它們覺得豆莢被狠狠一拉。它被摘下，握在人的手裏，接着它和其他飽滿的豆莢一起落進了一件外套的口袋。

"現在我們就要被打開了，"一顆豌豆說，這正是它們大家希望的。

"我很想知道，我們當中誰移動得最遠，"五顆豌豆中最小的一顆說，"這個我們很快就可以看到。"

"要發生的事情總會發生，"最大的一顆豌豆說。

豆莢爆開時"劈啪"一聲，五顆豌豆就滾到明亮的陽光中。它們躺在一個孩子的手裏。是個小男孩緊緊握住它們，説它們正好給他的射豆槍當子彈用。他馬上裝上一顆，射它出去了。

　　"如今我在飛到廣闊的世界裏去，"這顆豌豆説，"你有本領就來抓住我吧。"它一下子就飛掉了。

　　"我，"第二顆豌豆説，"要一直飛到太陽上去，那是誰都看到的一個豆莢，正好適合我。"它飛走了。

　　"我們到哪裏就在哪裏睡覺，"接下來兩顆豌豆説，"不過我們還是先得向前滾一下。"它們真的掉到了地板上，在進射豆槍以前滾了一陣，儘管如此，還是被裝進了射豆槍。"我們要比其他豌豆飛得遠，"它們説。

　　"要發生的事總會發生，"最後一顆豌豆從射豆槍裏射出去時大聲説，它説話間飛到閣樓窗下一塊舊木板上，落到一個幾乎滿是青苔和軟泥的小裂縫裏。青苔在它周圍把它埋了，它留在那裏像一個囚徒，但是上帝並不是沒有看到它。

　　"要發生的事總會發生，"它心裏説。

　　這小閣樓裏住着一個貧窮的女人，她出去打掃爐子、劈木柴和做諸如此類的苦工，因為她強壯又勤勞。但她一直這麼貧窮，家裏躺着她唯一的女兒。她發育不全，很孱弱，終年臥床，看起來半死不活。

　　"她要到她的妹妹那裏去了，"那女人説。"我生過兩個孩子，養活兩個可不容易，但是好心的上帝幫了我的忙，接走了其中一個撫養。現在我很高興養着留給我的另一個，但是我想兩姊妹不能分開，我生病的這一個很快也要到天上她妹妹那裏去了。"但是這生病的女孩依然活着，在她的母親離家去工作時，她整天安靜耐心地躺着。

春天到了，一天大清早，陽光明亮地照進小窗，投射到房間地板上。正當母親要出去工作的時候，生病的女孩盯着窗最下面一塊玻璃看，大聲說："媽媽，在窗上朝裏面探頭的那綠色小東西會是甚麼呢？它在風裏晃來晃去的。"

母親走到窗口，把窗打開一半。"噢！"她說。"真有那麼一顆小豌豆，它生了根，長出了綠葉子。它怎麼會鑽進這裂縫的呢？現在好了，這裏有一個小花園給你散散心啦。"於是生病女孩的床移到更近窗戶的位置，這樣她就能看到那發芽的植物，而母親則工作去了。

"媽媽，我相信我會好起來的，"生病的女孩在晚上說，"今天太陽照進來又亮又溫暖，小豆長得那麼好。我也會好起來的，那就又可以到外面溫暖的陽光裏去了。"

"願上帝保佑！"母親說，但是她不相信會能這樣。不過，這小豆既然給了她的孩子這麼美好的求生希望，她於是用一根小棍子支撐起那綠色植物，這樣它就不會被風吹斷了。她又在窗臺上拴一根細繩子，把它牽到窗框的上端，好讓這顆豆的卷鬚繞着它向上爬。卷鬚爬上去了，真可以看到這顆豌豆一天一天在長大。

"現在這裏真的要有一朵花了，"有一天母親說，如今她終於開始希望她生病的女兒會當真好起來。她想起這孩子這些日子說話更加快樂，最近幾天早晨，她在床上已經坐了起來，用閃亮的眼睛去看她那只有一顆豌豆的小花園。一個星期以後，這一直臥床不起的孩子能坐上整整一個鐘頭了，靠近打開的窗，在溫暖的陽光中感到十分快樂，而外面長着那顆小豌豆，在它上面，一朵粉紅色的豌豆花已經盛開。小女孩彎下身體去輕輕地吻那些細嫩的花瓣。這一天對她來說簡直就是一個節慶。

"是我們的天父親自種了這顆豌豆，讓它生長，讓它枝繁葉茂，把快樂帶給你，把希望帶給我，我幸運的孩子，"開心的母親說，她對着這朵花微笑，就像它是上帝派來的天使。

但是其他幾顆豌豆又怎麼樣了呢？飛到廣闊世界去，説"你有本領就來抓住我吧"的那顆豌豆落到一座房子屋頂的水槽裏，在一隻鴿子的嘴巴裏結束了它的旅行。那兩顆懶豌豆也只走了那麼遠，因為它們也被鴿子吃掉了，不過它們到底還是有點用處。但是第四顆，要到達太陽的那一顆，落到了一個污水池裏，在污水裏躺了許多天、許多星期，直到脹得大大。

"我胖得夠了，現在剛剛好，"這顆豌豆説，"我想我最後會胖得爆開，我想一顆豌豆頂多也只能做到這樣。在我們那豆莢裏的五顆豌豆當中，我最了不起了。"污水池贊成它的看法。

但是那小女孩站在打開的閣樓窗戶，眼睛閃亮，臉蛋透出健康紅潤的面色，在豌豆花上合起瘦削的雙手，感謝上帝所做的一切。

"我贊同我那顆豌豆，"污水池説。

# 20
# 她是個廢物

**市**長站在開着的窗前面。他看起來很瀟灑,因為他別着
胸針的襯衫褶邊和褶襇花邊都十分漂亮。他把他的下
巴刮得特別光滑,雖然他微微割破了自己一點,在那上面貼了一
小片報紙。"聽着,小傢伙!"他叫道。

他對着講話的男孩不是別人,而是一個貧窮洗衣婦的兒子,
他正好在這房子前面走過。他停下來,恭恭敬敬地摘下他的鴨舌
帽。鴨舌帽的帽舌已經從中間斷掉,這樣他很容易就能捲起帽子
放到他的衣袋裏去。他穿着他那不體面但乾淨、補得很好的衣
服,腳上蹬着沉重的木頭鞋,站在市長面前,看起來謙恭得好像
面對着國王本人。

"你是個有禮貌的好孩子,"市長説。"我想你的母親正忙着
在下面河邊洗衣服,你一定是在給她送去你衣袋裏的東西。對你
母親來説這是非常不好的。那裏面你弄到了多少?"

"只有半斤,"孩子用害怕的聲音吞吞吐吐地説。

"今天早晨她已經喝過這麼多了吧?"

"不,那是昨天,"孩子回答説。

"兩個半斤就是整整一斤了,"市長説。"她是個廢物。這些
人,真是可悲。你去對你的母親説,她應該為她自己感到羞恥。

你可不要變成酒鬼，但是我想你會的。可憐的孩子，好，現在走吧。"

孩子繼續走他的路，手裏拿着他的鴨舌帽，風吹拂着他的金髮，把一縷縷髮絲吹得豎了起來。他在街角拐彎，走進通往河邊去的小巷。他母親正站在河水裏她的洗衣凳旁邊，用一根很重的木棍捶打着被單。磨坊的水閘門已經打開，當水很快地滾滾而來的時候，被單被流水帶走，幾乎把洗衣凳都掀翻了，因此洗衣婦不得不趴在它上面按住它。"我幾乎都要被沖走了，"她說。"你來得正好，我要點東西提提神。在水裏真冷，我已經在水裏站了六個鐘頭。你給我拿來甚麼了嗎？"

孩子從衣袋裏掏出瓶子，他母親馬上放它到嘴邊，喝了一點。

"啊，真是好東西，讓我多暖和啊，"她說。"它像頓熱飯一樣好，又沒那麼貴。喝一點吧，我的孩子。你看起來十分蒼白，衣服單薄，你都在發抖了，真正入秋天啦。噢，水多涼啊！但願我不會生病。不，我絕不可以怕生病。再給我來一點，你也可以喝一些，不過只是抿一抿，你絕不可以喝慣，我可憐的小寶貝。"她從河裏走上孩子站着的橋上，來到岸邊。水從圍着她身體的草蓆、從她的衣服上滴滴答答落下來。"我賣力工作，我兩隻可憐的手痛得要命，"她說，"但是我心甘情願這樣做，讓我可以誠實、正直地養大你，我的小寶貝。"

這時，一個比她年長的女人走向他們。她看起來很叫人難受，一條瘸腿，在她的一隻眼睛上垂下一大束假鬈髮，這隻眼是盲的。這鬈髮是要遮蓋這盲眼，但它只令這隻眼更加明顯。她是洗衣婦的朋友，鄰里稱她為"鬈髮瘸腿瑪莎"。"哦，你這可憐的東西，你怎麼會站在水裏工作！"她大聲說道。"你確實需要一些東西來給你帶來一點溫暖，然而惡意的人因為你喝幾滴酒就大吵大嚷。"然後瑪莎在幾分鐘內告訴洗衣婦，市長對洗衣婦兒子說的話，這些話她無意中聽到了。而且她非常生氣的是，竟然有人可以對一個孩子說他母親的壞話，就如市長所做，就只因為他母親喝了幾滴酒。她更生氣的是，在那一天，市長將要舉行一場晚宴，在那裏會有酒，而且是烈酒，一瓶一瓶地喝掉。"許多人會比他們該喝的喝更多，但他們不叫這做飲酒！他們沒做錯，你就是廢物！"瑪莎憤怒地喊道。

"他是那樣對你說的嗎，我的孩子？"洗衣婦說，說話時嘴唇在顫抖。"他說你有個是廢物的媽媽。不過他也許是對的，但是他不該把這話說給我的孩子聽。在那個家我經歷了多少事啊！"

"不是嗎？"瑪莎說。"我記得那個市長的父母還活着的時候，你在他家打工，住在那房子裏，那是多少年前的事情啦。打從那以後不知多少鹽吃了下去，人們大概很渴了，"瑪莎微笑起來。"市長今天的盛大晚宴本該延期，但是消息來得太晚了。那僕人告訴我說，菜都已經做好，才接到信說市長在哥本哈根的弟弟死了。"

"死了！"洗衣婦叫起來，面色一下子蒼白得像死人。

"是的，沒錯，"瑪莎回答說，"不過你為甚麼為這事這樣傷心啊？我想你許多年前就認識他，你還在那裏打工的時候。"

"他死了嗎？"她大聲說。"噢，他是那麼一個善良好心的人，像他那樣的人還真不多，"她說話時淚水滾下她的臉頰。接着她叫道："噢，天啊，我覺得很不舒服，周圍的東西都在打轉，我受不了啦。瓶子空了嗎？"她說着，靠在木板上。

"天啊，你真病了，"那女人說。"快，振作起來，也許一會就好。不對，我看你真的病了，我最好還是送你回家去。"

"不過我洗的東西在那裏。"

"我會收拾它們。來吧，把你的手臂給我。孩子可以留在這裏看着那些東西，我再回來把它們洗完，衣服並不多。"

洗衣婦的腿在發抖，她說："我在冷水裏站得太久了，從早晨起一整天沒吃過東西。噢，仁慈的上帝啊，幫助我回家吧，我全身燒得滾燙。噢，我可憐的孩子，"她痛哭起來。而他，可憐的孩子，一個人坐在河邊，緊靠濕被單，守着它們，也在哭。

兩個女人走得非常慢。洗衣婦搖搖晃晃、跌跌撞撞地走過小巷，繞過街角，走進市長住的那條街。當她來到市長那座房子的門口時，她在行人路上暈倒了。許多人過來圍住她，瘸腿瑪莎跑進那座房子求救。市長和他那些客人來到窗前。

"哦，是那個洗衣婦，"他說，"她喝多了。她是個廢物。對她那個漂亮的年幼兒子來說真是一件傷心事情。我倒很喜歡那個孩子，不過他的母親是個廢物。"

過了一會洗衣婦自己恢復了知覺，大家扶她回到她那可憐的住處，放她到床上。體貼的瑪莎給她熱了一杯啤酒，在裏面加入牛油和糖，她認為這是最好的藥，然後趕到河邊又是洗又是絞。說實在的，洗得很不好，但是她已經盡了力。接着她把洗過的被單拉上岸，就那麼濕漉漉的放到籃子裏。天黑前她和洗衣婦一起坐在那可憐的小房間裏。市長的廚師給她一些烤馬鈴薯和一塊很好的肥肉帶給病人。這些東西瑪莎和孩子吃得津津有味，但是病人説，她只要聞聞它們的氣味已是夠有營養的。過了一會，孩子上床了，就睡在他媽媽躺着的同一張床上。不過他睡在她的腳下，蓋一張用藍色和白色破布拼起來的舊被子。這時候洗衣婦覺得好了些。熱啤酒使她有了點力氣，好食物的香味也使她愉快起來。

"多謝你，你這好人，"她對瑪莎説。"現在孩子睡着了，我來告訴你一切。他很快就睡着。他閉上眼睛躺在那裏，樣子多麼溫柔可愛啊！他不知道他的母親吃了多大的苦，老天保佑他永遠不會知道。我在顧問官，即是市長的父親那裏當僕人，正好碰上他最小的兒子，那位學生，回家來。那時候我是個年輕野女孩，但是很老實，這一點我可以對天發誓。那學生快樂、勇敢、溫和、親切。他身上的每一滴血都是美好而高尚的，天底下沒有更好的人了。他是這一家的少爺，而我只是一個僕人，但是他真誠地愛我，並把這件事告訴了他的母親。對他來説，他母親是人世間的天使，她是那麼聰明美麗。他要去旅行，臨行前他把一枚金戒指戴到我的手指上。他一走出房子，我的太太就把我叫來。她溫和而莊重地拉我到她的身邊，像一個天使那樣對我説話。她清楚地讓我知道他和我之間在精神上和實質上的差別。'他現在喜歡你漂亮的臉，'她説，'但是美貌是不長久的。你沒有像他那樣受過教育。你們在學識和身份上都不相稱，不幸就在於此。我是尊重窮人的，'她説下去。'在上帝面前，他們可能比許多富人具有更高的地位，但是在這裏人世間，我們必須小心不要誤入歧途，不然我們的打算就會落空，就像一輛馬車行駛在一條危險的路上翻車一樣。我認識一個很好的人，他是工匠，他想要娶你。我說的是艾力，那個做手套的師傅。他死了老婆，沒有孩子，境遇很好。你考慮一下好嗎？'她說的每一個字像尖刀一樣刺痛我的心，但是我知道她是對的，這想法沉重地壓在我的心頭上。我吻了她的手，流下痛苦的眼淚，回到我的房間撲倒在床，哭得更傷心了。我熬過了一個可怕的長夜，上帝知道我受了多大的折磨，我是怎樣地掙扎。接下來的禮拜天我去教堂祈求上帝指引我。就像是天意，我一走出教堂，艾力就向我走來，於是我心中的疑慮全消。我們在身份和境遇上都相對。他甚至還可以說是一個有錢的人。我走到他面前，握住他的手，說道：'你對我的心依然沒有變嗎？''是的，永遠不會變，'他說。'那麼你願意和一個尊敬你但不愛你的女孩結婚嗎？不過愛情以後可能會產生。''是的，愛情以後會產生，'他說。於是我們談妥了，我回到太太的家裏。我把她兒子給我的金戒指藏在懷裏。白天我不能戴它在我的手上，只能在晚上，當我上床時，我把戒指吻了又吻，直到嘴唇都要流出血來。然後我把戒指還給太太，告訴她說，我和手套師傅的結婚公告將在下星期發佈。於是太太擁抱我，吻我。她沒有說我是'廢物'，大概我那時比現在更有用一些，但是我當時對這世界上的不幸還一無所知。我們在米迦勒節　結了婚，第一年我們一切順利。我們有一個伙計和一個學徒，而瑪莎你也來做了我們的僕人。"

"啊，對，你是一位美麗的好太太，"瑪莎說，"我永遠不會忘記你和你丈夫對我有多麼好。"

"不錯，你和我們在一起那幾年是快樂的日子，雖然我們起先沒有孩子。我再也沒有和那學生見過面。但是我見過他一次，不過他沒有看見我。他回來參加他母親的葬禮。我看見他站在他母親的墳前，看起來臉色蒼白得像死人，十分痛苦，因為那是他的母親。過了一些時候，他的父親也死了，那時他在國外沒有回家。我知道他一直沒有結婚，我相信他成了一名律師。他已經忘記我了，即使我們見面，他也不會認出我，因為我已經失去我的美貌，也許這樣更好。"接着她談了她苦難的日子，這時不幸落到了他們夫婦頭上。

"我們有了五百元，"她說，"街上有一座房子要出售，售價是兩百元，因此我們想，我們值得買下它，拆掉並在原地造一座新的，於是我們把它買下來了。營造商和木匠估計造新房子要花一千零二十元。艾力很有信用，因此他在首都借到了錢。但是帶錢回來給他的船長遇到了沉船事故，錢也丟了。就在這時候，如今睡在這裏的我那小寶貝出世了，我的丈夫患上了嚴重的長期病患。有九個月我不得不服侍他穿衣服和脫衣服。我們不但還不出錢，還借了更多債，我們所有的一切都失去了，賣掉了，接着我的丈夫去世了。打從那以後，我為了孩子工作、苦幹和拼命。我不分粗細衣物都拿來又擦又洗，但我沒有辦法改善生活，這是上帝的旨意。在他認為合適的時候，他會帶我到他那裏去，但是我知道他永遠不會遺棄我的孩子。接着她睡着了。天亮時她覺得精神好得多，認為有足夠的力氣繼續做她的工作。但是她剛踏到冷水裏，只感到一陣頭暈。她的手在空中亂抓，向前踏了一步，隨即倒了下來。她的頭跌在地上，但是雙腳在水裏，只用一束乾草繫在腳上的兩隻木頭鞋被水沖走了。當瑪莎來這裏給她送點咖啡的時候，看到她正是這個樣子。

就在這時候，市長派人到她家，要她務必馬上去見他，他有話要跟她説。但是太晚了，一個外科醫生被請來給她在手臂上放血，但是這個可憐的女人已經死了。

"她喝酒喝死了，"殘酷的市長説。在報告他弟弟死訊的信裏寫明，他遺囑中要贈予曾給他母親當女僕的手套匠寡婦六百元，這筆遺贈應根據實際需要，以或大或小的數目付給寡婦或者她的孩子。

"我記得我弟弟和她有過點甚麼事，"市長説。"她死了倒是件好事，因為這孩子現在可以得到全部錢了。我要把他交給老實人家領養，使他能成為一個正派的工人。願上帝賜福這些話。"於是市長把孩子叫來，答應照顧他，但極其殘酷無情地加上一句，説他的母親死了是一件好事，因為"她是個廢物"。人們抬她到教堂墓地，埋葬窮人的教堂墓地。瑪莎在墳上撒上黃沙，在上面栽了一棵玫瑰樹，孩子站在她身邊。

"噢，我可憐的媽媽！"他叫道，同時熱淚滾下他的兩頰。"他們説她是個廢物，這是真的嗎？"

"不，這當然不是真的，"老女僕回答説，抬起眼睛朝天上看。"她非常有用。我在許多年前就知道這一點，在她生命的最後一夜以後，我比以前更加確信這一點。我説她是一個好人，一個可敬的人，在天上的上帝知道我説的是真話，儘管世上的人到現在還會説她是個廢物。"

# 21

# 笨蛋漢斯

在遙遠的地方有一座豪華的古宅，古宅裏住着它的老主人，老主人有兩個兒子，這兩個年輕人都自以為聰明透頂。他們要遠道去向國王的女兒求婚，因為這位女孩公開宣佈，她要物色一個説話最有條理的小伙子做自己的丈夫。

於是這兩位天才為求婚準備了整整一個星期，他們就只能有這麼多時間。不過這點時間也足夠了，因為他們本來就大有學問，人人都知道這多麼有用處。其中一個早把整本拉丁文字典，還有這小鎮整整三年的日報，全都背得滾瓜爛熟，熟得要順着背就順着背，要倒着背就倒着背，都一樣背誦如流。另一個則精通公司法，每一家公司應該知道的所有條文他都爛熟於胸。因此他自認為可以暢談國家大事，在議會可以阻撓別人的行動。外加他還會一件事，就是在背帶上繡上玫瑰和別的花，還有阿拉伯式花紋，因為他是一個手指靈活的雅士。

"我會得到公主！"他們兩個都這樣嚷着説。於是他們的老父親給了他們一人一匹駿馬。會背字典和報紙的那個年輕人得到一匹黑馬，對公司法無所不曉的那個年輕人得到一匹奶白色的馬。接着他們用魚油抹抹嘴角，這樣他們就會變得油嘴滑舌，能説會道了。所有僕人都站在下面院子裏看着他們上馬，這時候碰巧第三個兒子來了。古宅老主人其實有三個兒子，不過沒有人把這第三個兒子和他兩個哥哥算在一起，因為他沒有他們有學問，說實在的，大家叫他做"笨蛋漢斯"。

"喂！"笨蛋漢斯說，"你們這是到哪裏去啊？我說你們都穿上了最好的衣服！"

"我們上皇宮去向國王的女兒求婚。你沒聽說過全國都知道的佈告嗎？"於是他們把事情一五一十地告訴了他。

"啊！我也要去！"笨蛋漢斯叫起來，他的兩個哥哥對他哈哈大笑，接着騎馬走了。

"我的好爸爸，"漢斯說，"我也要一匹馬。我太想娶老婆了！如果那女孩要我，她可以得到我；如果她不要我，我還是要得到她。她反正要成為我的人！"

"不要胡說八道，"老紳士回答說。"你別想從我這裏得到馬。你不會講話，你說話沒有條理。你的兩個哥哥和你完全不一樣。"

"好吧，"笨蛋漢斯說，"如果我不能得到一匹馬，我就騎公羊去，牠本來就是我的，牠照樣能帶我去。"

他這麼說就這麼辦。他騎上公羊，用腳跟夾着牠的身體，就順着大街像颶風一樣飛快地跑起來了。

"呵！這才騎得痛快呢！我來了！"笨蛋漢斯大喊大叫，還唱起歌來，直唱得他的歌聲在四面八方發出迴響。

他的兩個哥哥在他前面騎馬走得很慢。他們一言不發，因為他們各自埋頭在想他們臨時可能要講的漂亮言詞，這些話必須預先好好地準備妥當。

"喂！"笨蛋漢斯在後面叫道。"我來了！看我在大路上找到了甚麼。"他給他們看是甚麼，是隻死烏鴉。

"笨蛋！"兩個哥哥說，"你要拿牠來做甚麼？"

"拿這隻烏鴉做甚麼嗎？那還用說，我要送牠給公主。"

"好，你就送吧，"他們說，然後哈哈大笑着騎馬走了。

"喂，我又來了！來看看我這一回找到了甚麼，這樣的東西在大路上不是每天都能找到！"

兩個哥哥回過頭去看他這一回又找到甚麼。

"笨蛋！"他們叫道。"那只是一隻舊木頭鞋，而且鞋面都沒有了。你要把這個也送給公主嗎？"

"那還用說，我當然送，"笨蛋漢斯回答說。兩個哥哥又哈哈大笑着騎馬走了。就這樣，他們走在他前面很遠。但是……

"喂 —— 呵啦啦！"又是笨蛋漢斯。"事情越來越妙了，"他叫道。"萬歲！這真是一流。"

"怎麼，這一回你又找到甚麼了？"兩個哥哥問道。

"噢，"笨蛋漢斯說，"我幾乎沒法對你們說。公主見了會多高興啊！"

"呸！"兩個哥哥說，"那不過是在溝裏挖上來的泥濘。"

"對，當然是泥濘，"笨蛋漢斯說，"是一種最好的泥濘。看，它那麼濕漉漉，從人的手指間流過。"他裝了一衣袋的爛泥濘。

但是他的兩個哥哥不聽他的話，放馬飛奔，直跑得馬蹄下火星直冒，比傑克早了整整一個小時到城門口。這時候，在城門口每個求婚的人都獲派編號，他們一到就馬上讓他們排隊，六個人一排，擠得他們手臂都沒法動。這真是個謹慎的安排，因為他們如果稍微能動一動，哪怕只是因為其中一個站到另一個前面，就會動起拳頭來。

城裏所有的國民都大羣大羣地圍着皇宮，幾乎擠到窗底下，要看公主怎樣接待向她求婚的人。每一個求婚的人一進大廳，他的說話能力就好像喪失了，如同蠟燭光給吹滅了一樣。於是公主會說："他一點用處也沒有！帶他離開大廳吧！"

最後輪到會背字典的那個哥哥，但是他現在背不出來了，他已經把它忘得一乾二淨。地板好像隨着他的腳步響起回聲，大廳的天花板是鏡子做的，因此他看見他自己倒立着。窗口站着三個秘書和一個秘書長，他們每一個都正在記下說出來的每一個字，好把它印在報紙上，到街頭上去賣一個錢。這真是可怕的煎熬，再加上火爐裏火生得那麼旺，屋子裏好像熱燙燙。

"這裏熱得真可怕！"第一個哥哥說。

"對，"公主回答，"我父王今天要吃烤雞。"

"咩！"他站在那裏像隻羊咩咩。他對這樣的談話一點也沒有準備，雖然想講點風趣的話，但是一句也說不出來。"咩！"

"他一點用處也沒有！"公主說。"帶他出去！"

他因此只好走出大廳。這一回輪到第二個哥哥進來了。

"這裏熱得真可怕！"他說。

"對，我們今天在烤雞，"公主答道。

"甚麼……甚麼……你說甚……"他口吃着說，所有秘書記下來："甚麼……甚麼……你說甚……"

"他一點用處也沒有！"公主說。"帶他出去！"

這一回輪到了笨蛋漢斯。他騎着他那隻公羊進大廳。

"哎呀，這裏熱壞了。"

"對，因為我在烤雞，"公主回答説。

"啊，真幸運！"笨蛋漢斯大聲説。"因為我想你會讓我順便烤我的烏鴉吧？"

"十分歡迎，"公主説。"但是你有甚麼東西可以裝着牠烤嗎？因為我沒有煲也沒有煎鍋。"

"我當然有！"漢斯説。"這是個有鐵把手的煎鍋。"

他拿出了那隻舊木頭鞋，放烏鴉到裏面。

"哈，那倒是一道名菜！"公主説。"但是我們怎麼去找調味汁呢？"

"噢，我衣袋裏有，"漢斯説。"我多的是，丟掉點也無所謂，"他説着，從他的衣袋裏倒出一點爛泥濘。

"我喜歡這樣！"公主説。"你回答得出，你有話可説，因此你將做我的丈夫。不過你注意到沒有，我們説的每個字都記下來了，要在明天的報紙發表？你看那邊，你可以看到在每個窗戶有三個秘書和一個秘書長，要數老秘書長最糟糕，因為他甚麼也聽不懂。"

但是她説這番話只是想嚇嚇笨蛋漢斯。幾個秘書高興得發出很響的笑聲，每一個都從鋼筆上濺一滴墨水到地上。

"噢，那些人是紳士，對嗎？"漢斯説。"那麼我送我最好的東西給秘書長。"他説着，翻轉他的衣袋，把爛泥濘擲向秘書長一臉。

"做得真聰明，"公主説。"這樣我還做不到，不過遲早會學會的。"

這樣，笨蛋漢斯就當上了國王，得到了皇冠和妻子，坐上了王位。這份報紙油墨未乾，我們就從秘書長的印刷機和印刷廠拿到手，不過它們一點也靠不住。

# 22
# 瓶頸

**緊**靠街的轉角，在許多窮人的住屋中間，有一座特別高而窄的房子，它日久失修，四面八方都好像脱了臼似的。這房子裏住的都是窮人，而最窮的顯然是閣樓上的那一家。小窗前有一個歪斜的舊鳥籠掛在陽光裏，它裏面連個好好的水杯也沒有，當水杯用的是一個破瓶頸，倒過來，用塞子塞着下面的瓶口，讓它盛滿水。一位老女士坐在窗口，她剛在鳥籠上面掛上繁縷草，鳥籠裏的小朱頂雀從一根棲木跳到另一根棲木，吱吱喳喳快快樂樂唱着歌。

"是的，你的歌聲真不錯，"瓶頸説。當然，它不是真的和我們一樣説話，因為瓶頸不會説話，但是它在自己的心裏這樣説就像人有時在心裏説話那樣。

"是的，你完全可以唱歌，因為你的肢體完好無損。你應該體會一下，像我這樣失去了身體，只剩下一條頸和一個嘴，嘴上還塞着個塞子，這到底是甚麼滋味。我想沒錯，這一來你就不會唱了。不過有人能快快樂樂也很好。我卻沒有理由唱歌，即使我快樂，我現在也唱不出歌來。不過當我還是個完整的瓶子時，他們用個塞子把我一擦，我不是也唱了嗎？那時候，我通常獲稱為十全十美的雲雀。我記得那時我和毛皮商人一家出去野餐，那天他女兒正好訂婚，想起來好像還是昨天的事。我回憶一下，我一生經歷的事還真不少：我曾經到過火裏和水裏去，我曾經深深留在泥土裏，我曾經比大多數人到過更高的地方，而現在我在一個鳥籠外面，在這裏半空中，在陽光裏晃來晃去。噢，我的故事實在值得聽聽。不過我不把它説出聲來，這是由於一個很充份的理由，因為我不能説話。"

瓶頸於是開始講它那個的確十分出色的故事。不過，説實在的，它是在講給自己聽，或者至少是在自己的心裏想。這時小鳥在快活地唱牠自己的歌，下面街上人們坐車的坐車，走路的走路，來來往往，各想各的心事，或者也許根本甚麼也不想，但是瓶頸埋頭在想它自己的事情。它想起工廠裏那個烈火熊熊的熔爐，它就是在那工廠裏被吹出來而誕生的。它回憶起它被放進那個爐 —— 它的老家 —— 時它覺得有多熱，恨不得馬上再跳出來。但是過了一會爐子涼些了，它覺得非常舒服。它被放在一大排同爐的兄弟姊妹中間，其中有些被吹成香檳酒瓶，有些被吹成啤酒瓶，它們之間都有點區別。這個世界上常有這樣的事，啤酒瓶會裝上最貴重的酒，而香檳酒瓶卻裝上黑色塗料，但是人即使衰敗了也總能看出他出身好不好。貴族總是貴族，正如香檳酒瓶即使裝了黑色塗料還是香檳酒瓶一樣。當所有酒瓶裝箱時，我們這個酒瓶也裝在其中。那時候它沒有想過到頭來會成為一個瓶頸，或者用作鳥籠的盛水器，不過這也是一個光榮的位置，因為在世界上還有點用處。這瓶子裝箱以後再看不到天日，直到在酒商的地窖裏和其他瓶子一起被拆箱拿出來，接着它第一次被水沖洗，這給人一種很古怪的感覺。它就躺在那裏，空空的，塞子也還沒有，這時它有一種奇怪的心情，好像想要點甚麼，但是也不知道要甚麼。最後它被灌滿了貴重的美酒，塞了塞子，封了口。接着被貼上"上等"的標籤，就像在考試中得了第一名似的。再說，酒和酒瓶兩者都是好的，我們年輕時正是詩的時代。瓶裏響起了歌聲，唱着它不明白的東西，唱着陽光普照的青山，山上長着葡萄藤，快樂的葡萄園工人又是笑又是唱，嘻嘻哈哈。"啊，生活是多麼美好啊。"瓶子裏所有這些快樂歌聲就像年輕詩人腦裏的活動，它常常不明白它腦裏響起的那些聲音到底是甚麼意思。有一天早晨，這瓶子找到了買主，是那毛皮商人的學徒，他被派來買一瓶最好的酒。瓶子被放進食物籃，跟火腿、芝士和香腸放在一起。最好的新鮮牛油和最好的麵包是毛皮商人的女兒親手放進籃子的，因為是她裝籃子。她年輕貌美，棕色的眼睛笑吟吟，她的嘴角也一直帶笑，這微笑和眼睛上的一樣甜。她有一雙柔嫩的手，白得可愛，而她的脖子還要白。一眼就能看出來，她是個非常美麗的女孩，卻還沒有結婚。當一家人乘車到樹林中去時，食物籃放在她的膝上，瓶頸從白餐巾的摺口間朝外張望。瓶塞上有紅封蠟，瓶子一直向那年輕女孩的臉上看，還看坐在她旁邊的那個年輕水手的臉。他是她的年輕朋友，父親是一位肖像畫家。他最近考試獲得優等，成為大副，第二天早晨就要乘船遠航了。裝籃子時他們兩個就這件事情談了許多話，談話中，毛皮商人女兒的眼睛和嘴上沒有了那種十分高興的神情。這對年輕人漫步走到青翠的林中，交談着。他們談些甚麼呢？瓶子說不上來，因為它在食物籃裏。瓶子在籃子裏留了很久，等到它最後被拿出來時，它感到發生了甚麼喜事，因為人人都在笑，毛皮商人的女兒也笑了，但是她不說話，兩頰像兩朵紅玫瑰。接着她的父親拿起瓶子和拔瓶塞的鑽子。讓瓶塞第一次給拔掉，那是一種何等奇怪的感覺啊！在那以後，瓶子永遠忘不了那一時刻的場面。的確，當瓶塞飛出去的時候，它心中突然一陣震動，在酒斟到玻璃杯裏時，發出咯咯咯的聲音。

"祝未婚夫妻健康，"父親叫道，每一杯酒都乾了，這時年輕的水手親吻他美麗的未婚妻。

"祝你們兩個幸福快樂，"父親和母親兩老雙雙說，年輕水手又斟滿所有玻璃杯。

"安全返航，明年今天舉行婚禮，"他叫道。當大家又乾了杯以後，他拿起酒瓶，高高舉起它說："你在我一生這個最快樂的日子裏在場，你將不再被別人所用！"他說着，把酒瓶高高地扔上空中。

毛皮商人的女兒想，她再也不會看見這個酒瓶，但是她錯了。瓶子落到一個林中小湖泊邊的燈心草叢中。瓶頸記得很清楚它在那裏躺了有多久，誰也看不見它。"我給他們酒，可他們給我泥漿水，"它心裏說，"但是我想他們的本意是好的。"它再也看不到那對未婚夫妻，也看不到那對快樂的老夫妻，但是它好半天還聽到他們在歡慶和唱歌。最後終於來了兩個農家孩子，他們往蘆葦叢中窺看，發現了這個瓶子。他們於是把它拿起來帶回家，這樣它又一次有了歸宿。在他們那間木屋裏，這兩個孩子有一個哥哥，也是一個水手，他正準備去遠航。他昨天回來告別，他的母親這一刻忙得不可開交，正在為他收拾各種要帶出門的東西。晚上他的父親要帶這包東西進城去，再看看他的兒子，並代孩子的母親説句告別的話。這時一個小瓶子已經灌好攙上了白蘭地的藥草汁，裹起來了。但這時候兩個孩子回來了，拿着他們找到的這個更大更厚實的瓶子。這瓶子比那小瓶子可以多裝許多，人們都説白蘭地對胃病大有好處，特別是攙上了藥草汁以後。於是這個瓶子裏現在灌進去的已經不是原先裝的紅酒，而是苦的藥酒，但是它有時候極其有用——對胃來説。如今要送去的不是小瓶子，而是新的大瓶子了，因此這瓶子又一次上路。它被帶上了船（因為彼得·贊森是船上的一名水手），這正好就是那個年輕大副要乘的那艘船。不過大副沒有看到這瓶子，説實在的，即使看見了它也不會認得，或者猜到這就是曾經斟出酒來，為未婚夫妻的幸福，為預祝他開心快活返航回來後舉行婚禮而乾杯的那個瓶子。當然，瓶子再也斟不出酒來，但是它裝着同樣好的東西。因此，彼得·贊森每次拿它出來，他那些伙伴就稱它為“藥劑師”，因為它裝着醫治胃病的良藥，只要一滴尚存，彼得很樂意分一點給別人。這真是快樂的日子，用塞子一摩擦瓶子就唱歌，所以大家又稱它為“大雲雀”、“彼得·贊森的雲雀”。

漫長的一天天、一個個月過去，那瓶子早已空了，站在一個角落裏。有一天來了暴風雨——到底是在出航或是在回家的路上，它就説不出來了，因為它從來沒有上過岸。這是一場可怕的暴風雨，巨浪掀起，把船狂暴地搖來晃去。主桅折成幾段，船裂了口，抽水機也沒有用，而周圍黑得像在夜裏。在船沉下去的最後時刻，年輕的大副在一張紙上寫道：“我們在下沉。聽從上帝的旨意。”接着他寫下他未婚妻的名字、他自己的名字和船名。他隨即把這張紙塞進正好在他手頭的一個空瓶子裏，把塞子塞緊，扔到浪花飛濺的大海裏。他並不知道，這就是曾為他掛滿了快樂和希望的酒杯的同一個瓶子，如今他帶着他最後的祝福和死者的音信正在波浪上顛簸。船沉下去了，船員和它一起沉下去了。但是瓶子像一隻鳥兒那樣向前飛着，因為它裏面裝着一顆用愛心寫下的情信。當太陽升起和落下時，瓶子感到像在它最初存在的時刻，當時它在烈火熊熊的滾燙火爐裏渴望着飛走。它熬過了一場又一場暴風雨，又經歷了風平浪靜的順境，它沒有撞上礁石，也沒有被鯊魚吞噬，但漂流了一年多，有時向北，有時向南，流水帶它到哪裏就到哪裏。它可以算是自由自在了，但即使如此也是會厭倦的。那張字條，未婚夫給未婚妻的最後告別信，一旦到達她的手裏也只會帶來悲哀。但那雙手，那雙在她的訂婚日裏曾鋪枱布在翠綠林中的新鮮草地上的如此嬌嫩的手，它們在哪裏呢？啊，對啊，毛皮商的女兒在哪裏呢？離她家可能最近的那塊土地在哪裏呢？

瓶子不知道，它只是一味向前漂流，到頭來，一味這樣漂流變得厭倦了。不管怎麼說，漂流到底不是它的慣常工作。但是它只好漂流，直到最後漂到了陸地——一個陌生的國家。這個國家裏說的話瓶子一個字也聽不懂，這種話它以前從來沒有聽過，不會一種語言真是一個莫大的損失。瓶子從水裏被撈上來，每處都被仔細檢查過。它裏面裝的那封小信被發現了，拿出來被傳來傳去看，但是那裏的人怎麼也看不懂上面寫的是甚麼。他們可以斷定，這瓶子是從船上扔到水裏的，紙上寫着船發生了甚麼事情，只是寫的是甚麼呢？問題就在這裏，因此字條被重新放回瓶子裏，瓶子和紙一起放到城裏一座大房子的櫃子裏。只要有外國人來到這地方，那張紙就被拿出來翻來覆去看，到頭來，只是用鉛筆寫的地址都幾乎模糊得認不出來了，最後根本沒有人再能認出一個字母。瓶子在那櫃子裏留了整整一年，然後被送到上面閣樓，在那裏很快就罩滿了灰塵和蜘蛛網。唉！那時候它多麼經常地想起那些好日子——想起在清新的翠綠樹林裏，它曾斟出美酒；想到被浪頭搖來晃去時，它懷着一個秘密、一封信和一個最後的別離歎息。整整二十個年頭它就這樣站在閣樓上，要不是這座房子要重建，它也許還要留下去。當屋頂被拆掉時，瓶子被發現了。人們在講它，但是瓶子不明白他們在講它甚麼——這樣留在閣樓上，哪怕是留了二十年，也學不會一種語言。"如果我在下面房間裏，"瓶子想，"我也許就學會了。"現在它被洗刷一番，這樣做的確有必要，等到洗刷完，它看起來乾淨透明，覺得返老還童了，不過它那麼忠心耿耿地帶着的那張字條卻在洗刷時毀掉了。他們在瓶子裏裝滿種子，雖然它一點也不知道給它裝的是甚麼。接着他們緊緊地塞上塞子，小心地包好。連火把或者提燈的光也透不到它那裏，更不用說日光或者月光了。瓶子想："人旅行至少可以看到許多東西，而我卻甚麼也看不見。"不過它也做了一件同樣重要的事，它終於來到了它想到的地方，包裝被打開來。

"他們費了多少功夫才把那瓶子從那邊帶到這裏來啊！"有一個人說。"它很可能破了。"但是瓶子沒有破，更好的是，現在他們說的每一個字它都能聽懂。這種語言它在熔爐裏；在酒商那裏；在林中和船上都聽過——這是它能聽懂的唯一一種美好的熟悉語言。它已經回到家，那語言好像就是對它的歡迎。由於喜出望外，它覺得已經準備好從人的手上跳下來，幾乎沒注意到它的塞子已經拔掉，裏面裝的東西倒空，它被拿到了地窖，扔在那裏被忘掉了。"沒有地方比得上家鄉好，哪怕這是個地窖。"它想也沒想過它會在這裏一年一年住下去，它覺得太舒服了。它在地窖裏留了許多個漫長的歲月，直到最後有人來拿走瓶子，把我們的這一個也拿去了。

外面花園裏在開盛大的慶祝會。閃亮的燈籠掛在一棵樹連一棵樹的彩帶上，光從紙燈籠裏照射出來，使它們看起來像透明的鬱金香。這是一個美麗的夜晚，天氣溫和晴朗。星星閃爍着，一彎新月被滿月的影子圍繞，像是一個帶金邊的灰色球體。對於眼睛好的人來説，這是一幅美景。月光一直延伸到花園最僻靜的小徑，至少不使它僻靜得讓人在那裏迷路。花園的邊沿放着些瓶子，每個瓶子裏都有燈光，它們中間就有我們認識的那個瓶子，它的命運是有朝一日只剩了個瓶頸，作鳥籠的盛水杯之用。但當時對我們這個瓶子來説，這裏沒有一樣東西不顯得可愛，因為它又來到了翠綠的樹林之間，周圍喜氣洋洋，盡情歡樂。它又聽到了音樂聲和歌聲，以及人羣的低語聲和喧鬧聲，特別是在燈火閃耀，紙燈籠五光十色的花園那一部份。它自然是站在遠處的小徑上，不過那地方很適宜沉思。它帶着亮光，當場有用，同時又是一個點綴。在這樣的時刻很容易忘卻它曾在閣樓上留了二十年，能忘卻這個也是一件好事。靠近瓶子走過一對年輕男女，很像那訂了婚的一對 —— 大副和毛皮商的女兒，很久以前他們兩個也曾在林中散步。瓶子覺得它好像回到了過去。不但客人，其他的人也到花園裏來走走，讓他們目睹一下這番美景和慶祝場面。在這些外來的人中有一位老小姐，她看起來在這個世界上十分孤獨。

她和那瓶子一樣在想着青翠的樹林，想着一對和她本人密切相關的未婚夫妻。她在想着那個時刻，她一生中遇到的最快樂的時刻，她本人就是那對未婚夫妻中的一方，這樣的時刻是永遠不會忘記的，哪怕是一個女孩變成了像她現在這麼老。但是她認不出這瓶子，瓶子也沒有注意到這位老小姐。在這個世界上我們常常就跟他們兩個一樣，碰到了會相互錯過，即使兩個人住在同一個城市裏。

那瓶子從花園又送到一個酒商那裏，再一次灌滿酒，賣給了一個飛行員，他下個星期日要乘他的氣球飛到天上去。一大羣人前來觀看這個場面，軍樂隊早已安排好，許多別的準備也做好了。瓶子從籃子裏全都看見，它在籃子裏緊靠着一隻活兔子躺着。那兔子極其激動，因為它知道它要被帶上天去，再用降落傘放下來。不過瓶子不懂甚麼"上去"、"下來"，它只看到氣球越脹越大，直到大得不能再大了，然後開始上升，搖搖晃晃。接着繫住它的繩子割斷，氣球就帶着飛行員和裝着瓶子和兔子的籃子飛上天，這時音樂奏起來，所有人高呼："萬歲！"

"飛上天倒是一次了不起的旅行，"瓶子想。"這是一種新的航行方式，在這裏至少不怕撞到甚麼東西。"

成千上萬人在盯着氣球看，在花園的那位老小姐也看，因為她站在閣樓開着的窗旁邊。窗口掛着那個有隻朱頂雀的鳥籠，當時還沒有盛水杯，朱頂雀只好滿足於有一個舊杯子。窗臺上有一盆香桃木，它被稍微推向一邊，免得掉出去，因為老小姐正在把身體探出窗，好看得見。她清楚看到了氣球裏的飛行員，看到他怎樣用降落傘放下了兔子，接着他拿起瓶子喝酒，為所有觀眾的健康乾杯。乾完杯以後他把瓶子高高扔向空中。老小姐根本沒有想到，她年輕時，在青翠的樹林中，在那歡樂的幸福日子裏，她的朋友為了她向上扔的正好就是這個瓶子。瓶子卻沒時間去想，它突然間往上飛，還沒醒悟過來，已經到達了它從未達到的最高點。教堂尖頂和屋頂遠遠在它底下，下面的人小得不能再小。接着它開始下降，比兔子下降要快得多，還在空中翻着筋斗，覺得自己年輕極了，而且自由自在，雖然還裝着半瓶酒。但是這為時不久。這是一趟怎樣的旅行啊！所有人能夠看到這瓶子，因為太陽照在它上面。氣球已經遠去，瓶子很快也落得很遠，因為落在一個屋頂上，它碎成了碎片。不過這些碎片受到那麼大的撞擊，停也停不下來。它們繼續蹦蹦跳跳，滾個不停，最後落到院子裏，變成更小的碎片。只剩下瓶頸還保持完整，它斷得很整齊，像是用金剛石鋸下來的一樣。

“可以用它做一個餵鳥的盛水杯，”住在地窖的一個人說，但是住在地窖的那些人沒有一個有鳥或者鳥籠，也不可能指望他們只因為找到了一個可以做盛水杯的瓶頸就去買一隻鳥。但是住在閣樓上的老小姐有一隻鳥，她的確可能用得着它。於是那人在瓶口上塞上個塞子，把瓶頸送上去給她，也就像生活中常見的，本來最高的部份現在倒過來向下朝了，裏面裝滿了清水。接着他們掛它在小鳥的籠子裏，小鳥吱吱喳喳，從未唱得如此開心過。

“唉，你完全有理由唱歌，”瓶頸說，它被大家看成十分了不起的東西，因為它乘過氣球。關於它的歷史，大家知道的就只有這一點。如今它掛在鳥籠裏，可以聽到下面街上人們的喧鬧聲和低語聲，以及房間裏老小姐的談話聲。有一個老朋友剛來看她，她們談的不是瓶頸，而是窗戶的香桃木。

"不，你不必花上一塊錢去買你女兒的結婚花束，"老小姐說；"你可以有一個開滿鮮花的小花束。你看到那棵樹已經長得多麼漂亮嗎？它僅僅是從一根香桃木小樹枝栽起來的，就是我訂婚後那天你送給我的那根樹枝。我本要用它在一年後做我自己的結婚花束，但是那一天始終沒有到來。那雙將要成為我一生的光明和快樂的眼睛閉上了。我心愛的人在海底安眠，那棵香桃木已經成為老樹，而我是一個更老的女人。在你送給我的那根樹枝枯掉前，我折下一小枝，插它在泥裏。現在你看，它已經長成大樹，它的一束花作為你女兒的花束，最後終於出現在一個婚禮上。"

當老小姐講到她年輕時代的愛人和林中訂婚的事情時，她的眼睛裏含着眼淚。許多思緒湧上心頭，但是她永遠沒有想到，就在她身邊，就在那窗戶，是那些往日的一個紀念物——那瓶頸。在她訂婚那一天，當塞子砰的一聲飛出來的時候，那瓶子曾發出一聲歡呼。但是瓶頸沒有認出老小姐，它沒有在聽她說甚麼，也許因為他正在埋頭想着她。

# 23

# 老橡樹最後的夢

離大海不遠，高高位於陡岸上，樹林裏聳立着一棵很老很老的橡樹。它正好三百六十五歲，但是這段漫長的時間對於這樹來説，只等於我們同樣數目的天數。我們白天醒着，夜裏睡覺，並在這時候做我們的夢。樹不同，它一年中三季醒着，一刻也不睡，直到冬季降臨。冬季是它休息的時間，是它春、夏、秋這漫長的一日之後的夜晚。在溫暖的夏天，蜉蝣這種只活一天的昆蟲在這老橡樹周圍飛來飛去，享受生活，感到幸福，有時一隻這種小昆蟲停在它的一片新鮮的大葉子上，橡樹總是説："可憐的小昆蟲！你的一生就只有一天。多麼短啊。這一定是極其悲哀的。"

"悲哀！你這話是甚麼意思？"小昆蟲總是回答説。"我周圍的一切是那麼出奇地光輝、溫暖和美麗，叫我快樂極了。"

"但只有一天，接着全完了。"

"完了！"小昆蟲答道。"完了是甚麼意思？你也要完了嗎？"

"不，我大概要活你的日子的千萬倍，我的一天有整整幾季長，這實在長得你永遠也算不出來。"

"算不出來？那麼我真不了解你。你可能有千萬個我的日子，但是我有千萬個片刻可以逍遙自在，快快活活。當你死了以後，世界所有的美景也就停止存在了嗎？"

"不，"橡樹回答說，"它們當然存在得長久得多，甚至比我能想像的更長。""好，"小昆蟲說，"那麼我們活的時間是一樣的，只是我們計算方法不同罷了。"於是小昆蟲在空中又跳舞又飛翔，為自己如薄紗和絲絨的精緻翅膀感到高興，為溫暖的微風感到高興，它帶來三葉草田與野玫瑰、接骨木花與花園樹籬上的忍冬花，以及野百里香、櫻草花與薄荷的芳香，所有這些香氣幾乎香得使這小昆蟲陶醉了。這長長的美麗一天是如此充滿快樂和甜蜜的喜悅，等到太陽下山時，牠感到一切快樂和享受使自己累極了。牠的翅膀再也不能承受自己，牠慢慢滑翔下來，輕輕落到晃動的柔嫩草葉上，在還能點頭的時候點了點牠的小腦袋，然後安靜甜蜜地睡了，小昆蟲就這樣死了。

"可憐的小蜉蝣！"橡樹說。"短促得那麼可怕的一生啊！"就這樣，夏季裏每一天重複着同樣的舞蹈，問着同樣的問題，聽到同樣的回答。蜉蝣一代又一代沒完沒了地繼續着同樣的事情，他們全都感到同樣的快樂、同樣的幸福。

橡樹就這樣一直醒着，度過了它春天的早晨、夏天的中午和秋天的晚上。如今它的休息時候、它的夜臨近了，冬天正在到來。暴風雨已經在歌唱："晚安，晚安！"這裏一片葉子落下，那裏一片葉子落下。"我們來搖你，讓你發睏。好好睡吧，好好睡吧。我們唱歌催你入睡，搖你催你安眠，這對你那些老樹枝有好處，它們甚至會樂得吱嘎響。好好睡吧，好好睡吧，這是你的第三百六十五個夜。準確來說，你只是世界上的一個小寶寶。好好睡吧，雲將在你身上灑下雪，那可是很好的被子，暖乎乎的，還蓋住你的腳。願你睡個好覺，做個好夢。"橡樹站在那裏，脫下身上所有葉子，留下來休息一整個漫長的冬天，做許多夢，夢見它一生中發生過的種種事情，就像人做夢一樣。這棵巨大的樹曾經很小很小，在搖籃中它還只是一顆果實。按照人類的計算方法，它如今正處在它存在的第四個世紀。它是這森林中最巨大、最好的樹。它的樹頂聳立在其他所有樹之上，在海上遠遠就可以看到它，因此對於水手來說它成了地標。它不知道有多少雙眼睛急着在尋找它。斑鳩在它最高的樹枝上築巢，杜鵑鳥經常在那裏唱歌，牠那為大家所熟悉的旋律在丫枝間迴響。到了秋天，當樹葉看起來像銅片一樣的時候，候鳥在飛渡大海之前會停在它的樹枝上。但如今是冬天了，樹站在那裏光禿禿得連一片葉子也沒有，因此人人可以看到，從樹幹上伸出來的樹枝是多麼蜿蜒扭曲。烏鴉和禿鼻烏鴉輪流蹲在它們上面，相互訴說正在開始的苦日子，冬天覓食該有多困難。

就在聖誕節左右的時候，老橡樹做了一個夢。這樹無疑有一種節日已經來臨的感覺，它在夢中覺得聽到周圍所有教堂的鐘都響起來了，然而它感到這時候似乎是美麗的夏日，又柔和又溫暖。它巨大的樹頂上張蓋着鮮嫩的綠葉；陽光在枝葉間戲耍，空氣充滿花草的芳香；彩蝶相互追逐；夏蠅在它周圍跳舞，好像世界只是為了牠們跳舞和尋歡作樂而創造的。橡樹一生中每年發生的一切，好像節慶的巡遊隊伍那樣在它面前一一經過。他看到古代的騎士和貴婦騎着他們的駿馬穿過森林，他們的帽上飄動着羽毛，手腕上停着獵鷹。狩獵的號角吹響，獵犬汪汪叫。它看到穿彩色衣服和閃光盔甲，手持矛和斧槍的敵方武士搭起帳篷，不久以後又拆掉它們。營火又重新燃燒起來，人們在好客的大樹冠下唱歌和睡覺。它看到情侶們靠近它在月下談笑風生，在它樹幹的灰綠色樹皮刻上他們姓名的第一個字母。有一次，不過那是好多好多年以前了，高興的旅人把結他和風弦琴掛在它的樹枝上，現在它們，好像又掛在那裏了，它可以聽到絕妙的琴聲。斑鳩咕咕叫着像是表達這樹的感情，杜鵑鳥叫起來告訴它還有多少個夏日它要過。接着，似乎新的生命在透過樹根、樹幹和樹葉的每一根纖維向上升，甚至一直升到頂上那些樹枝。橡樹感覺到自己在伸展和擴張，而通過泥土下的根，流動着生命的溫暖活力。等到它長得越來越高，力氣也大起來了，它頂上那些樹枝就變得更粗大滾圓。隨着它日漸成長，它也越來越得意了，油然產生了一個歡快的渴望，就是要長得越來越高，甚至高得碰到溫暖明亮的太陽。它最高的那些樹枝已經穿過雲層，雲朵飄在它們底下像是一羣羣候鳥或者巨大的白天鵝。每一片葉子似乎能夠看見東西，它好像有了眼睛一樣。天上的星星在大白天也能看到，它們又大又閃爍發光，像些明亮柔和的眼睛。它們使人回憶起熟悉的孩子目光，或曾在老橡樹樹枝下約會那些情侶的目光。對於老橡樹來說，這些時刻都充滿了不起的和平快樂和幸福，然而在這幸福之中，橡樹又感到一種渴望，渴望它腳下所有的樹木、灌木和花草也能和它一樣長得更高，看到一切美景，享受同樣的幸福。如果其他樹木，不論大樹小樹，不能一起分享這種幸福，這巨大雄偉的橡樹在它的幸福中是不可能十分快樂的。這種渴望的感覺，通過每一根樹枝、每一片樹葉在顫動，熱烈得彷彿它們是人心臟的纖維。樹冠搖來晃去，彎下來，似乎它在無言的渴望中，正尋找着甚麼東西。這時候傳來了百里香的香氣，隨之而來的是更濃烈的忍冬和紫羅蘭的香氣，它覺得它聽到了杜鵑鳥的歌聲。最後它的渴望滿足了。林中樹木的綠色樹冠直沖雲端，橡樹低頭看到它們在上升，越長越高。灌木和花草向上飛長，有些甚至拔了自己的根，好長得更快。長得最快的是樺樹。它細長的樹幹像閃電一樣，彎彎曲曲飛快生長。樹枝在它四周展開有如綠色的薄紗和旗幟。樹林中每一種植物，連棕色的羽狀燈心草，都跟大夥一起向上生長，同時鳥兒唱着歌向上騰飛。在一片像綠色長緞帶飄在空中的草葉上，蹲着一隻蚱蜢，牠正用腿梳理自己的翅膀。甲蟲嗚嗚哼，蜜蜂嗡嗡響，鳥兒唱歌，各發各的聲音，空氣中充滿了歌聲和快樂的響聲。

"但是長在水邊的那小藍花在哪裏？"橡樹問道。"還有紫色的風鈴草，還有雛菊？"你看橡樹要它們全都和它在一起。

"我們在這裏，我們在這裏呢，"響起說話聲和歌聲。

"但是這個夏天的漂亮百里香呢，它在哪裏啊？還有去年蓋滿大地的鈴蘭呢？還有開漂亮的花的野蘋果樹，以及年年在林中盛開似錦的繁花呢？甚至如今僅僅在發芽的，也可以和我們在一起。"

"我們在這裏，我們在這裏呢，"空中更高的地方傳來聲音，好像它們先行長到那裏去了。

"啊，這太漂亮了，漂亮得叫人不相信，"橡樹用快活的聲調說。"不管是大是小，它們都在我這裏了，一棵也沒有漏掉。這樣的幸福能夠想像出來嗎？這幾乎像是不可能的。"

"在天上永生的上帝這裏，這是能夠想像的，這是可能的，"空中傳來這回答。

還在向上生長的老橡樹這時感到它腳下的根從泥土中鬆開了。

"這樣不錯，這樣最好了，"橡樹説，"現在沒有羈絆牽制着我。我可以飛到燦爛和光明的最高點。我愛的一切花草樹木，不管大小，全都跟我在一起。一切，所有一切都在這裏。"這就是老橡樹做的夢：它夢見在聖誕節的時候，一場強大的風暴掃過陸地和海洋。大海向岸邊滾滾而來。樹上聽到了破碎的聲音。在夢中它正從泥土鬆開的那一刻，也就是它的根真正從地面拔起的時候。它摔倒了──它的三百六十五年就像蜉蝣的一天過去。聖誕節那天早晨，太陽升起時，風暴已經停止。所有教堂響起節日的鐘聲，從每一個壁爐，甚至是最小的小屋的壁爐，煙升到藍天，就像德魯伊　祭壇上的感恩祭的煙一樣。大海逐漸變得平靜，在夜裏一艘大船經歷了暴風雨，所有旗幟都展示出來，作為歡樂和喜慶的象徵。"樹倒了！老橡樹──海岸的地標！"水手們驚叫道。"它一定是在昨晚的風暴中倒下了。誰可以取代它？唉！可沒有。"這就是對老橡樹的葬禮演説，簡短但意義深遠。老橡樹躺在冰雪覆蓋的海岸上，在它上面響起了一首來自船上的歌，歌裏唱着聖誕的歡樂、人們靈魂的救贖，以及基督贖罪寶血帶來的永生。

"高聲唱吧，在這快樂的早晨，

一切都圓滿了，因為基督已經誕生；

讓我們把快樂的歌高聲唱出吧，

'感謝和讚美基督，哈利路亞！'"

古老的聖誕頌歌就這樣響徹上空，船上每一個人都感到透過歌聲和祈禱，他們的思緒飛揚起來，甚至像老橡樹在它聖誕節凌晨，那最後一個美麗的夢中所感覺到的那樣向上飛升。

# 24
# 孩子話

有一個富商，家裏開兒童派對，來了有錢人和大人物的孩子。這商人是個有學問的人，因為他父親送他上大學，考試也及格了。他父親起初只是個賣牛的商販，但一向誠實勤奮，因此賺了錢，而他兒子，就是那個商人，又增加了他的家產。他不但聰明，而且心地也好。不過大家都講他的錢，鮮有講起他的善心。各種各樣的人來拜訪商人，大都是出身好又有知識的人，但也有些人這兩種優點都沒有。

這是個孩子聚會，說的都是些童言童語，自然總是想到甚麼就說甚麼。孩子裏有個漂亮小女孩，她驕傲得很，但這是僕人教出來，不是她父母教出來，她父母是極有頭腦的人。

她父親是一位皇室侍從官，這是宮廷裏很高的職位，這一點小女孩知道。"我是一個宮廷裏的孩子，"她說。她本也有可能只是一個地窖裏的孩子，因為沒有人能決定自己的出身。反正她告訴其他孩子她出身好，說出身不好的人在世上無法出頭。讀書和勤奮毫無用處，因為一個人出身不好就永遠一事無成。"那些姓名以'森'收尾的人，"她說，"根本永遠不成大器。我們必須把手叉在腰上，讓手肘尖尖地伸出來，好讓這些甚麼'森'離我們遠一點。"她說着，把兩隻美麗的手臂叉在腰上，讓手肘尖尖地伸出來，示範給大家看該怎樣做。她那兩隻小手臂真是非常美麗，因為她是個樣子可愛的孩子。

但是商人的小女兒聽了這番話十分生氣，因為她父親的姓是彼得森，她知道這個姓是用"森"收尾的，因此她盡可能用驕傲的語氣說："但我爸爸買得起一百塊錢糖果，把它們派給孩子們。你爸爸能做到嗎？"

"我爸爸能做到，而且我爸爸，"報紙編輯的小女兒說，"我爸爸能把你爸爸和所有人的爸爸登到報紙上。我媽媽說各種各樣的人都怕他，因為他利用報紙為所欲為。"這小女孩看起來無比驕傲，好像她是一個真正的公主，理應可以很驕傲。

但是半開着的房門外有一個窮孩子，他正從門縫望進來。他太低賤了，甚至不獲允許進房間。他一直在替女廚師轉烤肉叉，女廚師於是讓他站在門外偷看一下在房間裏玩得那麼開心、衣着漂亮的孩子們。對他來說，這就很了不起了。"噢，如果我能是他們當中的一個就好了，"他想，就在這時候，他聽到關於姓的話，這就足以使他更加傷心。他在家裏的父母連買份報紙的錢也沒有，更不要說在報上寫文章了。最糟糕的是，他父親的姓，自然還有他自己的姓，正是用"森"收尾的，因此他永遠不會有出頭之日，想到這一點他真難過極了。然而他終究來到了世界上，生活階層無可選擇，因此他也只好認命。

這是那天晚上發生的事。

許多年過去，孩子們都長大成人了。

在城裏有一座富麗堂皇的房子，裏面擺滿各種美麗和貴重的東西。人人都想去看看，甚至周圍農村的人也來請求參觀一下裏面的珍寶。

我們在上面說着童言童語的孩子當中，誰能夠擁有這房子呢？有人也許以為這很容易猜出來。不，不對，不那麼容易。這房子是那天晚上站在門外的那個窮孩子的。他當真成了個大人物，雖然他的姓以"森"收尾，因為他姓托瓦爾森　。

至於另外三個孩子 —— 出身好、富有和知識上有優勢的孩子 —— 她們受到世人尊敬，因為其出身和地位使他們不愁吃喝，而沒有理由為了多年前那個晚上的所說所想譴責自己。畢竟，童言無忌嘛。

# 25

# 老頭子做的事總是對的

我來給你講個我小時候聽到的故事。每次我想起這個故事，總覺得它越來越可愛，因為故事也和許多人一樣——越老越好。

我毫不懷疑你曾去過鄉下，看過很古老的農舍，它的乾草屋頂上，亂長着青苔和小植物。三角牆的屋脊上有個鸛鳥巢，因為我們沒有鸛鳥是不行的。房子的牆歪斜着，窗都很低，而且只有一扇是做出來讓人打開的。烤爐從牆上突出來像個大圓瘤。一棵接骨木樹懸在圍籬上，而枝葉底下，圍籬腳邊有一個水池，水池裏有幾隻鴨子在戲水，還有一隻看院子的狗，誰來了牠都汪汪叫。在一條鄉村小道旁邊，就建着這樣的一座農舍。農舍裏住着一對老夫妻，一個農民和他的老伴。儘管他們的財產那麼少，有一樣東西他們卻是不能沒有的，那就是馬，牠全靠吃着在大路邊找到的草才能努力活下去。老農民騎這匹馬到鎮上去，他的鄰居們常向他借馬來用，作為回報就給老夫妻兩人幫點忙。過了一些日子，他們想這匹馬該拿去賣了，或者用牠換點對他們可能更有用的東西。但這東西是甚麼呢？

"這個你最在行，老頭子，"他的老伴說。"今天有市集，你騎着牠到鎮上，賣了牠賺點錢，或者換點好東西吧。不管你怎樣做，對我來說都是不會錯的，你就騎馬到市集去吧。"

於是她給他繫上頸巾，因為她繫得比他好，而且能打個漂亮的蝴蝶結。她還用掌心擦他的帽子再給了他一個吻。然後他騎上那匹要賣掉或者換點甚麼東西的馬走了。一點也不假，老頭子知道他要去做甚麼。這時太陽曬得很熱，天上一點雲也看不到，路上灰塵滾滾，因為許多人都去趕市集，他們駕着車，或者騎着馬，或者一路上走着，沒有可以遮擋炎熱太陽的遮蔭處。在人羣中有一個人耗盡力氣在走着，趕一頭母牛到市集上去，母牛在同類中可算最漂亮。

"我斷定牠能出好奶，"老農民心裏説。"用馬換頭母牛是個好交易。喂，你這位趕牛的，"他説。"你聽我説，我敢説馬比牛更值錢，但我不在乎這個，母牛我更用得着。因此，如果你願意，我們就來交換吧。"

"我當然願意，"那人説。

交易就這樣做成了。交換好以後，老農民本來可以回家，因為他出來要辦的事已經辦完。但他原先就拿定主意要上市集，所以他決定還是去，就算去看看也好。於是他趕着牛朝鎮上走。他牽着母牛，滿心堅定大步走着，不多一會就趕上了一個趕着一頭羊的人。那是一頭很好的肥羊，身上的毛漂亮極了。

"我很想有那麼一頭羊，"老農民心裏説。"我家的圍籬旁邊有很多青草可以給牠吃，冬天可以留牠在我們的房間裏，有一頭羊也許比有一頭母牛更有好處。我該交換嗎？"

趕羊的人巴不得交換，這筆交易很快就做成了。接着我們這位老農民趕着羊，沿着大路繼續向前走。不久他又趕上一個人，這人從田地裏上大路來，胳肢窩裏夾着一隻大鵝。

"你夾着一隻多重的傢伙啊！"老農民説，"牠毛又多，長得又肥，用一根繩拴着，或者讓牠在我們那裏玩水，看着倒挺不錯。那對我的老伴會很有用，她能從中獲得種種好處。她多少次説過：'我們現在有隻鵝就好了！'如今正是個機會。可能的話，我要給她弄到這隻鵝。我們交換好嗎？我用羊換你的鵝，你肯交換就實在太感謝你了。"

那人一點也不反對，於是成交了，我們的老農民就擁有了這隻鵝。這時候他已經離鎮上非常近。大路上越來越擠，人和牲口好像潮湧一樣。牲口走在小路上和樹籬旁。在收稅關卡，牠們甚至走到收稅人的馬鈴薯田裏去了。那裏有一隻雞，走來走去，一副昂首闊步的模樣，一隻腳被一根繩拴着，因為怕牠會被人羣嚇跑不見了。雞的尾巴毛很短，牠眨着兩隻眼睛，"咯咯咯咯"地叫，看起來很狡猾。牠叫這麼兩聲，心裏到底在想甚麼，這我就無法告訴你了。不過我們那位好心人一看到牠，心裏就想："哎呀，這是我一輩子所見最漂亮的雞。依我説，牠比我們那位牧師的傳種母雞還要漂亮。我很想得到這隻雞。雞總能啄到身邊幾顆穀粒，幾乎可以自己養活自己。如果我能用我的雞換牠我想這倒是一椿好交易。我們交換好嗎？"他問那收稅人。

"交換嘛，"那人重複了一遍，"好，那倒也不壞。"

於是他們成交了，收稅關卡的收稅人拿到鵝，老農民拿走雞。在他到市集的路上，他真正做了一大批交易，現在又熱又累。他想弄點東西吃，買杯麥芽酒提提神，於是他轉身向一家酒館走去。他正要進酒館，酒館伙計正好出來，他們在門口遇上了。酒館伙計背着一袋東西。"你那袋裏裝的是甚麼啊？"老農民問道。

"爛蘋果，"伙計回答説，"整整一袋爛蘋果，餵豬正好。"

"哎呀，那太糟蹋東西了，"老農民聽了説，"我倒想拿它們回家去給我老伴。去年草地旁那棵老蘋果樹只結了一個蘋果，我們放它在碗櫥裏保存着，直到它最後乾了，爛了。那總是一份財產啊，我老伴説。這一下她可以看到一大筆財產啦，整整一口袋。我很想拿它們回去給她看看。"

"給你這袋蘋果，你給我甚麼呢？"酒館伙計問道。

"我給你甚麼？好吧，我換我的雞給你。"

於是他給了酒館伙計那隻雞，換來了那些爛蘋果，拿它們到酒館裏。他在火爐邊小心放好那袋爛蘋果，然後去找張桌子坐下。但是火爐是熱的，這一點他卻沒有想到。現場有許多客人、馬販子、趕牲口的人和兩個英國人。這兩個英國人錢多得衣袋都鼓起來，好像快要爆裂了。他們還喜歡打賭，這個你馬上就要聽到。

"噓 —— 噓 —— 噓，噓 —— 噓 —— 噓。"火爐旁邊會是甚麼呢？蘋果都開始烤熟了。"那是甚麼？"一個人説。

"哈，你們知道嗎……"我們的老農民説，接着他把馬換牛，一直換到蘋果的整個故事告訴了他們。

"好啊，等到你回家，你那位老太太要狠狠給你一頓臭罵了，"一個英國人説。"會大吵一場嗎？"

"甚麼！給我甚麼？"老農民説。"哼，她會親我，並且説：'老頭子做的事總是對的。'"

"讓我們來打個賭吧，"兩個英國人說。"我們跟你打賭一桶金幣，一百鎊金幣對一百磅蘋果。"

"不，一斗金幣就好了，"農民回答道。"我只有一斗蘋果可以賭，我額外押上自己和老伴，我想這會增加籌碼。"

"好！一言為定！"於是這場打賭就這麼定了。

接着酒館老闆的馬車來到門口，兩位英國人和那老農民坐上去，他們駕車走了，很快就來到老農民的農舍停下。"晚上好，老太婆。""晚上好，老頭子。""我換了東西回來。"

"啊，很好，你做的事你心中有數，"老太婆說。接着她擁抱他，既不去注意那兩個陌生人，也不去注意那袋東西。

"我把馬換了一頭母牛。"

"謝謝上帝，"她說。"現在我們可以有許多牛奶，有許多牛油，有許多芝士吃了。這是一樁再好不過的交易。"

"是的，不過我把母牛又換了一頭羊。"

"哎呀，那就更好啦！"他老伴叫道。"你總是甚麼都想到了，我們有足夠的牧草養一頭羊。這一下就有羊奶、羊奶芝士、羊毛外套和羊毛襪了！母牛可生產不出這些東西，牛的毛只會落掉，你想得太周到了！"

"不過我把羊又換了一隻鵝。"

"那麼我們今年可以吃烤鵝了。親愛的老頭子，你總是想出點甚麼來讓我高興。這真叫人快活。我們可以用根繩子拴着鵝的腿，讓牠走來走去，這樣牠在烤以前就變得更加肥。"

"不過我把鵝又換了一隻雞。"

"一隻雞！好，換得好，"老太婆回答說。"雞會生蛋孵小雞，這樣我們就有小雞，很快就有一個養雞場了。噢，這正是我想要的。”

“不錯，不過我把雞又換了一袋乾癟的蘋果。”

“甚麼！為了這件事我真得親親你！”他老伴説。“我親愛的好老公，現在我來告訴你一件事。你知道嗎，今天早晨你幾乎一走我就開始動腦筋，今天晚上能給你甚麼好吃的呢，於是我想到煎蛋和煙肉，配上香草。雞蛋和煙肉我都有，但我要找香草。於是我到校長家，我知道他們香草多的是，可是校長太太真小氣，儘管她笑得那麼甜。我求她借我一把香草。‘借’她説。‘我沒有甚麼可借的，我園子根本甚麼也長不出來，哪怕是一個乾癟的蘋果。我連一個乾癟的蘋果也不能借給你，我親愛的老太太。’但但現在我能借十個給她，甚至整整一袋了，這真叫我高興，我想想都要笑出來啦，”説着，她給了他一個熱烈的吻。

“很好，我喜歡這一切，”兩個英國人都説。“老是走下坡路，卻老是快活，看到這樣的事值得花這筆錢。”於是他們付一百一十二鎊金幣給這位不管做甚麼都不會挨罵，而只會得到親吻的老農民。

是的，妻子看在眼裏並且心裏認定她丈夫最懂事，不管做的甚麼事都是對的，就是最好的報酬。

這就是我小時候聽到的一個故事。現在你也聽到了，知道了“老頭子做的事總是對的”。

# 26

# 蝸牛和玫瑰樹

花園周圍有一道榛樹樹籬。樹籬外面是田野和草原，那裏有牛有羊，但是花園當中有一棵玫瑰樹，開着花，樹下有一隻蝸牛，他的殼裏面有一大堆東西，那就是他自己。

"只等我的時候一到，"他說，"我要比玫瑰花開、榛樹結果和牛羊產奶做更多事。"

"我對你有很大希望，"玫瑰樹說。"請問一句，甚麼時候能夠兌現呢？"

"我要等我的時機到來，"蝸牛說。"你總是那麼急。急也沒有用。"

第二年蝸牛幾乎又躺在老地方，在玫瑰樹下曬太陽。玫瑰樹又長出花苞，開出玫瑰花，他們依舊鮮豔美麗。蝸牛把半個身體鑽出他的殼，伸出觸角，又把他們縮進去了。

"一切就和去年一樣！毫無進步。玫瑰樹只管開他的玫瑰花，沒有進展。"

夏天和秋天過去了。玫瑰樹開花結苞，直到天下起雪來，天氣變得濕冷。這時他垂下頭，而蝸牛已經鑽到了地下。

新的一年開始。玫瑰花又出現了，蝸牛也是。

"你如今是棵老玫瑰樹啦，"蝸牛說。"你必須趕快準備死了。你已把自己的一切全給了世界。那是不是很有價值，這問題我還沒時間思考。但有一點是清楚的，就是你對自身的發展絲毫沒有做過甚麼工作，否則你會產生一點其他東西。你有甚麼要辯護呢？你現在很快就要凋零，只剩下一根光桿。你明白我的意思嗎？"

"你嚇死我了，"玫瑰樹說。"我從來沒有想過這一點。"

"是的，你根本沒有費過心思來想問題。你曾經考慮過你為甚麼要開花，你的花是怎樣開出來嗎？為甚麼只是這樣而不是另一種模樣呢？"

"沒有，"玫瑰樹說，"我充滿喜樂來開花，因為我不得不這樣做。太陽照耀、溫暖着我，空氣使我清新。我喝晶瑩的露水和賦予生機的雨水，我呼吸着，我活着！我從泥土裏得到力量，也從天空得到力量。我感到周而復始、源源不絕的喜悅，因此我非繼續開花不可。那就是我的命，我只能這樣做。"

"你倒是過着一種非常輕鬆的生活，"蝸牛說。

"一點也不錯。生命賦予我的夠多了，"玫瑰樹說。"但是給予你的還要多。你獲得的是深思的性格、令世界驚奇且有極高天賦的心靈。"

"我一點也不打算像你那樣做，"蝸牛說。"世界和我沒有關係。我為甚麼要關心世界呢？我自己的事已經夠我費心，夠我想了。"

"但是生而在世，不應該把我們最好的東西給予別人，盡我們的力量作出貢獻嗎？不錯，我只能夠給予玫瑰花。但是，你如此得天獨厚，你給了世界甚麼呢？你將給它甚麼呢？"

"我給了甚麼？我將給予甚麼？我鄙視世界，它毫無意義，亦和我一點關係也沒有。依我説，你可以繼續開你的玫瑰花，別的事你都不會做。讓榛樹去結果吧，讓牛羊去產奶吧。它們有各自的天地。我的內心也有我的小天地。我縮進我的小宇宙，棲息於此，世界和我沒有關係。"

蝸牛説着，就縮進他的房子，關上了門。

"真可惜，"玫瑰樹説。"即使我再想也不能鑽到自己裏面去，我必須繼續開花。然後它們落下花瓣，隨風飛走。但是我曾看過一朵玫瑰花被夾在那位太太的讚美詩集裏，一朵落在一位漂亮的年輕女孩胸前，還有一朵被一個生活快樂的孩子親吻。那使我覺得快樂，這是真正的幸福。這是我的一些回憶，我的生活。"

於是玫瑰樹繼續純粹地開着花，而蝸牛懶散地躺在他的房子裏，世界與他毫無關係。

一年一年過去了。

蝸牛在泥土中變成了泥土，玫瑰樹也一樣，甚至夾在讚美詩集裏那朵玫瑰花也早枯萎了，但是花園中有其他玫瑰樹和蝸牛。蝸牛鑽進他們的房子，向世界啐他們的唾沫，因為世界和他們沒有關係。

我們要把這故事從頭讀一遍嗎？它還是那樣的。

# 27
# 一個銀幣

從前有一個銀幣，它跳着叫着從鑄幣廠裏出來："萬歲！現在我要到外面廣大的世界去了。"一點不假，它確實到了外面廣大的世界。孩子們用溫暖的手握着它，吝嗇鬼用冰涼的手狠狠地抓着它，老年人把它翻來翻去，天知道有多少次年輕人拿它到手就花掉。這硬幣是銀做的，含銅極少，在鑄造它的這個國家流通了一年，它自覺在這個世界上已經周遊得夠遠了。然而有一天它才真是到廣大的世界去，因為這時候它屬於一位紳士，這位紳士正好要出國旅行。紳士動身時沒有發覺這銀幣在他的錢包底，直到有一天他拿它出來才看到了。"怎麼，"他叫起來，"這裏有一個從國內帶來的銀幣。那麼，現在它必須和我一起去旅行了！"當這銀幣被重新放回錢包裏的時候，它高興得跳起來，發出了叮噹聲。

如今它和一些外國朋友在一起，這些外國朋友老是進進出出，一個替換一個，但是這從家鄉來的銀幣卻總被放回去，只好留在錢包裏，這真是一種特殊待遇。許多個禮拜過去，在此期間，這銀幣在錢包裏走了很遠，卻一點也不知道自己是在甚麼地方。它發現其他的硬幣有法國的、有意大利的。一個硬幣說它們是在這座城裏，另一個硬幣說它們是在那座城裏，但是銀幣弄不清楚，也想像不出它們説的是甚麼意思。一個人如果被裝在布袋裏，他當然看不到外面世界，銀幣的遭遇實際上便是如此。但是有一天它正躺在錢包裏，發現錢包沒有關緊，於是它爬近錢包口去看外面一眼。他自然一點也沒有想到接下來會出甚麼事，但它太好奇了，好奇常常會為自己帶來懲罰。它太急着要看，離開錢包口太近，一下子就滑到外面，落進了褲袋。晚上當錢包被掏出來的時候，銀幣就被留在它落下去的褲袋角。等到衣服被拿到走廊，銀幣落到了地板上，沒有人聽見和注意到。第二天早晨，衣服被送回房間，那紳士穿上它們就動身了，但是銀幣就這樣留在地板上。過了些時候它被人發現，當作可以使用的硬幣，和其他三個硬幣放在一起。"啊，"銀幣想，"這太叫人高興了。我現在可以去看看世界，認識認識別國的人，學學外國的風俗習慣了。"

"你説那是一個銀幣？"隨即有人説。"那不是這個國家的真銀幣，是假的，它不能用。"

後來銀幣自己講這個故事時，就從這裏開始。

"'假的！不能用！'他説。這句話像把尖刀不斷刺透我的心。我知道這樣的鏗鏘聲是真正的銀幣才有的，我也知道我有真正的鋼印。這些人一定是全弄錯了，要不然他們就不是在説我。但他們是指我，他們是説我是'假的，不能用'。

"'那麼我必須暗中用它出去，'得到我的那個人説。於是我要在暗中被打發掉，而在光天化日之下再次受到羞辱。

"'假的！不能用！'噢，我必須設法溜走，我想。人們每一次試圖把我當作本國硬幣狡猾地用出去時，我都在他們的手指間發抖。唉！我真是個倒霉的銀幣！我的銀子、我的鋼印和我真正的價值在這裏有甚麼用呢，所有這些東西在這裏都一文不值。在世人的眼睛裏，一個人的價值只是根據對他形成的看法而定。感到良心責備和因做壞事而偷偷摸摸一定是很可怕的事。至於我，儘管我是無辜的，但只要他們拿我出來，我在他們的眼前就不禁發抖，因為我知道我會被當為以假亂真的東西，被人扔回桌子上。到頭來我被付給了一位貧窮的老太太，我是她辛辛苦苦工作了一整天才拿到手的工錢。但是她沒有辦法再用我出去，沒有人肯收下我。對於老太太來說，我成了最不幸的一個銀幣。'我不得不塞這個銀幣給甚麼人，'她説，'我心再好也不能存下一個假銀幣。它可以給那有錢的麵包師傅，他比我更能承受這個損失。不過，做這種事始終是不對的。'

"'唉！'我對自己歎了一口氣。'我也要成為這位可憐老太太良心上的負擔嗎？在我的老年，我是這樣完全變了嗎？'老太太把我遞給那個有錢的麵包師傅，但是他對流通貨幣太熟悉了，一接到我，馬上把我幾乎扔到老太太的臉上。她用我買不到麵包，我從心底裏感到難過，我竟給人造成那麼大的麻煩，並被作為一個被拋棄的硬幣對待。我年輕時曾因為自信自己的價值，深知自己有真正的鋼印，而感到那麼快活。一個沒人要的可憐銀幣會多傷心，我現在就是那麼傷心。老太太又帶我回家，非常認真地看着我説：'不，我不再用你去騙任何人了。我要在你身上鑽個洞，這樣人人都能知道你是個沒有價值的假東西。不過，我為甚麼要那樣做呢？你很可能是一個吉祥的銀幣。我剛想到這一點，我相信是這樣。對，我來在這銀幣上鑽個洞，'她説，'再在上面穿一根線，然後給我隔壁的小女孩，讓她作為一個吉祥的銀幣掛在脖子上。'就這樣,她在我身上鑽了一個洞。

"在我身上鑽一個洞實在不是味兒,但想到這是出於好意,我就能夠作出很大的忍耐。一根線穿過了洞,我成了一個徽章。他們把我掛在一個小女孩的脖子上,小女孩對我笑,吻我,我在一個孩子溫暖、天真的胸口上躺了一整夜。

"早晨小女孩的母親用雙手指夾住我,對我起了某種想法,這我很快就發現了。她首先找來一把剪刀,剪斷了線。

"'吉祥銀幣!'她說,'這正是我要試一試的。'接着她放我到醋裏,直到我全身發綠,然後她用水泥把洞填好,稍微擦擦我使我亮起來,傍晚到賣彩票的人那裏用我這枚帶來運氣的銀幣給自己買了一張彩票。真像是事事都給我添麻煩。賣彩票的人那麼用力地撳我,我想我都要斷裂了。我曾被說成是假的,我曾被扔掉,這個我知道。周圍有那麼多銀幣和銅幣,上面鑄着各種各樣的字和鋼印。我很清楚它們是多麼神氣,因此我因無比慚愧而避開它們。有幾個人正好和賣彩票的人在一起,這些人似乎有許多事要做,於是我悄悄地落到一個箱子裏,夾在幾個硬幣中間。"

"那張彩票是不是中了獎,我不知道。但這一件事我是知道的,幾天以後我被認出來是個假銀幣,擱到了一邊。發生的每一件事情似乎都增加我的痛苦。即使一個人有好的品性,但是人家說他怎麼樣他也無法否認,因為他並不能對自己作出公正的評判。"

"一年過去了,我就這樣不斷從一隻手轉到另一隻手。我老是遭到咒罵,老是被不悦的表情看着,不受任何人信任,但是我相信我自己,而不信任世界上的人。對,那是個非常黑暗的時期。"

"終於有一天我被轉到了一個旅行者手裏，他是個外國人，正是從自己國家帶我出來的那個人。他實在是夠單純和老實，把我當成了流通的銀幣。但是他也打算把我用出去嗎？我又要聽到大叫'假的！不能用'嗎？這位旅行者仔細地反覆看了我一遍。'我還把你當作真的銀幣呢，'他説。接着他突然笑逐顏開。我在任何別人的臉上也沒有看到過像在他臉上的那種微笑。'這真是太奇怪了，'他説，'這是我自己國家的銀幣啊，是我家鄉的一個上好的真銀幣啊。有人在它上面鑽了一個洞，這裏的人肯定會説它是假的。多麼奇怪，它回到了我的手裏。我要帶它回國，帶回我的家。'

"我一聽到這句話，高興得渾身發抖。我又一次被稱為一個上好的真銀幣，而且要回到我自己的家，那裏每一個人都認識我，知道我是用好銀子鑄造的，上面蓋有真鋼印。我高興得真想迸發出火花，但迸發火花在任何時候都不是我的天性。鋼能這樣做，銀子卻不能。我被包在乾淨的白紙裏，這樣我就不會和別的硬幣混在一起遺失掉了。當碰到特殊場合，碰巧遇到有人從我的國家來時，我被拿出來，並受到稱讚。他們説我非常有趣，有一點實在很值得注意，那些有趣的東西常常不為自己説一句話。

"最後我到了家。我所有的擔心和害怕都結束了。我重新快活非凡，因為我不是好的銀幣嗎，我不是有真的鋼印嗎？我不用再忍受羞辱或者失望，儘管我上面的確有一個洞，好像我是假的。但只要一個人有真材實料，遭到懷疑根本不算甚麼，每一個人應該保持行為正直，因為到時一切都會真相大白。這是我的堅定信念，"銀幣説。

# 28

# 茶壺

從前有一個驕傲的茶壺，它因為自己是瓷做的而感到驕傲，也因為有長壺嘴和大把手而感到驕傲。它前後都有東西——壺嘴在前，把手在後——它老是不離口的就是這兩樣東西。但是它不提它的壺蓋，因為壺蓋裂開了，用鉚釘接好，毛病很多，我們可不愛談自己的毛病，不過別人會談。杯子、牛奶盅和糖缸，這一整套茶具想着壺蓋的毛病的時候多得多，談它比談完好的把手和漂亮的壺嘴更多，茶壺知道這一點。

"我知道它們，"它心裏說。"我也知道我的缺點，我認為我知道自己的缺點就是我的謙虛、我的謙遜。我們全都有不少缺點，但是與此同時，我們也有優點。杯子有把手，糖缸有蓋子，我兩樣都有，而且我還多一樣，這一樣它們永遠不會有，那就是我有一個壺嘴在前，這就使我成為茶桌上的女王。我賜福給乾渴的人類，在我裏面，中國茶葉給予無味的開水香氣。"

茶壺在它的青春時期就是這樣講話的。它站在準備好茶點的桌上，被最嬌嫩的手拿起來。但是那隻最嬌嫩的手卻非常笨拙。茶壺落了下來，壺嘴斷了，把手斷了。蓋子就不必再提，關於它已經說得夠了。

茶壺昏倒在地，開水從它裏面流了出來。它感到巨大的恥辱，但最糟糕的是大家都笑它，只笑它，卻不去笑那隻笨拙的手。

"我將永遠忘不了這件事！"茶壺後來回想往事時說。"他們叫我做破爛的東西，扔在一個角落，第二天給了一個來討飯的女人。我降為貧民，裏外都無話可說，但我在那裏日子卻好起來了。一樣東西可以一下子變了個樣。

"他們把泥土裝到我裏面，對於一個茶壺來說這無疑是被埋葬，但是他們在這泥土裏種下一個花的球莖。誰把它種在這裏，誰把它給了我，我都不知道，但是它被種在這裏了，代替了中國茶葉和開水、斷掉了的把手和壺嘴。

"球莖躺在泥土裏，躺在我的裏面，它變成了我的心，我鮮活的心，一樣我以前從未有過的東西。我有了生命，我有了力量，我的脈搏跳動了。球莖發了芽，思想和感覺湧現並開花。"

"我看到了它，我孕育了它，我在它的喜悅中忘記了自己。為了別人而忘掉自己是一件幸福的事！花沒有感謝我，甚至沒有想到我。人人欣賞它，稱讚它。這使我感到非常高興，這一定使它更為高興！有一天，我聽到有人說這花應該有一個更好的花盆。我的背被重重捶打，受盡折磨，然後花被放入一個更好的花盆裏。我被扔到院子裏，躺在那裏成了陶瓷碎片。但我擁有記憶，我永不會失去它。"

# 29
# 蠟燭

$\large\text{從}$前有一支大蠟燭，它把自己的價值看得最高。

"我，"它說，"是用最純正的蠟做出來，用最好的模子澆出來的。我發出來的光比任何燭都亮，我燒的時間比所有燭都長。我是屬於水晶吊燈或者銀燭臺的。"

"你是多麼可人的東西啊，"脂油蠟燭說。"我不過是脂油做的，但是想到我比廉價的細燭條好得多，我又感到安慰了，它只在油脂裏浸過兩次，我卻浸了八次，才成為一支體面的粗油燭。我感到很滿足。不錯，用蠟做比用脂油做要好要幸運得多，但是出身不能由自己選擇，你的位置是在大廳堂和水晶吊燈在一起，我的位置卻只是在廚房。不過廚房也是個好地方。屋子裏所有的食物都是從那裏出來的。"

"世界上有比食物重要的東西，"蠟燭說。"上流社會！看他們閃閃發亮，並且讓自己發亮！我和我家族的所有蠟燭都受到了邀請，要去參加就在今晚舉行的舞會。"

它話剛說完，所有蠟燭就被拿走。但是那支油燭也沒留下。家裏的女主人用嬌美的手拿起了它，拿它到廚房去，一個男孩正在那裏等着，他手裏拿着一籃子女主人給他的馬鈴薯和幾個蘋果。

"這支油燭也給你，我的小朋友，"她對他說。"夜深了你母親可以點着它工作。”

這位太太的小女兒緊靠着她母親站着，當她聽到“夜深”這字眼時，她高興地説，“我也要等到夜深！今天晚上我們有舞會，我要紮上我的大紅腰帶！”她的臉閃着愉悦的亮光。沒有蠟燭能發出孩子眼睛那種光輝。

“這真是我的福氣，”油燭心裏想。“我絕不會忘掉她的樣子，而我肯定再也看不到了。”

他們放油燭進籃子，蓋上籃蓋。孩子帶着它走了。

“他會帶我到哪裏去呢？”油燭想。“我可能要和窮人一起過，他們連個銅燭臺都沒有，而蠟燭則坐在銀燭臺上，看着所有高貴的人。照耀高貴的人該多好啊，不過我生來就是脂油做的，也就只能如此。”

於是這油燭來到窮人手中。他們是一個寡婦和三個孩子，住在那富人家對面一個低矮的小房間裏。

“上帝保佑善良的夫人，她給我們所有這些東西，”寡婦説。“多好的油燭啊，它可以在夜裏點到很晚。”

她劃了一根火柴點燃它。

“呸，呸，”油燭説。“點燃我的火柴氣味真糟糕啊，在對門那富貴人家的蠟燭才不會有如此遭遇。”

那一邊的蠟燭也都點亮了。它們把外面的街也照得通亮，馬車隆隆地送來了參加舞會的優雅客人。音樂奏起來了。

“現在舞會開始了，”油燭注意到。它想起富有小女孩那張比所有蠟燭的光更亮的小臉。“那景象我再也看不到了。”

這時窮人家最小的女兒用雙臂摟過哥哥和姐姐的脖子。她要告訴他們的話太重要了，因此只能悄悄地說。"今晚我們會吃到——想想看吧——今晚會吃到熱的馬鈴薯！"

她的臉放射出幸福的光芒，油燭也正好把光照耀到她臉上。它看到她幸福快樂得就像當時富人家那小女孩說："我們今晚有舞會，我要紮上我的大紅腰帶！"

"這跟吃到熱馬鈴薯一樣快樂。"油燭想。"這裏的孩子也是同樣快樂的。"它打了個噴嚏，油脂滴滴答答地落下了，一支油燭也只能做到這樣。

桌子擺好了，馬鈴薯吃完了。它們多麼好吃啊！這真是一頓盛宴。一人還分到一個蘋果，最小的孩子作謝恩禱告：

"親愛的上帝，多謝你又滋養了我們。阿門。"

"媽媽，我說得好嗎？"小女孩問道。

"不要說這樣的話，"她的媽媽對她說。"只要感謝好心的上帝讓你吃飽就是了。"

孩子們上床，媽媽吻他們道晚安，他們很快就睡着了。他們的媽媽坐到夜深，縫衣服來養活他們和自己。富人家中透出亮光，傳出音樂。但是頭頂上的星光同樣明亮和神聖，照耀着所有房子，不分貧富。

"這是一個了不起的夜晚，"油燭心裏說，"蠟燭在它的銀燭臺上能有更美好的時光嗎？在我點完以前，我倒很想知道。"

它想起兩個快樂的孩子，一張臉被蠟燭照亮，另一張臉在油燭的光中閃亮。

對，這就是整個故事！

30

# 老約翰妮講的故事

風在那棵老柳樹間呼嘯，彷彿在聽一首歌，風吟唱那故事，樹則講述它。如果你聽不懂，就去問濟貧院裏的老約翰妮吧。她了解這裏，她是在這個教區出生的。

許多年前，當那條舊公路還在這裏時，這棵樹就已經很大，很惹人注目了。它那時和現在一樣矗立在裁縫那座用石灰水刷白的木屋前面，靠近水溝。水溝那時候很寬，牛羣也到那裏來喝水，夏天的時候，農家孩子常光着身體在那邊跑來跑去，在水裏划船。樹下有一塊大石鑿出來的里程碑，里程碑現在翻倒了，上面長出懸鈎子矮樹叢。

新公路如今築在那個富有農民的農莊的另一邊，舊公路成了田間小路，水溝也成了長滿浮萍的水潭，如果一隻青蛙跳進去，浮萍散開，就會看到黑色的死水。水溝周圍不斷生長着睡菜和黃色的鳶尾花。

裁縫的房子又舊又歪，屋頂成了青苔和長生草的溫床。鴿棚已經塌了，椋鳥在那裏築起了牠們的巢。燕子一個接一個掛牠們的巢在房子的三角牆上和整個屋簷下，好像幸運之神本身住在那裏似的。

幸運之神確曾眷顧這裏，但現在這是一個孤寂的地方。這裏孤零零地住着那個優柔寡斷的"可憐的拉斯木斯"，大家都這樣叫他。他在這裏出生，他也在這裏遊玩，曾滿草原跳，跳過樹籬，他小時候還曾跳到水溝裏去玩水，曾爬上那棵老樹。老樹會自豪和優美地伸展它那些大樹枝，就像現在也伸展它們一樣，不過暴風雨早已將樹幹彎曲了一點，時日也給了它一道裂口。自此以後，狂風和惡劣天氣不斷把泥土填進裂口，那裏長出了草和植物。對，甚至一棵小唐棣也在那裏安身。

春天燕子飛來時，繞着這棵樹和那屋頂飛，修補牠們的舊鳥窩，可憐的拉斯木斯卻放任他自己的小窩自己傾頹。他的格言是："那有甚麼用處呢？"這也是他父親的格言。

他就這樣留在他這個家裏。燕子飛走了，但牠們總會回來，多忠誠的鳥兒！椋鳥飛走了，但牠也會回來，又吹口哨似的吱吱喳喳唱牠的歌。拉斯木斯曾經也會唱，但是他現在不吹口哨也不唱歌了。

風那時候也在那棵老柳樹間呼嘯，就像現在一樣，一點不假，就彷彿在聽一首歌。風吟唱那故事，樹則講述它。如果你聽不懂，就去問濟貧院裏的老約翰妮吧。她了解這裏，多年前的事情她全知道，她就像一本歷史書，上面有銘文，也有古老的回憶。

當這房子還是嶄新完好的時候，鄉村裁縫伊瓦爾·奧爾塞和他的妻子瑪倫搬了進去，他們兩個都是勤勞忠厚的普通人。那時候老約翰妮還是個孩子，是個木頭鞋工匠的女兒，他可算是這教區最窮的人之一了。小約翰妮從瑪倫那裏得到許多好吃的三文治，因為瑪倫不缺食物。地主太太喜歡瑪倫，因為瑪倫總是嘻嘻哈哈，那麼快活，從不垂頭喪氣。她舌燦蓮花，手也巧得很，她動手縫紉和她動嘴一樣快，而且她對家務和孩子們關懷備至。她生的孩子接近一打，一共十一個，第十二個胎死腹中了。

"窮人總是孩子一大窩，"地主哇哇叫。"如果能像小貓那樣淹死他們，只留下一兩個最強壯的，就不會那麼不幸了！"

"上帝會發慈悲的！"裁縫的妻子說。"孩子們是上帝的賜予，他們使家庭那麼快樂。多一個孩子是多一份祈禱。如果日子不好過，有許多張嘴要餵，那麼，就應該更努力工作，老老實實想想辦法。只要我們不洩氣，我們的上帝是不會辜負我們的。"

地主太太同意裁縫妻子的話，她善意地點點頭，拍拍瑪倫的臉頰。她常常這樣做，是的，還吻過她，但那是在她年紀還很小，瑪倫當她奶媽的時候，她們兩個很親熱，這種感情沒有變過。

每年聖誕，莊園會送過冬的食物到裁縫家來 —— 一大桶肉、一頭豬、兩隻鵝、一小桶牛油、芝士，還有蘋果。這的確大大增加了他們儲存的食物。伊瓦爾·奧爾塞看起來也十分高興，但是他那句老格言很快又來了："那有甚麼用處呢？"

房子乾淨又整潔，窗上掛着窗簾，還放着花，有康乃馨和鳳仙花。一幅鑲在畫框裏的刺繡懸掛着，緊靠着它是一首押韻的情詩，是瑪倫·奧爾塞自己寫的，她很會押韻。她為他們家姓奧爾塞甚至有點自豪，在丹麥語裏只有這個字和"波爾塞"（香腸）押韻。"這至少勝過其他人，"她說道，並哈哈笑起來。她總是情緒很好，從來不像她丈夫那樣說："那有甚麼用處呢？"她的格言是："相信自己和我們的上帝。"她也這麼做了，這使一家人團聚在一起，孩子們茁壯成長，長大到在家裏留不下去了，就去闖世界，都幹得很興旺發達。

拉斯木斯是她最小的孩子，這孩子長得那麼漂亮，首都一位肖像畫大師還借他去當模特兒畫了一幅畫，在這幅畫裏他渾身赤條條，就如來到世界時那樣子。那幅畫如今正掛在皇宮裏。地主太太看過這幅畫，雖然小拉斯木斯身上甚麼也沒有穿，但是她還是認出他來了。

　　但是現在困難的日子到了。裁縫雙手患風濕病，腫得很厲害，醫生全沒有辦法，連懂一點"醫道"的靈媒斯坦也幫不了忙。

　　"一個人千萬不要洩氣，"瑪倫説。"垂頭喪氣毫無用處。現在我們再沒有爸爸的雙手來幫忙了，我必須加快我雙手的速度。小拉斯木斯也能操針。"他已經坐在縫紉桌旁，吹着口哨唱着歌。他是個快活的孩子。"不過他不該在那裏坐一整天，"母親説，"這對於孩子會是罪過，他也要到處玩玩跳跳。"

　　鞋匠家的約翰妮是他的遊戲好伙伴，她家比拉斯木斯家還要窮，她長得不好看，她光着腳走來走去，衣服破破爛爛，因為沒有人給她補衣服，又沒有想到要給自己補一補，她年紀還小，在上帝的陽光中快活得像隻小鳥。

　　拉斯木斯和約翰妮在那棵大柳樹下面的里程碑旁邊玩。他雄心壯志，有一天要成為一個著名的裁縫，住到城裏去，那裏有一些裁縫老闆僱用十來個裁縫，這是他從父親那裏聽來的。他要去那裏先當學徒，然後成為裁縫老闆，到那時候約翰妮可以去看他。如果到那時候她會下廚，她可以給他們大夥做飯，她還可以有一個她單獨住的大房間。這種事約翰妮連想也不敢想，可是拉斯木斯相信他會做到。他們坐在老樹下，風在樹枝和樹葉間呼嘯，好像是風在唱歌，樹在説話。

秋天樹葉落光了，雨從光禿禿的樹枝上落下來。"它們會再次變綠的，"奧爾塞媽媽說。

"那有甚麼用處呢？"她的丈夫說。"新的一年來了，我們的生活又有新煩惱。"

"放食物的櫃子裝得滿滿的，"他妻子說。"為了這件事我們要感謝我們好心的太太。我身體健康，精力充沛。再發牢騷就是罪過了。"

莊園主人和他太太在鄉下過了聖誕節，但是在新年過後的那個禮拜，他們進城去了，到那裏熱熱鬧鬧、快快活活過一個冬天。他們甚至要參加國王本人的招待會和舞會。這太太帶了兩套法國來的華貴衣服，它們的質料是那麼好，式樣是那麼新潮，縫製是那麼精妙，這樣華貴的衣服裁縫的妻子瑪倫還從來沒有見過。她問太太可否帶她丈夫到她家來一次，讓他也看一下她的衣服，開開眼界。一個鄉下裁縫絕不可能見過這樣的衣服，她說。他總算看到它們了，一句話也沒有說，直到回到家才開口，說的又是他那句老話："那有甚麼用處呢？"這一回他說對了。

莊園主人和他太太進了城，舞會和狂歡開始了，但是就在這輝煌時刻，莊園主人卻死了，於是太太穿不成她這些華麗的衣服。她太悲痛了，從頭到腳穿上了黑色喪服，連一塊白花邊披肩也看不到。所有僕人也都穿黑衣服，大馬車也罩上了黑布。

這是一個冰冷的夜，雪閃爍着，星星閃鑠着，沉重的靈車把遺體從城裏送回鄉下的教堂，他將葬在那裏家庭墳地的墓穴。管事和教區執事騎着馬，舉着火把，在墓地的大門口等着。教堂點起了燈，牧師站在教堂開着的門前迎接遺體。棺材被送上高壇，所有送喪的人跟在後面。牧師講了話，讚美詩唱過了，太太也在教堂裏。她坐一輛蒙着黑紗、裏外都是黑色的大馬車來，這樣的車教區以前還沒有見過。

整個冬天人們都在談論這難忘的哀悼場面，這真正是一個"貴族的葬禮"。

"一看就知道這人有多重要，"村裏人說。"他生來高貴，死了埋葬也得高貴。"

"這對他有甚麼用處呢？"那裁縫說。"現在他既沒有了生命，也沒有了財產。我們至少還有其中一樣。"

"不要說這種話！"瑪倫說。"他在天國裏得到了永生。"

"這話是誰告訴你的，瑪倫？"裁縫說。"死人是很好的肥料，但是這個人高貴得甚至不能給泥土任何好處，他必須躺在教堂的墓穴裏。"

"不要說得那麼不敬！"瑪倫說。"我跟你再說一遍，他得到了永生！"

"這話是誰告訴你的，瑪倫？"裁縫又重複一次。瑪倫把她的圍裙蓋在小拉斯木斯頭上，不能讓他聽到這種話。她帶他到外面的泥炭屋裏去，哭了起來。

"你在那裏聽到的話，小拉斯木斯，不是你爸爸說的，是魔鬼經過這房間，用你爸爸的聲音說出來的。現在你唸主禱文吧。我們兩個一起唸。"她把孩子的雙手交疊起來。"現在我又高興了，"她說。"對你自己和對我們的上帝要有信心。"

一年喪期滿了，如今寡婦太太只穿半孝，但她心中十分快樂。傳說有人在追求她，她已經在考慮再嫁了。瑪倫知道一點，牧師知道得更多一些。

在棕枝主日那天，寡婦跟未婚夫的結婚公告要在佈道後發佈了。他是木雕師或者說是雕塑家。他職業的名稱是甚麼，人們無從得知。當時沒多少人聽說過托瓦爾森和他的藝術。未來的莊園主人不是貴族，但他仍然是一個優雅高貴的人。他們說，他的職業人們不理解。他雕出塑像，擅長自己的工作，而且年輕英俊。"那有甚麼用處呢？"裁縫說。

就這樣，在棕枝主日那天，結婚公告在佈道壇上發佈了。接下來是唱讚美詩和領受聖餐。裁縫、他妻子和小拉斯木斯都在教堂裏。雙親去領聖餐時，拉斯木斯坐在座位上，因為他還沒有領受堅信禮。近來裁縫家缺衣服，但衣服翻了又翻，補了又補。這一回他們都穿上了新衣服，但都是黑布做的，像在葬禮上一樣。他們穿的衣服就是用靈車上的黑布做的。裁縫做了上衣和褲子，瑪倫做了高領連衣裙，拉斯木斯做了套可以一直穿到領受堅信禮的正裝。靈車內外的布都用上了。沒有人需要知道這些布以前是用來做甚麼的，但是人們很快就會知道了。

那個靈媒，還有兩個同樣通神但不靠此吃飯的女人，都說這種衣服會給家中帶來疾病。"穿用靈車布做衣服的人無一不是自掘墳墓。"木頭鞋工匠家的約翰妮一聽到這種話就哭起來。碰巧裁縫從那天開始病重，直到看來十分明顯：他要遭到這個命運了。結果證明的確如此。

在聖三一主日之後的那個星期日，奧爾塞裁縫去世了，留下瑪倫安排所有事情。她做到了，對自己和我們的上帝保有信心。

下一年拉斯木斯領受了堅信禮，於是他準備進城跟一個裁縫老闆當學徒，這不是一個僱有十名裁縫的裁縫老闆，而只僱了一名，小拉斯木斯可以算半個。他很高興，看起來的確高興，但是約翰妮哭了，她比原先自己想的更喜歡他。裁縫的妻子在那舊房子裏留下來，繼續做她的工作。

新的"國王公路"就是在這時候開通的，柳樹和裁縫家旁邊的那條舊公路就成了田間小路，水溝剩下的那潭水上長滿了浮萍。里程碑也翻倒了，因為它甚麼也不能表示了，但是那棵樹保持着它的健壯和美麗，風在它的枝葉間呼嘯、離開。

燕子都飛走了，那椋鳥也飛走了，不過牠們春天又回來了。當牠們第四次回來的時候，拉斯木斯也回到了他的家，他當學徒已經出師，成了一個英俊但瘦削的小伙子。現在他可以背上背包到外國去開開眼界了，那是他朝思暮想的。但是他的母親捨不得他走，家是最好的地方！其他孩子全都在外四散，他是最小的，房子將要給他。如果他在附近走走，他可以拿到很多工作做——當一個流動裁縫，在這個農莊做兩星期，在那個農莊做兩星期，那也是周遊啊。拉斯木斯終於聽從了他母親的勸告。

於是他又睡在他出生地的屋頂底下，他又坐在那棵老柳樹底下聽它呼嘯。他長得的確好看，能像小鳥那樣吹口哨，能唱新的舊的歌。

他很受所有大農莊歡迎，特別是在克勞斯‧漢臣的農莊，他是這教區第二富有的農民。他的女兒艾斯看起來像一朵最美麗的花，她總是笑呵呵，有些人壞得拿她開玩笑，這不過是為了炫耀她美麗的牙齒。她實在快活，總是有興緻開玩笑，樣樣事情都合她的意。

她喜歡拉斯木斯，他也喜歡她，但他們沒有互露心聲。因此他總是陰沉沉的，他的性格像父親多於像母親。只有艾斯在場的時候他的心情才會好起來，這時候他們相視而笑，説笑話，開彼此玩笑。但是雖然機會很多，他對自己的愛卻一字不提。"那有甚麼用處呢？"這就是他的想法。"她父母為她物色會帶來好處的婚姻，我卻不能給她好處。我最聰明的做法就是離開。"但是他離不開，就好像艾斯用線拴住了他似的。他就像艾斯的一隻受過訓練的鳥兒，他唱歌吹口哨都為了討她喜歡，聽她的意思。

約翰妮，那個鞋匠的女兒，如今就在這個農莊裏當女僕，做些普通工作。她在大草地上駕駛裝牛奶的大車，她和其他女孩在那裏擠奶。對，需要時她還要駕駛裝肥料的大車。她從不到客廳裏來，不常見到拉斯木斯或者艾斯，但是她聽説他們兩個好得像訂了婚似的。

"現在拉斯木斯要交上好運了，"她説。"這件事我不能妒忌他。"她的眼睛濕了，但是實在沒甚麼可以哭。

城裏有個市集，克勞斯·漢臣駕車上那裏去，拉斯木斯跟着去了，他坐在艾斯旁邊，雙雙同去同回。他愛她都愛得沖昏頭腦了，但是這件事他一個字也沒有説出來。

"這件事他應該對我説句甚麼，"女孩心裏説，這是對的。"如果他不説，我要嚇得他説出來。"

不久農莊裏傳言，教區裏那最有錢的農場主已經向艾斯求婚。他的確是求婚了，但沒有人知道她怎麼回答。

於是拉斯木斯腦裏各種念頭在翻騰。

有一天晚上，艾斯在手指上戴上一隻金戒指，問拉斯木斯這表示甚麼意思。

"訂了婚，"他説。

"你覺得是跟誰？"她問道。

"跟那個有錢的農場主？"他説。

"對了，你猜中了，"她點頭説着，溜走了。

但是他也溜走了，他像發了瘋一樣回到母親的房子收拾背包，他要離家到外面廣闊的世界去，連他母親的眼淚也阻止不了他。

他為自己從老柳樹上砍了一根手杖，裝出心情很好的樣子吹起了口哨。他要去看看整個美麗的世界。

"我非常難過，"母親説。"不過我想，你離開對你來説是最聰明和最好的做法，因此我只好接受了。對自己和我們的上帝要有信心，那麼我將看到你快快活活地回來。"

他沿着那條新公路走，看見約翰妮趕着一車垃圾過來。約翰妮沒有看到他，他也不想被她看到，於是在樹籬後面坐下。他在那裏被遮住，約翰妮駕駛着車經過了。

他到廣闊的世界裏去了，沒有人知道他在哪裏。他母親想："在不到一年他一定會回來的。現在他要看新事物，要想新事物了，但是接下來他會重返舊路，舊痕跡用熨斗也熨不掉。他的性格太像他父親了，我真希望他有我的性格，可憐的孩子！但是他一定會回家的，他不能忘記我或者這房子。"

母親可以等上一年，艾斯只等了一個月就偷偷地去找那個靈媒斯坦·馬斯達特，她除了懂點"醫道"以外，還會用塔羅牌和咖啡渣算吉凶，除了主禱文還知道其他更多東西。她自然就知道拉斯木斯現在身在何處，她是在咖啡渣渣中看出來的。他正在一個外國城市，只是城市的名字她沒能看出來，這個城市裏有許多大兵和美女。他正在考慮或者當兵，或者在年輕女孩中找一個結婚。

聽了這件事艾斯受不了，她情願拿出她全部的儲蓄去買他回來，不過不能讓任何人知道那是她做的。

斯坦保證他會回來，她可以施一種魔法，一種對他來說很危險但有效的魔法。這是最後一個補救辦法了。她要為他燒滾一鍋魔湯，然後，不管他在世界上甚麼地方，他不得不回到有一鍋魔湯在燒滾、有他的愛人在等着他的家裏來，可能要等幾個月，但是他只要還活着就一定會回來。他會日夜得不到安寧和休息，不得不漂洋過海、翻山越嶺，不管天氣是好是壞，哪怕腳都累壞了，也得趕着回家來。他會回家的，他必須回家。

這時候是上弦月，斯坦說正該趁這時候施魔法。這一陣是暴風雨天氣，老柳樹裂開了。斯坦砍下一根柳枝，打成一個結。它一定能幫助把拉斯木斯引回他母親的家來。她從屋頂採下青苔和長生草放到燉在火上的鍋裏。艾斯還必須從詩篇裏撕下一頁放進去，她隨手撕下了最後一頁，是個勘誤表。"那也行！"斯坦說着，也扔它到鍋裏去了。

鍋裏放進了許多各式各樣的東西，這鍋東西要不停地燒，一直燒到拉斯木斯回來。斯坦房間裏那隻黑公雞的紅雞冠被扔到鍋裏去了，艾斯那枚大金戒指也到鍋裏去了，斯坦還預先告訴她，她再也拿不回了。斯坦靈力實在太強了。扔進鍋的東西多得我們無法一一列舉，鍋子就在火焰上，或者在發光的炭上，或者在熾熱的灰燼上一直燒個不停。這件事只有她和艾斯兩個人知道。

每逢月圓月缺，艾斯都到她這裏來問：“你看到他來了嗎？”

“我知道的事情很多，”斯坦説，“我看見的東西很多，但是我看不見他要走的路有多長。現在他在過第一重山；現在他正在惡劣的天氣中渡海。路很長，還要穿過一座座森林。他腳上起了泡，他骨頭都在發燒，但是他必須向前走。”

“不，不，”艾斯説。“我為他感到難過。”

“他現在沒有辦法停下來了，因為我們如果讓他停下來，他就要倒下來死在路上！”

一年過去了，月亮照下來，又圓又大，風在老樹上呼嘯，彩虹在明亮的月光中橫過天際。

“那徵兆證明了我的話，”斯坦説。“現在拉斯木斯要回來了。”

但是他沒有回來。

“等待的時間是漫長的，”斯坦説。

“現在我等累了，”艾斯説。如今她很少來看斯坦，不再送東西給她。她的心變得輕鬆，有一天早晨，教區裏大家都知道艾斯已經答應了那個富有農場主的求婚。她到那裏去看了房子和田產，看了牛羣，看了家中的財物。一切情況良好，舉行婚禮的日子沒有理由再等下去了。

盛大的慶祝一連舉行了三天。大家跟着笛子和小提琴的音樂跳舞。教區裏沒有一個人被忘記邀請。奧爾塞媽媽也去了，當慶祝會結束，主人謝過客人，喇叭已經吹過的時候，她帶着宴會剩下來的東西回家了。

她本來只用一個插銷把門拴住。插銷給拔掉了，門開着，房間裏坐着拉斯木斯。他回家了，就在這個時候回來了。上帝啊，看他那副模樣！他只有皮包着骨頭，他又蒼白又黃。

　　"拉斯木斯！"他的母親説。"我看到的是你嗎？你看起來多麼糟啊！但是你終於回來了，我太高興了。"

　　她給他吃她從宴會帶回來的美食，一塊烤肉和一塊結婚蛋糕。

　　他説他近來老是想念母親，想家和那棵老柳樹。非常奇怪，他經常夢見這棵樹和光着腳的小約翰妮。他一點沒有提到艾斯，他病了，只好上床休息去。

　　但是我們不相信他回來都是由於那鍋子，或者那鍋子對他施展了甚麼魔法。這件事只有斯坦和艾斯相信，但是她們不説出來。

　　拉斯木斯躺在那裏發燒——他得了種傳染病。因此沒有人到裁縫的房子來，只除了約翰妮，那鞋匠的女兒。當她看到拉斯木斯有多悲慘的時候，她哭了。

　　醫生給他開了藥方到藥房去配。他不肯吃藥。"那有甚麼用處呢？"他説。

　　"吃了藥你就會好，"他的母親説。"對你自己和我們的上帝要有信心！只要我能看到你身上重新長出肉來，聽見你吹口哨和唱歌，我情願獻出我的生命。"

　　拉斯木斯的病醫好了，但是他母親生病了。我們的上帝召喚去的是她，而不是他。

　　在家裏孤孤單單的，他越來越窮。"他已筋疲力盡，"教區裏大家説。"可憐的拉斯木斯。"是他在旅行中過着的放蕩生活，而不是燒滾的黑鍋吸去了他的精力，使他的身體留下痛苦。他的頭髮變得稀疏灰白了。他懶得去工作。"那有甚麼用處呢？"他說。他情願上酒館而不去教堂。

一個秋天傍晚，他在風雨中搖搖晃晃地沿着泥濘的路從酒館回家，這時候他的母親早已去世，躺在她的墳墓裏了。燕子和椋鳥那麼忠誠的動物也飛走了。只有約翰妮，那鞋匠的女兒沒有走。她在路上追上了他，接着陪他走了一段路。

"要振作起來，拉斯木斯。"

"那有甚麼用處呢？"他說。

"你說的話太可怕了，"她說。"要記住你母親的話：'對你自己和我們的上帝要有信心。'你沒有這樣做，拉斯木斯，但是你必須這樣做，你會這樣做的。永遠不要再說：'那有甚麼用處呢？'因為這樣你就甚麼也不做了。"

她一直送他到他家門口，然後才離開他。他沒有留在屋裏，他走到外面那棵老柳樹下，坐在那塊翻倒的里程石碑上。

風在樹枝間呼嘯，聽起來像唱歌，像說話。

拉斯木斯回答它，他說出聲來，但是除了樹和呼嘯的風，沒有人聽見。

"我太冷了。該去上床了。睡覺吧，睡覺吧！"

他走了，但不是朝房子走，而是走過那條水溝，在那裏他搖晃一下，跌倒了。雨傾盆而下，風像冰一樣冷，但是他感覺不到。當太陽升起，烏鴉飛過香蒲時，他醒來了，病得快死。萬一他的頭是在腳的地方，他就永遠起不來了，綠色的浮萍就會成為他的裹屍衣。

那天稍晚一些時候，約翰妮到裁縫的房子來。她照料他，她好不容易送他進醫院。

"我們從小就相識，"她說。"你母親給我喝的和吃的，這些我永遠無法報答她。你的身體會好起來的，你會成為一個有信心活下去的人！"

我們的上帝要他活下去。但是他的健康和精神時好時壞。

燕子和椋鳥回來了，飛走了，又回來了。拉斯木斯看起來比他的歲數老。他一個人坐在他越來越破舊的房子裏。他很窮，現在比約翰妮還要窮。

"你沒有信仰，"她說，"如果我們不相信上帝，那我們還有甚麼呢？你應該去領受聖餐，"她說，"你領受堅信禮以後還沒有去過教堂。"

"那有甚麼用處呢？"他說。

"如果你這樣說也這樣相信，那就算了吧。上帝不要一個不情願的客人坐在他的桌旁。但是想想你母親和你的童年吧。你曾是一個虔誠的好孩子。讓我讀一首詩篇給你聽。"

"那有甚麼用處呢？"他說。

"它總能使我得到安慰，"她回答。

"約翰妮，你真變成一個聖徒了。"他用暗淡和疲倦的眼睛看着她。

於是約翰妮讀詩篇，但不是對着書讀，因為她手頭沒有書，她是背出來的。

"都是些美麗的話，"他說，"但是我不能全部聽懂你說的，我覺得頭多麼重。"

拉斯木斯已經成了一個老人。不過艾斯，如果我們還可以提一提她的話，也不再年輕了。拉斯木斯從來不提她。她已經是一個祖母，她的孫女是一個沒有禮貌的小女孩。

這小女孩正和別的孩子在村子裏玩。拉斯木斯拄着他的手杖走過來，他停下腳步看孩子們玩，對她們微笑，他想起了往昔的日子。艾斯的孫女指着他，"可憐的拉斯木斯！"她尖聲叫道。其他的小女孩們也學她的樣。"可憐的拉斯木斯！"她們吼道，尖叫着並追着這位老人。這是一個灰色陰暗的日子，接下來許多天都這樣，但是在這些灰色陰暗的日子之後，迎來了一個陽光明媚的日子。

那是美麗的聖靈降臨節早晨。教堂裝飾着綠色的白樺樹枝，樹林氣息充斥殿內，陽光落在教堂長椅上。大祭壇上燃點起蠟燭，聖餐正在舉行。約翰妮是跪着的眾人之一，但拉斯木斯並不在其中。上帝那天早上召喚他了。

承蒙上帝天恩和慈悲。

自那以後，許多年過去了。裁縫的房子仍舊在那裏，但是裏面沒有人住。只要碰到一個暴風雨之夜，它就會倒塌。水溝長滿了香蒲和睡菜，風在那棵老樹間呼嘯，彷彿在聽一首歌，風吟唱那故事，樹講述它。如果你聽不懂，就去問濟貧院裏的老約翰妮吧。

她仍舊住在那裏，唱她的詩篇，她曾讀給拉斯木斯聽的那一首。她想起他，為他向我們的上帝禱告 —— 她，這位忠誠的人，她能夠講出過去的日子，講出在那棵老柳樹間呼嘯着的記憶。

# 31
# 園丁和貴族人家

離城約十五里，矗立着一座古宅，有厚牆、塔樓和尖尖的三角牆。住在這古宅裏的是一個富貴人家，但也只有夏天來住。他們擁有不同莊園，這是最好和最美麗的一座。從外表看它像是剛完工，裏面佈置得舒適方便。這一家的盾徽刻在大門頂的石頭上，盾徽和陽臺周圍爬着美麗的玫瑰花，院子鋪着青草，這裏有紅山楂、白山楂，連溫室外面都長滿了奇花異草。這古宅的主人有一個非常有經驗的園丁。看看這些花圃、果園和菜地真是件賞心樂事。古宅原來的花園一部份仍在，幾排密密的黃楊樹都修剪成皇冠和金字塔的形狀。這些樹籬後面有兩棵參天古樹，幾乎總是沒有葉子，很容易叫人想到，風暴或者水龍捲把大堆大堆泥土撒到它們的樹枝上了，但每一堆泥土都只是一個鳥巢。自遙遠的過去起，一大羣吱吱喳喳的烏鴉和白嘴鴉就在這裏築起了牠們的巢，這成了一座鳥城，而這些鳥成了鳥城的主人。牠們不把古宅的主人——古宅最古老的家族——放在眼內，也不放現在的主人在眼內——這對牠們毫無價值，但牠們容忍着這些在牠們之下遊走的生物，即使他們有時用槍打牠們，嚇得烏鴉的背脊骨直哆嗦，飛起來大叫："嘎！嘎！"

園丁常對這貴族人家說該砍掉這兩棵古樹，它們並不好看，砍掉它們也就擺脫掉那些吱吱喳喳的鳥，這樣牠們大概會另找住處。但是這家人既不想放棄樹，也不想放棄這成羣的鳥，那是過去美好時代的遺產，應該好好保存作為紀念。

主人說，"要知道，那兩棵樹是今天的鳥繼承的遺產，就讓它們保留着吧，我的好拉臣！"拉臣是這個園丁的名字，但跟這個故事絕少關係。"你要工作的地方還不夠嗎，小拉臣？你不是有花園、溫室、果園和菜園了嗎？"他照料着它們，把它們安排得井井有條，充滿愛心和很有經驗地種植它們，這一點貴族一家人都知道。但是在他面前，他們也不掩飾，常常在別人家看到一些花，吃到一些水果比他們自己花園裏種出來的好，這很叫園丁難過，因為他總希望盡力做好工作，而他的確也盡力了。他是一個好心腸、勤懇和盡職的工人。

有一天，這貴族家的人叫他來，很和氣地說，前一天在某個有名望的朋友家裏吃到一些蘋果和梨，汁水那麼多，香味那麼好，他們和所有其他客人全都讚賞不已。大家疑心這些水果不是本地的，他們應該引進並移植到這裏，只要氣候條件允許。只知道這些水果是在城裏某個最好的水果商那裏買來的，他們決定讓園丁到那裏去查問這些蘋果和梨來自何處，訂購一些插條回來嫁接。園丁正好很熟悉那位水果商，因為他正把古宅花園裏多餘的水果賣給他。園丁進城去問這個水果商，那些眾口交譽的蘋果和梨他是從哪裏買來的。

"怎麼，就是你自己那個花園產的啊，"水果商說着，給他看蘋果和梨，他一看就馬上認出來了。園丁覺得多麼高興啊！他趕緊回來告訴主人，蘋果和梨都是他們自己的花園裏種出來的。但他不相信！

"那不可能。拉臣！你能從水果商那裏拿到這件事的書面保證嗎？"是的，他能夠，他拿書面保證回來了。

"這的確了不起！"貴族家人説。

現在每天在桌上擺上大盤大盤在他們自己花園所種的出色的蘋果和梨。這些水果還一筐筐、一桶桶地送給城裏和城外的朋友，對了，甚至運到外國。這件事使這一家人十分快活，不過他們認為，這當然是因為近兩年夏天水果生長特別好，全國各地水果都長得非常好。

過了一些時候，這家人到宮廷參加了一個晚宴。第二天他們叫來園丁。在皇家飯桌上他們吃到了皇家溫室種出來的西瓜，汁水多，香得不得了。"你必須去見宮廷園丁，讓他拿這些珍貴甜瓜種子給你。"

"但是宮廷園丁的甜瓜種子是從我們這裏拿去的！"園丁很高興地説。

"那麼，這個人懂得怎樣把瓜果培養得更好！"那家人説。"每一個瓜都非常好吃。"

"那我真正能夠感到自豪了！"園丁説。"我必須告訴老爺太太你們，宮廷園丁今年種瓜運氣不好，他看到我們這裏的瓜樣子那麼漂亮，嚐了嚐，給皇宮訂了三個。"

"拉臣，你不是要對我們説，那些西瓜是從我們花園買去的吧？"

"真的，我敢這樣説，"園丁説。於是園丁去看宮廷園丁，從他那裏拿到了一張書面保證，皇家餐桌上的甜瓜是從古宅這裏買的。對於這家人來說，這真正是一件大出意料之外的事。他們並不打算保持低調，把甜瓜種子派得又遠又廣，如同早些時候他們派嫁接枝條那樣。這家人後來聽說這些枝條生根發芽了，結出優質的果子。這個品種就以這家古宅命名，這個名字傳到了英國、德國和法國。

這件事是誰也沒有想過的。

"但願園丁不要自以為了不起，"這家人說。但是園丁另有想法。他現在力求讓大家知道他是國內最好的園丁之一，每年從各種園藝品種中出產一些優良產品。這一點他做到了。但他常聽說，他最早培植出來的水果，那些蘋果和梨，始終是最好的，但所有後來改良的品種就差多了。甜瓜的確非常好，不過它們是屬另一個種類的。他的草莓可以說是鮮美的，不過不比別的花園種的好。等到有一年他蘿蔔種得不大好，大家就光說這些不成功的蘿蔔，而不提他改良了的好產品。

這家人倒好像感到鬆了口氣似的說："今年種得不好啊，小拉臣！"是的，他們好像十分高興似的說："今年沒有種好！"

園丁一星期兩次送鮮花到他們的客廳來，高雅的搭配讓顏色看起來更鮮豔。

"你有很好的審美力，拉臣，"貴族家人說，"但那是出於我們的上帝所賜，而不是出於你自己！"

有一天園丁端進來一個水晶大鉢，裏面漂着一片白色睡蓮花瓣，上面放着一朵美麗的藍花，大得和向日葵一樣，長而厚實的莖枝垂延至水中。

"印度蓮花！"這家人叫起來。他們從來沒有見過這樣的花。

白天它放在陽光裏，傍晚它放在人造光底下。看到它的人個個覺得它異常美麗和非比尋常。是的，連國內最高貴的年輕小姐，那聰明和仁慈的公主也這麼說。古宅主人認為這是一種榮幸，把花送了給她，公主帶它到皇宮去了。接着貴族家人到他們的花園要採一朵同樣的花，但是怎麼也找不到。於是他們叫園丁來，問他這朵藍色的蓮花放到哪裏了。

"我們一直在找這種花，但是找不到，"他說。"我到過溫室了，在花園裏也找了一遍！"

"噢，不，它不在那些地方，"園丁說。"它只是菜園裏一種普通的花，不過看吧，它不是很漂亮嗎！它看起來就像藍色的仙人掌，然而它只是洋薊花！"

"你一開頭就該告訴我們了！"貴族家人說。"我們自然以為它是一種罕見的外國花。你在年輕的公主面前嘲弄了我們！她看到我們家這花，認為它很美麗。她雖然精通植物學，但不認識這花，那當然，科學和蔬菜完全無關。你怎麼可以這樣做呢，我的好拉臣！放這樣的花在我們的客廳裏就夠讓我們丟臉了！"

於是，來自菜園那朵美麗的花，從客廳給拿走，它不屬這個地方。不錯，貴族家人馬上去向公主道歉，告訴她這花只是一種蔬菜，園丁竟異想天開拿它來陳列，為此他已被嚴厲訓斥了。

"那太不應該了，非常不公平，"公主說。"他真正打開了我們眼界，使我們在意想不到的地方看到了美麗的花。只要洋薊開花，我們的宮廷園丁就將每天送一朵到我的私人房間去！"

貴族家人通知園丁，他可以再給他們送來一朵新鮮的洋薊花。"它的確漂亮！"他們說。"無比出眾！"園丁受到了稱讚。

"拉臣喜歡獲稱讚，"貴族家人說。"他像個寵壞了的孩子。"

秋天裏來了一場風暴，夜間更是加劇了，樹林邊許多大樹被連根拔掉。有一件事對於這家貴族來說是巨大的悲痛，而對於園丁來說則是喜事，那兩棵大樹連同所有鳥巢被吹倒了。風暴期間，古宅裏可以聽到烏鴉和白嘴鴉用翅膀敲擊窗時嘎嘎的尖叫聲。

"現在你當然快活了，拉臣！"貴族家人說。"暴風吹倒了那兩棵樹，鳥也飛到樹林裏去了。這裏再沒有舊時留下來的東西可看了，全都消失了，我們非常難過！"

園丁甚麼也沒有說，但他想起了久已存在於他腦裏的一件事，就是怎樣利用那塊陽光照耀着了不起的地方，讓這塊地方可以修飾花園，成為這家人的驕傲。那兩棵大樹倒下來時壓塌了那些非常古老的，修剪得非常別緻的黃楊樹籬。

他在這裏移栽了許多其他花園中看不到的植物。他弄了一面土牆，上面移植了各種各樣從本地田野上和樹林裏移來的植物。沒有園丁曾想到可以種在宅邸花園裏的植物他都種了，並完全根據植物各自的需要，給每一棵植物合適的土壤、陽光或樹蔭。他愛護它們，它們全都長得非常好。來自日德蘭半島荒野的杜松樹長得就像意大利柏樹的形狀和顏色。閃亮多刺的鐵海棠，在寒冬及夏日之下一樣青蔥，非常賞心悅目。前地種植了各種各樣的蕨類植物：其中一些看起來好像是棕櫚樹的後代；其他則好像是被稱為"維納斯金鎖"或"少女金髮"的美麗植物的親本。這裏長着被忽視的牛蒡，它生氣勃勃，十分美麗，即使紮成一束也很好看。牛蒡長在一片乾燥的地方，但下面潮濕的土壤裏長出了款冬。它也是一種被人忽視的植物，但它長長的莖和大片的葉卻最是優美，就像個六英尺高、有很多分支、花朵對花朵的大燭臺，抬舉着田間不起眼的毛蕊花。這裏有香車葉和山谷百合，野生馬蹄蓮和精緻的三葉酢漿草。這勝景真是奇觀！

前面長着一排排從法國土地上移植來的小梨樹，拴到鋼絲上。由於得到充足的陽光和很好的照料，它們很快就結出果子，和在它們本國的一樣大，一樣多汁。在兩棵無葉古樹的原址豎起了一根高高的旗杆，上面丹麥國旗在自豪地飄揚。緊靠着它立着另一根旗杆，在夏天和收穫季節，在它周圍，啤酒花藤的卷鬚纏繞着它那些芳香的花球，而在冬天，它上面按照老習慣懸掛着一束束燕麥，讓鳥兒在歡樂的聖誕節期間可以開懷大吃。

“我們的好拉臣老來變得多愁善感了，”這家人說，“不過他對我們是忠心和依戀的！”

一份畫報登了幅古宅新年時的畫，上面畫上了旗杆和為鳥兒而設的燕麥束。報上說，古宅保持這種古老美好的風俗，實在值得讚揚。

“拉臣做的任何事情，”貴族人家說，“他們全都竭力支持。他是一個幸運的人。有他為我們工作是我們的驕傲！”

但是他們一點也不為此感到驕傲。他們深知他們是這古宅的主人，他們可以告誡拉臣，不過他們不會這樣做。他們是好人，世界上像他們這種好人多得很，對所有拉臣這種人來說，這是一椿幸事。

不錯，這就是園丁和貴族人家的故事。現在你可以細味一下！

## 註解

1　基督教大齋節首日的前一天，按傳統習俗當天吃薄餅，故俗稱為 "薄餅日"
　　（Pancake Day）。

2　《聖經》記載，雅各曾夢見天梯，天使沿梯子上去下來，並且上帝也站在梯
　　子上面（創世紀 28：10-17）。

3　基督教節日，西方教會定為每年的 9 月 29 日，紀念天使長米迦勒，也是
　　財政年度的四個季度結算日之一。

4　古代凱爾特人的一種宗教。

5　丹麥雕塑家。